بسم الله الرحمن الرحيم

The Publications of the Presidency of Religious Affairs: 1035

Professional Books: 77

Redaction
Vanessa ROSE

Proofreading
Ayşe Zuhal SARI

Graphic
Emre YILDIZ
Uğur ALTUNTOP

Press
Korza Yayın Basım A.Ş.
Phone: 0312 342 22 08

ANKARA • 2015

2015-06-Y-0003-301
ISBN: 978-975-19-6322-2
Certification Number: 12930

High Board of Religious Affairs Decision: 06.09.1990/82

Contack us
General Directorate of Religious Publications
Department of Printed Publications
Phone: (+90.312) 295 72 93-94
Fax: (+90.312) 284 72 88
e-mail: diniyayinlar@diyanet.gov.tr

Delivery And Sale
Directorate of Revolving Funds
Phone: (0.312) 295 71 53 - 295 71 56
Fax: (0.312) 285 18 54
e-mail: dosim@diyanet.gov.tr

BASIC RELIGIOUS KNOWLEDGE

FAITH – WORSHIP – MORALITY - BIOGRAPHY OF THE PROPHET

Seyfettin YAZICI
Retired Member of High Board of Religious Affairs of the Presidency of Religious Affairs of Turkiye

(Translated by Adem Çetinay)

PUBLICATION OF PRESIDENCY OF RELIGIOUS AFFAIRS

TABLE OF CONTENTS

FAITH

UNIT VI - FAITH IN PROPHETS

UNIT VII - FAITH IN JUDGMENT DAY

UNIT VIII - FAITH IN QADAR & QADA

WORSHIP

UNIT I - WORSHIP

UNIT II - ISLAM

UNIT V - PRAYER (II)

UNIT VI - SAWM (FASTING)

UNIT VII - ZAKAT

UNIT VIII - BATTLES OF OUR PROPHET (Sall Allāhu 'alay-hi wa -sallam) (II)

FOREWORD

It is incumbent upon all Muslims to possess accurate and adequate knowledge about their religion.

The first and foremost duty of a Muslim is to have faith in Allah and then to observe religious commandments.

The fruits of the tree of faith, which is nourished by worship, are good morals. A good Muslim is a person who performs his/her duties of worship towards Allah and behaves well towards people.

For good morality, our best role model is our beloved Prophet Muhammad (Salla Allāhu ʿalay-hi wa-sallam). Therefore, learning moral duties and the exemplary life of our Prophet carries special importance for all Muslims.

This book, which contains basic knowledge on such topics as faith, worship, morality and siyar (the Prophetic biography), was prepared with particular attention to the syllabi used in Qur'an classes. It was purposely composed in a simple language, so that our young generations in particular could easily grasp the topics under discussion. Additionally, the book has several illustrations that demonstrate how ablution (wudu) and prayers are performed; it will make it easy for the new-learners to pray.

I ask Allah the Almighty that Muslims of all ages will benefit substantially from this book.

Work is from us, success is from Allah.

Seyfettin YAZICI
6 August 1990
ANKARA

CHAPTER ONE
FAITH

UNIT I

ISLAM AND ITS CHARACTERISTICS

Topics:

- *What is religion?*
- *Islam's place among religions*
- *The aims of Islam*
- *The characteristics of Islam*
- *Characteristics that make Islam universal*

WHAT IS RELIGION?

Religion is the divine law which provides a rational human being with a guideline for the attainment of happiness and tranquility in this world and in the hereafter.

Religions are divided into three types:

1) The true religion:

This is the religion of Allah that has been conveyed to people through prophets and that has not been altered or spoilt in any way until today. The only religion that fits into this category is our religion, Islam.

2) Corrupted religions:

These are religions of Allah that have been altered and corrupted by people over time, even though they were conveyed to people through prophets.

3) Superstitious religions:

These are men-made religions. They do not have any relationship with the religions that were delivered by prophets.

ISLAM'S PLACE AMONG RELIGIONS

The first human being, Adam (alayhi al-salām) is also the first prophet. The first religion of humankind is also the true religion. All the prophets who came after the Prophet Adam up until the Prophet Jesus conveyed to people the belief in the oneness of Allah. They also taught mankind how to worship Allah. However, the principals of faith and the religious rulings that were conveyed by the Prophets have been corrupted with time.

Consequently, Allah the Almighty sent the last and the perfect religion, Islam to humankind through the last Prophet Muhammad (Salla Allāhu ʿalay-hi wa-sallam). Islam is the only true religion in the world today. Superstitious religions have no value in the sight of Allah. The one and only religion according to Allah is Islam.

Allah (j.j.)[1] informed us about this in the Holy Qur'an as follows:

"Indeed, the religion in the sight of Allah is Islam." [2]

"And whoever desires other than Islam as a religion – it will never be accepted from him, and he, in the hereafter, will be among the losers."[3]

My religion is supreme; I love my religion
I hold it above all religions, praise it,

***

Islam is my religion; the most beautiful of all religions.
The oneness of Allah is the foundation of our religion,

***

We say "Allah is one", we say "Allah."
We do not know any other words other than "Allah is one."

***

My Prophet "Muhammad", the sun of two worlds,
None of the Prophets is His equal.

***

He is the one that has brought this religion to us from our Lord;
This religion pours divine light, upon us from the sky.

***

This religion says to be clean! This religion says to be right!
Is there another path better than this religion?

***

Our book is the Qur'an; we recite it every moment,
Praise to Allah we are Muslims, Muslims.

M. Ş. YALTKAYA

1. Jalla Jalalahu
2. Ali 'Imran, 3/19
3. Ali 'Imran, 3/85

THE AIM OF ISLAM

The rulings of Islam aim to make people happy. People who act according to these rulings will achieve happiness both in this world and in the hereafter.

Rulings in Islam have three dimensions:

1) Faith: A person can self-actualize himself by believing in the fundamental principles of faith, and by cleansing the heart from incorrect beliefs and adorning it with true beliefs.

2) Deeds (Amal): Deeds are the actions that people undertake. Rulings in relation to deeds are divided into two:

a) The duties to worship Allah.

b) Rulings that regulate relations among people.

3) Morality: Rulings that regulate our thoughts and behavior towards other people.

THE CHARACTERISTICS OF ISLAM

Islam is the last religion and so, there will be no other religion after it. Its rulings will be valid until the Judgment Day. Muhammad (Salla Allāhu ʿalay-hi wa-sallam), who conveyed the religion of Islam to people, is the last Prophet and no other prophet will come after him.

Islam is a universal religion. Whilst the previous prophets conveyed religion to particular nations, Islam was sent to the whole of humankind.

The rulings of Islam are perfect and can fulfil all of the needs of humankind.

Islam accepts all of the prophets and divine books that Allah sent previously.

Islam abrogated rulings enforced by the religions that the previous prophets conveyed. This is because they were sent to particular nations for a limited period. Whereas Islam is the religion that was sent to the whole of humankind, and it will continue to exist without alteration until the Day of Judgment.

THE CHARACTERISTICS THAT MAKE ISLAM UNIVERSAL

There are many characteristics that make Islam universal. Some of these are as follows:

1. Islam is the last religion sent to the whole of humankind:

Islam is the last divine religion sent to the whole of humankind, and it will continue to exist until the end of time. Thus, our Prophet, with the aim of conveying the message of Islam to all nations, sent letters calling upon all of the neighboring emperors and kings to accept Islam.

2. Islam is a religion of reason and knowledge:

Islam places great importance on reason and sanity. Being sane is one of the conditions for a person to be held accountable for religious obligations. Attaching much importance on knowledge, our religion commands reading and learning and informs that learning is fard (obligatory) for every Muslim.

3. Islam is a religion for both this world and the hereafter:

The aim of Islam is to bring people happiness both in this world and in the eternal life of the hereafter. By providing necessary principles that answereds nees of individuals and communities in every age, our religion ensured people's happiness in this world and in the hereafter.

The following Prophetic tradition summarizes the Islamic principle of how to strike a balance between this world and the hereafter: "Work for this world as if you are never going to die, work for the hereafter as if you are going to die tomorrow."

4. Islam is a religion of simplicity:

Islam favors simplicity over difficulty. The commandments of our religion aim to make us more mature and prepare us for an exalted life. Our religion requires us to perform worship according to our strength and abilities.

For example, a traveler may reduce all obligatory four-*ra'kah* prayers to two-*ra'kah*s during his/her trip. Moreover, a person may perform his/her prayers in a sitting position, if he/she cannot stay in a standing position. People who do not have enough strength or are sick during Ramadan can fast (*sawm*) after they recover. Those who have no hope of recovering from their illness and the elderly can pay a certain amount of money (i.e. *fidya*), in order to compensate for their religious obligation of fasting. Likewise, there are several other cases when Islam allows Muslims to perform their religious duties in a more simplified manner in accordance with their strength and capacity.

5. There is no extremism in Islam:

Islamic rulings are the most compatible ones for the human mind and disposition. Our duty is to comply with those rulings.

Islam recommends modesty. Therefore, it is not acceptable to be harsh on oneself and live a purely ascetic life by avoiding worldly blessings that are *halal* (permissible).

6. **Islam is a religion of peace and love:**

One of the other aims of Islam is to place love and respect for others into people's heart. With this objective in mind, our religion has developed many rules, and made respect and love for others requirement for being a true Muslim.

QUESTIONS

1) What is religion?

2) How many types of religion are there?

3) Explain Islam's place among religions.

4) What is Islam's aim and how many parts are the rulings of Islam comprised of?

5) What are the characteristics of Islam?

6) What are the characteristics that make Islam universal?

UNIT II

FAITH

Topics:

- *Kalimah al-Fawheed and kalimah al-Shahada*
- The pillars of faith
- *Ijmali* faith
- *Tafsili* faith
- Types of people according to their beliefs.
- Tranquility and happiness provided to people by faith
- The relationship between faith and deeds
- The conditions for acceptable and true faith

KALIMAH AL-TAWHEED

لَآاِلٰهَ اِلَّا اللهُ مُحَمَّدٌ رَسُولُ اللهِ

Pronunciation: **"Lâ-ilâha illallah, Muhammadur Rasulullah"**

Meaning: "There is no God except Allah; Muhammad (salla Allāhu ʿalay-hi wa-sallam) is His messenger."

KALIMAH AL-SHAHADA

اَشْهَدُ اَنْ لَآاِلٰهَ اِلَّا اللهُ وَ اَشْهَدُ اَنَّ مُحَمَّداً عَبْدُهُ وَ رَسُولُهُ

Pronunciation: **"Ash-hadu an lâ-ilâha illallah Wa ash-hadu anna Muhammadan abduhu wa Rasulu."**

Meaning: "I bear witness that there is no God except Allah, and I bear witness that Muhammad (Salla Allāhu ʿalay-hi wa-sallam) is the servant and messenger of Allah."

THE PRINCIPALS OF FAITH

Literally, faith means to "believe in something."

As a religious term, faith means, “belief in the message that our Prophet Muhammad (salla Allāhu ʿalay-hi wa-sallam) brought from Allah and uttering this belief with the tongue.”

Faith is divided into two:

a) *Ijmali* faith,

b) *Tafsili* faith.

***a) Ijmali* faith:** Belief in Allah and that Muhammad (salla Allāhu ʿalay-hi wa-sallam) is Allah’s messenger. It is called “*ijmali faith*”, which means “belief as a whole”, because it is the summary of the things to believe in our religion.

The principals of faith are expressed both as a whole and as a summary in *kalimah al-tawheed* and *kalimah al-shahada*. People enter Islam if they utter either *kalimah al-tawheed* or *kalimah al-shahada* with their tongue and believe in them with their heart. However, a Muslim should not be content with this alone, he/she should learn the details of the principals of faith.

***b) Tafsili* faith:** Belief in each of the pillars of faith individually.

The pillars of faith are also called the conditions of faith.

There are six conditions of faith and they are to believe in:

1) Allah,
2) Allah’s angels,
3) Allah’s books,
4) Allah’s prophets,
5) The Judgment day,
6) Destiny, and a belief that good and evil are from Allah.

The prayer of *Amantu* contains all the conditions of faith. Every Muslim should learn *Amantu* and its meaning. *Amantu* is:

اٰمَنْتُ بِاللّٰهِ وَمَلٰٓئِكَتِهٖ وَكُتُبِهٖ وَرُسُلِهٖ وَالْيَوْمِ الْاٰخِرِ وَبِالْقَدَرِ خَيْرِهٖ وَشَرِّهٖ مِنَ اللّٰهِ تَعَالٰى
وَالْبَعْثُ بَعْدَ الْمَوْتِ حَقٌّ اَشْهَدُ اَنْ لَٓا اِلٰهَ اِلَّا اللّٰهُ وَاَشْهَدُ اَنَّ مُحَمَّدًا عَبْدُهُ وَرَسُولُهُ

Pronunciation: **"Amantu billahi wa malaikatihi wa kutubihi wa rusulihi wal-yawmil-akhiri wa bil-qadari khayrihi wa sharrihi minallahi taala wal-ba'thu ba'dal-mawti haqqun ash-hadu an la ilaha illallah wa ash-hadu anna Muhammadan abduhu wa rasuluh."**

Meaning: I believe in Allah, the angels of Allah, the books of Allah, the Prophets of Allah, the day of judgment, destiny: I believe that goodness and harm is from Allah. To arise from the dead is true. I bear witness that there is no god except Allah, and I bear witness that Muhammad (salla Allāhu ʿalay-hi wa-sallam) is the servant and messenger of Allah."

POEM

Allah is one in essence, speech, language and in voice!
While my spirit remains, Allah is one!
We came like this; we wish to leave like this...
Allah is one, in our first and last breaths.

Emin Ali SİPAHİ

TYPES OF PEOPLE ACCORDING TO THEIR BELIEFS

People are divided into three groups according to their beliefs

1) Believers (*mu'min*): These are the people who believe in the existence and oneness of Allah and believe that Muhammad (salla Allāhu ʿalay-hi wa-sallam) is Allah's messenger with their hearts and express this belief with their tongue.

2) Hypocrites (*munafiq*): These are the people who do not believe in the existence and oneness of Allah nor that Muhammad (salla Allāhu ʿalay-hi wa-sallam) is Allah's messenger in their hearts, yet they express this belief with their tongue.

3) Infidel (*kafir*): These are the people who do not believe in the existence and oneness of Allah nor that Muhammad (salla Allāhu ʿalay-hi wa-sallam) is Allah's messenger in their hearts and express this non-belief with their tongue.

Those who are believers will attain a life of endless happiness in paradise. Hypocrites and infidels will not enter, paradise; rather they will suffer the penalty of non-belief in hell.

TRANQUILITY AND HAPPINESS PROVIDED BY FAITH

A human being comprises of a body and a soul. Just as our body requires food and drink, so does our soul, it requires sustenance.

Strong belief is the soul's most important sustenance. A person who believes and trusts Allah gains great strength because humans are always in need of Allah's help. It is a source of tranquility and credence to believe in the Exalted Being that we are in need.

Allah the Almighty commands:

"Verily, in the remembrance of Allah do hearts find rest." [1]

Faith rescues a person from loneliness and emptiness. Faith is the sustenance of our souls, the light of our hearts. A faithless person is a soul without sustenance, a heart in darkness and is void of the biggest support that is Allah.

In life, a person encounters various difficulties, and in these times, the believers whose hearts are devout do not fall into despair. Rather, they take refuge in Allah, awaiting the outcome with patience and trust. It gives a person great happiness to be attached to such a powerful friend with love and respect.

However, faithless people fall into despair and suffer in times of hardship. Hoping to escape their troubles, they look to find comfort in alcohol and drugs that drags them into greater problems. Thus, they lose happiness in both this world and the hereafter.

THE RELATIONSHIP BETWEEN FAITH AND DEEDS

A Muslim does not leave Islam or become an infidel by not performing worship. They are still Muslims as long as they have faith in their hearts and do not deny religious judgmentst. However, they commit a sin and deserve punishment because they have not performed their duties of worship as commanded by Allah.

Religious practices enable faith to mature and strengthen. They are a means to escape punishment in the hereafter and to attain the blessings

1. Ar-Ra'd, 13/28

of paradise. To abandon religious practices and only be content with faith causes a person's faith to weaken and his/her divine light of faith to be extinguished.

This can be explained with the following example:

Faith is like an exposed burning lamp. The lamp must be protected with a glass lantern to avoid it being extinguished. If the lamp continues to burn unprotected in this way, it could be blown out by a slight breeze. Belief is a burning light in our hearts. Its protector is religious practice. We protect our faith and fulfill our duties towards Allah by performing prayer, fasting and engaging in other religious practices.

If religious practices are not performed, the light of faith will be unprotected like the burning of an exposed lamp. It could burn out one day. If faith disappears, it means to lose the keys to paradise, which are the most important asset of a Muslim. Consequently, religious practices have a very important place in protecting our faith and for attaining eternal life in paradise.

THE CONDITIONS FOR AN ACCEPTABLE AND VALID FAITH

Three conditions must be satisfied for faith to be acceptable and valid:

One cannot start believing in a state of hopelessness. There is no benefit for an unbeliever to begin believing upon realizing the existence of punishment at the time of death.

A Muslim should not deny, by word or action, any religious rulings. For example, if a person believes in all of the religious commandments but denies one, he would lose his faith because we believe in Islam as a whole and denying one condition of faith means denying all.

A Muslim must accept that all religious rulings are suitable for Muslims. Disliking any religious rulings would cause one to lose his/her faith.

For a Muslim, the most important asset is faith. A person who attains faith will likewise attain tranquility and bliss in this world and eternal happiness in the hereafter. However, it is a condition to carry this faith until our last breath.

The faith that a person possessed previously will be of no benefit if they depart this world as an unbeliever. Therefore, we must strive hard to protect our faith until our last breath and avoid words or actions that could harm our faith, and even if we do sothat, we must immediately repent and seek forgiveness from Allah.

QUESTIONS

1) Recite *kalimah al-tawheed* and *kalimah al-shahada* without error and mention their meanings.

2) Into how many part are the principals of faith divided?

3) How would you define *ijmali* faith?

4) How would you define *tafsili* faith?

5) Recite 'Amantu' and give its meaning, please.

6) Can you explain how many types of people are there in accordance with their beliefs?

7) What is the tranquility and happiness that faith provides people? Explain, please.

8) Explain the relationship between faith and religious deeds.

9) What are the conditions of an acceptable and valid faith?

UNIT III

FAITH IN ALLAH

Topics:

- The existence and oneness of Allah
- The attributes of Allah
- The love of Allah
- A faithful young girl (Reading)

THE EXISTENCE AND ONENESS OF ALLAH

The first of the six conditions of faith is to believe in Allah. The first and most important duty of a person who is rational and who has reached the age of puberty is to believe in the existence and oneness of Allah.

When we look around us, we see that nothing happens on its own. This illustrates the existence of a craftsman who created a beautiful work of art. For example, the person who makes the watch that we use is a craftsman, the work of art paintings that decorate the walls in our rooms is an artist. Is there not a master of the buildings that we live? Undoubtedly, there is.

In that case, the universe is founded on a delicate scale that operates on a perfect system and there is a creator of human, who is the most beautiful work of art. This creator is Allah, the owner of endless strength and force. The harmony and the perfect order of the universe show the existence and oneness of Allah.

Our first duty is to genuinely believe in Allah, our creator who allows us to live.

We must learn the attributes of Allah in order to believe in Him correctly and know our supreme creator in the best manner possible.

THE ATTRIBUTES OF ALLAH

Allah has 14 attributes. Six of these are called *zati* attributes and eight of them are called *subuti* attributes.

Zati attributes:

***1) Wujud*:** To exist. Allah exists and His absence is unthinkable.

2) Qidaam: There is no beginning to Allah's existence. Allah is not a being that came into existence later. He was there when there was nothing else.

3) Baqa: There is no end to the existence of Allah. Allah's existence will continue after everything else.

4) Wahdaniyyah: It means the oneness of Allah. Allah is one. He has no replicas, equivalents or partners.

5) Mukhalafath-un lil hawadith: Does not resemble things created afterwards. Allah does not look like any of His creations.

6) Qiyam bi nafsihi: The existence of Allah is through Himself. Allah is not in need of anything, everything is in need of Him.

Subuti Attributes:

1) Hayaat: To be alive. Allah is always alive.

2) Ilm: Knowledge. Allah knows everything that is secret and open, past and present. He also knows what passes through the heart.

3) Sami': To hear. Allah hears everything.

***4) Basar*:** To see. Allah sees everything.

5) Iraade: To will. Allah wills and does what He wills.

6) Qudrah: Unlimited Power. Allah is the owner of endless force; His power is enough for everything.

***7) Kalaam*:** To say. Allah is the owner of words; He has announced His word to the Prophets. The Qur'an is Allah's word.

8) Takween: To create. Allah is the creator. He is the creator of everything in the universe. If Allah wishes to create something, He says for it to be, and then it happens spontaneously. He can also eradicate anything that exists whenever He wishes.

A Muslim believes in Allah as follows:

- Allah exists and is one. The existence of Allah has no beginning or end. Allah does not resemble any of His creations. Allah's existence is through Him. Allah is not in need of anything, everything is in need of Him.
- Allah is always alive. Allah knows everything, hears everything and sees everything.

- Allah wishes, does what He wishes and no one can interfere with His doings.

- Allah is the owner of strength and power. His power is enough for everything.

- Allah is the creator. He creates what He wishes from nothing and eradicates what He wishes. Everything in the universe is through His creation. There is reason in all His creation.

- Allah's word exists. He announced His word to the Prophets and informed them of His commandments. The supreme book of our religion is the Qur'an, Allah's word.

- A person who truly believes in Allah in such a manner attains his/her true value by taking his/her honorable place amongst all creations. This belief cleanses a person's heart from bad thoughts while decorating it with good thoughts and beautiful habits.

- Even though a person may be in a place where no one else can see him/her, he/she should not engage in any behavior that is immoral or inappropriate. This is because we believe that Allah sees and knows everything all the time. Faith in Allah is the source of all goodness.

THE LOVE OF ALLAH

We have been created in a position much more superior to other creations. Allah has provided us with eyes to see, ears to hear, a tongue to speak, hands that can do various jobs and feet to walk, and our bodies are equipped with wisdom and intelligence.

Allah has equipped the earth with various blessings for us to live healthy and happy fulfilling all of our needs from the air we breathe to the water we drink. A person who cannot breathe any air for a short period will not live; he will lose his life. If we think about all these blessings that we are in need of, we understand how much goodness comes to us from Allah.

Allah the Almighty commands:

"And if you should count the blessings of Allah, you could not enumerate them." [1]

1. Ibrahim, 14/34

People like it when others do a favor to them. In that case, Allah is the one whom we must love the most. This is because His goodness towards us is so much that we could not enumerate it. Therefore, we must love Allah a lot. Love cannot be shown just by words. People show respect to the ones they love; they do not do anything that their loved ones would dislike. The love of Allah occurs by remembering His sacred name with respect, willingly carrying out the worship duties commanded and refraining from the things He has prohibited (haram).

If we do this, if we prove that we truly love Him, Allah will in return love us and bestow upon us much more blessings in the hereafter than in this world.

The greatest happiness for a person is to be one of the people whom Allah loves.

ALLAH

The creator of the earth and the sky,
Ornaments the trees,
Blossoms the flowers,
It is one Allah, one Allah
***
Feeds every animal,
Allows every person to live,
Protects this homeland,
It is one Allah, one Allah
***
Allah is ready everywhere,
Sees what I do,
Hears what I say,
He exists, He is one and big,
I love Allah,
I obey His every word.

Sabri Cemil YALKUT

READING:

A faithful young girl

Milkmen were prohibited from adding water to the milk by the Caliph Umar during his reign and this order was announced everywhere. One night, while walking around checking the city's public order in Madinah, the Caliph got tired. He leaned on the wall of a house to rest. He heard the following conversation coming from the house between a mother and a daughter:

Mother:

Come, my daughter: get up and put some water in the milk.

Girl:

Do you not know that the Caliph prohibited adding water to milk?

Mother:

Yes, I know.

Girl:

In that case, how can I do something that has been prohibited by the Caliph?

Mother:

Get up and put water in the milk. How is Umar going to see you?

Girl:

Umar may not see but my Lord will. I swear that I will not do something in a place that cannot be seen if I cannot do it in a place that can be seen.

After hearing this discussion, the Caliph Umar returned his home. He then married this well-mannered poor girl with high morals to his son Asim.

See the positive influence in the actions of a person who believes in Allah.

QUESTIONS

1) What is a person's first duty?
2) How many attributes does Allah have?
3) Name the *zati* attributes of Allah.
4) Name the *subuti* attributes of Allah.
5) How should a Muslim believe in Allah?

UNIT IV

FAITH IN ANGELS

Topics:

- The entity and attributes of angels
- The names of the archangels and their duties
- The benefits of believing in angels

THE ENTITY AND ATTRIBUTES OF ANGELS

The second condition of faith is to believe in angels. Angels are beings created from divine light. They do not eat or drink, nor are they male or female.

Angels are the beloved servants of Allah. They execute Allah's commands flawlessly; they do not commit any sins.

Allah the Almighty has created beings in various forms. Some of these forms can be seen by us and others cannot. Some beings cannot be seen by humans. This is because a human's eye has not been created to see everything; rather its ability to see is limited.

For example, just as we cannot see very small substances, we can also not see the air, wind, our souls or our minds. The electric current that passes through wire cannot be seen either. However, we know that it exists but we cannot actually see it. Therefore, angels are the beings that exist even though they cannot be seen by us.

We cannot see angels because they are subtle beings created from divine light. Yet, we believe in their existence because Allah the Almighty informed us of the existence of angels in the Qur'an. Our Prophet has seen angels and He has also informed us of them. Everything Allah the Almighty and our beloved Prophet notified us about is correct. Consequently, we faithfully believe with certainty in the existence of angels.

THE NAMES OF ARCHANGELS AND THEIR DUTIES

Angels: They exist on earth, in the sky, in our environment and everywhere. Their numbers are only known by Allah. They each have a duty entrusted to them by Allah.

Some of them uninterruptedly worship Allah. Some are charged with the duty of managing and coordinating the universe. They perform the big tasks that the powers of people cannot complete.

There are angels who are sent to help believers in troublesome times, preaching goodness to people and protect them from harm. Allah the Almighty has shown His endless power with the existence of angels.

Archangels and their duties

1) Jibril: The greatest of angels. Has a responsibility in acting as a messenger between Allah and His Prophets, revealing Allah's books to the Prophets. Jibril brought our book, the Qur'an to our Prophet from Allah.

2) Mikail: has a responsibility in managing the nature. (Like the pouring of rain, the blowing of the wind, the growing of crops etc.)

3) Israfil: has a responbility in dealing with the apocalypse and the resurrection of people.

4) Azrael: has a responsibility in taking the lives of people who have reached the end of their lifespan.

In addition to the above mentioned Archangels, some of the other angels are as follows:

***Kiraman Katibin*:** They are two angels. One stays on a person's right side and the other on his left. The one on the right records the good deeds performed and the one on the left records the bad deeds performed. Thus, a "Book of Deeds" is compiled for every person where good and bad deeds are recorded.

***Munkar & Nakir*:** They are the two angels tasked with asking questions to people in the grave after they die.

***Ridwan*:** The head angel in paradise.

***Maalik*:** The head of all the angels in hell.

THE BENEFITS OF BELIEVING IN ANGELS

There are angels who never leave us, they are with us at all times and places. As mentioned earlier, the duties of the angels named "Kiraman Katibin" are to record all the good and bad deeds that we do. Therefore, a person is not alone even if there is not anyone else nearby. There are angels that always observe and record everything that a person does.

A Muslim who believes in angels cannot engage in mischief by saying "No-one can see me; I'll do whatever I want to." This is because no matter where they are, they know that there are angels observing and recording all the good and bad deeds. Thus, our faith in angels prevents us from doing harm to others.

In addition to these, there are other angels that protect us from harm and lead us to goodness. An example of goodness and beauty in this world is an angel and an example of evilness and ugliness is satan. An angel calls a person to goodness, whereas satan calls to evil.

For example, when we come across a poor person who is hungry and in need of assistance, a feeling of pity appears. A secret voice calls out to us to "help the poor person." This is the voice of an angel. Meanwhile, a different voice inside us tries to discourage us from helping the poor by whispering, "If you help, your money will decrease, desist from helping." This whisper is the voice of satan.

In this situation, we should comply with the voice that calls upon us to help the poor. This is the voice of a friend who likes kindness and calls upon us to do good deeds. Complying this will lead us to good deeds and is a means to earn reward. We must refrain from complying with the voice of satan because he will hinder us from kindness and try to deceive us into committing sin.

It can be seen that believing in angels enables us to avoid harm to others and it beautifies our morality.

Our Prophet (salla Allāhu ʿalay-hi wa-sallam) commands the following:

"Both satan and angels bring something to the heart of a person. Satan's duty is to call upon mischief and ward off rightness. The duty of an angel is to call upon rightness, goodness and keep the believer away from mischief.

Whoever hears a voice inside them calling for goodness should know that this is the voice of an angel. They should immediately obey and give thanks to Allah.

And whoever hears a voice inside them calling for mischief should know that this is the voice of satan. They should move away from them and take refuge in Allah."[1]

QUESTIONS

1) What kind of creations are angels?
2) Why can we not see angels?
3) What are the names of the archangels and what are their duties?
4) Explain the benefits of believing in angels.

1. Tirmidhi

UNIT V

FAITH IN BOOKS

Topics:

- The nature and types of revelations
- Divine books and Pages
- The Revelation of the holy Qur'an
- The script of the holy Qur'an and how it was transformed into a book
- The characteristics of the holy Qur'an
- Our duties towards the holy Qur'an
- Sacred statements by our Prophet about the virtues of reciting the Qur'an (Reading)

THE NATURE OF REVELATIONS

Revelation literally means to notify something quickly and secretly to someone. In a religious context, it means an expression of certain knowledge notified to the prophets directly by Allah or through a messenger.

This is one of the special ways by which Allah notifies his chosen servants of His commands. Allah has made His word heard to the prophets through various types of revelations.

TYPES OF REVELATIONS

1) Faithful dreams: Allah has notified the Prophets the messages that He wishes through true dreams. The first revelation that came to our Prophet was a true dream and each dream He saw turned out to be true.

2) Through inspiration: Allah put the message He wishes into the hearts of the prophets directly without intermediaries.

3) Words from behind a curtain: To hear Allah's words directly as if they come from behind a curtain, without seeing the teller.

4) A revelation through an intermediary (Angel): Allah the Almighty has notified His words through an angel to His Prophets.

The angel notifying Allah's word to prophets would sometimes appear in their own forms. Or the angel would appear in the form of a person, so that everyone could see and hear the angel.

Sometimes, an angel would notify a revelation to Prophets without being seen.

Most of the Qur'anic verses were revealed to our Prophet through an intermediary angel. The angel who brought the Qur'an from Allah to our Prophet is the archangel Jibril.

DIVINE BOOKS AND PAGES

The third of six conditions of faith is to believe in Allah's books. Allah the Almighty has sent books to His servants conveyed by the prophets. These books deliver Allah's commandments and prohibitions to us; teach us the duties that servants must perform and the ways to obtain happiness in this world and in the hereafter.

We Muslims believe in all of the books sent to all of the Prophets. However, the divine books before the Qur'an have been corrupted and changed by people over time. It is for this reason that we believe in their uncorrupted form as sent to the Prophets and not in their current corrupted states. Only the Qur'an has been under the divine protection, and never been changed until today.

Some books sent by Allah to Prophets are small booklets, consisting of only a few pages. They are called **"SUHUF"**, which literally means "pages."

The other books are called the "Four Major Books."

Pages were sent to the following Prophets:

1) 10 pages to Adam alayhi as-salām.

2) 50 pages to Shith alayhi as-salām.

3) 30 pages to Idris alayhi as-salām.

4) 10 pages to Ibrahim alayhi as-salām.

And the four great books that were:

1) The Torah to Musa Alayhi s-salām.

2) The Zabur (Psalms) to Da'ud Alayhi s-salām.

3) The Bible to Isa Alayhi s-salām.

4) The Qur'an to our Prophet Hazrat Muhammad (Sall Allāhu ʿalay-hi wa-sallam).

THE REVELATION OF THE HOLY QUR'AN

Shortly before Prophethood was bestowed upon our Prophet Muhammad (Salla Allāhu ʿalay-hi wa-sallam), He retired to the cave of Hira, located at Jabal al-Nour (The Mountain of Light) close to Makkah, and occupied himself with the thinking of Allah's greatness.

When Muhammad (Sall Allāhu ʿalay-hi wa-sallam)retired to the cave of Hira, on one of the Monday nights in the month of Ramadan in 610, He turned to Allah with all His heart and mind. It was at this time that, with Allah's command, the archangel Jibril (alayhi as-salām) went to our Prophet and said, **"Read."** This command was repeated three times. When our beloved Prophet said, **"What should I read"**, Jibril (Alayhi s-salām) delivered the first five verses of the Quran to him. Thus, the first revelation was received and the Qur'an began to be formed.

POEM

"The most glittering light manifested by Allah,
The sunshine of the Qur'an was born; the night of interregnum came to an end."

When the first revelation was received, our Prophet (Sall Allāhu ʿalay-hi wa-sallam) was forty years old. The meaning of those first five verses of suraht Al-'Alaq is as follows:

1) Recite in the name of your Lord who created.

2) Created man from a clinging substance.

3) Recite, your Lord is the most Generous.

4) Who taught by the pen -

5) Taught man that which he knew not.

It was disclosed to Muhammad (Salla Allāhu ʿalay-hi wa-sallam) with the revelation of the Qur'an that He was the last Prophet. The Qur'an was delivered in parts in over 23 years, sometimes verse by verse and sometimes chapter-by-chapter (*surah*). Verses were mostly revealed as a response to a question or an incident. The question or incident that caused the verse to be revealed is called *"reason for revelation" (sabab al-nuzul)*.

The last verse to be revealed in the Qur'an was verse 281 of surah Al-Baqarah, which means:

"And fear a Day when you will be returned to Allah. Then every person will be compensated for what he earned, and they will not be treated unjustly."

THE SCRIPT OF THE HOLY QUR'AN AND HOW IT WAS TRANSFORMED INTO A BOOK

As the verses of the Qur'an were revealed, our Prophet (salla Allāhu ʿalay-hi wa-sallam) called upon the scribes who wrote down the revelation and showed them which verses were part of which chapters and in what order. The revelation scribes would write as it was shown to them. Some of the companions of our Prophet memorized the verses revealed. By this way, the Qur'an was conserved both in writing and in memory since the time of our Prophet.

Since verses were still being revealed during the life of our Prophet, the written pages had not yet formed into a book. The Qur'an was completed when the revelations ended.

After the death of our Prophet (salla Allāhu ʿalay-hi wa-sallam), the Caliph Abu Bakr established a commission of the leading Companions. This commission gathered the individual pages of the Qur'an together and compared them with the verses memorized by the Companions and transformed them into a book. This collection was called the book, or "*Mushaf*."

In th is process, the chapters were arranged in the order shown by our Prophet. This *mushaf* is preserved by Abu Bakr.

As Islam spread, copies of the Qur'an were produced and sent to various Islamic nations by the third Chaliph Uthman.

Thus, the Qur'an was conserved as it was revealed to our Prophet without any change until the present day and it will remain the same until Judgment Day. The Qur'an that we have today is the same copy that was written and memorized during the time of our Prophet, transformed into a book during the time of Abu Bakr and reproduced during Uthman's era.

THE CHARACTERISTICS OF THE HOLY QUR'AN

The Qur'an is a holy book that was sent to Muslims by Allah through the last and greatest Prophet.

There are many special characteristics that differentiate the Qur'an from the other divine books.

The main attributes are:

a) The Qur'an has reached us without any change as it was revealed to our Prophet. This will continue until the Day of Judgment.

Some sacred books had been completely lost and yet some others had been altered or corrupted by people. None of them were preserved in the form that Allah sent to us.

Allah the almighty gave an assurance with the following verse that He will protect the Qur'an:

Indeed, it is We who sent down the Qur'an and indeed, We will be its guardian. [1]

Allah the Almighty protected our sacred book the Holy Qur'an to this day and will continue to protect it until the Day of Judgment.

b) The Qur'an was revealed part by part in verses and chapters in response to the questions and the incidents. This ensured that we could easily memorize and understand it.

c) The Qur'an is the last divine book, and no other book will be sent. The rulings of the Qur'an are valid until Judgment Day and they will not be changed.

d) The Qur'an is a book sent to all of humankind. It is equipped with the truth and wisdom to meet the needs of each century. Whereas other sacred books were sent to specific nations.

e) The Qur'an is our Prophet's greatest miracle, a unique miracle with its words, its meanings and the lofty truth it carries.

1. Al-Hijr, 15/9

OUR DUTIES TOWARDS THE HOLY QUR'AN

1) Every Muslim must know that the Qur'an is the word of Allah and must recite it without error following the rules of *tajweed.*

2) We are allowed to hold the Qur'an while we are in a state of ablution and commence reciting it with the *basmala*. We should face the *qibla* when possible when reciting the Qur'an and try to learn the meaning of it.

3) We should recite the Qur'an in clean places and not next to people who are busy with other things or people who are not listening.

4) We should listen with respect to others who are reciting the Qur'an.

5) We should keep the Qur'an in clean and high places without placing it in lower places.

6) We should do the things that the Qur'an commands and refrain from the things that it tells us not to do. We should act in accordance with the morals and principals laid down in the Qur'an.

SUPREME QUR'AN

Supreme Qur'an
Supreme Qur'an
From Allah it was
Brought to our Prophet...

***

You are the light of the world,
The enlightenment of the soul,
On Judgment Day you are
The refuge of faith...

***

Supreme Qur'an
Supreme Qur'an
You, more than anything else
I respect and love...

Gökhan EVLIYAOĞLU

READING:

The sacred words of our Prophet regarding the virtues of reciting the Qur'an:

"The most auspicious among you are those who learn the Qur'an and teach it."

***

"There is merit for whoever reads a letter of the Qur'an, the book of Allah. Each merit is to be given multiplied by ten times."

***

"A multitude of merits will be given to whoever listens to one verse of the Qur'an, the book of Allah. And there will be a divine light on the Day of Judgment for those who recite one verse of the book of Allah."

***

"Recite the Qur'an, for it will become an intercessor for the reader on Day of Judgment."

***

"Whoever reads the Qur'an and acts according to it, their mother and father will be adorned on the day of judgment with a crown of light whose gleam is like that of the sun. Now, you calculate the merits of acting accordingly."

***

Our Prophet (salla Allāhu ʿalay-hi wa-sallam) said to Abu Dharr:

"Learning one verse of the Qur'an, the book of Allah before leaving home in the morning is more auspicious for you than 100 ra'kahs of nafl prayer."

***

"Whoever reads the Quran and memorizes it believing its halal to be halal and regards its haram to be haram, Allah will place him in paradise and accept intercession for ten of his relatives deserving Hell."[2]

---

2. Et – Terğib ve't-Terhib Volume 2, Page 342 onwards.

QUESTIONS

1) What does revelation mean?

2) Explain the different types of revelations.

3) Explain the types of revelations that our Prophet received.

4) What type of revelation was the Qur'an that was sent to our Prophet by Allah?

5) Which Prophets were sent divine books and booklets?

6) How was the Qur'an delivered and what were the first verses that were revealed?

7) Explain how the Qur'an was written.

8) What does the word *Mushaf* refer to?

9) What are the attributes of the Qur'an?

10) What are our duties towards the Quran?

11) Memorize five hadiths regarding the virtues of reciting the Qur'an.

UNIT VI

FAITH IN PROPHETS

Topics:

- Prophethood and the need for Prophets
- Duties and attributes of Prophets
- Names of Prophets mentioned in the Qur'an
- Common principals of the religions delivered by Prophets
- What does miracle and *karamah* (divine blessing) mean?
- Miracles of our Prophet
- Attributes of our Prophet
- Hazrat Muhammad (salla Allāhu ʿalay-hi wa-sallam) being the last Prophet
- What did they say about our Prophet (Reading)?

PROPHETHOOD AND THE NEED FOR PROPHETS

The fourth of the six conditions of faith is to believe in Prophets. Prophets are messengers between Allah and people. For this duty, Allah chooses the most worthy servants. Prophets were sent to people as a guide because people need guides.

Because even if people could understand the existence of Allah with their own intelligence, they could not comprehend His lofty attributes. They cannot know how Allah should be worshipped, what life in the hereafter looks like, who will be rewarded there, who will be punished and how we achieve happiness in this world and in the hereafter.

Allah the Almighty charged His Prophets with the duty of teaching this truth to people and showing the ways of achieving happiness in this world and in the hereafter.

THE DUTIES OF PROPHETS

Prophets introduced Allah to people in the best possible way, teaching them the principals of belief and forms of worship. They explained the principals of religious rulings and good morality. Their words and actions were role models to people.

Prophets carried out their duties in the most difficult conditions. They showed miracles, brought about extraordinary events to prove to the disbelievers that they were Prophets. They gave good news to those performing Allah's commandment with paradise and notified those who did not with the penalty of torment in hell.

Prophets are role models who are chosen by Allah from amongst people who possess all kinds of good morality.

The necessary attributes of a Prophet:

1) Sidq: It means truthful. Prophets are people of immense truth. They would never lie. What they said happened, happened, and what they say will happen, will certainly happen.

2) Amanah: It means to be reliable. Prophets are people who are reliable in all matters. They will never betray that which has been entrusted to them.

3) Fatanah: It means to be smart and shrewd. Prophets are people who are smart, shrewd and of high intelligence.

4) Ismah: It means to not commit sin. Prophets do not commit any sin either privately or publically.

5) Tabligh: It means to inform. Prophets inform people of religious rulings received from Allah without any alteration.

THE NAMES OF PROPHETS MENTIONED IN THE QUR'AN

The first Prophet is Adam (alayhi as-salām) and the last Prophet is the Prophet Muhammad (salla Allāhu ʿalay-hi wa-sallam). There have been many Prophets who have come between these two. Of the Prophets, 25 of them have been mentioned in the Qur'an. However, the actual number of Prophets is much bigger than 25. We believe in the Prophets mentioned in the Qur'an without differentiation together with the other Prophets and, their numbers are only known by Allah.

The following Prophets are mentioned in the Qur'an:

Adam, 2) Idris, 3) Nuh, 4) Hud, 5) Salih, 6), Ibrahim, 7), Lut 8) Isma'il, 9), Ishaq 10) Ya'qub, 11) Yusuf, 12) Shu'aib, 13) Musa, 14), Harun 15) Da'ud, 16) Sulaiman, 17) Ayyub, 18) Dhul-kifl, 19) Yunus, 20) Elias, 21) Al-Yas'a, 22) Zakariyyah, 23) Yahya, 24) Isa, 25) Muhammad (Sall Allāhu ʿalay-hi wa-sallam).

COMMON PRINCIPALS OF THE RELIGIONS DELIVERED BY PROPHETS

The religion that Allah instructed His Prophets in is the right religion. There are some principals that do not change within right religions. These are:

1) The principals of faith
2) Religious practices
3) Moral rules

As times change, some religious rulings and practices have also changed in accordance with people's situations and needs and eventually took the perfect shape with the arrival of our Prophet Muhammad (salla Allāhu ʿalay-hi wa-sallam).

WHAT DOES MIRACLE AND *KARAMAH* MEAN

Miracle: These are extraordinary events that Prophets used with the help of Allah to prove that they were Prophets. Miracles are deeds of Prophets. Other people are incapable of carrying out extraordinary events.

Displaying miracles are reserved for Prophets. They occur with the permission and power of Allah.

All Prophets have displayed miracles as a divine deed in order to prove they are Prophets. They have silenced the disbelievers with such miracles.

Karamah: They are extraordinary events triggered by those who are close to Allah (*wali*), with Allah's help. Such extraordinary events are considered *karamah* for the friends of Allah and considered as the miracles the Prophets they are tied.

MIRACLES OF OUR PROPHET

Our Prophet Muhammad (salla Allāhu ʿalay-hi wa-sallam) performed several miracles with the aim of proving that He was sent by Allah.

Some of these are as follows:

a) One day as the *asr* prayer was approaching; our Prophet could not find water for ablution. Upon this, a container with a little bit of water was brought to Him. Our Prophet (salla Allāhu ʿalay-hi wa-sallam) placed His hand in the container with water and water started gushing out between His fingers. It continued until the congregation of about three hundred people who were there completed their ablution.

b) At the masjid in Madinah, our dignified Prophet (salla Allāhu ʿalayhi wa-sallam) used to talk to the congregation on top of a date tree log. As the Muslims increased, our Prophet had made for Him a three-step pulpit to talk from a higher place. One Jumu'ah when He started reciting the *khutbah* from this pulpit, it was heard that the date tree log that was on the other side of the masjid started howling like the outcry of a camel that lost its offspring, because it was separated from our Prophet. The howling of the log ceased when the Prophet, who noticed this, stepped down from the pulpit and picked up the log and caressed it.

c) One night, the Prophet Muhammad was taken with an animal called Buraq from the Masjid al-Haram in Makkah to Masjid al-Aqsa in Jerusalem approximately one and half years after the *Hijrah*. From there He was raised to the skies together with Jibril (alayhi as-salām). The journey that our Prophet went upon as Allah's guest is an unprecedented event in the universe and it happened in a short span of time. The limitless power of Allah in this event is known as the miracle of 'Isra' (The night journey).

d) The greatest and most permanent miracle of our Prophet is the Qur'an. It is a unique miracle that caresses our spirits by its recitation giving tranquility to the hearts, its countless wisdom full of lofty meaning, its eternal principals that bring happiness to people and real science that holds a light to all ages.

ATTRIBUTES OF OUR PROPHET

Allah the Almighty commands the following:

"And We have not sent you except comprehensively to humankind as a bringer of good tidings and a warner." [1]

"Say O Muhammad! O humankind, indeed I am the messenger of Allah to you all." [2]

1. Al-Saba, 34/28
2. Al-'Araf, 7/158

As Muslims, we believe in all Prophets without any differentiation. However, our Prophet Muhammad (salla Allāhu ʿalay-hi wa-sallam) has a superior place and attributes amongst the other Prophets.

These main attributes are as follows:

1) Our Prophet (salla Allāhu ʿalay-hi wa-sallam) is the most loved servant of Allah, the greatest and virtuous of all creations.

2) He is the last Prophet and no other Prophet will come after Him.

3) He is a Prophet for all of humankind.

4) His prophethood includes all periods of time until the Day of Judgment. The duties of the other Prophets were for specific periods of time.

5) The Islam that our Prophet conveyed will continue until the Day of Judgment.

HAZRAT MUHAMMAD (salla Allāhu ʿalay-hi wa-sallam) BEING THE LAST PROPHET

Allah the Almighty commands the following:

"He is the Messenger of Allah and last of the Prophets." [3]

Our Prophet Muhammad (salla Allāhu ʿalay-hi wa-sallam) is the greatest and last of all Prophets.

The Islam that he conveyed is the last religion. The Qur'an that he conveyed on behalf of Allah is the last book of Allah that calls out to all of humankind religion.

The door to prophethood has been closed with the arrival of Muhammad (salla Allāhu ʿalay-hi wa-sallam). He is a Prophet to all nations on Earth. This truth is openly expressed in the Qur'an.

The previous Prophets were sent to specific communities. They resembled a lamp illuminating inside a house. As for our Prophet, who was sent to all of humankind, he is like the sun that brightens the world. After the sun rises, there is no need for any more lamps.

3. Al-'Ahzab, 33/40

SHORT DUA

Make us walk, O Allah,
Through your road of inextinguishable divine light...
Do not ever separate us,
From your love, your Prophet...

***

We know your kindness,
Will not lessen from any of your servants...
The weak and helpless,
Holding and guiding them...

***

Repentance will not be devoid,
From your favor and acceptance...
Make us walk, O Allah,
From the road of your Prophet...

E. Ali SİPAHİ

READING:

What they said regarding our Prophet...

"Hazrat Muhammad is the greatest human being in the history of humankind."

In his historical research book titled "The 100 most influential people in the history of humankind", an American scholar named Michael H. Hart wrote that, of the most influential 100 people in history and the present day, the Prophet Muhammad (salla Allāhu ʿalay-hi wa-sallam) is the world's greatest figure.

The book that the American scholar wrote was published in October 1978 and caused great interest. In his work, the book's writer Prof. Dr. Michael H. Hart proves that the greatest figure is the Prophet Muhammad (salla Allāhu ʿalay-hi wa-sallam) as follows:

"The fact that I have chosen the Prophet Muhammad at the head of the list of the most influential figures in this world may amaze some readers. It may open the road for some people to ask questions. However, from a

religious and worldly perspective, Muhammad is the only figure who have reached the height of success.

(Diyanet Newspaper 15 January 1979, Issue 205)

***

Prince Bismark, a German diplomat said the following with great respect about our beloved Prophet:

"O Muhammad, I am sorry that I could not be a contemporary to you....

Humankind has seen an eminent force like you only once and will not see it again afterwards. In your formidable presence, I bow to you with deep respect."

***

Alex Lovazon, a French philosopher says:

"The Qur'an that was sent to Muhammad is a brilliant book filled with wisdom for the guidance of people. There is no doubt that Muhammad is a true Prophet."

***

The famous Russian author Tolstoy said the following:

"The Prophet Muhammad (salla Allāhu ʿalay-hi wa-sallam) is a great reformer. He has provided a great service to humankind. He united His community with the true divine light. This honor to Him itself is enough. He saved them without the spilling of blood and attained peace. He opened the roads of advancement to them. A great person like Him is worthy of all kinds of respect."

QUESTIONS

1) Who are prophets and why is there a need for them?

2) What are the duties of prophets?

3) Count the required attributes of prophets.

4) Which prophets are mentioned in the Qur'an and who is the first and last prophets?

5) What principals are the same in the religions conveyed by the prophets?

6) What is a miracle and *karamah*?

7) Explain three of our Prophet's miracles.

8) How is the Qur'an a miracle?

9) Explain the attributes of our Prophet.

10) Explain how our Prophet is the last Prophet.

UNIT VII

FAITH IN JUDGMENT DAY

Topics:

- What does faith in Judgment Day mean?
- Benefits of faith in the hereafter
- Death, the grave and doomsday
- Reward, penalty, paradise and hell

WHAT DOES FAITH IN JUDGMENT DAY MEAN?

The fifth condition of faith is to "Believe in Judgment Day." Just as there is an end to people and other life forms, there will also be an end to the world one day. When the time determined by Allah arrives, the angel Israfil will blow the **trumpet of doom**. All living creatures will die (except those Allah wishes otherwise) with the effect of this awful noise. The natural order in the Earth and the skies will be destroyed and the universe will take a new form.

After a period, known as Judgment Day, Israfil will, with the command of Allah blow the trumpet of doom for a second time. All people will then rise from the dead and will be called to a meeting place called "Armageddon." Here, everyone will be brought into the presence of Allah and will be interrogated about the things that they did in this world.

Each person will be handed their book of deeds that records the kindness and the harm that they did as written by the *Kiraman Katibin* angels. Everyone will see and read what they did in this world in their book of deeds.

All worldly offences committed whether publically or privately will be revealed, kindness and harm will be measured on the sensitive scales of justice and human beings will see the response of what they did in this world.

A person will reap in the hereafter what they sow in this world. Divine justice will find its place and no one will be inflicted with injustice.

Our beloved Prophet advised as follows:

"On the Day of Judgment, a person cannot move from Allah's presence until they have been interrogated about four things:

- Where they spent their life,

- Where they wore out your body,

- Where they earned and spent their wealth,

- What deeds they did with their knowledge." [1]

This time, which commences with the rise from the dead and continues until eternity, is called Judgment Day. That is why this is one of the most important principals of faith to believe that people will rise again from the dead and enter the eternal life.

BENEFITS OF FAITH IN THE HEREAFTER

a) To believe in Judgment Day helps a person achieve a feeling of responsibility. A person who carries the feeling of responsibility pays attention to their actions.

To believe in Judgment Day means to believe that we will rise from the grave after dying and give account in the presence of Allah for all we did in this world. It is to believe that the doers of good will see reward and the doers of harm will be punished. This belief ensures that a person refrains from doing harm and it makes them owners of morality and virtues by directing them to goodness and rightness. No person will harm anybody else in a community where such belief exists. They will show respect for each other's rights and perform as many good deeds as possible. These actions will develop reciprocal love and feelings of trust amongst people. Belief in the hereafter plays a very important role in individuals having good morality, providing safety and tranquility in the community.

b) A person who believes in the hereafter will prepare for an exulted and endless life in this temporary world. A person embarking on a long journey will make preparations and take enough money with him/her for spending. He/She will not depart for the journey without preparing and having enough money.

However, the road in the hereafter continues after we die, it is much longer and more important than those journeys across this world.

1. Et-Terğib ve't- Terhib Volume 1, Page 125.

Therefore, we must make preparations and acquire much more provisions for the hereafter.

A person who believes in the hereafter prepares for it by performing Allah's commands and avoiding His prohibitions. Those who depart for a journey after preparing will pass through to an exalted life. Allah the Almighty wants us to make preparations by stating, "Acquire provisions."

Those who do not prepare for the hereafter will see the truth at the time of their death and will want to return to this worldly life to perform Allah's commands. However, this request will not be accepted because the opportunity has passed. This situation is described in the Qur'an as follows: **"When death comes to one of them, he says, My Lord! Send me back so that I may do good in that which I have left behind."** [2]

c) Believing in Judgment Day consoles people and diminishes sadness.

Such as:

There are many nice people in the world who die without seeing reward for their goodness or suffer injustice without obtaining their rights and where many cruel people die without receiving a penalty. Judgment Day is a day where the just and the unjust, the good and the bad will be distinguished and everyone will receive their recompense with exactitude.

Divine justice will find its place on Judgment Day. The doers of good will receive their reward in abundance. Those being wronged will get their rewards in full. The evil doers will not keep their doings; they will get the penalty they deserve. It is this belief that gives people tranquility and hope.

DEATH

Every person lives in this world for a prescribed period. When this time elapses, people die. A human being is a creation of the coming together of the body and soul. The soul gives liveliness and movement to our bodies. The soul separates from the body when the time allocated by Allah arrives. The event of the soul separating from the body is called "**death**." Death is ordained for all humans. There is no escape from this.

This truth is expressed in the Qur'an as follows:

2. Al-Mu'minun, 23/99-100
3. Ali 'Imran. 3/185

"Every soul will taste death." [3]

"Wherever you may be, death will overtake you, even if you should be within towers of lofty construction." [4]

Death does not mean to disappear. It is the transition from this temporary world to eternal life in the hereafter. Death for those carrying out their duties towards Allah is a door opened to obtain a more exalted life.

THE GRAVE

The period of time from when a person dies until they rise again from the grave on Judgment Day is known as "life in the grave." The place they will exist during this time is called the "grave." When a person dies, their body decomposes and mixes with the earth, but the soul that separates from the body does not. When people are placed inside the grave, they are questioned by the angels called *Munkar and Nakir*. For those who answer correctly, their graves will be a resting place, yet it will be a place of torture for those who cannot provide answers.

Our Prophet (salla Allāhu ʿalay-hi wa-sallam) explains the status of the grave as follows:

"The grave is either a piece of the gardens of paradise or a pit in the pits of hell." [5]

The grave is a resting place in the gardens of paradise for those who carry out good deeds and perform their duties towards Allah whereas it will be torture in the pits of hell for those who do not.

THE DAY OF JUDGMENT

As we stated earlier, when the appointed time from Allah comes, of the four archangels, Israfil will blow an instrument called the "trumpet of doom" which will make an awful noise. All living creatures will die as a consequence of this noise creating important changes in the universe.

Namely:

4. An-Nisa, 4/78
5. Keşfu'l-Hafa, Volume 2, Page 90.

The sky will crack; the sun, which illuminates our day, will be folded losing its light. There will be a moon eclipse and the moon will merge with the sun.

The stars that shine in the sky will burn out and pour down like pieces of hail. A horrendous earthquake will shake the earth, the seas will merge and mountains will be broken off and thrown like cotton. Briefly: the current order of the universe will be destroyed and the earth and sky will take a different form.

This big event is called Judgment Day. Only Allah knows when it will take place.

REWARD, PENALTY, PARADISE AND HELL

"Reward" is recompense for the doing of good, whereas the recompense for doing bad is "Penalty."

People have been sent to this world as part of a test. They have been informed of the duties for which they are accountable. Those who fulfil Allah's commands, avoid His prohibitions and do good to people will achieve success in the examination and as recompense will be rewarded greatly. Everyone will receive recompense in full in the hereafter for what they do in this world.

Allah the Almighty commands:

"And We place the scales of justice for the Day of Judgment, so no soul will be treated unjustly at all." [6]

"So whoever does an atom's weight of good will see it, And whoever does an atom's weight of evil will see it." [7]

Paradise is a place of reward prepared for believers.

There are blessings in paradise which no person has even dreamed of, which eyes of this world have not seen and ears have not heard. Paradise is a place of unique beauty where people will continuously find everything that they enjoy and that pass through their hearts. Everything there is in accordance with people's desires; whatever they wish for will be instantly ready next to them.

6. Al-'Anbiya, 21/47
7. Az-Zalzalah, 99/7-8

There is no sickness, fear or sadness in paradise. People will always remain young and never age there. Life in paradise is eternal. There is no death. Those who enter there will not exit, they will find whatever their hearts desire, they will reside there with pleasure and joy until eternity.

On this topic, the holy Qur'an commands:

"But they who believe and do righteous deeds - those are the companions of paradise; they will remain therein eternally."[8]

"There they will have all that they desire, and with Us is more." [9]

The recompense of actions for those who do not perform their duties towards Allah, who do not avoid the haram and those who harm others, will be penalized in hell.

Hell is a place where faithless people and people who commit sin, even if they are believers, will be penalized by fire. People who die without faith will remain here eternally. Even though they believe, those who do not act according to the commandments of Allah, who do not fulfil their religious duties will remain in hell for a defined period and will later exit and enter paradise. The infidels and hypocrites will remain in hell eternally.

The status of infidels and hypocrites are explained in the Qur'an as follows:

"And those who disbelieve and deny Our signs - those will be companions of the Fire; they will remain there eternally." [10]

"Indeed, the hypocrites will be in the lowest depths of the Fire - and never will you find for them a helper ."[11]

QUESTIONS

1) What does Judgment Day mean?
2) Explain briefly the benefits of having faith in the hereafter.
3) What does death mean?
4) What will life in the grave be like?
5) What does Judgment Day mean?
6) Explain the meaning of the words reward and penalty.
7) What is paradise and hell? Who have they been prepared for?

---

8. Al-Baqarah, 2/82
9. Qaf, 50/35
10. Al-Baqarah, 2/39
11. An-Nisa, 4/145

UNIT VIII

FAITH IN QADAR & QADA

Topics:

- What are *qadar* and *qada*?
- A person's responsibilities
- Benefits of having faith in *qadar* and *qada*
- Sustenance and time of death
- *Tawakkul* and working
- The importance of working in Islam
- Let's plant trees (Reading)

WHAT ARE QADAR AND QADA

The sixth condition of faith is to believe that *qadar* and *qada*, goodness and harm is with the will of Allah.

The meaning of *qadar* and *qada* as religious terms:

***Qadar*:** is for Allah to know everything from the past eternity; and to determine when, where and how things will occur.

***Qada*:** is the creation of the things that Allah has predestined from the past for eternity.

If we liken *qadar* to a plan, *qada* is the making of it in accordance with the plan. Everything that occurs in the universe is by means of Allah's knowledge, will and creating. There is no other creator except Him.

It means to have faith in *qadar* and *qada*, goodness and evil, everything that is good and bad is due to Allah's will, determination and the creation when the time comes.

A PERSON'S RESPONSIBILITIES

There are two parts to people's responsibilities:

Firstly, it is the things that occur through Allah's creation outside their own will. It is like the shaking of a hand when sick, or the functioning of the heart or one's height being short or long.

These occur directly with the will and creation of Allah and people are not accountable for these things.

Secondly, the things created by Allah which are tied to the will of a person. It is with the will of a person and the creation of Allah that a person sits down and stands up, walks and moves their limbs.. People are accountable for these things.

Everything is ordained and created by Allah. However, Allah gives people freedom to choose and the will power to decide whether to do something. If a person chooses to perform good deeds with this will power and uses his/her strength to do this, Allah will create the goodness. If a person chooses to do harm and uses his/her strength to do this, Allah will create the evil.

It can be seen that Allah creates whatever a person wants to do. Good and evil is from Allah. The meaning of this statement is that goodness and harm is part of Allah's creation.

The reason why a person is being held accountable for their actions is the fact that he possesses a freedom to choose and use his power to do the things he chooses. It is for this reason that a person is accountable for everything he does with his own will power. He will see reward for the good that he did and penalty if he committed any harm.

THE BENEFITS OF HAVING FAITH IN *QADAR* AND *QADA*

A person who believes in *qadar* understands that everything in the universe occurs according to Allah's will and creation. However, they also know that they have been given the freedom to choose and the power to do things. A person who possesses this belief, strives to achieve success in life and is undaunted by anything. This is because if people direct their freedom and power to do something, they believe that Allah will create that thing and lead them to achieve success.

Because a person knows that they will be accountable for the things they do through their own will, they choose to use their freedom to do good things. They avoid things that incur divine punishment. Thus, the belief in *qadar* increases a person's power to work and earns them the feeling of accountability.

A person who believes in *qadar* does not become pessimistic or be of low morale if they do not achieve success in their activities or if they encounter disaster. This is because there is purpose and wisdom in everything Allah does. Since a person is a creature who was created with limited ability of understanding such a purpose, he has no responsibility for things outside of his ability, bows to Allah's will and takes refuge in Him. This belief gives comfort to a person and allays any sadness.

The belief in *qadar* teaches us that everything in the universe has been created in accordance with a plan and purpose and that there is a reason for everything.

With this belief, a person investigates ways and reasons to achieve success and works hard to perform the duties assigned to them.

SUSTENANCE (Rizq)

All the things that living creatures eat, drink and utilize are called sustenance. The source of sustenance for all living creatures is Allah. Allah the Almighty commands:

"And there is no creature on earth but its sustenance is due from Allah." [1]

Allah has preordained and determined everyone's sustenance. However, a person is responsible for seeking and finding sustenance. A person's duty is to earn sustenance by *halal* means in accordance with Allah's commands. Allah will provide sustenance to people in any way they choose. While earning their sustenance, if a person uses his will power for evil and consumes what is haram will be punished because of those mistakes.

TIME OF DEATH

Allah created humankind from nothing, allowed them to live and foreordained how long a person will live. A lifespan is the limited period between a person's birth and death. Time of death is the time where the worldly life ends.

Allah preordained how long everyone will live, and when, where and how they will die. Whatever death's reason, time of death is one, its cause is

1. Hud, 11/6

unvarying. A person dies when the determined time of death arrives. Allah the Almighty informs us that the time of death will not change in the Qur'an as follows:

"And when their term comes, neither can they delay nor can they advance it an hour." [2]

The duty that falls upon us: To protect our health, avoid things that put our lives in danger, not to waste our limited time in this world for nothing, to live life in this world as if we were never going to die and to work for the hereafter as if we were going to die tomorrow.

A person should perform his duties on time without leaving it for the future, as he does not know when his life will cease and when death will arrive.

TAWAKKUL AND WORKING

Tawakkul is to put one's trust in and await results from Allah after making every effort within his power in relation to any task.

Let me explain this with an example:

A farmer who wants good crop from his farm firstly ploughs his field nicely, then sows the seed, spreads the fertilizer and if required, waters it. After taking all sorts of measures to protect the crop from damage, he leaves the rest to Allah, trusting Him. The farmer has then done all that he can. Now, he has to trust in Allah and wait for results from Him for the crop to grow and give products. This is true *tawakkul.*

Wanting something to happen without working for it and awaiting results from Allah is not *tawakkul*. This thought is wrong and an unsuitable behavior for a Muslim.

Our Prophet (salla Allāhu ʿalay-hi wa-sallam) stated the following to a person who left his camel outside without tying it and said I have *tawakkul* in Allah: **"First tie your camel then have *tawakkul* in Allah."**[3] It is understood from the words of our Prophet that a Muslim must first do all that he can within his power and then have *tawakkul* in Allah.

2. An-Nahl 16/61
3. Keşfu'l-Hafa, Volume 1, Page 144

Just as performing prayer and fasting are religious duties, working to earn a livelihood is a task that has the value of worship.

Allah the Almighty commands: **"And when the prayer has been concluded, disperse within the land and seek from the bounty of Allah."** [4]

Our beloved Prophet informed us that it is a religious imperative (*fard*) to seek *halal* earnings. [5] Umar stated:

"None of you should say to Allah give me sustenance whilst abandoning the seeking of it. You know that gold or silver does not fall from the sky." [6]

It can be seen that working is a command of our ,religion; it is a Muslim's duty. To be successful with a task, we should do everything that we can which is within our power and then wait for Allah in order for us to achieve success.

THE IMPORTANCE OF WORKING IN ISLAM

The main aim of Islam, the last and the perfect religion, is the happiness of humankind. This happiness is not one sided or unbalanced.

Islam has shown people ways of being happy both in this world and in the hereafter. Happiness in this world and the hereafter is achieved by working. For this reason, a Muslim must work for both. It is also a command of our religion to earn and work for this world.

Allah the Almighty emphasizes the importance of working in the Qur'an as: **"And that there is not for man except that good for which he works."** [7]

Our beloved Prophet stated, **"The most auspicious food a person eats is one achieved with his own effort. Allah's Prophet Da'ud (alayhi al-salām) also made a living with his own effort."** [8]

Our religion has placed great importance on working and has valued the deriving of halal earnings as worship.

4. Al-Jumu'ah, 62/10
5. Keşfu'l-Hafa, Volume 3, Page 46.
6. Şehru Ayni-İlm, Volume 1, Page 182
7. An-Najm, 53/39
8. Riyadh us Salihen, Volume 1, Page 569.

One day at a place where our Prophet was located they saw a powerful and strong person walking by. The Companions who saw this asked, **"O Allah's messenger, if only this person would work for the sake of Allah."**

Upon this, our Prophet (salla Allāhu ʿalay-hi wa-sallam) stated: **"If this man has left his home to earn bread for his small children, then he is on Allah's path. He is again on Allah's path if he has left home to fulfil the needs of his elderly mother and father. He is on Allah's path if he has left to earn his own bread. If he has left for show then, he is on the path of satan."**[9]

The two of the five conditions of Islam, zakat and hajj are worships that are compulsory for wealthy Muslims. Wealth is achieved by working. A person who works is a useful person because he is useful to himself, his family and his nation.

Our Prophet has expressed this truth by stating: **"The best person is the one who is the most beneficial to people."** [10]

Our Prophet always recommended us to work and asked us to go forward every day, stating: **"Whoever lives two days the same is deceived."** [11]

A Muslim from Madinah came to the Prophet asking for assistance. Our Prophet asked him:

- Do not you have anything at home? He replied:

- We have a mat that we pull over us and lies on the floor, and a pot that we drink water from. Our Prophet replied:

- Go and bring them to me. The man went home and brought them back to the Prophet. Our Prophet asked:

- Who will buy these? One of the Muslims said:

- O Allah's messenger, I will buy them for one dirham. Our Prophet asked:

- Is there anyone willing to pay more? Another person said:

- I will pay two dirhams for these. Our Prophet gave these to that man. He then turned to the first man that had come to him:

---

9. Et-Terğib ve't-terhib, Volume 2, Page 524.
10. 250 Khadith, Page 121
11. Keşfu'l-Hafa, Volume 2, Page 233

- Take these (dirhams), buy food for home with one and an axe with the other, and then bring it to me. Our Prophet put a handle on the axe that the man had brought with his own hands and said:

- Now go and cut some wood from the mountains and sell it. I do not want to see you around here for fifteen days.

The man returned fifteen days later. He had earned ten dirhams, bought some food with a portion of it and some clothing. Thereupon, our Prophet said:

Working like this is better than begging. Because on the Day of Judgment, those who beg will have black stains on their faces. [12]

With these words, our Prophet has shown us the way to be happy in this world and the hereafter. He stated:

"The best of you is one who does not abandon the hereafter for this world, who doesn't abandon this world for the hereafter but works for both without being a burden on people." [13]

In that case, a Muslim must work for both this world and the hereafter, moving ahead each day. This is a command of our religion.

Do not think that your ancestors slept for centuries;
Where would you then find the homeland that you now have?
The remains that bleed from time to time on three continents are witnesses
That great generation of holy Muslim warriors did not rest even one day.

M.Akif ERSOY

READING:

Let us plant trees...

Our beloved Prophet (salla Allāhu ʿalay-hi wa-sallam) stated:

"If on the Day of Judgment one of you has a date sapling in hand, they should plant this immediately, not letting it go if they have the power to do so prior to Judgment Day breaking." [14]

12 Et-Terğib ve't-Terhib, Volume 2, Page 523.

13 Muhtaru'l-Ehadis

14 250 Hadith, Page 27.

"If a Muslim plants a tree or plants something else and a bird, a person or an animal eats from this then, this will be charity for one's self...[15]."

"If a person plants a tree then a reward is given in his book of deeds for the amount of fruit the tree gives." [16]

When Harun Rashid, one of the Abbasid Caliphs, saw an elderly person plant a small fruit sapling he said to them:

- Father! You are very old, why do you inconvenience yourself for you will not see the fruit of the tree that you plant?

The elderly man responded as follows:

- Those before us planted trees and we ate its fruit. Now we should plant trees so that those after us can eat it.

Harun Rashid was delighted with this response and gave the old man a handful of gold. The old man said:

- See my son, now I already have seen the fruits of the saplings that I planted.

With these words, Harun Rashid was pleased once again.

Trees and forests are a rich resource of this country. From the air that we breathe to the water that we drink, from the book that we read to the pencil that we write with, we see the byproducts of trees just about everywhere. For living things to be able to survive, the required oxygen is produced by forests almost like a factory; various animals and birds are also sheltered in its bosom. Forests also prevent the erosion of soil into the sea.

For this reason, without doubt, it is just as favorable to raise trees, as it is to raise children. However favorable it is to plant and tend to trees, it is equally sinful to cut trees and deforest.

Our Prophet stated the following: ***"Whoever cuts a live tree, Allah the Almighty will on the Day of Judgment throw that person upside down into hell."*** [17]

This hadith is an important warning to Muslims.

---

15. Tecrid-i Sarih Tercemesi ve Şerhi, Volume 7, Page 121.
16. Tecrid-i Sarih Tercemesi ve Şerhi, Volume 7, Page 122.
17. Feyzu'l-Kadir. Volume 6, Page 206.

How can a person cut down a tree unless it is a requirement? How can they be accountable for forests burning to ashes and many living creatures burning alive whilst taking shelter?

Those who demolish trees and forests cruelly will have to answer for this evil on Judgment Day where they will be inflicted with a deserved punishment. As Muslims, our duty is to obey the commands and recommendations of our Prophet, to plant and grow trees, to look after trees like children, to protect forests like our eye. Planting trees is as auspicious as worship. Besides, it is a patriotic duty. A citizen who carries the love of trees in their heart has expressed their feelings beautifully:

Like the hands of a person making dua, the appeal of the branches of a tree that reach towards the sky:

It is me that protects you from the cold nights of winter heating your home and protecting you from the sun on hot summer days.

It is I on the roof of your home, your door and the wood of the table.

I am the pencil, the paper and the faithful companion from the cradle to the grave.

I participate in your joy at birth, your service during life and your pain at death.

Save me from the blaze of the fire, the cutting of the axe and the teeth of the goat.

Because, I am the beauty of the country, the carnival and ornament of the land and the covering of the mountains.

Love me, so birds can sing on my branches, so the wind can sing songs in my head and so travelers can rest in my shade.

Do not burn me as rivers will become torrents and mountains will become bald. Fountains will dry and the land will become barren. May you burn cow dung and build from mud brick.

Listen to my advice; engage your axe on stone without touching a tree.

Do not burn me; do not sacrifice the creatures that I shelter.

May the biggest wish tree that severs from your heart be love.

How can we sacrifice or raise our hands to live trees where these feelings call out to us simply begging not to be sacrificed?

QUESTIONS

1) Describe what *qadar* and *qada* is.
2) How many parts is a person's work divided into?
3) Why are people accountable for what they do?
4) What are the benefits of having faith in *qadar* and *qada*?
5) Explain what sustenance and time of death is.
6) Explain the understanding of working and *tawakkul*.
7) Explain the importance of working in Islam.

CHAPTER TWO
WORSHIP

UNIT I

WORSHIP

Topics:

- What is worship and why do we worship?
- The types of worship
- The degrees and benefits of worship

WHAT IS WORSHIP?

Worship is to show honor and respect to Allah and fulfil a debt of gratitude for the countless blessings that He has given to us.

WHY DO WE WORSHIP?

Allah has created us from nothing. He is the source of our life. Allah the Almighty has equipped our bodies with perfect organs such as eyes that see, ears that hear and tongues that speak. He has elevated us to a loftier state being eminent amongst creations and being distinctive from other living things by giving us wisdom. Aside from this, He has provided us with countless blessings such as the air that we breathe and water that we drink in order to live.

Moreover, He did not leave us alone; He sent us Prophets and books showing the path to happiness in this world and the hereafter. For all this goodness, Allah has wanted us to recognize Him and worship Him. Let us think, we respect and thank our elders when we see goodness from them. If they give us a duty, we do it lovingly, do we not?

If that is the case, is not it necessary to give thanks to Allah the Almighty and perform lovingly the worship that He commanded? It is necessary, it is Allah who created us from nothing and provided us with countless blessings.

The purpose of our creation is to recognize and worship Allah. By performing our duties of worship, we fulfil our debt of gratitude to the blessings provided and attain His love. If we perform our duties of worship to Allah and attain His love, then He will provide much more worldly blessings in the hereafter and allow us to attain endless happiness in paradise.

TYPES OF WORSHIP

There are three kinds of worship:

1) Worship performed with the body: such as performing prayer and fasting.

Muslims must perform all acts of worship with the body by themselves. It is not lawful to appoint an agent on your behalf. A person cannot perform prayer or fast on behalf of another person.

2) Worship performed with wealth: such as giving *zakat* or sacrificing a *qurban*. A person can appoint an agent for worship performed with one's wealth.

3) Worship performed with both body and wealth: The pilgrimage is an act of worship like this.

Even though they have money to perform the pilgrimage, those who cannot perform it due to disability, illness or old age can appoint another person as an agent.

DEGREES OF WORSHIP

Worship is performed with three thoughts:

1) To Allah: As the only being worthy of worship and respect.

This is the highest degree of worship that is performed for fulfilling Allah's command without expecting a return.

2) Worship performed with the hope of entering paradise or fear of hell.

A person performing worship with this thought in mind would fulfil Allah's command. However, a person should not perform worship thinking of benefit but only for the sake of Allah.

3) To achieve a benefit in this world with the intention of worshipping for showing off.

This is the lowest degree of worship. It is not even correct to call this worship because there is no value in any worship not performed for Allah.

BENEFITS OF WORSHIP

Just as our bodies require nourishment, our spirits also require nourishment. Faith and worship are the nourishments of the spirit. Worship heightens our spirit, keeps us from evil, matures our morality and protects our faith, our most valuable asset.

There are times when people encounter various problems in life and when they are in a state of hopelessness and depression. In situations like these, people can take refuge in worship. People come closer to Allah as a result of worship. They take refuge in His mercy and attain tranquility. Just as worship has benefits for our spirits, it also has many benefits for our bodies.

A person who performs prayer must make *wudu* (ablution). To make *wudu* means to be cleansed a few times a day. We all know how useful cleanliness is for our health.

It is true that particular movements performed whilst performing prayer and the resting of the digestive system and some organs whilst fasting provide an important benefit to the health. There are many benefits from the worship of *zakat* for society from a social welfare perspective..

QUESTIONS

1) What is worship?
2) Why do we worship?
3) How many types of worship are there?
4) Explain the degrees of worship.
5) Explain the benefits of worship.

UNIT II

ISLAM

Topics:

- What does Islam mean?
- The pillars of Islam
- *Mukallaf* (accountable) and judgments concerning *mukallaf* people

WHAT DOES ISLAM MEAN?

Islam: Is to accept the truths that Allah notified to our Prophet Muhammad (salla Allāhu ʿalay-hi wa-sallam) and show our acceptance by obeying Him and His Prophet. In brief, Islam means to submit completely to Allah's will.

THE PILLARS OF ISLAM

There are five pillars in Islam:

1) To say kalimah al-shahada:

Kalimah al-shahada is to say "Ash-hadu an lâ-ilâha illallah Wa ash-hadu anna Muhammadan abduhu wa Rasulu".

Meaning: "I bear witness that there is no God except Allah, and I bear witness that Muhammad (Sall Allāhu ʿalay-hi wa-sallam) is the servant and messenger of Allah."

2) To perform prayer:

To perform prayer five times a day.

3) To fast:

To fast during the month of Ramadan every year.

4) To give *zakat*:

People who are wealthy in accordance to our religion give a certain amount of their property and wealth to the poor every year.

5) Hajj (the pilgrimage):

To perform the hajj by those who have the power and ability to do so once in a lifetime.

THE PILLARS OF ISLAM

Islam has five pillars;
Knowing is even bliss,
Whoever complies with these
Paradise opens to them...
***
The first pillar:
Kalimah al-Shahada;
From Allah, the only and greatest
There is no other God of course.
His last Prophet
The renowned supreme Muhammad
***
The second pillar is prayer.
What a beautiful worship it is.
Half an hour every day,
Turn of duty fits five times...
***
The third pillar is Ramadan
The intent is in the fast.
Without eating or drinking during the day
The length of time passes with joy...
***
The fourth pillar is zakat;
If Allah has given a fortune:
Divide its worth by forty,
Give it to someone as a gift...
***
To go to hajj once,
If it is in destiny.
The fifth pillar of Islam
To visit His Ka'bah

Gökhan EVLİYAOĞLU

WHO IS CALLED MUKALLAF?

Sane and post-pubescent people are called *mukallaf.*

A mukallaf is accountable to perform the commands of the religion and refrain from its prohibitions. There are two conditions required in order to be a *mukallaf*;

1) To be sane

2) To have reached puberty

People who are insane or children that have not reached puberty yet are not *mukallaf.*

The age of puberty varies according to the biology of a child and climatic conditions. Pubescence occurs between the ages of twelve and fifteen in males and between the ages of nine and fifteen for girls. Boys and girls who reach the age of fifteen without the signs of puberty are deemed to have reached puberty. They are *mukallaf* and must comply with religious commands and prohibitions.

JUDGMENTS CONCERNING MUKALLAF PEOPLE

There are eight judgments concerning *mukallaf* people. These are called *Af'al al-Mukallaf.*

1) Fard:

These are obligatory commandments, such as prayer, fasting, and *zakat*.

Fard judgment: Those who perform their *fard* duties receive reward in return for it. Those who do not without excuse will have earned punishment. Whoever denies a *fard* exits the religion.

Two types of *Fard*:

***a) Fard al-ayn*:** These are the commandments that are obligatory for every *mukallaf* person, such as five-time prayer.

***b) Fard al-kifayah*:** These are also obligatory commandments, but if some members of the community perform, then others would be relieved from them. The janazah prayer would be an example for this. In other words, when some Muslims perform their fard duty of the janazah prayer, that commandment would be fulfilled for the entire community.

2) Wajib:

Wajib is something that is not as certain as Fard but that has been commanded based on strong evidence. These are things such as the Eid prayer, giving *sadaqat al-fitr* and sacrificing a *qurban*.

Rulings of *wajib*:

People who perform that the *wajibs* gain reward. Those who do not without an excuse will be punished.

3) Sunnah

These are actions that our Prophet did with the intention of worship asides from what is *fard* and *wajib*.

Sunnah is divided into two:

a) *Sunnah muaqqadah*: Things that our Prophet did most of the times are called *sunnah muaqqadah*. Such as the *sunnahs* of Fajr, Zhuhr and Maghrib prayers.

b) *Sunnah ghair muaqqadah*: Things that our Prophet did from time to time are called *sunnah ghair muaqqadah*.

Rulings of sunnah:

People who perform the sunnah gain reward. They attain our Prophet's intercession. Those who abandon the sunnah knowingly, will be punished.

4) Mustahabb:

Mustahabb are things that our Prophet sometimes did and at other times did not do, such as the late morning prayer.

Rulings of *mustahabb*: People who perform actions that are *mustahabb* gain reward, but there is no punishment for those who do not.

5) Mubah

The things that people are free to do or not are called *mubah*. Actions such as sitting down, walking, and sleeping.

Rulings of *mubah*: People who perform actions that are *mubah* do not gain reward. Those who do not, do not commit sin.

6) Haram

The things that have been prohibited by our religion with certainty are called haram. Actions such as killing a person unjustly, stealing, drinking alcohol, gambling, eating pork and defying parents.

Rulings of *haram*: A person who performs an act that is haram requires punishment. Those who avoid *haram* due to the fear of Allah gain reward. Those who deny *haram* exit the religion.

7) Makruh

Actions that are disliked but not as severe as *haram*, the actions that our religion does not want us to engage in are called *makruh*.

Makruh is divided into two:

a) Karahah tahrimiyya = Makruh that is close to haram: Like not performing a *wajib*.

Ruling: People who avoid a *makruh* like this gains reward, yet those who perform commit sin.

b) Karahah tanzihiyya = Makruh that is close to halal: Like not performing actions that are *sunnah* and *mustahabb*.

Ruling: People who avoid *makruh* like this gain reward and those who do not, do not warrant any punishment.

8) Mufsid

The things that invalidate an ongoing worship. Actions like speaking whilst performing prayer, knowingly eating or drinking whilst fasting. Talking invalidates prayer and eating and drinking invalidates fasting.

Ruling: Punishment is required for invalidating worship knowingly and without a valid excuse.

QUESTIONS

1) What does Islam mean?

2) What are the pillars of Islam?
3) Who are *mukallafs*?
4) What is meant by pubescent age?
5) Explain the rulings in relation to *mukallaf.*

UNIT III

CLEANLINESS

Topics:

- Cleanliness and its importance in Islam
- Water in relation to cleanliness
- The virtue of *wudu*
- The *fards*, *sunnahs* and etiquettes of *wudu*
- How *wudu* is performed
- The *makruhs* of *wudu*, the things that invalidate *wudu*
- Things that cannot be performed without *wudu*
- Performing *masah* on socks
- Performing mash on dressings
- Ghusl
- The *fard* of *ghusl*, its *sunnah* and how it is performed
- The status of those with excuses
- Conditions specific to women
- The *fard* of *tayammum*, its *sunnah* and how it is performed
- Things that invalidate tayammum
- Environmental cleanliness (Reading)

CLEANLINESS AND ITS IMPORTANCE IN ISLAM

Islam has been founded upon cleanliness. To be a Muslim means to be a clean person. Those that are clean are loved by both Allah and people. Our supreme Lord commands the following in the holy Qur'an; **"Indeed, Allah loves those who are constantly repentant and loves those who clean themselves."** [1]

To be one of the loved ones of Allah, we must pay attention to cleanliness. Our beloved Prophet expressed the importance that our religion gives to cleanliness stating; **"Cleanliness is half of faith."** [2]

1. Al-Baqarah, 2/222
2. Meşariku'l-Envar, Volume 2, Page 107.

Muslims find themselves in the presence of Allah while performing prayer. Our bodies, clothing and the place of prayer must be clean in order to appear in Allah' presence. Our religion has placed great importance on internal cleanliness. Just as our body must be clean, our heart and spirit must also be clean.

WATER IN RELATION TO CLEANLINESS

There are two types of water:

a) Pure water:

This is water coming from rain, snow, lakes, rivers, seas, springs and wells. Nothing has been mixed with this water.

b) Restricted water:

This is water that is mixed with other substances such as rose water and grape water. Wudu and ghusl ablutions cannot be performed with this type of water.

From a cleanliness perspective, "Pure Water" is split into five parts:

1) The water which is both clean and cleansing and usage of which is not *makruh*:

This is water where their color, taste and smell remains unspoilt, and that their original structure has not been altered and that they have never been used. This water can be used for all types of cleaning. *Wudu* and *ghusl* can be performed with it and it can be used for cooking and drinking.

2) The water which is both clean and cleansing but usage of it iss *makruh*:

This is water that is left over from domestic animals such as cats and chickens and predatory birds like hawks and falcons. When there is other clean water, it is *makruh* to perform *wudu* and *ghusl* and to use these waters for drinking and cooking. When there is no other clean water, it is not *makruh* to use this type of water.

3) Water that is clean itself but does not cleanse:

These are waters used for *wudu* and *ghusl*. You cannot perform *wudu* or *ghusl* with this used water again.

4) Water that is not clean:

This is non-flowing water in which faeces has dropped. The leftover water from dogs, pigs and other predatory animals are not clean and cannot be used in any cleaning process.

5) Suspect water:

These are leftover waters from donkeys and mules. You can wash dirt with water like these. You cannot perform *wudu* or *ghusl* while there is other clean water available. If there is no other water available, you can perform *wudu*, *ghusl* and later *tayammum*. This is because we do not know whether these waters are clean or not and so their cleanliness is uncertain.

THE VIRTUE OF WUDU

Wudu is cleansing by washing and performing *masah* on specified organs in an appropriate manner. Our beloved Prophet has stated the following in relation to the virtue of *wudu* and its spiritual benefits:

"When a Muslim washes his hands in the course of *wudu*, the sins that he committed with his hands are forgiven; when he washes his face, the sins that he committed with his eyes; when he performs the *masah* on his head, the sins that he committed with his ears; when he washes his feet, the sins that he committed whilst walking with his feet are forgiven." [3]

"When one of you performs *wudu* completely, the eight gates of paradise opens and you may enter through the one that you wish if you say after *wudu*: "Ash-hadu an lâ-ilâha illallahu wahdahu la sharika lah wa ash-hadu anna Muhammadan abduhu wa Rasulu." [4]

Wudu has many benefits for our health. Muslims who perform *wudu* wash their organs continually because of the dirty contact of their surroundings. This protects him from many illnesses.

---

3. Et-Terğib ve't Terhib, volume 1, Page 155
4. Ibid., volume 1, Page 171

THE FARDS OF WUDU

The *fards* of *wudu* are four:

1) To wash the face once,

2) To wash the arms including the elbows once,

3) To perform the *masah* (wiping with wet hands) on one quarter of the head,

4) To wash feet together with heels once.

Wudu will not be valid if one of these *fard*s are incomplete.

THE SUNNAHS OF WUDU

1) Saying the *niyyah* (intention) to perform *wudu*,

2) To commence *wudu* with *Auzu* and the *Basmala*,

3) Firstly, to wash the hands up to the wrists,

4) To brush the teeth with a *miswak* (tooth-stick), a brush, or rub with fingers,

5) To wash the limbs in *wudu* consecutively, one organ should be washed before the other dries,

6) All limbs that are washed must be rubbed thoroughly,

7) To sip water into your mouth three times and then empty it,

8) To rinse the mouth thoroughly with water when you are not fasting,

9) To sniff water into the nose three times and to blow it out each time with the left hand, (To thoroughly sniff water into the nose when not fasting)

10) To make sure that the order of washing the *wudu* limbs and *masah* is in accordance with the above mentioned order,

11) To wash all required organs three times,

12) To always commence washing in *wudu* with the right side,

13) To commence with the fingers when washing the hands and feet,

14) To comb the beard with one's fingers for those that have thick beards,

15) To move the ring on one's finger,

16) To perform the *masah* of the two ears,

17) To perform the *masah* of the neck,

18) To perform the *masah* over the whole head,

19) To separate and space out all fingers and toes.

THE ETIQUETTES OF WUDU

1) To perform *wudu* and be ready for prayer prior to the prayer time,

2) To turn toward the *qibla* whilst performing *wudu*,

3) To sit at in high place,

4) Not to ask others for assistance whilst performing *wudu*,

5) Not to talk unless compelled to whilst performing *wudu*,

6) Not to waste *wudu* water by using too much, and not to use as little water as possible so the water does not flow off the *wudu* organs,

7) To recite the *kalimah al-shahada* by facing the *qibla* after *wudu*.

HOW WUDU IS PERFORMED

Firstly, turn towards the qibla if possible. State your intention by saying *"I intend to perform wudu for the consent of Allah"* and recite *"Auzu billahi Minash shaitanir rajeem, Bismillahir Rahmanir Raheem."*

Then, in order:

Wash your hands up to the wrists three times, if there is a ring on a finger then move it to ensure that the area under the ring is washed.

After this, sip water into your mouth three separate times from your right palm rinsing it properly on each occasion. Once aagain, with your right palm, sniff water into your nose three separate times and clean your nose with your left hand by blowing it.

Later, wash your face completely three times. After this, the right arm is firstly washed three times together with the elbows then, the left arm is washed together with the elbows three times.

After this, the hands are wet with new water; the *masah* is performed with the inside of the right hand by wiping the top of your head. The hands are then wet and the *masah* is performed on the insides of the ears with the index fingers and the outside of the ears with the thumbs. With the back of the three remaining fingers, the *masah* is performed on the behind of the neck.

After this, firstly the right foot and then the left foot together with the ankles are washed three times. Whilst washing the feet, it is appropriate to wash the toes starting from the small toe to the big toe on your right foot and then from the small toe to the big toe on the left foot.

We must pay attention to cleaning the toes thoroughly whilst washing the feet.

When *wudu* is completed, the *kalimah al-shahada* is recited by facing the *qibla*. The *fard*, *sunnah* and the etiquettes are fulfilled when the *wudu* is performed like this. There are *duas* that are recited whilst performing *wudu*.[5] It is very beautiful for these to be recited. The *wudu* would still be complete if they are not recited.[6]

THE MAKRUHS OF WUDU

The *makruh*s of *wudu* are the following:

1) To use more water than required,
2) To use less water than normal even though it is not required,
3) To splash the water on the limbs of *wudu* quickly,
4) To talk unnecessarily whilst performing *wudu*,
5) To perform *wudu* in a dirty area.

A person performing *wudu* should avoid these.

5. You can find the *duas* of *wudu* at the end of this book.
6. You can find pictorial instruction of how *wudu* is performed at the end of this book.

THINGS THAT INVALIDATE WUDU

The *wudu* of a person would be invalidated with the occurrence of one of the following situations:

1) If blood, pus or water is excreted from any part of the body,

2) A mouthful of vomit,

3) When spitting, if half or more than half of the spit is blood,

4) To go to the toilet (to urinate or defecate), to break wind,

5) To faint or be drunk,

6) To laugh whilst performing prayer (laughing outside of prayer does not invalidate *wudu*),

7) To sleep.

THINGS THAT CANNOT BE PERFORMED WITHOUT WUDU

1) You cannot perform prayer,

2) You cannot touch the holy Qur'an,

3) You cannot perform *sajdah al-tilawah*,

4) You cannot circumambulate the Ka'bah. (It is *wajib* to have performed *wudu* in order to circumambulate the Ka'bah)

TO PERFORM MASAH (WIPING) OVER SOCKS

It is sufficient for a person who wears socks (thin-soled boot) after performing *wudu* to be able to perform the *masah* over their socks at the following *wudu* if the socks have not been taken off. This is an ease granted to Muslims by our religion.

Residents (those who are not travelling) can perform *masah* over their socks during a 24-hour period. After this 24-hour period, the feet must be washed when the next *wudu* is performed. This period for those that are travelers, in a religious sense, is three days or 72 hours.

The *masah* is performed over socks as follows:

Once you have reached the stage of washing your feet after performing *wudu* as described above, you firstly wet your right hand and then with three fingers (with the fingers open), you perform the *masah* over the socks commencing from the tip of the right foot towards your ankle passing over the heel. Later, you wet the left hand and perform the *masah* over the left foot as described. The *masah* is not performed underneath the socks.

Conditions that make the *masah* acceptable:

The following conditions must be fulfilled in order for the *masah* to be performed and be lawful over socks:

1) The socks must be worn (after the feet have been washed) at the time of *wudu*,

2) The socks must cover the heels of the feet. You cannot perform the *masah* over socks that are below the heel,

3) The socks must be durable enough to withstand walking at least twelve thousand steps or more,

4) There must not be any holes, rips or tears in any sock exceeding the width of three fingers,

5) The socks must be thick enough to remain on the feet without laces,

6) The socks must not allow any water to be absorbed in from the outside.

You cannot perform *masah* over your feet if you have lost the front part of your sock where there is not at least three fingers remaining. You must wash your feet. You must wash both feet even if one sock is partially missing and the other is undamaged. It is not lawful to perform the *masah* over the undamaged foot alone.

Things that invalidate the *masah*:

1) The things that invalidate the *wudu*.

2) For this reason, you will be required to perform the *masah* over the socks when performing *wudu* again.

3) If the socks are taken off or removed from the feet.

4) In this case, if the person's *wudu* is valid, they only need to wash their feet. If only one sock is removed then it is necessary for both feet to be washed. If their *wudu* is invalid, they need to perform *wudu* and wash their feet.

TO PERFORM MASAH OVER A DRESSING

If there is a fracture on any part of the body or there is a dressing as a result of a wound, the dressing should be removed and inside of it should be washed when performing *wudu* or *ghusl*. You are not required to remove the dressing and wash the bottom of the wound if it is harmful to do so. In this situation, you wet your hand and perform the *masah* over the dressing once.

If there is no dressing over a wound where medication is applied then that part should be washed as long as it is not harmful to do so. If water will harm it then do not wash it, rather perform the *masah* over it. You can abandon this, too if performing the masah is also harmful.

GHUSL

Ghusl is washing the whole body without leaving any part dry.

The situations that require *ghusl* are:

1) A state of impurity (unclean body in Islam):

a) After sexual relations having reached puberty

b) Excretion of fluid from certain organs of both men and women whether asleep or awake

2) When a woman's menstruation ends each month

3) When the postpartum period ends after a woman has given birth

It is *fard* for people in this situation to perform *ghusl*. Those who do not perform *ghusl* cannot:

a) Perform prayer.

b) Recite the Qur'an.

c) Touch the Qur'an.

d) Circumambulate the Ka'bah.

e) Enter a mosque unless it is necessary.

Furthermore, women cannot fast during menstruation and the postpartum period.

It is *sunnah* to perform *ghusl* even though there is no condition requiring it on *jumu'ah*s and *Eid* prayers.

THE FARDS OF GHUSL

The *fards* of *ghusl* are three:

1) To sip water into the mouth and rinse up until the throat,

2) To sniff water into the nose and clean it,

3) To wash the whole body (without leaving any dry spots the size of the point of a needle).

THE SUNNAHS OF GHUSL

1) The main *sunnah* of *ghusl* are the following:

2) To commence *ghusl* with the *Basmala*,

3) To state your intention to perform *ghusl*,

4) To wash and clean beforehand any dirt or filth that may be on your body,

5) To wash your genitals,

6) To perform *wudu* prior to commencing *ghusl*,

7) After *wudu*, begin washing by pouring water three times over the head, then three times on the right shoulder, and three times on the left shoulder. Ensure that the water reaches the whole body each time it is poured.

8) To rub your body when you pour water.

9) To leave washing your feet to the end if water accumulates around your feet.

HOW GHUSL IS PERFORMED

First, recite the *Basmala* and state your intention. Wash your genitalia after washing your hands to the wrists.

After this, sip water in to your mouth from your right palm three times rinsing the mouth thoroughly each time until the throat. Those fasting must ensure that water does not escape to the throat. Then, sniff water into the nose three times with your right palm and clean your nose by blowing it out each time with the left hand.

After this, perform *wudu* as explained earlier. After the *wudu* is completed, begin washing by pouring water three times over the head, then three times on the right shoulder, and three times on the left shoulder. Each time you pour water on yourself, rub the body as far as your hands can reach. Wash the whole body three times without leaving any dry spots the size of the point of a needle.

While washing:

Special attention must be paid to ensure that the bottom of the belly button, the curves inside the ear, the ear piercing holes, between the teeth, moustache, hair and beard are wet. No *duas* are recited during *ghusl*, you do not turn towards the *qibla* unless you are covered or you should not talk unnecessarily. This is how *ghusl* is performed conforming to the *fard* and *sunnah*.

A person who is required to perform *ghusl* can perform it by sipping water into the mouth and nose rinsing it properly and then wetting their whole body by entering running water, the sea or a large pool.

THE STATUS OF THOSE WITH AN EXCUSE

If one of the things that invalidates *wudu* occurs continuously throughout the time of prayer, it is called an excuse. The person in this situation is called the owner of an excuse.

If a person's nose bleeds all the time due to an illness, or blood or any another type of discharge (drops of urine or puss) appear from any part of the body and if the discharge ceases within the time of prayer, *wudu* is performed and the prayer can be completed.

If the discharge continues throughout the whole time of prayer and there is not a pause long enough for *wudu* to be performed then, this person is considered to be the owner of an excuse.

If the discharge continues after the time of prayer, a person in this situation should perform the *wudu* and complete his prayer. A person can continue to perform prayer (such as *qada* and *nafila* prayers) within this prayer time period as much as he likes providing nothing else invalidates his *wudu* besides the continuing discharge.

The *wudu* of an excuse owner is invalidated when the time of that prayer expires. For as long as the condition of excuse continues, a person must perform *wudu* again after the time of prayer commences.

This is an ease that our religion has shown to excuse owners.

SPECIFIC CONDITIONS FOR WOMEN

There are three specific conditions for women:

1) Menstruation:

A specific state occurs to women when they reach puberty. This is called menstruation. Menstruation occurs every month at specific times and generally continues until the age of 55, or sometimes much earlier than this age.

The menstruation period differs from women to women. The shortest period is three and the longest is ten days. It is not mandatory for there to be continuous discharge during these days. Even if the discharge ceases from time to time, this period is still counted as part of the menstruation. As some things are *haram* for women during this period, they should know their days of menstruation well and must be careful.

On the days when women have their menstruation, they cannot:

1) Perform prayer,
2) Fast,
3) Recite the Qur'an,
4) Touch the holy Qur'an,

5) Perform the *tawaf* of the Ka'bah,

6) Enter a mosque,

7) Have sexual relations with their partner.

When the menstruation period ends, it is *fard* to perform the *ghusl*. Women do not need to make-up for the prayer missed during the period of menstruation as Allah almighty has absolved them. The fasting that they miss during the month of Ramadan is required as a *qada*, i.e. performed later on.

2) The postpartum period:

The specific condition of women after giving birth is called the postpartum period.

The postpartum period continues for a maximum period of forty days after childbirth. There is no limit for the minimum time. It can end prior to forty days. In this case, women can continue their worship after performing *ghusl*. They do not have to wait for the completion of the forty days. If the discharge ceases and then continues during the days of postpartum, this period is counted towards the days of the postpartum period.

The things that are *haram* during the menstruation period are also *haram* during the postpartum period.

It is *fard* to perform *ghusl* after the postpartum period is finished. The prayers that are missed during the postpartum period are not required to be performed later but the fasting that was missed must be made-up by *qada*.

3) **Istihaza:**

If the discharge lasts less than three days, this is not the menstruation ,period; rather it is counted as an excuse for women. Discharge that continue for more than ten days or a postpartum period that continue for more than forty days or discharges that appear whilst pregnant are also considered like that. This condition is called *istihaza*.

In situations like these, women perform prayer and fast. This is because these conditions are not menstruation or postpartum periods. It is considered a medical condition like a nose bleed.

TAYAMMUM

State your intention, place your hands on the clean earth, or on something of a similar nature, and then perform the *masah* over the face and arms. This is called *tayammum*. If you are unable to find water to perform *wudu* or *ghusl*, *tayammum* is performed in the place of *wudu* and *ghusl*.

FARDS OF TAYAMMUM

The *fard*s of *tayammum* are two:

1) To state the intention,

2) To hit your hands on clean earth or on something of a similar nature twice. After the first time you perform the masah over the face and then the arms the second time.

SUNNAHS OF TAYAMMUM

1) To firstly recite the *Basmala*,

2) To observe the order,

3) To perform it consecutively without pausing,

4) Firstly rub the hands forward when you hit the earth,

5) Then, rub the hands back,

6) To keep the fingers apart,

7) Shaking the dust off by hitting the hands together if they are dusty when raised.

HOW IS TAYAMMUM PERFORMED?

State your intention for the *tayammum*. With your fingers apart, hit your hands on clean earth or on something of a similar nature once. If the hands are overly dusty, then shake them off by hitting them together slightly.

Then, the *masah* is performed once over the face with the inside of the hands.

The hands are then hit on the earth again. The *masah* is then performed firstly with the left palm over the right arm together with the elbow. Then, perform the *masah* with the right palm over the left arm together with the elbow.

THINGS THAT INVALIDATE TAYAMMUM

1) The things that invalidate *wudu* also invalidate *tayammum*.

2) The *tayammum* is invalidated if water is found to perform *wudu* and *ghusl*.

3) If a person needs to perform *tayammum* because water cannot be touched on the body due to a wound or excuse, the *tayammum* is invalidated when the excuse is removed.

IN WHICH SITUATIONS IS TAYAMMUM PERFORMED?

1) When there is not enough clean water to perform *wudu* or *ghusl*,

2) In situations when there is water but it is not possible to use this water,

3) When all of the body or most of it has wounds and it is harmful to use water in these situations.

In order to perform worship, *tayammum* is an ease endowed to our beloved Prophet and to us Muslims by Allah the Almighty.

READING:

Environmental Cleanliness

Cleanliness does not only consist of our bodies, our clothes or inside our houses. The range of cleanliness in our religion is much broader. Environmental cleanliness not only concerns us but other people as well. Polluting the environment and disturbing others means to harm other people. However, a Muslim is a person who does not harm others or hurt any living things.

7. Tirmidhi, Adab

*Our Prophet has ordered that the surroundings of our houses must be cleaned by stating, **"Clean your courtyards."**[7]*

It is very bad to pollute a clean environment; it is ugly behavior and is unbecoming of a Muslim.

*Our Prophet stated, "**Refrain from being those that have been cursed.**"*

Thereupon a Companion asked:

'Who are these, oh Messenger of Allah?" He asked. Our Prophet replied:

> ***"Those who pollute the road that the public use and the shady places where they rest."**[8]*

Polluting the roads where people travel on, the places where they live and rest and disturbing them is not compatible with the morality of Islam.

A Muslim does not engage in any actions that discomforts other people. They must pay attention to the roads on which they travel back and forth each day ensuring that they are kept clean and well maintained. They must keep public places, parks, gardens and attractions clean and take care of them.

Our Prophet has shown how much importance he placed on the environment by forbidding urinating in still waters. He would personally clean off the spit off that he saw on the masjid walls by scraping and removing it with a piece of rock.

Our Prophet did not allow people to spit on the floor, so how is it possible for a Muslim to cause discomfort to other people by polluting the environment? How is it possible that a Muslim could be involved in actions that cause harm to others?

*Our Prophet stated: "**Whoever eats onions or garlic should stay away from us and our masjids.**"[9] Indeed, garlic and onions are halal foods. However, the smell of the mouths of people who eat these annoys other people. For this reason, we should not eat onions or garlic when going to mosques. If we had eaten them, then we should avoid others and not cause them any discomfort until the smell subsides.*

Allah the Almighty commands in the holy Qur'an that He loves those who observe cleanliness. In that case, let us keep our surroundings clean

9. Riyadh us Salihen, Volume. 3, Page. 282
10. Bukhari, Babu bed'il-Ezan.

and be one of the servants that Allah loves. People also like others who are clean. Let us try to earn the love of people by paying attention to cleanliness and not their hatred by polluting the environment.

QUESTIONS

1) Explain the importance that Islam gives to cleanliness.
2) From a cleanliness perspective, how many types of water are there?
3) Explain the virtue of *wudu*.
4) Explain the *fard*s of *wudu*, its *sunnah* and the rules of good manners.
5) How is *wudu* performed?
6) What are the *makruh* and the things that invalidate *wudu*?
7) What can a person without *wudu* not perform?
8) How is *masah* performed over socks?
9) In what situations is *masah* performed over dressings?
10) What is *ghusl* and what are the situations that require *ghusl*?
11) What cannot be performed in the situations of impurity?
12) What are the *fard*s of *ghusl* and the main *sunnah*s?
13) How is *ghusl* performed?
14) How do the owners of excuses act?
15) What are the specific conditions of women?
16) What is *tayammum*, what are the *fard*s of *tayammum* and its *sunnah*s?
17) How is *tayammum* performed?
18) In which situations is *tayammum* performed?

UNIT IV

PRAYER (I)

Topics:

- The importance of prayer, who is it *fard* for?
- Prayer times and times when it is unlawful to pray
- Types of prayer
- The *fards*, *wajibs* and *sunnahs* of prayer
- Things that invalidate prayer and the *makruhs* of prayer
- How prayer is performed five times a day
- How the *fajr* prayer is performed
- How the *zhuhr* prayer is performed
- How the *asr* prayer is performed
- How the *maghrib* prayer is performed
- How the *isha* prayer is performed
- How the *witr* prayer is performed
- What is recited after prayer?

THE IMPORTANCE OF PRAYER

The second condition of Islam's five pillars of faith is to perform prayer. A person's first duty is to believe in the existence of Allah, His oneness and the Prophethood of Muhammad. The most important *fard* after faith is prayer. The five daily prayers were made *fard* one and a half years prior to the *Hijrah* on the night of Mi'raj.

Prayer is a worship that cleans the spirit, enlightens the heart and increases the rank of a person in Allah's presence.

Our beloved Prophet indicated that prayer is a very important kind of worship in our religion by stating, "**Prayer is the pillar of religion**." [1] Prayer is a divine light that helps us achieve bodily and spiritual cleansing. As a result, Muslims purify themselves from sin and become worthy to enter paradise as a clean servant.

1. Keşfu'l-Hafa Volume, 2 Page. 31

On this topic, our Prophet (salla Allāhu ʿalay-hi wa-sallam) stated:

"If any one of you were to find a river in front of your door, and if you washed from that river five times a day, would there be any dirt left on you?"

The listeners answered:

"There would be no dirt left O Rasulullah!"

Our Prophet stated:

"Behold, prayer five times in a day is similar, Allah wipes away sins with prayer." [2]

Prayer protects people from committing sin by placing the fear of Allah in their hearts. This truth is told in the holy Qur'an as, "**Recite, [O Muhammad], what has been revealed to you of the Book and establish prayer. Indeed, prayer prohibits immorality and wrongdoing.**" [3]

A person who performs prayer justly prevents himself/herself from committing a sin, strengthens his/her faith and gains Allah's pleasure. The road of the radiance of paradise opens to him. Just as a Muslim is liable to perform prayer, he is also required to teach their children. Our beloved Prophet commands the following: **"Order your children to pray when they reach the age of seven."** [4]

If a mother and father teach their children to perform prayer at the age of seven, they will get used to it by the time they reach puberty.

PRAYER WILL NOT PLACE YOU IN THE WILD

Fajr, *Zhuhr*, *Asr*, *Maghrib*, *Isha* five times
Stand in prayer, shed all the dirt from inside you,

***

Radiance fills the inside of those who perform prayer,
The radiance in the face fades for those who do not perform prayer.

***

Prayer means, to appear in the presence of Allah,
To speak to Allah, to reach His divine light;

***

2. Bukhari, Volume. 2, Page. 475
3. Surah Al-'Ankabut, 29/45
4. Keşfu'l-Hafa, Volume. 2, Page. 203

Those who perform *wudu* and cleanse, be very clean early,
You should get used to cleanliness when you are a child.

M. Şerafettin YALTKAYA

WHO IS PRAYER A FARD FOR?

Three conditions should be fulfilled for prayer to be *fard*:

1) To be a Muslim.

2) To have reached puberty.

3) To be sane.

THE TIMES OF PRAYER

There are five times for prayer every day. These are *fajr*, *zhuhr*, *asr*, *maghrib*, and *isha* prayers. Each of these prayers has a particular time. It is required that all prayers are completed in its own set time. Just as it is unlawful to perform prayer before its appointed time, leaving it to after is a big sin. The holy Qur'an commands the following:

"Indeed, prayer has been decreed upon the believers a decree of specified times."[5]

The time of the *fajr* prayer: The period from the start of dawn until sunrise.

The time of the *zhuh*r prayer: From when the sun is right above us and the shade starts to stretch towards the east side (Except the shade that exists when the sun is right above) and continues until the time when the shade of everything is one or two times its own length.

The time of the *asr* prayer: From the end of the time of the *zhuhr* prayer until the sun sets.

The time of the *maghrib* prayer: Commences from sunset to the time when the redness of the sunset or the whiteness disappears afterwards.

The time of the *isha* prayer: Commences after the time of the *maghrib* prayer finishes and continues until the time when *fajr* prayer commences.

5. Surah An-Nisa', 4/103

The time of the *witr* prayer: The time for the *witr* prayer is the same as the *isha* prayer. However, *witr* must be performed after the *isha* prayer.

The time of the *jumu'ah* prayer: Is the time of the *zhuhr* prayer.

The time of the *tarawih* prayer: The time for the *tarawih* prayer is the same as the *isha* prayer.

The time of the *Eid* prayer: The time for the *Eid* prayer commences approximately 50 minutes from sunrise until the sun is right above.

TIMES WHEN IT IS UNLAWFUL TO PRAY

There are some times during the day when no forms of prayer are permitted. There are three times when it is unlawful to perform prayer:

1) When the sun is rising.

2) When the sun is at the top point just before it turns to the western side.

3) When the sun is setting.

It is only permitted to pray the *fard* of that day's *asr* prayer when the sun is setting.

TYPES OF PRAYER

Prayer is divided into three main types:

1) Fard prayers,

2) Wajib prayers,

3) Nafl prayers.

A) FARD PRAYERS:

These are the five daily prayers, *jumu'ah* and the *janazah* prayers.

The five daily prayers:

***1) FAJR* PRAYER**: 4 *ra'kahs*

2 *ra'kahs* of *sunnah*,

2 *ra'kahs* of *fard*.

2) ZHUHR* PRAYER: 10 *ra'kahs

4 *ra'kahs* of the first *sunnah*,

4 *ra'kahs* of *fard*,

2 *ra'kahs* of the final *sunnah*.

3) ASR PRAYER: 8 *ra'kahs*

4 *ra'kah*s of *sunnah*,

4 *ra'kah*s of *fard*.

***4) MAGHRIB* PRAYER: 5** *ra'kahs*

3 *ra'kah*s of *fard*,

2 *ra'kah*s of *sunnah*.

***5) ISHA* PRAYER: 10** *ra'kahs*

4 *ra'kah*s of the first *sunnah*,

4 *ra'kahs* of *fard*,

2 *ra'kah*s of the final *sunnah*.

***Fard* prayers besides the five daily prayers:**

***1) JUMU'AH* PRAYER**: 10 *ra'kah*s

4 *ra'kah*s of the first *sunnah*

2 *ra'kah*s of *fard*

4 *ra'kah*s of the final *sunnah*

***2) JANAZAH* PRAYER**: *Fard al-kifayah.*

***B) WAJIB* PRAYERS:**

***1) WITR* PRAYER**: 3 *ra'kah*s

***2) EID AL-FITR* PRAYER**: 2 *ra'kah*s

***3) EID AL-ADHA* PRAYER**: 2 *ra'kah*s

***NAFL* PRAYERS**:

"***Nafl* prayers**" are those which are performed other than *fard* or *wajib* prayers.

Nafl prayers are divided into two:

1) Nafl prayers that are performed in conjunction with *fard* prayers:

These are the *sunnah* prayers that are performed before and after the *fard* prayers, prayers performed during the night in the month of Ramadan and *tarawih* prayer are *sunnah muakkadah*.

2) Nafl prayer that are not in conjunction with *fard* prayers:

These are called *mustahabb* or *mandub* prayers. These are prayers performed at certain times with the intention of gaining reward.

Some examples include the following:

***1) Ishraq* prayer**: It is a prayer performed after sunrise and after the *makruh* period has passed. It is a minimum of two and a maximum of twelve *ra'kah*s.

***2) Tahajjud* prayer**: It is a prayer performed late in the night with a minimum of two and a maximum of eight *ra'kah*s.

***3) Tahiyyat al-masjid*:** It is a two-ra'kah prayer performed when entering masjids (if it is not a *makruh* time).

THE FARDS OF PRAYER

The *fard*s of prayer are 12. Six of these are the outside of the prayer and are called the "**conditions of prayer**." Six of these are inside of the prayer and are called the "**pillars *(rukns)* of prayer**."

For prayer to be valid, the twelve *fard*s must be completed in full.

Conditions of prayer:

1) Taharah min al-hadath:

To remove the spiritual dirt by performing *wudu* and if required by performing *ghusl*.

2) Taharah min al-najasah:

A person who is going to perform prayer must clean the body, clothes, and the place of prayer from dirt.

3) Satr al-'awrah:

A person performing prayer must cover the required body parts.

Men: To cover the body between the knees (including the knees) and the belly button,

Women: To cover the whole body except the face, hands, and feet.

4) Facing the *Qibla*: To perform prayer facing the *qibla*. The locus of the *qibla* is the Ka'bah, the first sacred building that was built in Mecca for the purpose of worship. The Ka'bah was constructed by the Prophets Ibrahim and Isma'il.

5) Waqt: To perform prayers within their own periods. It is not lawful to perform prayer prior to its appointed *waqt* (time).

6) Niyyah: To know which prayer one will perform and to confirm it with one's heart. It is *sunnah* to verbally state one's intention as to which prayer one will perform.

The *rukns* of prayer:

1) Takbir al-iftitah: To perform the *takbir* when commencing to pray.

2) Qiyam: To stand up during prayer.

3) Qira'at: To recite some Qur'an during prayer whilst standing.

4) Ruku': To bend over enough so the hands can reach the kneecaps.

5) Sujud: To place the feet, knees, hands and forehead on the ground.

6) Qa`idah akhirah: To sit down long enough at the end of prayer to recite "Al-taḥiyyāt."

THE *WAJIBS* OF PRAYER

1) To commence prayer with the phrase "Allāhu Akbar."

2) To recite Surah Al-Fatihah during the first two *ra'kah*s of *fard* prayers and all *ra'kah*s of *nafl* prayers.

3) To recite a surah or an ayah after al-Fatihah during the first two *ra'kahs* of *fard* prayers and all *ra'kahs* of *witr* and *nafl* prayers.

4) To recite al-Fatihah prior to the surah.

5) To place the forehead together with the nose on the ground during *sujud*.

6) To sit in the second *ra'kah* during all three and four *ra'kah* prayers (this is called *qa'dah 'ula* = first sitting).

7) To recite the *tashahhud* (*Al-taḥiyyāt*) during the first and final sitting.

8) For the imam to recite al-Fatihah aloud on each *ra'kah* when performing prayer with the congregation during *fajr*, *jumu'ah*, *Eid*, *tarawih* and *witr* prayers and during the first two *ra'kahs* of the *maghrib* and *isha* prayers and to recite quietly from within, the *zhuhr* and *asr* prayers.

9) The congregation that follows the imam must not recite the *Fatihah* and the *surah*. They must remain quiet.

10) To perform the *Qunut takbir* during the *witr* prayer and recite the *duas of Qunut*.

11) To take additional *takbirs* during *Eid* prayers.

12) Ta'dil al-arkan, namely to stand up straight when standing and be standing straight up during *ruku* (women stand a little slanted). To straighten thoroughly when arising from *ruku*, to sit down completely between the two *sajdas*.

13) To perform the *salām* to the right and then to the left at the end of prayer.

14) To perform the *Sajda al-Sahv* if there is an error.

(A *sajda al-sahvu* is required if a *fard* or *wajib* of prayer is performed late or if one of the *wajib* acts is abandoned. If a *wajib* act is abandoned on purpose, the prayer must be performed again.

THE SUNNAHS OF PRAYER

1) To raise the hands during *takbir* at the start of all prayers, during the *Qunut takbir* of the *witr* prayer and the additional *takbirs* of *Eid* prayers. (Men raise their thumbs to their earlobes; and women raise their hands with their fingertips in line with their shoulders).

2) To recite the *adhan* and *iqama* for the five daily prayers and *jumu'ah* prayer. (The *adhan* and *iqama* is not *sunnah* for women)

It is *mustahabb* to listen to the *adhan*. A person who hears the *adhan* should repeat the recited sentences of the *muazzin*. However, they should state "la hawla wa la quwwata illa billahil aliyyil'azim" when *Hayya 'ala s-salah* and *Hayya 'ala 'l-falah* is recited.

The following dua is recited after giving *salātu wa salām* to our Prophet following the recitation of the *adhan*:

اَللّٰهُمَّ رَبَّ هٰذِهِ الدَّعْوَةِ التَّامَّةِ وَ الصَّلاَةِ الْقَائِمَةِ اٰتِ مُحَمَّدًا اَلْوَسِيلَةَ وَ الْفَضِيلَةَ وَابْعَثْهُ
مَقَامًا مَحْمُودًا اَلَّذِي وَعَدْتَهُ

"Allahumma Rabba hadhihi-d-da' watit-tammati was-salātil qa'imati, ati Muhammadan al-Wasilata wal-Fadilata, wab' athhu Maqaman Mahmudan-il-ladhi wa' adtahu.

Meaning: O Allah! Lord of this perfect call and of the prayer that is going to be performed. Kindly give Muhammad (salla Allāhu ʿalay-hi wa-sallam) the right of intercession and superiority (a high degree in *jannah*) and bestow upon him the 'Maqaam al-Mahmuda' (the greatest position of intercession) which You promised him.

Our Prophet stated: **"Whoever recites this *dua* at the end of the *adhan* will gain right to my intercession on the Day of Judgment."** [6]

ADHAN

Allāhu Akbar - Allāhu Akbar
Allāhu Akbar - Allāhu Akbar

Ash-hadu an-la ilaha illa llah
Ash-hadu an-la ilaha illa llah

Ash-hadu anna Muhammadan-Rasulullah
Ash-hadu anna Muhammadan-Rasulullah

6. Riyadh us Salihen, Volume 2, Page. 371

Hayya 'ala s-salah, Hayya 'ala s-salah
Hayya 'ala 'l-falah, Hayya 'ala 'l-falah

As-Salātu Khayrun-minan Nawm[7]
As-Salātu Khayrun-minan Nawm

Allāhu akbar, Allāhu akbar
La ilaha illa-Allah

IQAMA

Allāhu akbar - Allāhu akbar
Allāhu akbar - Allāhu akbar

Ash-hadu an-la ilaha illa llah
Ash-hadu an-la ilaha illa llah

Ash-hadu anna Muhammadan-Rasulullah
Ash-hadu anna Muhammadan-Rasulullah

Hayya 'ala s-salah, Hayya 'ala s-salah
Hayya 'ala 'l-falah, Hayya 'ala 'l-falah

Qad qāma tis-salaah
Qad qāma tis-salaah

Allāhu akbar, Allāhu akbar
La ilaha illa-Allah

3) To recite *Subhanaka.*

4) To recite *Auzu* and the *Basmala* after *Subhanaka* on the first r*a'kah*. To recite *Basmala* before *Fatihah* during other ra'kahs.

5) To recite *Subhanaka*, *Auzu and the Basmala* silently.

6) For the congregation and the imam to say 'Amin' silently when the *Fatihah* is recited.

7) To pronounce all takbirs within the prayer apart from the *iftitah takbir*.

7. This part is only recited during the Fajr adhan.

8) To state “Sami Allāhu liman hamidah” when rising from *ruku*, and to say “Rabbana lakal hamd” after that.

9) To state “Subhana rabbi al azeem” three times at ruku and at each sajda state “Subhana rabbi al ala” three times.

10) For the distance between the feet to be four fingers apart during *qiyaam*.

11) To hold the knees during *ruku* and to keep the fingers apart when holding. (Ladies do not keep fingers apart and do not hold their knees; they just put their hands on the knees).

12) To keep the knees and elbows straight without bending it during *ruku*. (Ladies bend their knees and slant their backs up a little).

13) To touch the ground firstly with the knees, then hands and then face when performing the *sajda*. When rising from the *sajda*, first face, then hands and later knees, with hands placed on them, should be raised.

14) To place the hands on the thighs when sitting.

15) When sitting, to spread the left foot on the ground and sit on it and to keep upright the right foot and make the toes face the *qibla*. (Ladies spread their feet to the right side and sit on their buttocks).

16) To recite “Allahumma Salli” and “Allahumma Barik” after *Al-taḥiyyāt* during the final sitting and recite a *dua* (*dua* of “Rabbana atina..”.).

17) To turn your head firstly to the right and then the left when performing the *salām*.

18) To state “Assalamu alaikum wa rahmatullah” during the *salām*.

The Etiquettes of Prayer:

When performing prayer, to look at:

b) The place of sajda when standing,

c) Your feet at ruku,

d) Your lap when sitting,

e) Both sides of your nose at sajda, and

f) The shoulders when performing salām.

THINGS THAT INVALIDATE PRAYER

1) To speak during prayer.

2) To eat or drink anything.

3) To laugh enough that you are able to hear it (If people next to you can hear you laughing, then your *wudu* would also be invalidated).

4) To either give or receive a *salām* from someone.

5) To turn your chest away from the *qibla*.

6) To cry in relation to a pain of this world or say "Ah" (To cry due to a fear of Allah will not invalidate the prayer)

7) To try and cough when you do not need to. (Normal coughing which you cannot do anything about will not invalidate your prayer)

8) To try to do another work during prayer.

9) To blow at something.

10) To recite the Qur'an incorrectly enough to change its meaning.

11) To read the verses from the Qur'an.

12) To invalidate your *wudu* during prayer.

13) A person who has performed *tayammum* to see water during prayer, and for the *masah* period to end during prayer.

14) The sun rising during the *fajr* prayer.

15) For women and men to perform prayer in congregation side by side in an isle without a curtain or barrier in between.

16) For the parts that require covering during prayer to open and for this uncovering to remain long enough to perform a *rukn*.

THE MAKRUHS OF PRAYER

1) To play with your body or clothing during prayer, to crack your knuckles, to interconnect your fingers together and to place your hands by your side.

2) To yawn or stretch.

3) To close your eyes, to look left, right or above. (to turn your chest away from the *qibla* when looking will invalidate prayer)

4) To commence prayer with your sleeves rolled up. (women's prayer will be invalidated if they do this)

5) During prayer, to sit on your buttocks an, to crouch or sit with your knees upright without an excuse.

6) To perform prayer facing towards a person's face or a burning ember (performing prayer towards a lamp, candle or light is not makruh).

7) To wipe sweat or dust from your face, to scratch, to place rocks at the place of *sajda*. (It is not *makruh* if these are done due to an illness)

8) To abandon the *tasbih* during *ruku* and *sajda* or to recite them less than three times.

9) For there to be live pictures in front of or to the sides of a person performing prayer, or at the place of sajda on top of the picture of a person or animal (there is no objection to pictures of inanimate or abstract things such as a scenery or trees).

10) To lean on something during prayer.

11) To place only your forehead on the ground without putting your nose on it.

12) To put your hands on the ground before your knees when performing the *sajda*. To raise the knees before the hands when rising from the *sajda*. (It is not *makruh* if it is done due to an illness)

13) To perform prayer on the road, somewhere dirty, on a grave, somewhere close to dirt. Or to perform prayer in a place without the owner's permission.

14) To recite a longer verse or chapter in the second *ra'kah* than in the first.

15) To recite the same *surah* or verse in the two *ra'kah*s even though they know other chapter by heart.

16) In the second *ra'kah*, to recite a preceding *surah* or verse of the one recited in the first *ra'kah*.

To go from start to finish (from top to down) when reciting*surahs*. For example, it is correct to recite "Li ila fi" in the second *ra'kah* after reciting

"A lam tara" in the first *ra'kah* after the *Fatihah*. However, it is *makruh* to recite in reverse, "Li ila fi" in the first *ra'kah* and "A lam tara" in the second *ra'kah*.

17) To skip one v*surah* in the second *ra'kah* compared to the first.

Namely, it is makruh if "A lam tara" is recited in the first *ra'kah* and then "Ara ai tallazi" in the second by skipping "Li ila fi." However, it is not makruh to skip two or more *surahs*.

18) To place your jacket or coat on your shoulders whilst performing prayer.

19) To shut your eyes during prayer.

20) To perform prayer in an isle behind whilst there is an opening spot in the front isle in a *masjid*.

HOW TO PERFORM THE FIVE DAILY PRAYERS

For a prayer to be complete and in accordance with religious rulings, its *fard*s, *wajib*s and *sunnah*s must be performed in its proper place. One needs to avoid things that invalidate prayer and things that are *makruh*.

FAJR PARYER

Fajr prayer is four *ra'kah*s with two being *sunnah* and two being *fard*. First the *sunnah* is performed and then the *fard*.

How the *sunnah* of the *fajr* prayer is performed:

The First *Ra'kah*:

1) Face your feet towards the *qibla* when standing and have your feet four fingers apart.

The *Niyyah*:

2) State the *niyyah*, "I intend to perform the *sunnah* of today's *fajr* prayer for the consent of Allah"

The *Iftitah takbir*:

3) To take the *takbir* saying "Allāhu akbar"

(**When men make the *takbir***, the inside of the hands face the *qibla* while holding the fingers normally apart. The hands are raised so that the thumbs are raised to the height of the ear lobes).

(**When women make the *takbir*,** the inside of the hands face the *qibla* while holding the fingers normally apart and raising the hands on a level so that the fingertips reach shoulder height).

***Qiyaam*:**

4) Tie your hands after the *takbir*. Look at the place of *sajda* whilst standing.

(**Men**; place the palm of your right hand on top of your left hand and wrap your thumb and little finger of the right hand around the left wrist placing the hands just below the belly button).

(**Women**; place the right hand over the left hand and place one on top foof the other on your chest. Women do not wrap their fingers around the wrist like the men).

***Qira'at*:**

5) To recite in order whilst standing a) *Subhanaka*, b) *Auzu* and the *Basmala*, c) *Surah al-Fatihah*, d) a *surah* from the Qur'an.[8]

***Ruku*:**

6) Perform the *ruku* stating "Allāhu akbar" and state "Subhana rabbi al azeem" three times. Look at the tops of your feet while performing the *ruku*.

(Men hold their knees while the fingers are kept apart and the back is straight during *ruku*. They must keep the knees and elbows straight).

(In *ruku,* women bend their backs slightly whilst bending less than men do in *ruku*. They place the hands (without keeping the fingers apart) on the knees whilst bending the knees slightly.

8. Some of the *duas* and some *surahs* that are recited during prayer have been included at the end of this book.

Rising from *ruku*:

7) Rise to the feet from *ruku* stating "Sami Allāhu liman hamidah" and state "Rabbana lakal hamd" when standing upright.

***Sajda*:**

8) The *sajda* position is taken by stating "Allāhu akbar." The *sajda* is performed with the knees firstly touching the ground, then hands and then forehead. During the *sajda*, the head is placed in alignment between both hands. The feet are not raised while performing the *sajda*. During the *sajda,* you look at the sides of your nose. Here, "Subhana rabbi al ala" is recited three times.

(**Men**; Keep the elbows away from the sides during the *sajda* and keep the arms up above the ground. The feet are placed upright with the toes facing the *qibla*.

(**Women**; Keep the hands by the sides during the sajda. The feet are placed upright with the toes facing the qibla.

Sitting between the *sajda*s:

9) You sit up on your knees by raising your head from *sajda* by stating "Allāhu akbar." When sitting, the fingers are placed to the same level with the knees with the hands on the thighs whilst looking at your lap. Here, you sit for a period short enough to at least state "Subhanallah."

(**Men**: When sitting, spread their left foot on the ground, sit on it, keep the right foot uprights and make the toes face the *qibla.*)

(**Ladies**: spread their feet to the right side and sit like that.)

10) The second *sajda* is performed after stating "Allāhu akbar", and "Subhana rabbi al ala" is stated three times.

11) By stating "Allāhu akbar", you stand to commence the second *ra'kah* by tying your hands.

When rising from the sajda, you first raise your face, then hands and later your knees with your hands placed on them.

Everything done to this point from the *iftitah takbir* is called one *ra'kah*.

The second *ra'kah*:

1) Whilst standing, recite these in order: a) The *Basmala*, b) *Surah al-Fatihah*, c) a *surah* from the Qur'an.

2) Perform the *ruku* stating "Allāhu akbar" just as in the first *ra'kah* stating "Subhana rabbi al azeem" three times.

3) Rise to the feet from *ruku* stating "Sami Allāhu liman hamidah" and state "Rabbana lakal hamd" when standing upright.

4) Perform the *sajda* by stating "Allāhu akbar." Here, recite "Subhana rabbi al ala" three times.

5) Sit up on your knees from *sajda* by stating "Allāhu akbar." Here, sit for a period short enough to state "Subhanallah."

6) The second *sajda* is performed after stating "Allāhu akbar", and "Subhana rabbi al ala" is stated three times.

Al-Qa'da al-Akhira (Sitting at the end of prayer):

7) Sit up on your knees from the *sajda* stating "Allāhu akbar." When sitting, the fingers are placed to the same level with the knees with the hands on the thighs whilst looking at your lap.

(**Men**: when sitting, spread the left foot on the ground, sit on it, keep the right foot upright and make the toes face the *qibla.*)

(**Ladies**: spread their feet to the right side and sit like that).

8) To recite the *duas* in order during the sitting; a) *Al-taḥiyyāt*, b) *Allahumma Salli*, c) *Allahumma Barik*, d) *Rabbana atina*.

9) Giving the *salām* to the right side:

First, turn your head to the right and state "Assalamu alaikum wa rahmatullah." Look at the shoulder whilst giving the *salām*.

10) Giving the *salām* to the left side:

11) Then, turn the head to the left by stating "Assalamu alaikum wa rahmatullah." Thus, the second *ra'kah* of prayer is completed.

How the *fard* of the *fajr* prayer is performed:
Performing the *fard* of the *fajr* prayer is the same as the *sunnah*. However, the difference between the *sunnah* is to state the *niyyah* for the *fard* and for the men to recite the *iqama*.

The *niyyah* is stated for the *fard* of the *fajr* prayer as follows;
"I intend to perform the *fard* of today's *fajr* prayer for the consent of Allah"[9]

ZHUHR PRAYER

The *zhuhr* prayer is ten *ra'kahs* with four being the first *sunnah*, four *fard* and two *ra'kahs* as the final *sunnah*.

How the *sunnah* of the *zhuhr* prayer is performed:

The first *ra'kah*:

1) State the niyyah saying: "I intend to perform the *sunnah* of today's *zhuhr* prayer for the consent of Allah."

2) Make the *takbir* by saying "Allāhu akbar" and tie the hands.

3) Recite in order whilst standing; *Subhanaka*, *Auzu* and the *Basmala*, *Surah Al-Fatihah,* and a *surah* from the Qur'an.

4) Perform the *ruku* by stating "Allāhu akbar" and state "Subhana rabbi al azeem" three times.

5) Rise to the feet from the *ruku* by stating "Sami Allāhu liman hamidah" and state "Rabbana lakal hamd" when standing upright.

6) Perform the *sajda* by stating "Allāhu akbar" and recite "Subhana rabbi al ala" three times.

7) Sit up on your knees from the *sajda* by stating "Allāhu akbar."

8) Perform the second *sajda* after stating "Allāhu akbar" and state "Subhana rabbi al ala" three times.

9) After stating "Allāhu akbar", stand to commence the second *ra'kah* by tying your hands.

The second *ra'kah*:

1) Recite the *Basmala*, *Surah al-Fatihah* and a *surah* in order whilst standing.

2) Perform the *ruku* stating "Allāhu akbar" and after that, state "Subhana rabbi al azeem" three times.

9. The performing of the fajr prayer with pictures has been included at the end of this book.

3) Rise to the feet from *ruku* stating "Sami Allāhu liman hamidah" and state "Rabbana lakal hamd" when standing upright.

4) The *sajda* is performed by stating "Allāhu akbar." Here, "Subhana rabbi al ala" is recited three times.

5) Sit up on your knees from the *sajda* by stating "Allāhu akbar."

6) Perform the second *sajda* after stating "Allāhu akbar" and state "Subhana rabbi al ala" three times.

7) Sit up stating "Allāhu akbar" and recite "At-taḥiyyāt" (this is called the first sitting).

8) After "Allāhu akbar" is stated, stand to commence the third *ra'kah* by tying your hands.

The third *ra'kah*:

1) Recite the *Basmala*, *Surah al-Fatihah* and a *surah* in order.

2) Perform the *ruku* stating "Allāhu akbar" and state "Subhana rabbi al azeem" three times.

3) Rise to the feet from *ruku* stating "Sami Allāhu liman hamidah" and state "Rabbana lakal hamd" when standing upright.

4) The *sajda* is performed stating "Allāhu akbar." Here, "Subhana rabbi al ala" is stated three times.

5) Sit up on your knees from the *sajda* by stating "Allāhu akbar."

6) Again, the *sajda* is performed for the second time by stating "Allāhu akbar" and after "Subhana rabbi al ala" three times.

7) After "Allāhu akbar" is stated, you stand to commence the fourth *ra'kah* by tying your hands.

The fourth *ra'kah*:

1) Recite the *Basmala*, *Surah Al-Fatihah* and a *surah* in order.

2) Perform the *ruku* by stating "Allāhu akbar" and stating "Subhana rabbi al azeem" three times.

3) Rise to the feet from ruku by stating "Sami Allāhu liman hamidah" and state "Rabbana lakal hamd" when standing upright.

4) The *sajda* is performed by stating “Allāhu akbar.” Here, “Subhana rabbi al ala” is recited three times.

5) Sit up on your knees from *sajda* by stating “Allāhu akbar.”

6) Once again, the second *sajda* is performed by stating “Allāhu akbar” and after “Subhana rabbi al ala” three times.

7) Sit up by stating “Allāhu akbar.”

8) Recite the *duas Al-taḥiyyāt*, *Allahumma Salli*, *Allahumma Barik* and *Rabbana atina...* in order during the sitting.

9) First, turn the head to the right and state “Assalamu alaikum wa rahmatullah.” Then, turn the head to the left stating “Assalamu alaikum wa rahmatullah.”

How the fard of the *zhuhr* prayer is performed:

The first *ra'kah*:

1) Recite the *iqama*. (for men)

2) State the *niyyah* by saying: “I intend to perform the fard of today’s *zhuhr* prayer for the consent of Allah.”

3) Make the *iftitah takbir* by saying “Allāhu akbar” and tie the hands.

4) Recite *Subhanaka*, *Auzu* and *the Basmala*, *Surah Al-Fatihah* and a *surah* in order.

5) Perform the *ruku* by stating “Allāhu akbar” and state “Subhana rabbi al azeem” three times.

6) Rise to the feet from the *ruku* stating “Sami Allāhu liman hamidah” and state “Rabbana lakal hamd” when standing upright.

7) The *sajda* is performed stating “Allāhu akbar” and “Subhana rabbi al ala” is recited three times.

8) Sit up on your knees from the *sajda* by stating “Allāhu akbar.”

9) The second *sajda* is performed after stating “Allāhu akbar” and “Subhana rabbi al ala” is stated three times.

10) After “Allāhu akbar” is stated, you stand (to commence the second ra’kah) and fold your hands.

The second *ra'kah*:

1) Recite the *Basmala*, Surah al-Fatihah and a surah in order whilst standing.

2) Perform the ruku stating "Allāhu akbar" and state "Subhana rabbi al azeem" three times.

3) Rise to the feet from *ruku* stating "Sami Allāhu liman hamidah" and state "Rabbana lakal hamd" when standing upright.

4) The sajda is performed stating "Allāhu akbar." Here, "Subhana rabbi al ala" is recited three times.

5) Sit up on your knees from *sajda* by stating "Allāhu akbar."

6) The second *sajda* is performed after stating "Allāhu akbar" and "Subhana rabbi al ala" is stated three times.

7) Sit up stating "Allāhu akbar."

8) "Al-taḥiyyāt" is recited while sitting.

9) After "Allāhu akbar" is stated, you stand (to commence the third *ra'kah*) and fold your hands.

The third ra'kah:

1) Recite whilst standing Basmala and Surah Al-Fatihah.

2) Perform the ruku stating "Allāhu akbar" and state "Subhana rabbi al azeem" three times.

3) Rise to the feet from ruku stating "Sami Allāhu liman hamidah" and state "Rabbana lakal hamd" when standing upright.

4) The sajda is performed by stating "Allāhu akbar." Here, "Subhana rabbi al ala" is recited three times.

5) Sit up on your knees from the sajda by stating "Allāhu akbar."

6) Once again, the sajda is performed for the second time after stating "Allāhu akbar" and "Subhana rabbi al ala" is stated three times.

7) After "Allāhu akbar" is stated, you stand (to commence the fourth ra'kah) and tie your hands.

The fourth ra'kah:

1) Recite the Basmala and Surah al-Fatihah while standing.

2) Perform the ruku stating "Allāhu akbar" and "Subhana rabbi al azeem" three times.

3) Rise to the feet from ruku stating "Sami Allāhu liman hamidah" and state "Rabbana lakal hamd" when standing upright.

4) The sajda is performed stating "Allāhu akbar." Here, "Subhana rabbi al ala" is recited three times.

5) Sit up on your knees from the sajda by stating "Allāhu akbar."

6) Once again, the second sajda is performed by stating "Allāhu akbar" and after "Subhana rabbi al ala" three times.

7) Sit up stating "Allāhu akbar."

8) Recite the duas At-taḥiyyāt, Allahumma Salli, Allahumma Barik and Rabbana atina... in order during the sitting.

9) Firstly, turn the head to the right and state "Assalamu alaikum wa rahmatullah." Then, turn the head to the left stating "Assalamu alaikum wa rahmatullah."

This way, the fard of the zhuhr prayer is completed.

How the final sunnah of the zhuhr prayer is performed:

State the niyyah saying: "I intend to perform the final sunnah of today's zhuhr prayer for the consent of Allah."

Then, perform the two ra'kahs in exactly the same way as the sunnah of the fajr prayer.

THE ASR PRAYER

The asr prayer is eight ra'kahs with four being the first sunnah and four being the fard.

How the sunnah of the asr prayer is performed:

The First Ra'kah:

1) State the niyyah by saying: "I intend to perform the sunnah of today's asr prayer for the consent of Allah."

2) Make the iftitah takbir saying "Allāhu akbar" and tie your hands.

3) Recite *Subhanaka*, *Auzu* and *the Basmala*, Surah al-Fatihah and a surah in order whilst standing.

4) Perform the ruku stating "Allāhu akbar" and state "Subhana rabbi al azeem" three times.

5) Rise to the feet from ruku stating "Sami Allāhu liman hamidah" and state "Rabbana lakal hamd" when standing upright.

6) The sajda is performed stating "Allāhu akbar" and "Subhana rabbi al ala" is recited three times.

7) Sit up on your knees from sajda by stating "Allāhu akbar."

8) The second sajda is performed after stating "Allāhu akbar" and "Subhana rabbi al ala" is stated three times.

9) After "Allāhu akbar" is stated, stand to commence the second ra'kah by folding your hands.

The Second ra'kah:

1) Recite the Basmala, Surah Al-Fatihah and a surah in order whilst standing.

2) Perform the ruku stating "Allāhu akbar" and stating "Subhana rabbi al azeem" three times.

3) Rise to the feet from ruku stating "Sami Allāhu liman hamidah" and state "Rabbana lakal hamd" when standing upright.

4) The sajda is performed stating "Allāhu akbar." Here, "Subhana rabbi al ala" is recited three times.

5) Sit up on your knees from sajda by stating "Allāhu akbar."

6) The second sajda is performed after stating "Allāhu akbar" and "Subhana rabbi al ala" is stated three times.

7) Sit up stating "Allāhu akbar."

8) To recite in order during the sitting: a) At-taḥiyyāt, b) Allahumma Salli, c) Allahumma Barik.

9) After "Allāhu akbar" is stated, stand (to commence the third ra'kah) and fold your hands.

The third ra'kah:

1) To recite *Subhanaka*, *Auzu* and *the Basmala*, Surah Al-Fatihah and a surah in order whilst standing.

2) Perform the ruku stating "Allāhu akbar" and statestate "Subhana rabbi al azeem" three times.

3) Rise to the feet from the ruku stating "Sami Allāhu liman hamidah" and state "Rabbana lakal hamd" when standing upright.

4) The sajda is performed stating "Allāhu akbar." Here, "Subhana rabbi al ala" is recited three times.

5) Sit up on your knees from the sajda by stating "Allāhu akbar."

6) Again, the sajda is performed for the second time after stating "Allāhu akbar" and "Subhana rabbi al ala" is stated three times.

7) After "Allāhu akbar" is stated, stand (to commence the fourth ra'kah) and fold your hands.

The fourth ra'kah:

1) Recite the Basmala, Surah al-Fatihah and a surah while standing.

2) Perform the ruku stating "Allāhu akbar" and stating "Subhana rabbi al azeem" three times.

3) Rise to the feet from the ruku stating "Sami Allāhu liman hamidah" and state "Rabbana lakal hamd" when standing upright.

4) The sajda is performed stating "Allāhu akbar." Here, "Subhana rabbi al ala" is recited three times.

5) Sit up on your knees from sajda by stating "Allāhu akbar."

6) Once again, the second sajda is performed after stating "Allāhu akbar" and "Subhana rabbi al ala" is stated three times.

7) Sit up stating “Allāhu akbar.”

8) Recite the duas in order during the sitting; At-taḥiyyāt, Allahumma Salli, Allahumma Barik, Rabbana atina...

9) Firstly, turn your head to the right and state “Assalamu alaikum wa rahmatullah.” Then, turn the head to the left stating “Assalamu alaikum wa rahmatullah.”

The difference between the first sunnah of the zhuhr prayer and asr prayer is:

The first sunnah of the zhuhr prayer is a *sunnah muakkadah*. Only At-taḥiyyāt is recited during the sitting at the second *ra'kah* and when commencing the third *ra'kah*, Basmala, Fatihah and a *surah* is recited.

The sunnah of asr prayer is a *sunnah ghair muakkadah*. At the sitting of the second ra'kah, At-taḥiyyāt, Allahumma Salli and Allahumma Barik are recited. You first recite Subhanaka when you rise for the third ra'kah then, Auzu Basmala with Fatihah and a surah.

How the fard of the asr prayer is performed:

1) The iqama is performed. (for men)

2) State the niyyah saying: “I intend to perform the fard of today's asr prayer for the consent of Allah.”

The fard of the Asr prayer is performed exactly the same as the fard of the zhuhr prayer. The difference is just the niyyah.

THE MAGHRIB PRAYER

The Maghrib prayer is five ra'kahs with three being the fard and two ra'kahs the sunnah. The fard is performed first.

How the fard of the maghrib prayer is performed:

The first ra'kah:

1) The iqama is recited. (for men)

2) State the niyyah saying: “I intend to perform the fard of this evening's maghrib prayer for the consent of Allah.”

3) Take the iftitah takbir saying “Allāhu akbar” and tie the hands.

4) Recite in order whilst standing: Subhanaka, Auzu Basmala, Surah Al-Fatihah and a surah.

5) Perform the ruku stating “Allāhu akbar” and state “Subhana rabbi al azeem” three times.

6) Rise to the feet from ruku stating “Sami Allāhu liman hamidah” and state “Rabbana lakal hamd” when standing upright.

7) The sajda is performed stating “Allāhu akbar” and “Subhana rabbi al ala” is recited three times.

8) Sit up on your knees from sajda by stating “Allāhu akbar.”

9) The second sajda is performed after stating “Allāhu akbar” and “Subhana rabbi al ala” is stated three times.

10) After “Allāhu akbar” is stated, stand (to commence the second ra’kah) and tie your hands.

The second ra’kah:

1) Whilst standing, recite the Basmala, Surah Al-Fatihah and a surah.

2) Perform the ruku by stating “Allāhu akbar” stating “Subhana rabbi al azeem” three times.

3) Rise to the feet from ruku stating “Sami Allāhu liman hamidah” and state “Rabbana lakal hamd” when standing upright.

4) The sajda is performed stating “Allāhu akbar” and “Subhana rabbi al ala” is recited three times.

5) Sit up on your knees from sajda by stating “Allāhu akbar.”

6) The second sajda is performed after stating “Allāhu akbar” and “Subhana rabbi al ala” is stated three times.

7) Sit up from the sajda stating “Allāhu akbar.”

8) “Al-taḥiyyāt” is recited while sitting.

9) By stating “Allāhu akbar”, stand (to commence the third ra’kah) and tie your hands.

The third ra'kah:

1) Recite the Basmala and Surah Al-Fatihah whilst standing.

2) Perform the ruku stating "Allāhu akbar" and stating "Subhana rabbi al azeem" three times.

3) Rise to the feet from ruku stating "Sami Allāhu liman hamidah" and state "Rabbana lakal hamd" when standing upright.

4) The sajda is performed stating "Allāhu akbar." Here, "Subhana rabbi al ala" is recited three times.

5) Sit up on your knees from sajda by stating "Allāhu akbar."

6) Again, the second sajda is performed by stating "Allāhu akbar" and "Subhana rabbi al ala" three times.

7) Sit up stating "Allāhu akbar."

8) On this sitting, recite the duas Al-taḥiyyāt, Allahumma Salli, Allahumma Barik and Rabbana atina...

9) Firstly, turn the head to the right and state "Assalamu alaikum wa rahmatullah." Then, turn the head to the left stating "Assalamu alaikum wa rahmatullah."

How the sunnah of the maghrib prayer is performed:

State the niyyah saying, "I intend to perform the sunnah of this evening's maghrib prayer for the consent of Allah." The sunnah of the maghrib prayer is performed exactly like the two ra'kah sunnah of the fajr prayer.

THE ISHA PRAYER

The isha prayer is ten ra'kahs, with four being the first sunnah, four the fard and two ra'kahs the final sunnah.

How the first sunnah of the Isha prayer is performed:

State the niyyah saying: "I intend to perform the first sunnah of tonight's isha prayer for the consent of Allah."

After the niyyah, it is performed identically to the sunnah of the asr prayer. Both are *sunnah ghair muakkadah*. The difference between them both is just the niyyah.

How the fard of the Isha prayer is performed:

1) The iqama is recited. (for men)

2) State the niyyah by saying, "I intend to perform the fard of tonight's isha prayer for the consent of Allah."

After the niyyah, it is performed identically to the fard of the *zhuhr* prayer.

How the final sunnah of the isha prayer is performed:

State the niyyah by saying: "I intend to perform the final sunnah of tonight's isha prayer for the consent of Allah."

After the niyyah, it is performed identically to the sunnah of the fajr prayer.

HOW THE WITR PRAYER IS PERFORMED

The three-ra'kah witr prayer that is performed after the isha prayer has a difference when compared to the other prayers. The ruku is not performed immediately after reciting the Fatihah and a surah in the third ra'kah. When "Allāhu akbar" is stated, the hands are raised for the takbir, folded again and then Qunut duas are recited. After this, the ruku is performed.

Let us see how the witr prayer is performed after this explanation:

The First Ra'kah:

1) State the niyyah by saying, "I intend to perform tonight's Witr prayer for the consent of Allah."

2) Make the iftitah takbir by saying "Allāhu akbar" and tie the hands.

3) Recite in order whilst standing: Subhanaka, Auzu Basmala, Surah Al-Fatihah and a surah.

4) Perform the ruku stating "Allāhu akbar" and state "Subhana rabbi al azeem" three times.

5) Rise to the feet from ruku stating "Sami Allāhu liman hamidah" and state "Rabbana lakal hamd" when standing upright.

6) The sajda is performed stating "Allāhu akbar" and "Subhana rabbi al ala" is recited three times.

7) Sit up on your knees from sajda by stating "Allāhu akbar."

8) The second sajda is performed after stating "Allāhu akbar" and "Subhana rabbi al ala" is stated three times.

9) After "Allāhu akbar" is stated, stand (to commence the second ra'kah) and tie your hands.

Second Ra'kah:

1) Recite the Basmala, Surah Al-Fatihah and a surah in order whilst standing.

2) Perform the ruku stating "Allāhu akbar" stating "Subhana rabbi al azeem" three times.

3) Rise to the feet from the ruku stating "Sami Allāhu liman hamidah" and state "Rabbana lakal hamd" when standing upright.

4) The sajda is performed stating "Allāhu akbar." Here, "Subhana rabbi al ala" is recited three times.

5) Sit up on your knees from sajda by stating "Allāhu akbar."

6) The second sajda is performed after stating "Allāhu akbar" and "Subhana rabbi al ala" is stated three times.

7) Sit up stating "Allāhu akbar."

8) Recite Al-taḥiyyāt in this sitting.

9) After "Allāhu akbar" is stated, stand (to commence the third ra'kah) and tie your hands.

The third ra'kah:

1) Recite the Basmala, Surah Al-Fatihah and a surah while standing.

2) The hands are raised stating "Allāhu akbar" and the then re-tied.

3) Qunut duas are recited. (Those who do not know the Qunut duas can recite "Rabbana atina fid-dunya hasanatan wa fil 'akhirati hasanatan waqina 'adhaban-nar" instead.)

4) Perform the ruku stating "Allāhu akbar" and state "Subhana rabbi al azeem" three times.

5) Rise to the feet from the ruku stating "Sami Allāhu liman hamidah" and state "Rabbana lakal hamd" when standing upright.

6) The sajda is performed stating "Allāhu akbar." Here, "Subhana rabbi al ala" is recited three times.

7) Sit up on your knees from sajda by stating "Allāhu akbar."

8) Again, the second sajda is performed by stating "Allāhu akbar" and after "Subhana rabbi al ala" three times.

9) Sit up stating "Allāhu akbar" after the sajda.

10) To recite the duas Al-taḥiyyāt, Allahumma Salli, Allahumma Barik, Rabbana atina...in order during the sitting.

11) Firstly, turn the head to the right and state "Assalamu alaikum wa rahmatullah." Then, turn the head to the left stating "Assalamu alaikum wa rahmatullah."

WHAT IS RECITED AFTER THE PRAYER IS PERFORMED

After performing the salām during the fard prayer:

اَللّٰهُمَّ اَنْتَ السَّلاَمُ وَ مِنْكَ السَّلاَمُ تَبَارَكْتَ يَاذَا الْجِلاَلِ وَ الْاِكْرَامِ

"Allahumma anta-s-salāmu wa minka salām tabarakta ya dhal jalali wal ikram" is recited.

If there is no sunnah prayer after a fard prayer, (such as the Fajr and Asr prayers)

اَللّٰهُمَّ صَلِّ عَلَى سَيِّدِنَا مُحَمَّدٍ وَ عَلَى اٰلِ سَيِّدِنَا مُحَمَّدٍ

After that, by stating **"Allahumma salli 'ala Sayyidina Muhammadin wa `ala ali sayyidina Muhammad"**, prayer and salām is brought upon the Prophet. If there is a sunnah prayer after a fard prayer (such as Zhuhr, Maghrib, Isha) then, salātu salām is recited after the sunnah prayer is performed.

After the salātu salām:

سُبْحَانَ اللّٰهِ وَالْحَمْدُ لِلّٰهِ وَلَآ اِلٰهَ اِلاَّ اللّٰهُ وَاللّٰهُ اَكْبَرُ وَلاَ حَوْلَ وَلاَ قُوَّةَ اِلاَّ بِاللّٰهِ الْعَلِيِّ الْعَظِيمِ

"Subhanallahi walhamdulillahi wa la ilaha illallahu wallahu akbar wala hawla wala quwwata illa billahil aliyyil azeem" is recited.

After this, Ayat al-Kursi is recited after Auzu and the Basmala.

Ayat al-kursi:

اَللّٰهُ لَآ اِلٰهَ اِلَّا هُوَ اَلْحَيُّ الْقَيُّومُ لَا تَاْخُذُهُ سِنَةٌ وَلَا نَوْمٌ لَهُ مَا فِي السَّمٰوَاتِ وَمَا فِي الْاَرْضِ مَنْ ذَا الَّذِي يَشْفَعُ عِنْدَهُٓ اِلَّا بِاِذْنِهِ يَعْلَمُ مَا بَيْنَ اَيْدِيهِمْ وَمَا خَلْفَهُمْ وَلَا يُحِيطُونَ بِشَيْءٍ مِنْ عِلْمِهِٓ اِلَّا بِمَا شَآءَ وَسِعَ كُرْسِيُّهُ السَّمٰوَاتِ وَالْاَرْضَ وَلَا يَؤُدُهُ حِفْظُهُمَا وَهُوَ الْعَلِيُّ الْعَظِيمُ

Transliteration:

Allahu la illaha illa hu Wal Hayyul Qayyum. La te huzuhu sinetun wala nawm. Lahu ma fissemawati wa ma fil'ard. Men dhalladhiy y yeshfe'u indehu illa bi iznih. Ya'lemu ma beyne eydiyhim wa ma halfehum. Wa la yuhiytune bi shey'in min ilmihi illa bima sha-a. Wasia kursiyyuhu-s-semavati wal'ard. Wa la yeuduhu hifzuhuma. Wa hu wal aliyy ul aziym.

Meaning:

Allah - there is no deity except Him, the Ever-Living, the Sustainer of all existence. Neither drowsiness overtakes Him nor sleep. To Him belongs whatever is in the heavens and whatever is on the earth. Who is it that can intercede with Him except by His permission? He knows what is before them and what will be after them. They encompass not a thing of His knowledge except for what He wills. His Kursi extends over the heavens and the earth, and their preservation tires Him not. And He is the most High, the most Great.

After, in turn:

33 times, سُبْحَانَ اللّٰهِ "Subhanallah"

33 times, اَلْحَمْدُ لِلّٰهِ “Alhamdulillah”

33 times, اَللّٰهُ اَكْبَرُ “Allāhu akbar”

are recited.

Following these:

لَآ اِلٰهَ اِلاَّ اللّٰهُ وَحْدَهُ لاَ شَرِيكَ لَهُ لَهُ الْمُلْكُ وَلَهُ الْحَمْدُ وَهُوَ عَلَى كُلِّ شَيْءٍ قَدِيرٌ

“La illaha illallahu wah-dahu la sharika lah, Lahul-mulku wa lahul hamdu, wa huwa ‘ala Kul-li shay’in Qadeer” is stated and the hands are raised chest high for the dua.

The following duas with their meanings included, which were recommended by our Prophet, are recited:

“All praise is due to Allah, Lord of the worlds. Salāt and salām to our Prophet (salla Allāhu ʿalay-hi wa-sallam), those observing him and his Companions.

Oh Allah! We seek refuge in you from any difficulties that we cannot tolerate, from the shortages of this world and the hereafter, from destiny that will give us sadness and from grief that will please our enemies.

Oh Allah! Forgive our sins and preserve us, be content with us, accept our worships, place us in jannah, save us from the hellfire, correct all our tasks in this world and the hereafter. Help us to remember you, to give thanks to you and to make good worship.

Oh Allah! Make good the end of all our tasks and protect us from the sadness of this world and the torment of the hereafter.

Oh Allah! We seek the things that will take us to your forgiveness and things that are a cause for your mercy and we seek to stay away from all sins, we wish to acquire all the good and eventually enter jannah and be saved from hell.

Oh Allah! Please forgive all our sins without leaving any unforgiven, do not leave any sorrow, make us rejoice, give us the power and strength to pay our debts, meet all our requirements in this world and in the hereafter that meets your consent. The most gracious of all graciousness!

Oh Allah! Give us goodness and beauty in this world, give us goodness and beauty in the hereafter and forgive us with your mercy, protect us from the torment of hell. The most gracious of all graciousness!

Oh Our Lord! Forgive me, my mother, father and all Mu'min on the Day of Judgment with your mercy. The most gracious of all graciousness!

May salām be upon all Prophets, praise only to Allah, Lord of the worlds."

We end our dua with the following verse and wipe our hands over our face:

سُبْحَانَ رَبِّكَ رَبِّ الْعِزَّةِ عَمَّا يَصِفُونَۚ وَسَلَامٌ عَلَى الْمُرْسَلِينَۚ وَالْحَمْدُ لِلّٰهِ رَبِّ الْعَالَمِينَ

"Subhana rabbika rabbil izatti ama yasifun wa salamun allal mursalin wa alhamdu lillahi rabbil alaamin."

QUESTIONS

1) Explain the importance of prayer.

2) For whom is prayer a fard?

3) Count the prayer times and the times prayer is not performed.

4) How many types of prayer are there?

5) How many fards of prayer are there? Explain the fards outside of the prayer.

6) Explain the fards within the prayer.

7) What are the wajibs and sunnahs of prayer?

8) What things invalidate prayer?

9) What things are makruh during prayer?

10) What are the differences between how the four ra'kahs of fard and how four ra'kahs of sunnah are performed?

11) What are the differences between how a muakkadah sunnah and a ghair muakkadah sunnah are performed?

12) What is recited during the witr prayer when compared to other prayers?

13) What is recited after prayer is completed?

UNIT V

PRAYER (II)

Topics:

- The sajda al-sahvu
- The virtues of prayer in congregation
- The etiquettes of the mosque and the congregation, how prayer is performed in congregation
- Jumu'ah and jumu'ah prayer, how jumu'ah prayer is performed
- Eid prayers
- Takbir al-tashreeq
- The tarawih prayer
- Performing prayer whilst sitting or with implication
- The t'traveler's prayer
- The qada of past prayers
- The sajda al-tilawattilawah
- The janazah prayer

THE SAJDA AL-SAHR

Conditions that require a sajda al-sahvu:

Within prayer:

1) Performing one of the fards late due to forgetting,

2) Performing one of the wajibs late due to forgetting or not performing it at all due to forgetting.

It is wajib to perform the sajda al-sahv at the end of prayer to make up for any omissions. If one of the fards is forgotten or not performed knowingly, the prayer is invalidated and the sajda al-sahv cannot complete the prayer. Therefore, the prayer must be re-performed. A sajda al-sahv is not required if one of the wajibs are knowingly abandoned, the prayer must be re-performed.

When and how a sajda al-sahv is performed

If one of the fards or wajibs of prayer is performed late due to forgetfulness or if one of the wajibs are abandoned then, after reciting only Al-taḥiyyāt at the final sitting and giving the salām to the right:

Perform sajda by saying "Allāhu akbar." "Subhana rabbi al ala" is recited three times here. Later, sit up stating "Allāhu akbar" and then perform the second sajda saying "Subhana rabbi al ala" three times after stating "Allāhu akbar." Then, "Allāhu akbar" is stated again prior to standing up.

At this sitting, recite the duas Al-taḥiyyāt, Allahumma Salli, Allahumma Barik and Rabbana atina... Then, the salām is given to the right and then to the left. This is called sajda al-sahv.

THE VIRTUES OF PRAYER IN CONGREGATION

Our religion has placed great importance upon performing prayer in congregation. Muslims who perform prayer with the congregation get to meet with each other on a close basis. Those who do not know, benefit from those who do by gaining good habits and abandoning bad habits with time.

Reciprocal love occurs amongst Muslims who perform prayer in congregation, and emotions of brotherhood and solidarity are strengthened. Mu'mins who perform prayer like the angels in the presence of Allah, earn more reward than those who perform prayer alone.

Our Prophet gives glad tidings on this topic stating:

"The reward for performing prayer in congregation is twenty seven times more than the prayer performed alone."

"A person who performs isha prayer in congregation is like someone who performs prayer until the middle of the night. A person who performs the fajr prayer in congregation is like someone who performs prayer the whole night."

"If a person cleans oneself nicely at home and goes to a masjid to perform one of Allah's fards, one of the steps taken wipes away the sins and the other increase their rank."[1]

Fard prayers can be performed alone. However, it is a muakkadah sunnah to perform prayer in congregation. The unworldly reward of

1. Et-Terğib ve't-Terhib, Volume 1, Page 260 onwards

performing prayer at the mosque is great; it also plays a big role in keeping the community together.

The sunnah and nafl prayers cannot be performed with a congregation. However tarawih prayer can be performed either alone or in congregation even though it is sunnah. Witr, which is wajib is only performed in congregation in the month of Ramadan. Jumu'ah and Eid prayers are performed in congregation, as they cannot be performed alone.

ETIQUETTES OF THE MOSQUE AND THE CONGREGATION

Mosques are places where Muslims worship Allah. The mosques, which are the most dignified places on earth, are called "Allah's house." BelieverMu'mins that go to the mosques to worship are the visitors and guests of Allah. Just as homeowners provide offerings to guests, Allah the Almighty is going to give smu'mins that go to mosques a great reward.

Our Prophet has commanded the following on this topic: **"A person who performs a good *wudu* at home and goes to the mosque is the visitor of Allah. Allah is going to give offerings to those who visit."** [2]

It is a duty of every Muslim to show respect to mosques. These duties in brief are the following:

1) To enter the mosque with *wudu*, clean and smart clothes.

2) To enter the mosque with the right foot and recite salawat to our Prophet.

3) To exit the mosque with the left foot.

4) Not to step on the carpet or rugs with dirty feet or socks.

5) Not to sit in the mosque stretching out one's legs without an excuse, not to yell, scream or make a noise and avoid disrespectful actions like talking about worldly things.

6) Not to discomfort the congregation by eating onions or garlic, burping or actions that will disgust the people nearby.

2. Et-Terğib ve't-Terhib, Volume 1, Page 214

To listen to with intent and respect if the Qur'an is being recited at the mosque or if a sermon is being delivered. People who arrive at the mosque late should sit anywhere that is available and not inconvenience the congregation by trying to get to the front row.

Let us get to know mosques:

Mosques are inseparable parts of the Islamic community and symbols of an Islamic nation. Turks have placed great importance on building mosques throughout history. Even today, unique and unparalled masterpieces are being built everywhere in the world.

Mosque: A place where Muslims worship together is called a mosque.

Masjid: In some muslim countries, small mosques are called *masjid*s. Usually, only daily prayers are performed at *masjids*, not *jumu'ah* or *Eid* prayers.

Sometimes, big mosques such as Al-Masjidi Al-Nabawi, are called *masjid*s as well.

Parts of a mosque:

Mihrab: A niche, in front of a mosque, directed towards *qibla* (the direction of Mecca). It is a place where the imam leads the prayer.

Minbar: The high steps where the imam delivers the *khutbah* during *jumu'ah* and *Eid* prayers.

Kursi: A high seat place where sermons are delivered at mosques.

Minaret: A high structure like towers adjacent to the mosques for calling the *adhan*.

Sharafa: A protruding place built circumferentially around the minarets from where the adhan is recited. You get up there through stairs in the *minaret*. *Minarets* mainly have a *sharafa*. There are also *minarets* that have more than one sharafa.

Alem: A crescent moon hood on the tops of minarets.

HOW PRAYER IS PERFORMED WITH A CONGREGATION?

The status of those who follow the *imam* in the first *ra'kah* of prayer:

A person who will follow the imam in prayer as part of the congregation must make *niyyah* for the prayer about to be performed and to follow the imam. Let us see as an example how the *fard* of the *zhuhr* prayer will be performed:

1) Make the *niyyah* as follows: "I intend to perform the *fard* of today's *zhuhr* prayer for the consent of Allah, following the imam."

All prayers performed with the congregation following an imam must add the sentence "Following the imam" at the end of the *niyyah.*

2) When the imam makes the *takbir*, the congregation immediately follows by also making the *takbir*, ties their hands and silently recites "Subhanaka" and remains quite. The congregation does not recite anything else standing in any other *ra'kah* except to say "Amin" when the imam completes the *Fatihah.*

3) The congregation during *ruku* says "Subhana rabbi al azeem" three times. The imam stands up saying "Sami Allāhu liman hamidah" and then the congregation says "Rabbana lakal hamd."

On the *sajda*s, "Subhana rabbi al ala" is stated three times each.

4) On the sittings, the congregation and the imam recite the *duas* "At-taḥiyyāt, Allahumma Salli, Allahumma Barik, Rabbana atina and Rabbana'ghfirli" and then gives the *salām* with the imam.

A person who is performing prayer as part of a congregation following the imam must not move before the imam and must follow the commands of the imam when making the *takbir*, during *ruku*, when rising from *ruku*, when performing the *sajda*, when rising from the *sajda*, and when giving the *salām.*

A person is deemed to have completed the number of *ra'kah*s that the congregation completed if he joins in the prayer prior to the imam rising from the *ruku* of that particular *ra'kah.*

The situation of those who follow the imam from the second *ra'kah*:

A person who has not been able to catch the *ruku* of the first *ra'kah* must make *niyyah*, take the *takbir* and follow the imam from whence they arrived and continue the prayer with the imam. At the final sitting, they recite "Al-taḥiyyāt" and wait for the imam to give the *salām*. When the imam gives the *salām* to the right hand side, they rise to their feet saying "Allāhu akbar", then recite "Subhanaka", "Auzu" and the "Basmala", "Fatihah" and a *surah* to perform the *ra'kah* that was missed on their own. Later, they sit after performing the *ruku* and *sajda* reciting "Al-taḥiyyāt, Allahumma Salli, Allahumma Barik and the Rabbana atina dua." Then the prayer is completed after giving the *salām* firstly to the right and then the left.

The situation of those who follow the imam from the third *ra'kah*:

If you follow the imam by catching the third *ra'kah* of a prayer that carries four *ra'kahs*, at the final sitting, you recite "Al-taḥiyyāt" and wait for the imam to give the *salām*. When the imam gives the *salām* to the right hand side, you rise to your feet by saying "Allāhu akbar" and complete the two *ra'kah*s that were missed as follows:

Recite "Subhanaka", "Auzu" and the "Basmala" and "Fatihah" together with a *surah*, perform the ruku and sajda, and then stand again stating "Allāhu akbar." Perform the *ruku* and *sajda* again after stating the "Basmala" and reciting "Fatihah" and a *surah*. You then recite at the final sitting "Al-taḥiyyāt, Allahumma Salli, Allahumma Barik and the Rabbana atina dua" and then complete your prayer giving the *salām* firstly to the right and then the left.

A person who catches the prayer and follows the imam in the third *ra'kah* completes that *ra'kah* together with the imam in prayers that have three *ra'kah*s such as *maghrib* and *witr*. You recite "Al-taḥiyyāt" and wait for the imam to give the *salām*. When the imam gives the *salām* to the right side, you rise to your feet saying "Allāhu akbar" without giving the *salām*. Then, you recite "Subhanaka", "Auzu" and the "Basmala", "Fatihah" and a *surah,* and then perform the *ruku* and then sit after the *sajda*. Here, only "Al-taḥiyyāt" is recited before rising to your feet stating "Allāhu akbar." After stating the "Basmala" and reciting the "Fatihah" and a surah, perform the *ruku* and *sajda* and then sit down.

Prayer is then completed by reciting "Al-taḥiyyāt, Allahumma Salli, Allahumma Barik and the Rabbana atina dua" and then giving the *salām* firstly to the right and then the left.

The situation of those who follow the imam from the fourth *ra'kah* in four *ra'kah* prayers:

Once again, the fourth *ra'kah* is performed with the imam. Then you wait after reciting "Al-taḥiyyāt" at the final sitting. When the imam gives the *salām* to the right side, you rise to your feet saying "Allāhu akbar", here you recite "Subhanaka", "Auzu Basmala", "Fatihah" and a *surah*. Then you sit after performing the *ruku* and the *sajda*. Here, only "Al-taḥiyyāt" is recited before rising to your feet stating "Allāhu akbar." Then, whilst standing, state the "Basmala", recite the "Fatihah" and a *surah* and rise to the feet again after performing the *ruku* and *sajda* without sitting down. Then, recite only the Basmala and Fatihah and then sit down after performing the *ruku* and *sajda*. Prayer is then completed by reciting "Al-taḥiyyāt, Allahumma Salli, Allahumma Barik and the Rabbana atina dua" and then giving the *salām* firstly to the right and then the left.

A person who follows the imam in the fourth *ra'kah* after the imam rises from the *ruku*, rises to their feet saying "Allāhu akbar" when the imam gives the *salām* to the right. Then he completes all the *ra'kah*s on his own from start to finish.

JUMU'AH (FRIDAY) AND JUMU'AH PRAYER

The *jumu'ah* days are holy for Muslims. It is for this reason that Muslims should meet this day with the happiness of *Eid* and go to the mosque after washing, cleaning and wearing good clothing. Our Prophet (salla Allāhu ʿalay-hi wa-sallam) commands:

"If anyone performs *wudu* properly, then comes to the *jumu'ah* prayer, listens to the *khutbah* attentively and keeps silent, his sins between that *jumu'ah* and the following *jumu'ah* will be forgiven, with the addition of three more days." [3]

Jumu'ah prayer is ten *ra'kah*s, which consists of four *ra'kah*s for the first sunnah, two *fard*, and four for the last *sunnah*. *Jumu'ah* prayer is performed

---

3. Riyadh us Salihen, Volume 2, Page 440

at the time of *zhuhr* and it replaces that day's *zhuh*r prayer. The *fard* of *jumu'ah* prayer is performed with the congregation. It is not performed alone.

WHO IS JUMU'AH PRAYER A FARD FOR?

Six conditions must be met for the *jumu'ah* prayer to be fard for a person, asides from being a Muslim and reaching the age of wisdom and puberty.

Conditions of the *jumu'ah* prayer to be *fard*:

1) To be a male (it is not *fard* for females).
2) To be independent and free.
3) To be muqeem (to be a resident, not a visitor).
4) To be healthy.
5) Not to be blind.
6) To have healthy legs.

Jumu'ah prayer is not fard for those who does not meet one of these conditions. However, if a person in this situation goes to the mosque and performs jumu'ah then, this will count towards his *zhuhr* prayer of that day.

There are six conditions for the validity of *jumu'ah* prayer.

CONDITIONS FOR THE VALIDITY OF JUMU'AH PRAYER:

1) To perform *jumu'ah* at the time of *zhuhr* prayer.
2) For there to be a *khutbah* before prayer.
3) The place of prayer for *jumu'ah* must be open to everyone.
4) There must be at least three male people in the congregation in addition to the imam.
5) The person who leads the prayer must be assigned by the government or an authorized person.
6) The place where *jumu'ah* is performed must be a city or have the features of a city.

HOW JUMU'AH PRAYER IS PERFORMED

Four *ra'kah*s of the first *sunnah* are performed after the *adhan* for the *zhuhr* prayer is called on *jumu'ah*. The *niyyah* for this is as follows: "I intend to perform the first *sunnah* of today's *jumu'ah* prayer for the consent of Allah."

The way the first *sunnah* of the *jumu'ah* prayer is performed is the same as the *sunnah* of the *zhuhr* prayer. After the *sunnah* is performed, another *adhan* is called inside the mosque and the imam gives a *khutbah* on the *minbar*. The *iqama* is called out after the khutbah is completed. The two-*fard ra'kah*s of the *jumu'ah* prayer is performed with the congregation. The congregation behind the imam states the *niyyah* as follows: "I intend to perform the *fard* of today's *jumu'ah* prayer for the consent of Allah and I am following the imam."

The four *ra'kah*s of the final *sunnah*, is performed after the *fard*. This is performed identically to the first *sunnah* of the *jumu'ah* prayer. The *niyyah* is: "I intend to perform the final *sunnah* of today's Jumu'ah prayer for the consent of Allah."

This way, the *jumu'ah* prayer is completed.

After this, those who want to can perform the four *ra'kah*s of the *Zhuhr Akhir* (*final zhuhr*) and two *ra'kahs* of the *sunnah* of the *waqt*.

The *niyyah* for the final *zhuhr* prayer is as follows: "I intend to perform for the consent of Allah the final *zhuhr* prayer that I could reach and have not yet performed." The final *zhuhr* prayer can be performed like the four *ra'kah*s *fard* of *zhuhr* prayer or it is better and can be performed like the *sunnah*s where a surah is recited after the *Fatihah* for each of the four *ra'kah*s.

The *niyyah* of the two *ra'kah*s of the *sunnah* of the time is stated as follows: "I intend to perform the *sunnah* of time for the consent of Allah." This prayer is also performed like the *sunnah* of *fajr* prayer.

EID PRAYERS

Eid means a day of happiness. The *Eid* prayers performed with the congregation is a great indicator of the unity and solidarity amongst Muslims. *Eid* is an important day that brings Muslims closer with each other, removes any anger and displeasure and strengthens the ties of brotherhood. The days of Eid are the day of the feast for the believing Mu'min servants of Allah.

Muslims have two religious *Eid* celebrations every year:

1) Eid al-Fitr

2) Eid al-Adha

It is *wajib* to perform the *Eid* prayers for the people, to whom *jumu'ah* prayer is *fard*. The *Eid* prayer is two *ra'kah*s and is performed in congregation. There is no reciting of the *adhan* or the *iqama* during *Eid* prayers. The *Eid khutbah* is *sunnah* and it is delivered after prayer, whereas the *jumu'ah khutbah* is *fard* and is delivered before prayer.

The *Eid* prayers are different to other prayers where an additional six *takbirs* are performed with three being in the first *ra'kah* and three in the second *ra'kah*. These are called *zawaid takbir*s.

HOW EID PRAYERS ARE PERFORMED

Eid al-Fitr prayer:

The first *ra'kah*:

1) In a straight line, the congregation takes their place behind the imam and states their *niyyah*: "I intend to perform the *Eid al-Fitr* prayer for the consent of Allah following the imam."

2) When the imam raises his hands calling out "Allāhu akbar", the congregation also states "Allāhu akbar" raising their hands following the imam and then holds their hands together below the belly.

3) Both the imam and the congregation silently recite "Subhanaka." Then, three *takbir*s are performed. The *takbir*s are performed as follows:

The first takbir: The imam calls out "Allāhu akbar" in a loud voice and the congregation follows stating it silently (the same as the *iftitah takbir*) raising their hands and then relaxing them by their sides. There is a short pause here.

The second takbir: "Allāhu akbar" is pronounced out loud for the second time with the hands raised and then relaxed by the sides. There is a short pause just as with the first *takbir*.

The third takbir: Then, "Allāhu akbar" is called again; the hands are raised and then tied together without relaxing them by your side.

4) After this, the imam silently recites "Auzu-Basmala" and then recites the *Fatihah* and a *surah* out loud (the congregation listens silently to the imam without reciting anything).

5) After performing the *ruku* and *sajda,* the hands are held together when stood up.

The second *ra'kah*:

1) The imam silently states the "Basmala" and then recites the *Fatihah* and a surah out loudly. When the surah is completed, in a loud voice the imam calls out the *takbir* three times and the congregation follows silently (just as in the first *ra'kah*). After the third *takbir*, without the hands being tied the *ruku* is performed with the fourth *takbir*. Then, you sit after the *sajdas* are performed.

2) At the sitting, both the imam and the congregation recite the *duas Al-taḥiyyāt, Allahumma Salli, Allahumma Barik* and *Rabbana atina*. The prayer is completed after the *salām* is performed firstly to the right and then the left. A *khutbah* is then delivered after the prayer.

Eid al-Adha prayer:

1) The *niyyah* is stated: "I intend to perform the Eid al-Adha prayer for the consent of Allah following the imam."

2) The imam takes the *iftitah takbir* calling out "Allāhu akbar" with the congregation behind also stating "Allāhu akbar" when raising their hands and then holds them together below the naval.

After the *niyyah*, the prayer is performed identically to the *Eid al-Fitr* prayer and the *khutbah* is delivered when the prayer is completed.

TAKBIR AL TASHREEQ

The *takbir al-tashreeq* is recited after every *fard* prayer following the fajr prayer on the eve of *Eid al-Adha* until the *asr* prayer on the fourth day of *Eid* as follows:

"Allāhu akbar, Allāhu akbar, La Ilaha Illallahu, Wallahu Akbar, Allāhu akbar wa lillahilhamd."

It is *wajib* to perform these *takbir*s – which are called *Takbir al-Tashreeq*.

This *takbir* is *wajib* for the whole congregation, for those performing prayer alone, the traveler, the resident, the men and the women.

If the prayers that are left to *qada* during the days of *tashreeq* are performed during this period then, the *takbir al-tashreeq* must be performed. If the *qada* is performed after the days of *tashreeq* has ended then, the *takbir*s are not performed.

Our duties during *Eid*:

Some of the duties that must be carried out during *Eid* are: To wake up early on the morning of *Eid*, to take shower, to clean teeth, to wear best clothes and to go to the mosque having applied the best fragrances, to greet everyone met with a smiling face, to make the poor happy by helping them, to congratulate religious siblings for the *Eid*, to visit the elderly, to give charity on behalf of deceased relatives, to visit the grave sites whilst reciting the Qur'an and making dua, to leave quarrels, to make peace between those resentful and to make children happy with presents.

TARAWIH PRAYER

The *tarawih* prayer is twenty *ra'kah*s. This is *sunnah muakkadah* for both men and women. It is performed during the month of Ramadan. The *tarawih* prayer is also *sunnah* for those who do not fast due to illness or because they are a traveler. It is *sunnah* for the *tarawih* prayer to be performed at mosques together with the congregation. It can also be performed by oneself or with a congregation at home. However, it is more virtuous to perform this prayer at a mosque.

Our Prophet stated the following:

"Those who spend Ramadan nights with *ibadah* (observe the *tarawih* prayers) believing in the virtues and seeking his reward from Allah, will be forgiven from his past sins." [4]

How *tarawih* prayer is performed:

4. Riyadh us Salihen, Volume 2, Page 467

The *tarawih* prayer is performed after *isha* prayer. It is not lawful to perform this before *isha*. The *witr* prayer is performed after *tarawih* during the month of Ramadan but it can also be performed before.

The *tarawih* prayer is twenty *ra'kahs* and is performed by giving the *salām* at the end of two *ra'kahs* or at the end of four *ra'kahs*. In both situations, the prayer is continued until twenty *ra'kahs* are completed.

How the *tarawih* prayer is performed giving the *salām* every two *ra'kahs* with a congregation:

The *tarawih* prayer is performed after the *fard* and final *sunnah* of the *isha* prayer is completed.

The imam that will lead prayer states: "I intend to perform the Tarawih prayer for the consent of Allah and I will lead as an imam for anybody following my lead." taking the iftitah takbir and tying their hands together.

The congregation following the imam state the niyyah as: "I intend to perform the Tarawih prayer for the consent of Allah following the imam." and then takes the takbir stating "Allāhu akbar" after the imam's takbir and then ties their hands together.

After this, the imam and the congregation silently recite "Subhanaka." After Subhanaka is recited, (the congregation do not recite anything else whilst standing) the imam silently states the Auzu Basmala, recites aloud Surah Al-Fatihah and another surah. Then, together with the congregation, the ruku and sajdas are performed before rising for the second ra'kah.

Here, the imam again silently states the *Basmala* before reciting Surah Al-Fatihah and another surah. Then, performing the ruku and sajda's together with the congregation before remaining seated.

During this sitting, the imam and the congregation recite the duas Al-taḥiyyāt, Allahumma Salli, Allahumma Barik and Rabbana atina... and then give the salām. As such, two ra'kahs are performed.

Then, you stand and continue to perform two ra'kahs each as described above. The twenty ra'kahs are completed by continuing to complete ten of these two ra'kahs. After this, the three ra'kahs of the Witr prayer are performed.

How Tarawih prayer is performed giving the salām every two ra'kahs by one's self:

The niyyah is stated: "I intend to perform the Tarawih prayer for the consent of Allah." and the prayer is performed identically to the two ra'kahs of the sunnah of the Fajr prayer.

Two ra'kahs are performed until twenty ra'kahs are completed. Then, the three ra'kahs of the Witr prayer are performed after the Tarawih prayer is completed.

How the Tarawih prayer is performed giving the salām every four ra'kahs with a congregation:

The imam leading the prayer and the congregation states the niyyah and takes the iftitah takbir tying their hands together as described above. The imam and the congregation silently recite "Subhanaka" (the congregation does not recite anything else) the imam silently states the Auzu-Basmala, recites aloud Surah Al-Fatihah and another surah. Then, the ruku and sajdas are performed before rising for the second ra'kah.

Here, the imam silently states the *Basmala*, recites *Surah al-Fatihah* and another *surah,* performs the *ruku* and *sajdas* and sits. During this sitting at the end of the second *ra'kah*, the imam and the congregation recite the *duas Al-taḥiyyāt, Allahumma Salli, Allahumma Barik* and then rise for the third *ra'kah*.

At the start of the third *ra'kah*, both the imam and the congregation silently recite *Subhanaka*. Later, the imam silently states the *Auzu* and the *Basmala*, recites aloud *Surah al-Fatihah* and another *surah*. Later, the *ruku* and *sajda* are performed before rising for the fourth *ra'kah*.

The imam silently states the *Basmala*, recites *Surah al-Fatihah* aloud and another *surah* and then sits after performing *ruku* and *sajda*.

At this sitting, the imam and the congregation recite the *duas Al-taḥiyyāt*, *Allahumma Salli*, *Allahumma Barik* and *Rabbana atina*... and then give the *salām*. As such, the first four *ra'kah*s of the *tarawih* prayer is completed.

After this, they rise to their feet and continue to perform four *ra'kah*s as described above. The twenty *ra'kah*s are completed by performing four *ra'kah*s five times.

Then, the *witr* prayer is performed with the congregation.

How the *tarawih* prayer is performed by giving the *salām* for every four *ra'kah*s by oneself

The *niyyah* is stated: "I intend to perform the *tarawih* prayer for the consent of Allah." and the prayer is performed identically to the *sunnah* of the *asr* prayer. The difference between the two is just the *niyyah*. The twenty *ra'kah*s are completed like this four *ra'kah*s at a time. Following this, the *witr* prayer is performed.

PRAYER WHILST SITTING OR WITH IMPLICATIONS

There are no difficulties in Islam. Worship and prayer are designated in Islam in accordance with a person's strength and power. For example, a person who cannot perform prayer whilst standing can do it while seated. The *ruku* is performed by bending forward. After straightening from the *ruku*, the *sajda* is performed and the prayer is completed like this.

If the *sajda* cannot be performed by placing the forehead on the ground due to a lack of ability then they perform prayer with a gesture of their head. This is called "prayer with implication" as the *ruku* and *sajda* are performed by gesture leaning the head forward. A person in this condition leans his head forward a little during *ruku* and then a little further during the *sajda*. It will not be a valid prayer if the head leaning forward for the *sajda* is not further than the *ruku*.

If a sick person is not in a position to sit, they can perform prayer lying down as they wish and make gestures with the head. A person who does not have the ability to perform prayer with gestures of the head leaves the prayer for a later time.

THE PRAYER OF THE TRAVELER

A person who leaves their village or town to a place of 18 hours (with an average speed on foot) away (approximately 90 kilometers) is called a guest (traveler).

Just as a person who travels from their village or town of residence is a traveler until they reach their destination, they are still considered a guest if they decide to stay for less than 15 days. They are no longer deemed guests if they decide to stay at the place that they traveled to for more than 15 days.

Our religion provides some easiness to guests:

A traveler performs the four *ra'kah*s of the *fard* prayers as two *ra'kah*s. The two-*fard ra'kah*s of the *fajr* prayer, the three *ra'kah*s of the *fard* of the maghrib prayer and the witr prayers are performed in its entirety.

A guest who follows the lead of an imam who is not a guest performs four *ra'kah*s together. If a guest acts as the imam for followers that are not guests, the imam gives the *salām* at the end of the two *ra'kah*s. The congregation that are not guests, continue to perform prayer by themselves by completing the four *ra'kah*s. A guest performs the *qada* of four-*ra'kah* prayers missed during travels as two ra'kahs after the travel has been completed. A guest who wears socks together with their *wudu* performs the *masah* over the socks for three days and three nights.

A guest can either fast during the month of Ramadan or can fast when they return home. It is better for a traveler to fast if there is no difficulty in doing so. A traveler does not have to perform *jumu'ah* or *Eid* prayers. However, if they do perform it, it is accepted. If they cannot perform the *jumu'ah* prayer then, they can perform the *zhuhr* prayer.

This is the ease provided to guests by our religion by taking the circumstances of the traveler into account.

THE QADA OF THE PAST PRAYERS

To perform a prayer within the appointed time is called "**Ada**." To perform after the appointed time period has elapsed is called "**Qada**." It is a great sin to leave prayer until after the time period has elapsed knowingly and without excuse. The missed prayer can be fulfilled by performing *qada*. However, we must ask for forgiveness from Allah the Almighty as it has been left for later.

Qada can be performed for all of the five daily *fard* prayers and the *witr* prayer. *Qada* cannot be performed for the *sunnah* prayers. A person who has not performed the *fajr* prayer within the appointed time can perform *qada* for the *sunnah* and the *fard* until the midmorning. There is no appointed time to perform *qada* prayers. It can be performed during the day or night. It cannot be performed at the three *makruh* times which are when the sun is rising, when it is at its highest point and when it is setting.

If a person is not sure which days and which prayer they wish to perform a past *qada* prayer for then, they should state their *niyyah* as follows: "I intend to perform the *fard* of the first *fajr* prayer left as *qada* for the consent of Allah." For other prayers, you make the *niyyah* for the first *zhuhr* left, the first *asr*, the first *maghrib*, the first *isha* and the first *witr* prayer. Alternatively, you can make *niyyah* for the last *fajr* prayer left as *qada*, the last *zhuhr*, the last *asr*, the last *maghrib*, the last *isha* or the last *witr* prayer.

THE SAJDA AL-TILAWAT

Sajda al-tilawah is to show our respect to Allah. There are fourteen *sajda ayahs* in the holy Qur'an. It is *wajib* for someone who recites or hears this to perform a *sajda*.

It is required that the *sajda al-tilawah* be performed during prayer if a *sajda ayah* is recited during prayer. If after the *sajda ayah*, the recitation of the Qur'an is going to be continued, you should perform the *sajda al-tilawah* immediately and then continue to recite the Qur'an after standing up.

If the Qur'an recitation is not going to be continued after the *sajda ayah* then, one, two or at the most three *ayahs* are recited before the *ruku* and *sajda* are performed. A separate *sajda al-tilawah* is not required.

If a person who is not in the prayer congregation hears the *sajda ayah* recited during prayer, they must also perform the *sajda*. If a person who is performing prayer hears the *sajda ayah* recited by another person, then, it is required that they perform the *sajda al-tilawah* after the prayer has finished.

A person who recites the *sajda ayah* must perform the sajda al-tilawah during prayer, not after the prayer has finished. If an imam recites a *sajda ayah* during prayer then, both he and the congregation that is following him must perform the *sajda al-tilawah*. The *sajda al-tilawah* is *wajib* for all people who are *mukallaf* (responsible) but it is not *wajib* for women during their menstruation and postpartum period.

HOW SAJDA AL-TILAWAT IS PERFORMED OUTSIDE OF THE PRAYER:

First, turn toward the *qibla*. Without raising your hands and with the *niyyah* of a *sajda al- tilawah, "Allāhu akbar"* is stated before performing the *sajda*. In the *sajda*, you state *"Subhana rabbi al ala"* three times and then rise up stating *"Allāhu akbar."* It is mustahabb to say *"Gufranaka rabbana wa ilaykal masir"* when standing up. The *sajda* is only performed once and no *salām* is required.

The *sajda ayah*s in the Holy Qur'an are in the following fourteen *surah*s:

1) Surah Al-'A`rāf	(Ayah 206)	8) Surah An-Naml	(Ayah 25)
2) Surah Ar-Ra`d	(Ayah 15)	9) Surah As-Sajdah	(Ayah 15)
3) Surah An-Naĥl	(Ayah 48)	10) Surah Sād	(Ayah 24)
4) Surah Al-'Isrā'	(Ayah 107)	11) Surah Fussilat	(Ayah 37)
5) Surah Maryam	(Ayah 58)	12) Surah An-Najm	(Ayah 62)
6) Surah Al-Ĥaj	(Ayah 18)	13) Surah Al-'Inshiqāq	(Ayah 21)
7) Surah Al-Furqān	(Ayah 60)	14) Surah Al-`Alaq	(Ayah 19)

JANAZAH PRAYER

The *janazah* prayer is *fard kifayah*. It is a *dua* for the deceased. It is to ask for the forgiveness of the sins and faults of our religious brother or sister from Allah and to carry out our last duty.

Whose *janazah* prayer can be performed?

Six conditions should be fulfilled for the performance of a *janazah* prayer for the deceased. These conditions are:

1) For the deceased to be a Muslim,

2) To be clean (For example, the body should be wrapped in a *kafan* (shroud) after being washed),

3) To be in front of the congregation,

4) For the deceased to have their whole body, more than half of theirhis body or half their body with their head exposed.

5) For the person to perform the *janazah* prayer to be on his/her feet (if not disabled).

6) For the deceased not to be placed on the ground, on shoulders or on animals.

If some Muslims perform this prayer, others are not required to do so, as the *janazah* prayer is *fard kifayah*. A congregation is not required for *janazah* prayers. If only a man or a woman performs the *janazah* prayer, the fard is fulfilled. The things that invalidate other prayers also invalidate *janazah* prayers. The janazah prayer can be performed at all times except in the three *makruh* times.

The *rukn*s of the *janazah* prayer are four *takbir*s and qiyaam. It is *wajib* to perform a salām. There is no *ruku* or *sajda* when performing a *janazah* prayer.

The *sunnahs* of the *janazah* prayer:

1) The imam leading the prayer must stand in parallel to the deceased's chest.

2) To recite "S*ubhanaka"* after the first *takbir*.

3) To recite *"Allahumma Salli and Allahumma Barik"* after the second *takbir*.

4) To recite a *dua* after the third *takbir*.

HOW THE JANAZAH PRAYER IS PERFORMED

The body is placed on a *musalla* stone (high stone table) where prayer will be performed after it is washed and placed in a *kafan*. The *janazah* is placed in front of the congregation. The imam leading the prayer stands in line with the deceased's chest. The congregation stands in lines behind the imam facing the *qibla* whilst standing. It is *mustahabb* for the congregation to be in three lines.

When performing the *niyyah*, you must specify whether the deceased is a man, woman, boy or girl.

The imam leading the prayer makes the *niyyah* as follows: *"I intend to perform for the consent of Allah the janazah prayer that is ready, and make dua for this male (if the deceased is a male)."*

If it is a deceased woman: "To make dua for this woman",

If it is a boy: "To make dua for this boy",

If it is a girl: "To make dua for this girl" is stated.

The congregation behind the imam states the *niyyah* as: *"I intend to perform for the consent of Allah the janazah prayer that is ready and make dua for this male (if the deceased is a male) following the imam."*

If the *janazah* is for a woman: "To make dua for this woman",

If the *janazah* is for a boy: "To make dua for this boy",

If the *janazah* is for a girl: "To make dua for this girl" is stated.

If a person of the congregation is unaware as to whether the deceased is a male or female, they make *niyyah* as follows: *"I intend to perform for the consent of Allah this janazah prayer which the imam will lead, to make dua for the deceased following the imam."*

After the *niyyah*, the imam in a loud voice and the congregation following silently take the *takbir* stating *"Allāhu akbar."* Like all the other prayers, the hands are raised to the height of the ears and then held below the naval.

Both the imam and congregation silently recite *Subhanaka*. Unlike the other prayers where *"wa jalla sanauk"* is not recited, it is recited with this.

After reciting subhanaka without raising the hands, the imam takes the second takbir aloud stating *"Allāhu akbar"* and the congregation does so silently. Both the imam and the congregation then silently recite *"Allahumma Salli and Allahumma Barik."*

Then, without raising the hands *"Allāhu akbar"* is recited again taking the third takbir and the *janazah dua* is recited. Those who do not know the *janazah dua* can recite *Qunut duas* instead. Those who do not know the *Qunut duas* can recite the following *ayah*: *"Rabbana atina fid-dunya hasanatan wa fil 'akhirati hasanatan waqina 'adhaban-nar."*

After this, the fourth *takbir* is taken stating *"Allāhu akbar"* without raising the hands and then without stating anything, the head is turned to the right stating *"Assalamu alaikum wa rahmatullah."* Then the head is turned to the left stating *"Assalamu alaikum wa rahmatullah"* and the *janazah* prayer is completed.

The *dua* recited after the third *takbir* during the *janazah* prayer:
This *dua* is recited for all *janazahs*:

اَللّٰهُمَّ اغْفِرْ لِحَيِّنَا وَمَيِّتِنَا وَشَاهِدِنَا وَغَا ئِبِنَا وَذَكَرِنَا وَأُنْثَانَ وَصَغِيرِنَا وَكَبِيرِنَا

اَللّٰهُمَّ مَنْ اَحْيَيْتَهُ مِنَّا فَاَحْيِهِ عَلَى الْإِسْلَامِ وَمَنْ تَوَفَّيْتَهُ مِنَّا فَتَوَفَّهُ عَلَى الْإِيمَانِ

Pronunciation: **"Allahumma`ghfirli-hayyina wa mayyitina wa shahidina wa ghaibina wa dhakarina wa unthana wa saghirina wa kabirina.**

Allahumma, man ahyaytahu minna fa-ahyihi ala`l-islam wa man tawaffaytahu minna fa-tawaffahu ala`l-iman."

Meaning: *O Allah! Forgive our living and our dead, those who are present and those who are absent, our young and our old, our males and our females.*

O Allah! Create the generation that will come from us into the religion of Islam. Of us whose death has arrived, let them die in a state of faith.

After this *dua*, one of the following *duas* can be recited depending on the situation of the *janazah* as follows:

1) This *dua* is recited if the *janazah* is for a male:

وَخُصَّ هٰذَا الْمَيِّتَةَ بِالرَّوْحِ وَالرَّاحَةِ وَالرَّحْمَةِ وَالْمَغْفِرَةِ وَالرِّضْوَانِ اَللّٰهُمَّ اِنْ كَانَ مُحْسِنًا فَزِدْ فِى اِحْسَانِهِ وَاِنْ كَانَ مُسِيئًا فَتَجَاوَزْ عَنْهُ وَلَقِّهِ الْاَمْنَ وَالْبُشْرٰى وَالْكَرَامَةَ وَالزُّلْفٰى بِرَحْمَتِكَ يَا اَرْحَمَ الرَّاحِمِينَ

Pronunciation: **Ve khussa hadha` l-mayyita bir-rawhi wa`r-rahati wa`r-rahmati wa`l-maghfirati ve`r-ridwan. Allahumma in kana muhsinan fa-zid fi ihsanihi wa in kana musian fa-tajawaz anhu wa laqqihi`l-amna wa` l-bushra wa`l-karamata wa`z-zulfa bi-rahmatika ya arhama`r-rahimin.**

Meaning: *My Lord, grant this dead person in clean air eternal rest, endless mercy, the forgiveness of sins and a life in jannah.*

Oh Allah, if this dead person is a person who acted well, then give him his reward in abundance; and if he acted wrongly, then abandon his punishment! Forgive his sins. Grant him security from the things he is worried, glad tidings, the honor of the hereafter and allow him to reach a high rank.

Oh Allah, the most merciful of all.

2) This *dua* is recited if the *janazah* is for a female:

وَخُصَّ هَذِهِ الْمَيِّتَةَ بِالرَّوْحِ وَالرَّاحَةِ وَ الْمَغْفِرَةِ وَ الرِّضْوَانِ اَللّٰهُمَّ اِنْ كَانَتْ مُحْسِنَةً فَزِدْ فِي اِحْسَانِهَا وَ اِنْ كَانَتْ مُسِيئَةً فَتَجَاوَزْ عَنْهَا وَ لَقِّهَا الْاَمْنَ وَ الْبُشْرَى وَ الْكَرَامَةَ وَ الزُّلْفَى بِرَحْمَتِكَ يَا اَرْحَمَ الرَّاحِمِينَ

Pronunciation: **Ve khussa hadihil` l-mayyitata bir-rawhi wa`r-rahati wa`l-maghfirati ve`r-ridwan... Allahumma in kanat muhsinatan fa-zid fi ihsaniha wa in kanat musiatan fa-tajawaz anha wa laqqihe`l-amna wa` l-bushra wa`l-karamata wa`z-zulfa bi-rahmatika ya arhama`r-rahimin.**

Meaning: *My Lord, grant this dead person in clean air eternal rest, endless mercy, the forgiveness of sins and a life in jannah.*

Oh Allah, if this dead person is a person who acted well, then give her reward in abundance; and if she acted wrongly, then abandon her punishment! Forgive sher sins. Grant her security from the things she is worried, glad tidings, the honor of the hereafter and allow her to reach a high rank. Oh Allah, the most merciful of all.

3) This dua is recited if the *janazah* is for a boy:

اَللّٰهُمَّ اجْعَلْهُ لَنَا فَرَطًا وَاجْعَلْهُ لَنَا اَجْرًا وَ ذُخْرًا وَجْعَلْهُ لَنَا شَافِعًا وَمُشَفَّعًا

Pronunciation: **"Allahummaj'alhu lana faratan vaj'alhu lana ajran va zuhran vaj'alhu lana shafi'an ve mushaffa'a."**

Meaning: O Allah! Allow this child to be a gift of the hereafter welcoming us to *jannah*...

O Allah! Allow this child to be an intercessor for us and make his intercession acceptable.

4) This dua is recited if the *janazah* is for a girl:

اَللّٰهُمَّ اجْعَلْهَا لَنَا فَرَطًا وَاجْعَلْهَا لَنَا اَجْرًا وَذُخْرًا وَجْعَلْهَا لَنَا شَافِعَةً وَمُشَفَّعَةً

Pronunciation: **"Allahummaj'alha lana faratan vaj'alha lana ajran va zuhran vaj'alha lana shafi'atan ve mushaffa'a."**

Meaning: Oh Allah! Allow this child to be a gift of the hereafter welcoming us to *jannah*...

Oh Allah! Allow this child to be an intercessor for us and make her intercession acceptable.

Those who do not know the *janazah duas* can read this *ayah* with the *niyyah* of a *dua*:

رَبَّنَا اٰتِنَا فِي الدُّنْيَا حَسَنَةً وَفِي الْاٰخِرَةِ حَسَنَةً وَقِنَا عَذَابَ النَّارِ

Pronunciation: **Rabbana atina fid-dunya hasanatan wa fil 'akhirati hasanatan waqina 'adhaban-nar**

Meaning: Our Lord! Grant us good in this world and good in the hereafter, and save us from the chastisement of the hell fire.

QUESTIONS

1) What does sajda al-sahv refer to and in what conditions is it performed?

2) Explain the virtues of prayer in congregation.

3) What should we pay attention to at mosques?

4) Explain the different sections of a mosque.

5) How does a person who follows the lead of an imam perform prayer in congregation?

6) To whom is *jumu'ah* prayer *fard*?

7) How many *ra'kahs* is *jumu'ah* prayer?

8) To whom are *Eid* prayers *wajib*?

9) What are the differences of the *Eid* prayer compared to other prayers?

10) Explain the *takbir al-tashreeq*.

11) Explain what the duties are during *Eid*.

12) Explain the virtues of *tarawih* prayer.

13) How is the *tarawih* prayer performed?

14) How is prayer performed whilst sitting or with implications?

15) Whom does a "traveler" refer to, and how do they perform prayer?

16) What do “ada” and “qada” refer to, and how are past prayers performed?

17) What is *sajda al-tilawah* and how is it performed?

18) For whom can *janazah* prayer be performed?

19) How is the *niyyah* stated for the *janazah* prayer, how is the *janazah* prayer performed?

UNIT VI

SAWM (FASTING)

Topics:

- The importance and benefits of fasting
- For whom is Ramadan fasting a *fard*?
- The virtues of *suhur*, *iftar* and *iftar dua*
- When and how is the niyyah stated for fasting?
- Types of fasting
- Excuses that make not fasting during Ramadan Permissible and *fidya*
- Rulings for not fasting during Ramadan without an excuse
- Things that require *qada* and penance for invalidating the fast
- Things that do not invalidate fasting
- Things that are *makruh* for people who are fasting
- Things that are not *makruh* for people who are fasting

THE IMPORTANCE OF FASTING

The third of the five conditions of Islam is to fast during the month of Ramadan.

The Ramadan fast became *fard* in the second year of the *Hijrah*.

Fasting starts from the beginning of dawn until sunset during which one cannot eat, drink or engage in any kind of sexual relations.

Some years, the month of Ramadan lasts 29 days, and some years it lasts 30 days. The fasting is complete even when Ramadan lasts 29 days. Because, what is *fard* is to fast the whole month. Our Prophet observed nine Ramadans in his life. Of these, four were 29 days and five were 30 days.

The month of Ramadan is a blessed month and is holy for Muslims. The religion of Islam was sent down in this month, and our supreme book, the holy Qur'an, which illuminated the world, began to be revealed during this month. Night of *Qadr*, which is more auspicious than a thousand months, is within this month. The fasting that cleanses our soul and body is performed during this month.

Allah the Almighty commands: **"O you who have believed, decreed upon you is fasting as it was decreed upon those before you. Maybe you will avoid and abstain."** [1]

Fasting is a type of worship that prevents us from committing sins in this world, protects us from the hellfire in the hereafter and is a means for our sins to be forgiven. Our beloved Prophet gives the following good news: **"Whoever fasts Ramadan out of faith expecting reward from Allah, Allah forgives all his past sins."** [2]

THE BENEFITS OF FASTING

a) Fasting improves our morality:

Fasting always reminds us of Allah and develops feelings of responsibility. It cleanses our hearts from negative feelings and protects us from doing evil acts to others. By providing us with the best moral codes, fasting can turn us into exceptional people. Fasting protects the eyes from looking at what is *haram*, the tongue from lies and nasty words, the ears from listening to *haram*, the stomach from eating *haram*, and the hands from carrying out bad deeds and the feet from going to bad places.

The wisdom behind fasting being a *fard* is to perform our duty of servitude to Allah and abstain from bad things.

b) Fasting develops the emotions of mercy and empathy:

A wealthy person who does not know what hunger is cannot understand how the poor suffer from hunger and hardship. However, if this person fasts, he/she can understand the meaning of hunger and empathize with the poor's hardship. As a result, they reach out to needy people and resolve their hardships.

c) Fasting teaches people the value of blessings (*ni'mah*):

A person can only understand the true value of the blessings that he/she possesses when they lose them. By then, however, it is too late. The value of blessings can be better understood when a person abstains from them for a period by fasting. This understanding teaches people how to better protect their blessings and how to give thanks to Allah for them.

---

1. Surah Al-Baqarah 2/183
2. Riyadh us Salihen, Volume 2, Page 489

d) Fasting makes a person healthier:

On this topic, our beloved Prophet commands: **"Fast and you will find health."** [3]After working for eleven months, the digestive system rests thanks to fasting. It then continues its functions revitalized after Ramadan. Scientists point out several benefits of fasting for our body. The Nobel Prize winner for medicine, the famous French scientist Doctor Aleksi Karel, said the following in relation to fasting: "During fasting, the body uses stored nutrition which is replaced by new nutrition. Thus, the body is regenerated. From a health perspective, fasting is very beneficial for our body." [4]

e) Fasting teaches people patience:

A person who gets used to fasting perseveres with the difficulties that he/she faces in life. He/she can stand up to adversaries and knows how to endure the difficulties that may arise as a result of their stance.

FOR WHOM IS RAMADAN FASTING A *FARD*?

The following conditions must be fulfilled for fasting to be a *fard*:

1) To be a Muslim,
2) To be sane,
3) To have reached puberty.

It is *fard* for every sane male and female Muslim who has reached the age of puberty to fast during the month of Ramadan. This is an established command by Allah. It is not a *fard* for those children who have not yet reached puberty to fast. However, it is good for children to get accustomed to fasting gradually.

Women who are on their postpartum period or monthly periods cannot fast or perform prayer. When these conditions are not present, they are able to fast to make up for what was previously missed as *qada*. However, it is not required that the prayers that they missed be performed.

---

3. Keşfu'l-Hafa, Volume 2, Page 33.
4. Life Encyclopedia, Fasting clause.

THE VIRTUE OF SUHUR AND IFTAR

It is *mustahabb* to get up and eat at *suhur*. Our beloved Prophet stated: **"Eat food at *suhur* because there is blessing in the food at *suhur*."**[5] The food at *suhur* gives one strength for the fast. The time of *suhur* is one of the times that prayers are accepted. A person who wakes up at *suhur* to fast should make *dua* for what they wish and should ask Allah to forgive their sins.

A person who completes the worship of fasting until the time of *iftar* feels great happiness and joy. They will taste the greatest joy and reward for the fasting performed on the day of judgment at the time of entering Allah's presence.

Our Prophet commands the following: **"There are two joys for a person who fasts: One is at the time of *iftar* and the other is the time when they meet Allah."**[6] Our Prophet notified us that the *dua*s made at the time of *iftar* will not be refused and will be accepted by Allah.

The *Dua* of *Iftar*:

It is *sunnah* to recite this *dua* at the time of *iftar*:

"Allahumma laka sumtu wa bika amantu wa `alayka tawakkaltu wa `ala rizqika aftartu Wa sawmal ghadi min shahri Ramadana nawaitu, faghfirli ma kaddamtu wa ma ahhartu."

Meaning: *"O Allah, I have fasted for You, believed in You, placed my trust in You, and broken my fast on your provision. I intend to keep the fast tomorrow for the month of Ramadan. Now forgive my past and future sins!"*

WHEN AND HOW IS THE NIYYAH STATED FOR FASTING?

It is a requirement to state the *niyyah* for a fast to be valid. A fast without *niyyah* is not acceptable.

The *niyyah* for the Ramadan fast can be stated from *maghrib* time to the following mid-morning:

5. Riyadh us Salihen, Volume 2, Page 495
6.. Et-Terğib ve't-Terhib, Volume 2, Page 81

Normally, the *niyyah* for fasting is stated after the meal at *suhur* is eaten. However, a person who awakens after dawn and misses *suhur* can state his/her *niyyah* until mid-morning even though the sun has risen, as long as that person did nothing to invalidate the fast after dawn.

A person who does not want to wake up for *suhur* can make the *niyyah* for the following day's fast after *maghrib*. They are not required to wake up and make the *niyyah* again. A person who awakens for *suhur* and forgets to make *niyyah* can still make the *niyyah* when they remember until mid-morning. Those who make *niyyah* late like this do not lose anything from their fast. The *niyyah* for fasting cannot be made after mid-morning. When making *qada* for the missed fasts of Ramadan, the *niyyah* must be made from the evening. The expiation fast is also like this. The *niyyah* for these fasts cannot be made after dawn.

The *niyyah* is made with the heart. If a person considers in their heart that they will fast tomorrow, that person has made *niyyah*. It is also a *niyyah* if a person wakes up for *suhur* with the thought of fasting. It is enough to make the *niyyah* to fast with one's heart. However, it is better to make the *niyyah* with the tongue as well as the heart. For this reason, a person who is going to fast should make the *niyyah* both with their heart and verbally by stating: "I intend to fast tomorrow for Ramadan."

TYPES OF FASTING

There are six types of fasting:

1) Fasting that is *fard*: The Ramadan fasts, the *qada* fasts and expiation (*kaffarah*) fasts are *fard*.

2) Fasting that is *wajib*: The *nazhr* fasts and spoiled *nafl* fasts are *wajib*.

3) Fasting that is *sunnah*: It is *sunnah* to fast on the ninth and tenth day or the tenth and eleventh day of the month of Muharram.

4) Fasting that is *mustahabb*: It is *mustahabb* to fast on the thirteenth, fourteenth and fifteenth days of the lunar month, on Mondays and Thursdays and for six days in the month of Shawwal after Ramadan.

5) Fasting that is *makruh*: It is *makruh* to fast only on the tenth day of the month of Muharram or to fast only on *jumu'ah*s or Saturdays.

6) Fasting that is haram: It is haram to fast on the first day of *Eid al-Fitr* and on the four days of *Eid al-Adha*. This is because the days of *Eid* are feast days provided by Allah to His servants. It is not appropriate to abstain from Allah's feast.

EXCUSES THAT MAKE NOT FASTING DURING RAMADAN PERMISSIBLE

It is a sin not to fast during the month of Ramadan without an excuse and so it is penalized. However, a person does not have to fast or can break a fast if one of the conditions below apply.

1) Sickness: A sick person does not have to fast if they are afraid that their sickness will increase. When the sick person is better, the missed fasts can be performed by *qada*.

2) Travelling: A person travelling in excess of ninety kilometers during the month of Ramadan does not have to fast. They can perform *qada* of the Ramadan fast when their travels have been completed. It is however, better for the traveler to fast if fasting will not be too difficult.

3) Difficult times: A person can spoil their fast if there is a danger to a person's life or if their body is threatened by harm. The broken fast can be performed later.

4) To be pregnant or breast--feeding: A woman who is pregnant or is breast--feeding does not have to fast if she is afraid of harming herself or her child.

5) Severe hunger or thirst: A person can break their fast if they believe that hunger or thirst will spoil their mind or that their body will suffer severe harm. Later, the fasts that were missed can be performed by *qada*.

6) Old age and weakness: A person does not have to fast if their body deteriorates from day to day or if they cannot endure it due to old age. As they cannot perform *qada* later on, they need to pay a *fidya* for each day missed.

FIDYA

A weak person or a person of old age who cannot fast and who do not have any hopes of getting better can pay a *fidya* for each missed day of fasting during Ramadan. The amount of *fidya* is equivalent to the *zakat al-fitr*. This *fidya* can be paid at the beginning, during or end of Ramadan.

The *fidya* can be paid altogether to one poor person or separately to several poor people. If the people who are in such a position cannot pay the *fidya,* they can seek forgiveness from Allah. Old people who do not have the strength to fast or the sick who have no hope of getting better in the future must perform the *qada* of fasting if they are able to fast later. The *fidya* previously paid is not accepted and will be counted as a *nafl* donation.

RULINGS FOR NOT FASTING DURING RAMADAN WITHOUT AN EXCUSE

To fast during the month of Ramadan is an established command by Allah. Muslims must fulfil the requirements of this command. A Muslim who does not make the *niyyah* to fast and eats and drinks without excuse during the month of Ramadan must only perform the *qada* of fasting for each day missed. A penance is not required. Because penance is for spoiling the fast, not for not fasting.

A person who does not fast during Ramadan without an excuse commits a sin and is then responsible to Allah. Therefore, they must repent and seek Allah's forgiveness and perform the *qada* fast immediately.

THINGS THAT REQUIRE BOTH *QADA* AND PENANCE FOR INVALIDATING A FAST

Whilst fasting, to consciously and intentionally:

1) Eat or drink (either food or medicine)

2) Have sexual relations

3) Smoke

Qada: To fast for each day a fast is invalidated.

Penance: To fast for two months or sixty consecutive days for invalidating one day of fast.

The fast of a person who makes a *niyyah*, commences to fast during the month of Ramadan and invalidates this fast knowingly without an excuse by eating, drinking or having sexual relations is invalidated. This invalidated fast must be replaced by *qada* and a penance is also required as the fast was invalidated knowingly and without an excuse.

The penalty in this world of a commenced fast that has been invalidated is a penance. If a penance fast is paused for any reason or is lacking, this must be performed again from the start for sixty days without a break. Women whose penance fast is interrupted by their period, do not fast on these days. They continue and complete their penance fast of sixty days consecutively when their period has finished.

THINGS THAT ONLY REQUIRE *QADA* FOR INVALIDATING A FAST

1) To swallow things that aren't usually eaten and that are not used medicinally (such as dirt, paper and cotton),

2) To inhale medicine through the nose,

3) To drop oil into the ear,

4) For water to enter into the throat through the mouth or nose accidentally whilst performing *wudu*,

5) To swallow the saliva in which the color of a piece of string taken into mouth mixed,

6) To forcefully invalidate the fast,

7) For someone else to pour water down one's throat whilst sleeping,

8) To vomit at least a mouthful (voluntarily),

9) To break the fast prior to sunset believing that the sun had already set,

10) To eat after the time of dawn believing that the time had not yet come.

THINGS THAT DO NOT INVALIDATE A FAST

1) To eat or drink forgetfully whilst fasting. (If you realize that you are fasting whilst you are eating or drinking, you should immediately wash out your mouth after remembering. The fast is not invalidated even if food goes down your throat).

2) To let water in the ear,

3) To drop medication into the eyes,

4) To have bath in the morning when it was required to at night,

5) To vomit involuntarily,

6) To have a wet dream (to be unclean Islamically where ablution is required),

7) To give blood,

8) For dust or smoke to enter the throat unintentionally,

9) To swallow one's own saliva.

THINGS THAT ARE *MAKRUH* WHILST FASTING

1) To taste something without swallowing it (e.g. if a husband causes problems because of excessive salt in the food prepared by his wife, then his wife can taste the food without swallowing it),

2) To gather one's saliva in one's mouth and to swallow it (if the saliva is swallowed after it is spit out, then, the fast will be invalidated),

3) To give blood if it will make one weak and to be involved in heavy work.

THINGS THAT ARE NOT *MAKRUH* WHILST FASTING

1) To smell things such as roses or musk,

2) To brush one's teeth,

3) To rinse one's mouth,

4) To sniff water up into the nose,

5) To wash or bath.

QUESTIONS

1) What does fasting mean?

2) Explain the benefits of fasting.

3) For whom is fasting a *fard*?

4) Memorize the *iftar* dua.

5) When and how is the *niyyah* for fasting performed?

6) How many types of fasting are there?

7) What are the excuses that make not fasting during Ramadan allowable?

8) What does *fidya* mean, who is required to pay the *fidya*?

9) What does *qada* and penance mean?

10) What are the things that invalidate a fast and require one to perform both *qada* and penance?

11) What are the things that invalidate a fast but only require *qada*?

12) What are things that do not invalidate a fast?

13) What are the things that are *makruh* and not *makruh* for the person fasting?

UNIT VII

ZAKAT

Topics:

- The importance and benefits of *zakat*
- Who must give *zakat*?
- *What is Nisab*?
- To whom is *zakat* given?
- Who can zakat not be given to
- Assets that do not reguire zakat
- Assets that reguire zakat and the zakat amounts
- *Sadaqat al-Fitr* (*Fitra*)

THE IMPORTANCE AND BENEFITS OF *ZAKAT*

The fourth condition of Islam is to give *zakat*. It became *fard* prior to fasting in the second year of the *Hijrah*. It is a type of worship that is performed with wealth.

Zakat is for a wealthy person (according to religious rules) to give one fortieth of his money to a poor Muslim. *Zakat* is mentioned together with prayer thirty seven times in the holy Qur'an, which shows the importance of *zakat* in our religion.

Zakat both cleans the heart from the illness of stinginess and it cleans the wealth of the rights of the poor over it. It is a type of worship that develops compassion and mercy among the wealthy. The jealousy and envy in the hearts of the poor are removed due to *zakat* and replaced with feelings of love and respect towards the wealthy who provide financial assistance to them. The unity and brotherhood of the community is strengthened.

Islam cures the problems of a community and meets many fundamental needs. Zakat is a command from Allah and is a form of social assistance. *Zakat* allows one's wealth to grow and increase. *Zakat* prevents wealth from disappearing and from the harm of bad people. Our beloved Prophet commands: **"Protect your wealth with *zakat*."** [1]

1. Et-Terğib ve't-Terhib, Volume 1, Page 520

Zakat is a measure in Islam of whether we are sincere. A person who gives *zakat* shows how sincere he is at being a servant of Allah. It fulfils the duty of thanks towards our Lord who has given us this blessing.

A wealthy person who gives *zakat*, who helps the needy and puts a smile on the face of the poor is a loving and helpful person.

WHO MUST GIVE ZAKAT?

The people who fulfil the following conditions are obliged to pay zakat:

1) To be a Muslim,

2) To be sane,

3) To have reached the age of puberty,

4) To be free and independent,

5) To be religiously wealthy (To have at least the *nisab* amount of wealth after essential necessities and debts are met),

6) To have the property or money to give zakat,

   a) To have reached the *nisab* amount (the value of 80.18 grams of gold),

   b) To have owned wealth for at least one lunar year,

   c) For the wealth to have be actually or legally increasing.

WHAT IS NISAB?

Nisab is the measurement of wealth by our religion after taking debts and essential necessities into consideration. Whoever has at least this amount or more of property or money is considered religiously wealthy.

It is required to have at least the *nisab* amount of property or money to pay the *fitra* or to sacrifice a *qurban*. However, it is not necessary for one year to pass on the ownership of the property or money or to be increasing.

TO WHOM IS ZAKAT GIVEN?

The following are the people who zakat can be given to:

1) The poor: People who are not classified as wealthy. People who do not own the minimum *nisab* amount in wealth.

2) The destitute: People who do not own anything.

3) People in debt: People who do not own more wealth than their debts.

4) Traveler: A traveler is a wealthy person who is away from their homeland without money. A person who has nothing in hand. (*Zakat* can be paid to these people, in an enough amount so that they can reach their homeland).

5) Those on Allah's path: These are people who are stranded without money when travelling for jihad or performing hajj and those who have left their jobs for the advancement of education.

We should observe the following order when giving *zakat*:

First our siblings, the children of our siblings, uncles, aunts followed by other relatives and neighbors. After this, we can give to the poor in our neighborhood and the country we live. It is better to give the *zakat* to poor people in order to cover their actual needs rather than people who will spend the *zakat* on sinful activities and waste it.

WHO CAN ZAKAT NOT BE GIVEN TO

Zakat cannot be given to the following:

1) Mother, father, grandmother and grandfather,

2) Son, the children of your son, daughter, the children of your daughter and the children born from these children,

3) The wealthy,

4) Non-Muslims,

5) A spouse.

ASSETS THAT DO NOT REQUIRE *ZAKAT*

Zakat is not required to be given for the assets that are necessary for the need of a person or his dependents. These assets are called "*hawaij asliyyah*." These are mainly:

The homes that you live in, your furniture, clothing, vehicles, books that are not for commerce, instruments of an artist, food and ornaments that are not on sale such as pearls, diamonds and emeralds with the exception of gold and silver.

ASSETS THAT REQUIRE *ZAKAT* AND THE *ZAKAT* AMOUNTS

The *nisab* of the assets that require *zakat* and the *zakat* amount are as follows:

1) **Gold**: One fortieth of at least 80.18 grams or more,

2) **Silver**: One fortieth of at least 561 grams or more,

3) **Money**: One fortieth of the minimum *nisab* amount or more. (The basic measurement of the *nisab* amount for *zakat* is to own the equivalent of at least 80.18 grams of gold).

4) **Trade assets**: One fortieth of at least the *nisab* amount or more of the equivalent value of all trade assets.

5) **Sheep and goats**: One sheep or goat for every forty of them.

6) **Cattle**: One calf at least one year old for every thirty cattle.

7) **Camel**: One sheep or goat for every five camels.

The amount of *zakat* changes as the number of animals increase. The *zakat* from crops attained from the land is different.

Just as the *zakat* of the assets mentioned above can be paid in their kind, it can also be given by way of cash of the equivalent value.

The condition of the zakat to be valid is *niyyah*. When a wealthy person gives *zakat* to a poor person, they must make the *niyyah* with their heart. It is not required to be stated with the tongue.

SADAQAT AL-FITR (Fitra)

It is *wajib* for a Muslim to give *sadaqat al-fitr* if they have at least the *nisab* amount of property or its equivalent of money after deducting their debts and essential needs. This is briefly called "*Fitra*." For *sadaqat al-fitr* to be *wajib*, it is not necessary for one year to pass on the ownership of the property or money or for it to be increasing.

Fitra is a *sadaqah* that is given to the poor in the month of Ramadan. It is good to give this prior to *Eid*. It can be given on *Eid* or even later. It is *wajib* for a person who is defined as wealthy in religious terms to give *fitra* for them and their children that have not yet attained puberty.

The *fitra* amount for the four types of food products listed below is:

Type:	Amount:
1) Wheat	1460 Grams
2) Barley	2920 Grams
3) Dried Grapes	2920 Grams
4) Dates	2920 Grams

Just as these products can be given themselves, you can also give the equivalent value of money. It is more appropriate to give whatever is more useful to the poor. One *fitra* can only be given to one poor person. It cannot be divided into two. More than one *fitra* can be given to the same poor person. *Fitra* is given with *niyyah*. However, you do not need to advise the poor recipient that this is *fitra*. It is acceptable to make the *niyyah* inside you.

The poor person to whom the *zakat* can be given to can also receive the *fitra*. People who do not fast during Ramadan with valid reason must also give the *fitra* if they own at least the *nisab* amount of property or money.

Wealthy Muslims who give the *fitra* allow the poor to experience the joys of *Eid*. Thus, they would have paid their debt and done good deeds. Giving the *fitra* is a cause to have the fasting accepted, and to evade the violence of death and chastisement in the grave.

QUESTIONS

1) Briefly explain the benefits of *zakat*.
2) For whom is *zakat* a *fard*?
3) To whom can *zakat* be given?
4) To whom can *zakat* not be given?
5) Which goods do not require *zakat*?
6) How much *zakat* is given for each type of good?
7) What is *nisab*?
8) What is *sadaqat al-fitr*?

UNIT VIII

HAJJ

Topics:

- The importance and benefits of *hajj*
- Who is hajj a *fard* for and when?
- Fards of Hajj
- The types of *hajj*
- Ihram, *talbiyah*, *tawaf*, *sa'y* and *waqfa*
- How is *hajj* performed
- *Umrah*

THE IMPORTANCE AND BENEFITS OF HAJJ

The fifth condition of Islam is *hajj*. *Hajj* is to visit specific holy places at specific times.

Hajj became *fard* in the ninth year of the *hijrah. Hajj* is a worship performed with both wealth and the body. It is *fard* for Muslims who fulfil certain conditions to perform *hajj* at least once in a lifetime. Like all of Allah's commandments, there is much wisdom and benefit in performing the *hajj* duty.

Muslims who face Allah strengthen the brotherhood in Islam when they come together with the single aim where different languages and colors, and people of various countries to this holy land. It allows Muslims to meet each other and to find solutions to each other's sorrow and hardship.

All Muslims whether rich or poor must enter a state of *ihram* with the same clothing that instils the thought of equality amongst people and reminds them of the day of judgment. The *hajj* journey increases one's knowledge and manners whilst helping form a habit to withstand difficulty. It decreases our dependence on wealth whilst developing the emotions of help and mercy towards the poor and destitute.

To see the holy places where our beloved Prophet was born and grew up and where Islam began to spread across the universe, gives moral excitement to the soul and strengthens religious emotions. A person feels closer to Allah at holy places where extra rewards are given to the worship performed.

Many sins (except the rights of the servants of Allah) are forgiven for those who perform the hajj pilgrimage duty for the sake of Allah and refrain from harming people. On this topic, our beloved Prophet stated:

"Whoever performs *hajj* for Allah's pleasure, avoids bad expressions and actions, will return back home free from all sins as he was in the day his mother gave birth to him."[1]

WHO IS *HAJJ* FARD FOR AND WHEN

It is *fard* to perform *hajj* for those who fulfil the conditions below:

1) To be sane,

2) To have reached the age of puberty,

3) To be a Muslim,

4) To be free (not be enslaved),

5) To know that *hajj* is *fard*. (This condition is for non-Muslim countries where people have accepted Islam. It is not an excuse not to know that *hajj* is *fard* for Muslims living in Islamic countries).

6) To have enough money to cover the essential needs of one's family until one returns from *hajj*.

7) To have enough money to cover the travel expenses to make the *hajj* pilgrimage with an appropriate vehicle.

8) To arrive at the appropriate time in order to perform the *hajj* duty.

In addition to the conditions stated, the following conditions are required to personally perform the *hajj* duty. These are called the conditions to perform the *hajj*.

The conditions of performing *hajj*:

1) To be physically healthy, (Not be blind, paralyzed, sick or too elderly to endure the *hajj* pilgrimage).

2) Not to experience any obstacles preventing one from performing the hajj pilgrimage, (like being in prison)

3) To have road security,

1. Riyad al-Salihin, Volume II, p. 521

4) If a woman is going to hajj, the husband must be with his wife or she must have someone with her that is unlawful for them to marry. [2]

5) For the waiting period (when a woman is divorced or when her husband dies, she must wait for a prescribed period before she can remarry) of a woman who is divorced or whose husband has passed away to have finished.

It is *fard* for a person who has the conditions mentioned to perform the *hajj* pilgrimage in the next *hajj* season.

FARDS OF HAJJ

The *fard*s of *hajj* are three, one is a condition and two are pillars:

1) Enter into the state of *iḥrām* (condition),

2) Waqfa (Stand) at Arafat, and

3) Tawaf (Circumambulating) the *Ka'ba*.

TYPES OF HAJJ

There are three types of *hajj*:

1) Ifrad hajj: The *hajj* performed without *umrah*. A *hajj* candidate enters into the state of *iḥrām,* makes *niyyah* for only the hajj and completes the hajj mission. It is not *wajib* for an *ifrad* hajj to sacrifice a *qurban*.

2) Tamattu hajj: Enter into the state of *iḥrām* separately to perform the umrah and hajj. The hajj candidate firstly enters into the state of *iḥrām* and performs the umrah mission and exit the iḥrām state. When the day arrives, he/she enters into the *iḥrām* state again and performs the hajj mission. It is *wajib* to sacrifice a *qurban* for *tamattu* hajj.

3) Qiran hajj: To perform the *umrah* and hajj with a single *iḥrām*. When a hajj candidate enters into *iḥrām*, he makes the *niyyah* for both the *umrah* and the hajj. He first performs the *umrah* but does not exit the *iḥrām* state and then performs the hajj. It is *wajib* to sacrifice a *qurban* for the *qiran hajj*.

---

2. According to the Shafi`i madhab, a woman who does not have her husband or a lawful person (*mahram*) with her, can still perform the *fard* hajj pilgrimage, by being accompanied by two or more reliable women.

A person who wants to perform *hajj* can choose and perform one of these three types of pilgrimages. The *hajj* duty is fulfilled by whichever method is performed appropriately.

IHRAM, TALBIYAH, TAWAF, SA'Y AND WAQFA

Ihram: Some of the deeds and actions that are normally halal are deemed *haram* for a certain period for people who perform the hajj and *umrah*. A person enters into a state of ihram when he makes the *niyyah* and state the *talbiyah* to perform hajj or *umrah*.

Talbiyah: is to state in a loud voice whilst in *ihram*: **"Labbayk Allāhumma Labbayk. Labbayka Lā Sharīka Laka Labbayk. Innal 'Ḥamda, Wa'n Ni'mata, Laka wal Mulk, Lā Sharīka Lak.**" Women state the *talbiyah* in a softer voice.

Tawaf: To circumambulate the *Ka'bah* seven times.

Sa'y: is to walk quickly back and forth seven times between the hills of Safa and Marwah located next to the *Ka'bah*. Of the seven times, four times are between Safa and Marwah and three times between Marwah and Safa.

Waqfa: is to pause at Arafat and Muzdalifah for a while at certain times whilst performing the *hajj*. The *waqfa* at Arafat is *fard* and the *waqfa* at Muzdalifah is *wajib*.

HOW IS *HAJJ* PERFORMED?

A person who wants to perform the *hajj* must procure *halal* wealth for this sacred duty. If they have debts, they fulfil those debts with the debtor and forgive each other's rights. They repent and ask for forgiveness of their sins from Allah. If there is any worship that has been left for *qada*, they should be performed as much as possible. They perform two *ra'kahs* of prayer at home before they leave. They proceed to depart by asking family members, friends and relatives for the forgiveness of each other's rights. During the travel and *hajj* worship, you should refrain from offending others with bad words or actions.

The place to enter *ihram* is at the boundary of *Miqat*. Prior to coming, people should first clip their nails and clean their bodies if required, and perform the *ghusl* if possible, or the *wudu*. Men take off all of their clothing and wrap themselves into the two-piece cloth called "*izar*" and "*rida.*" During the period of ihram, their feet and head must remain uncovered. When women enter *ihram*, they do not take off their clothing.

After this, they perform two *ra'kah*s of prayer with the *niyyah* of the *ihram sunnah* at the *miqat* boundary, make the *niyyah* to perform the hajj and state the *talbiyah*. Thus, people enter the state of ihram. As long as the state of ihram continues, they should refrain from the things that are prohibited in ihram.

When they arrive in Makkah, they should perform *ghusl* or *wudu*. They should later proceed to the Haram Sharif and perform the *tawaf al-qudum* and then two *ra'kah*s of *tawaf* prayer followed by the *sa'y* between Safa and Marwah. After this, the hajj candidate remains in Makkah. It is very meritorious to perform the prayers at the Haram Sharif whilst in Makkah and to perform supererogatory *tawaf* as the opportunities arise.

People go to Arafat on the day of *tarwiyah*, which is the day before *arafa*. They stay at Arafat until the sun sets on the day of *arafa*. The time is utilized with worship and *dua*. Here, the *zhuhr* and *asr* prayers are combined and performed together with the congregation at *zhuhr*. This is called "*jama' taqdim*." The *waqfa* is performed after *zhuhr*. You proceed to "Muzdalifah" after the sun sets without performing the *maghrib* prayer.

The *maghrib* and *isha* prayers are performed at the time of *isha* together with the congregation. This is called "jama' ta'khir." The *hajj* participants that spend the night at Muzdalifah collect rocks that are used to stone the devil.

On the morning of *Eid*, the *fajr* prayer is performed early and the "Muzdalifah" *waqfa* is performed. After the day has brightened, they move towards Mina.

On the first day of *Eid*, people:

1) First, throw seven stones at the large *jamrah(Jamrah of Aqaba)*.

2) Then, shave their hair and exit *ihram*. (As it is not *wajib* to sacrifice for those performing the *ifrad hajj*, they exit ihram after stoning the large *jamrah* and shaving their hair. Those performing the *tamattu* or *qiran hajj* exit ihram after stoning the large *jamrah*, sacrificing the *qurban* and shaving the hair).

3) If time and opportunity exist, the *fard tawaf al-ziyārah* should be performed by going to Makkah.

On the second day of *Eid*: First, throw seven stones each at the small, medium and *aqaba jamrah*s. Those who did not perform the *tawaf al-ziyārah* on the first day of *Eid*, should perform it on the second day.

On the third day of *Eid*: *Hajj* participants again throw seven stones each at the small, medium and large *jamrah*s. On the same day when they return to Makkah from Mina, the *hajj* duty is completed after the *tawaf al-wada* is performed.

The practice described was the *ifrad hajj*. There are some differences in performing the *tamattu* and *qiran hajj*.

Tamattu hajj: A person who wants to perform the *tamattu hajj* enters into the state of *ihram* for *umrah* at the *miqat* boundary. When they arrive at Makkah and complete the *umrah*, they shave their head and exit *ihram*. They wait at Makkah not in a state of ihram until the day of *tarwiyah* (one day before the day of *arafa*). On the day of *tarwiyah*, they enter into the state of ihram once again and perform the duties as explained above.

The difference with the *ifrad hajj* is:

1) After stoning the large *jamrah* on the first day of *Eid*, the *qurban* is sacrificed then the hair is shaved and the state of *ihram* is exited.

2) After the *tawaf az-ziyārah*, the *sa'y* of the *hajj* is performed.

Qiran hajj: A person who wants to perform the *qiran hajj* enters into *ihram* for both the *hajj* and the *umrah* together at the *miqat* boundary.

They first perform the *umrah* when they arrive at Makkah. After the *umrah* is completed, the *tawaf al-qudum* for the *hajj* and then the *sa'y* of the *hajj* is performed. However, they do not exit *ihram*. They wait in a state of *ihram* until the day of *tarwiyah*, proceed to Arafat, and perform the *hajj* duties as described. The difference between the *qiran hajj* and *ifrad hajj* is: They sacrifice the *qurban* after throwing stones at the large *jamrah* on the first day of *Eid* and then exit *ihram* by shaving their hair.

UMRAH

As performing an *umrah* is not tied to a specific time of year, it consists of entering into the state of *ihram*, performing the *tawaf*, the *sa'y* and shaving the hair.

Umrah is *sunnah*. There is no specific time to perform *umrah*. Asides from the day of Arafa, and the days of *Eid*, *umrah* can be performed at any time of the year except during these five days.

Performing the *umrah*

A person who wants to perform an *umrah* must carry out the necessary cleanliness outside the *miqat* boundaries. Later, they need to enter a state of *ihram* by making the *niyyah* and stating the *talbiyah*. When they arrive in Makkah, they perform the *umrah tawaf*. When the *tawaf* is completed, they perform two *ra'kah*s of *tawaf* prayer. Later, they perform the *sa'y* of the *umrah* between Safa and Marwah. The hair is shaved and ihram is exited when the *sa'y* is completed. As such, the *umrah* is completed.

QUESTIONS

1) What does *hajj* mean?
2) Briefly explain the benefits of *hajj*.
3) Who is *hajj* a *fard* for?
4) How many types of *hajj* are there?
5) In which type of *hajj* is sacrificing a *qurban* not *wajib*?
6) What do *ihram*, *talbiyah*, *tawaf*, *sa'y* and *waqfa* refer to?
7) What is *umrah*?

UNIT IX

QURBAN

Topics:

- The importance of sacrificing a *qurban*
- Who should sacrifice a *qurban*?
- When and how is a *qurban* sacrificed?
- Things we can do with the *qurban* meat and skin
- Animals that are lawful and unlawful to be sacrificed as a *qurban*
- The meat of animals that can and cannot be eaten
- Nazhr Qurban
- Types of oath and its rulings

THE IMPORTANCE OF SACRIFICING A *QURBAN*

Qurban is to sacrifice an animal at specific times with the *niyyah* of worship.

Sacrificing a *qurban* is a worship that is performed by wealth and it is a *wajib*. It was commanded in the second year of the *hijrah*. It is a sacrifice done for Allah's sake in fulfilling a debt of gratitude for the blessings given by Him.

The sacrificing of the *qurban* by wealthy people for the benefit of the poor strengthens the emotions of love and brotherhood amongst Muslims. Wealthy people rejoice together with the poor. The joy that comes with the *qurban* sacrifice increases the community's tranquility and the happiness.

Our beloved Prophet shows the importance of the duty of sacrificing a *qurban* by the wealthy stating "**Whoever finds wealth and does not sacrifice a *qurban* should not come near our masjids.**" [1]

WHO SHOULD SACRIFICE A *QURBAN*?

It is *wajib* to sacrifice a *qurban* for those who fulfil the conditions below:

1) To be a Muslim,

1. Et-Terğib ve't-Terhib, Volume 2, Page 155

2) To be sane,

3) To have reached puberty,

4) To be a free man or woman ,

5) To be a resident (not to be a guest),

6) To have at least the *nisab* amount of wealth or money (it is not necessary for a year to pass on the wealth when calculating the *nisab* amount for the *qurban*).

WHEN AND HOW IS A *QURBAN* SACRIFICED?

The time to sacrifice a *qurban* is on the first, the second and the third day of *Eid*. A *qurban* cannot be sacrificed after Maghrib of the third day.

You should act kindly to an animal when taking it to be sacrificed, not pushing and shoving it. The knife should be well sharpened so as not to cause the animal any pain and if possible, the owner should sacrifice it. If the owner cannot, then they can get someone else to sacrifice it.

The *qurban* that will be sacrificed is laid on its left side facing toward the *qibla*. The person sacrificing the animal states "Bismillah Allāhu akbar" while cutting it. The sacrifice is finished after cutting the gullet underneath the chin, the air pipe and the jugular vein. It is *makruh* to separate the head from the body or to skin the animal whilst the animal is still alive. If the Basmala is not stated on purpose when the *qurban* is sacrificed then, the meat of the animal cannot be eaten.

THINGS WE CAN DO WITH THE *QURBAN* MEAT AND SKIN

Not only can the person who sacrifices the *qurban* eat from its meat, they can also feed others with it.

The *qurban* meat should be split into three parts: One part should be distributed to the poor that cannot afford to sacrifice a *qurban*, another part should be gifted to relatives and friends and the remainder should be set aside for family members. It is lawful to give away the *qurban* completely. The *qurban* meat or its skin cannot be sold nor can a butcher's fee be paid from this. Just as it is lawful to make a *sajjada* or something to be used at home with the skin of the *qurban*, it is also lawful to give the skin to a poor person or to a charitable organization.

ANIMALS THAT ARE LAWFUL AND UNLAWFUL TO BE SACRIFICED

Of the animals, only sheep, goats, cattle, buffalo and camels can be sacrificed as *qurban*. Of these, the sheep and goat must be at least 12 months old, the cattle and buffalo two years old and camels must be at least five years old. However, if a sheep that is only six months old yet looks as if it is 12 months old, it can be sacrificed. This situation does not apply to goats; they must be at least 12 months old.

Sheep and goats can only be a *qurban* for one person. Cattle, buffalo and camels can be sacrificed for one to seven people. Of these, it is not an obstacle for the animal to be sacrificed because it does not have horns, if the horns are a little broken, if some of its teeth are falling out or if it is hobbling.

An animal cannot be sacrificed if any of the following faults apply:

1) If either one or two eyes are blind,

2) If one or both horns are broken from its root,

3) If more than half of an ear or tail is ruptured,

4) If they are crippled enough that they cannot step on one leg,

5) If the animal is missing an ear or tail from birth,

6) If most of the teeth have fallen out and it cannot feed itself,

7) One that is sick,

8) One that is weak to the degree that the bone marrow has withered,

9) Ones that have ruptured teats,

10) If one teat of a sheep or goat is dry or if two teats of cattle types are dry.

Furthermore, chickens, roosters and other feral animals cannot be sacrificed as *qurban*.

WHICH ANIMALS' MEAT CAN BE EATEN?

As long as animals such as a sheep, goat, cattle, buffalo, camel, chicken, goose, duck, giraffe, emu, grouse, pigeon, quail, peacock, swallow, owl, rabbit, crane, sparrow and starling are sacrificed in the correct manner, their meat can be eaten. Furthermore, all fish types that live in the water can be eaten.

WHICH ANIMALS' MEAT CANNOT BE EATEN

Predator animals that catch and hunt with their molar teeth, rip apart and defend themselves cannot be eaten such as a wolf, bear, lion, tiger, squirrel, weasel, monkey, pig, hyena, cat, dog, elephant, lizard and fox,.

The meat of horse, mule and donkey cannot be eaten. Animals that hunt with their nails and birds that eat carcass and dirt cannot be eaten as well. Such as, an eagle, kite, vulture, stork, raven, hawk, falcon, bat, and crow.

Animals that look hideous from birth such as a rat, scorpion, snake, lizard, frog, land and sea turtles, mole, hedgehog, snail, worm, maggot, all types of flies, insects, bees and butterflies cannot be eaten.

Sea animals that do not look like fish cannot be eaten. Crab, mussel, oyster and lobster also cannot be eaten.

NAZHR QURBAN

Nazhr is something that a person makes wajib upon himself/herself when he/ she is not obliged to do.

***Nazhr* is divided into two:**

1) *Nazhr* made by not tying to anything else:

If a person makes a *nazhr* stating that: "I am going to sacrifice a *qurban* for the sake of Allah" then, it becomes *wajib* for that person to sacrifice the *qurban* and can be fulfilled at any time.

2) *Nazhr* made by tying to something either happening or not happening:

For example: If a person states "I will sacrifice a *qurban* for the sake of Allah if my patient recovers." and the person actually does recover, it becomes wajib for that person to sacrifice a *qurban*. It is not valid to sacrifice a *qurban* before the stated *nazhr* occurs.

Nazhr can only be made with animals eligible for *qurban*, animals such as chickens and roosters cannot be *nazhr qurbans*.

Just as the meat of the *nazhr qurban* cannot be eaten by the people themselves, it cannot also be eaten by his spouse, father, mother, grandfather, grandmother, children and grandchildren and people who are considered wealthy who own the *nisab* amount of money. The whole of the *nazhr qurban* must be distributed to the poor.

The ruling for sacrificing a *qurban* for the deceased

A person who wishes to sacrifice a *qurban* for a deceased person must do this during the days of Eid al-Adha. A person himself can eat from this *qurban* and can also give it to others.

If a person who dies has left a testament for a *qurban* to be sacrificed then, the person sacrificing it cannot eat from its meat. All the meat must be distributed to the poor.

TYPES OF OATH AND ITS RULINGS

To make an oath is to mention the name of Allah in order to strengthen one's word.

There are three types of oaths:

1) Lagw: It is an oath made by inadvertently lying. It is like a person making an oath thinking that they do not have money stating: "Wallahi I do not have any money" yet they do. There is no penance required for an oath like this.

***2) Ghamus*:** It is an oath made by deliberately lying. It is like saying, "Wallahi I saw it" even though he did not, or "Wallahi I paid it" even though he did not. It is a great sin to deliberately make an oath that is untrue. A person must repent and ask for forgiveness for a sin like this to be forgiven.

If a person causes injustice by lying like this then, the rights of it should be returned to the rightful owner. Penance is not required for oaths like this. This is because penance is not enough to be saved from a sin like this.

3) Mun'aqia: It is an oath made if you will or will not do something in the future. Like making oaths such as, "Wallahi I will pay my debt tomorrow" or "Wallahi I will not speak to that person." If a person fulfils their oath then, penance is not required. However, if a person makes an oath and cannot fulfil his promise then, his oath is broken and he/she must give penance as punishment.

Penance for an oath:

A person making an oath on whether they will or won't do something in the future must pay on the broken oath penance by ,clothing ten poor people or paying ten people the value of the amount of the *fitra*. People who cannot afford to pay this must fast for three consecutive days as penance.

QUESTIONS

1) For whom is it *wajib* to sacrifice a *qurban*?

2) When should a *qurban* be sacrificed?

3) What should be done in relation to the meat and skin of the *qurban*?

4) Which animals are lawful and unlawful to be sacrificed?

5) What is a *nazhr qurban* and when is it sacrificed? What should be done with the *nazhr qurban*'s meat and skin?

6) Which of the animals' meats can and cannot be eaten?

7) What does an oath refer to and how many types of oaths are there?

8) Explain the expiation of an oath.

UNIT X

HOLY DAYS AND NIGHTS

Topics:

- The days of *Jumu'ah* and *Eid*
- *Mawlid al-Nabi*
- The nights of *Raghaib* and *Mi'raj*
- The nights of *Bera'at* and *Qadr*

THE DAYS OF *JUMU'AH*

The days of *Jumu'ah* are days of *Eid*. The *Jumu'ah* prayer is performed with the congregation. For this reason, Muslims find opportunity to gather, meet and greet. Muslims who gather each week increase their bonds of friendship, which strengthens their solidarity and togetherness.

Jumu'ah is a very auspicious and virtuous day on which very important events have occurred. Our Prophet commanded:

"The most auspicious day that the sun has risen on is *Jumu'ah*. On this day, Adam (*alayhi al-salām*) was created; he was placed in paradise and was removed from paradise." [1]

"There is a point in time during the day of *Jumu'ah* when Allah will accept the wishes of any *Mu'min*." [2]

THE DAYS OF *EID*

There are two religious *Eid*s each year:

1) Eid al-Fitr

2) Eid al-Adha

Eid is a day of happiness. Muslims who perform their duties by fasting during the month of Ramadan fulfilling Allah's command, sacrificing an animal in the name of Allah during *Eid al-Adha* and perform the *Eid* prayers with the congregation live the joy and happiness of performing their duty.

1. Riyadh us Salihen, Volume 2, Page 439
2. Ibid., Volume 2, Page 444

A helping hand is extended to the poor during Ramadan with *zakat*, *fitra* and *qurban* meat during *Eid al-Adha*. Thus, the true meaning of love and respect arises between the rich and poor.

Mothers, fathers and the elders are visited on the days of *Eid*, the offended make peace and friendship is reinforced with an exchange of presents amongst relatives. The common joy shared by the community strengthens the religious and national emotions. The tranquility brought by *Eid* relieves the fatigue for Muslims and the sorrow is forgotten.

Mu'mins congratulate each other during *Eid*s and send their greetings to those who live afar in order to please them. Graveyards are visited and *dua* is made for the dead. Their spirits are gratified by reciting Qur'an and giving *sadaqah*.

The days of *Eid* are a feast for Allah's Mu'min servants. These days should be enjoyed in accordance with proper behavior in order to gain Allah's consent.

MAWLID AL-NABI

Our Prophet Muhammad (salla Allāhu ʿalay-hi wa-sallam), the last and greatest Prophet sent as a savior to humankind, was born on the 12th night of the lunar month of Rabi' al-Awwal in the year 571. This holy night is called "Mawlid al-Nabi."

In the era He was born, the world was filled with ignorance, cruelty and indecency. Belief in Allah had been forgotten, humankind was in a dark and dismal position and the world was in an unlivable state.

The world was enlightened with the birth of our beloved Prophet. Hearts were filled with a divine light and the belief of Allah's oneness. Equality, justice and brotherhood arrived. Communities that believed in him attained true tranquility. The night he was born was an auspicious and holy beginning for the salvation of humankind.

This night has been celebrated amongst Muslims with great excitement for hundreds of years. Our beloved Prophet is remembered with deep respect. A *mawlid* book called "Vesiletun' Necat" written by the great Turkish scholar Suleyman Celebi is a valuable piece of work that brings mention to his birth, superiority and miracles in the best way.

On the anniversary of the birth of the Prophet, the *mawlid*s recited should be listened with respect. Reciting *salātu salām* for His spirit is undoubtedly an expression of immense love and loyalty towards our beloved Prophet.

Besides, it is one of our first duties to learn His morality and take His life that is filled with virtue as an example. In that way, we will actually attain His love and satisfaction.

THE NIGHT OF RAGHAIB

From a moral perspective, the months of Rajab, Sha'ban and Ramadan, which are known as "The Holy three months", are more superior and more abundant. When the month of Rajab arrived our Prophet used to make *dua* as follows:

"O Allah! Make Rajab and Sha'ban holy and allow us to reach Ramadan." [3]

The first night of *Jumu'ah* in the month of Rajab is known as "The night of *Raghaib*." This is a night on which Allah's mercy and forgiveness is abundant, and *dua*s are accepted. Our beloved Prophet commanded the following:

"There are five nights on which *duas* made will not be rejected (will be accepted). These are:

- **The first night of *Jumu'ah* in Rajab**
- **The fifteenth night of Sha'ban,**
- **The nights of *Jumu'ah*,**
- **The night of *Eid al-Fitr*, and**
- **The night of *Eid al-Adha*."** [4]

THE NIGHT OF MI'RAJ

On the invitation of Allah, one night our beloved Prophet was taken from Masjid al-Haram in Makkah to Masjid al-Aqsa in Jerusalem. From there they surpassed all the skies together with Jibril and ascended to the place

3. Cami'us – Sağir, Volume V, p. 131
4. Ibid, Volume III, p. 454

of Sidrat al-Muntaha. Our Prophet (salla Allāhu ʿalay-hi wa-sallam) went further from here and met with Allah almighty without an intermedium.

The section of the sacred journey from Makkah to Jerusalem is called "Isra"and the section that continues after Jerusalem is called Mi'raj. Our Prophet brought the five daily prayers to His *ummah* as a gift from Mi'raj.

The Mi'raj event is one of the greatest miracles of our Prophet. It occurred one and a half years prior to the *Hijrah* on the 27th night of Rajab.

THE NIGHT OF *BERA'AT*

The fifteenth night of Sha'ban is the "Night of Bera'at." *Bera'at* means to escape from debt, blame and punishment. The night of *Bera'at* means to atone for one's sins.

This is a night where Allah the Almighty exonerates believersMu'mins that turn towards Him seeking forgiveness. Our beloved Prophet commanded that we remain awake on this night and submit our wishes to Allah stating:

"When the fifteenth night of Sha'ban arrives, spend that night in worship and fast during the day. Because on that night, Allah the Almighty commands until the sun rises and mercy descends on the world;

- **Will anyone seek forgiveness, so that he may be forgiven?**
- **Will anyone wish for their livelihood, so that it may be given?**
- **Will anyone demand a cure, so that he may recover?**
- **Will anyone wish for something, so that his request may be granted"**

Now then, we should give an ear to the glad tidings of our Lord and benefit from this opportunity.

THE NIGHT OF QADR

The 27th night of Ramadan is the "Night of Qadr."

Our religion's holy book, which indicates the ways for people to be happy in this world and the hereafter, commenced its revelation in the month of Ramadan on the night of Qadr. The duty of Prophethood was given Muhammad (salla Allāhu ʿalay-hi wa-sallam) on this night and the

Islamic sun rose on this night. Great honor was given to the night of Qadr due to the important events that occurred.

The holy Qur'an openly informs us that the night of Qadr is more auspicious than a thousand months. Our beloved Prophet commands the virtues of this night as follows:

"Whoever spends the night of Qadr in worship believing in its virtue and anticipates the reward from Allah will have all their past sins forgiven." [5]

The night of Qadr is a grace and is an endless mercy of work from Allah the Almighty to us Mu'mins. We should take advantage of this night in the best way by performing prayer for the consent of Allah, reciting the Qur'an and making *dua*.[6]

One day, Aisha asked our Prophet:

- O Rasulullah: If I come across the night of Qadr, how should I make dua?

Our Prophet replied:

- **"Say: O my Lord, you are oft forgiving, you love to forgive, forgive me."**[7]

Let us repeat the dua that our beloved Prophet has taught us on the night of Qadr.

We should make use of these holy nights by performing prayer for the consent of Allah, reciting the Qur'an, reciting *salātu wa salām* to our Prophet, seeking forgiveness of our sins from Allah, making *dua* for our wishes in this world and the hereafter and, by making the poor happy with the charity that we give.

---

5. Et-Terğib ve't-Terhib, Volume 2, Page 119
6. Riyadh us Salihen, Volume 2, Page 464
7. Riyadh us Salihen, Volume 2, Page 467

QUESTIONS

1) Explain the virtues of *Jumu'ah*.

2) How many religious *Eids* are there in a year? What is the importance of *Eid*?

3) Explain what *Mawlid al-Nabi* is.

4) What is the night of Raghaib?

5) Explain the importance of the night of Mi'raj.

6) When is the night of Bera'at? Explain its virtues.

7) Explain the virtues of the night of Qadr.

8) What should be done on the holy nights?

CHAPTER THREE
MORALITY (AKHLAQ)

UNIT I

ISLAM AND MORALITY

Topics:

- Description of morality
- Morality in Islam
- The role of belief and worship in having good morality
- The best example of good morality is Prophet Muhammad (salla Allāhu ʿalay-hi wa-sallam)
- The importance of morality for individuals
- Business life and good morality
- Does morality change?
- High value Islam Places on Reason and Science

DESCRIPTION OF MORALITY

Morality are habits settled in a person's soul. These habits bring about our acts and actions without even thinking about it.

Habits settled in our souls are divided into two parts:

1) Good habits,

2) Bad habits.

The actions of our organs are tied to our spirits. If good habits are settled in our spirits then, the acts and actions of our organs are good. These are called **good morality**. If bad habits are settled in our spirits then, the actions become bad. These are called **bad morality**. For our actions to be good and our morality to be exemplary, we must cleanse our souls from bad habits and settle in good habits.

We reap what we sow. Wheat grows from a wheat seed and barley from barley seed. It can be seen that whatever seed you plant in the ground, a plant corresponding to that seed will grow. If we plant good habit seeds to the depths of our souls, these seeds appear as good morality in our organs. If we plant bad habit seeds in our souls, then these seeds will appear as bad habits in our organs.

MORALITY IN ISLAM

Islam places great importance and value on morality. The aim of Islam is to bring people to possess good morals by making them mature. Islam means good morality. Our Prophet (salla Allāhu ʿalay-hi wa-sallam) commanded the following:

"I was sent to complete good morality."[1] A Muslim's value is measured by his good morals. Our Prophet brings this truth to light by stating,

"The most amiable of you and the closest to me on the day of judgment is the one with good morality." [2]

Our Prophet was asked:

"Who are the most beloved servants in the eyes of Allah?"

Our Prophet replied:

"The ones who have good morality." [3] Just as worship is a commandment of our religion, so is fulfilling our moral duties. One of the aims of Islamic worship is to avoid people from being harmed and make them owners of good morality.

ROLE OF BELIEF AND WORSHIP IN HAVING GOOD MORALITY

A person who has true belief believes in the fact that Allah will see all of their actions and these actions will be recorded by the angels. They know that all their actions in this world will need to be accounted for in the hereafter. They believe with certainty that those who perform good deeds will see the benefits and those who do harm will suffer its penalty.

Allah the Almighty commands in the holy Qur'an that:

"Whoever does an atom's weight of good will see it, And whoever does an atom's weight of evil will see it." [4]

This belief will keep a person away from evil and turn them towards doing well. You should not expect good from people without a perceived benefit

1. Keşfu'l-Hafa, Volume 1, Page 211
2. Riyadh us Salihen, Volume 2, Page 54
3. Selection of Hadiths, Page 32
4. Surah Az-Zalzalah, 99/7-8

where they do not carry the emotions of belief and responsibility in their hearts. These people will carry out all sorts of harm at every opportunity.

Whereas a Muslim who has strong belief in their heart pays attention to their actions. They do not harm others. They carry out good deeds as much as possible. Worship strengthens the faith in our hearts and allows us to possess good deeds.

Five prayers always remind us of Allah and deter us from all misbehavior. Fasting develops feelings of compassion and mercy, protects our hand from the forbidden and our tongue from lies. *Zakat* saves us from stinginess, it develops the feelings of kindness and helpfulness to others, makes people useful to the society.

Thus, the faith that is fed by the worship gives our organs the fruit of good morals and therefore, humans gain their real value. People who do not possess good morality are like a plant that does not flower or give fruits.

THE BEST EXAMPLE OF GOOD MORALITY IS PROPHET MUHAMMAD (salla Allāhu ʿalay-hi wa-sallam)

The Prophet Muhammad (salla Allāhu ʿalay-hi wa-sallam) was brought up with the teachings of Allah. He is a Prophet with high morals. He obtained his morality from the Qur'an and gathered all the goodness in him. When Aisha was asked what the Prophet's morals were like, she gave the following response:

"The Qur'an was His morality."[5]

Our Prophet taught the duties of good morals towards others and personally practiced them himself. He never strayed from the straight path, never strayed from the truth and his good morals and good deeds were an example to people. Allah the Almighty in the Qur'an commands: **"Indeed in the Messenger of Allah you have a good example to follow."** [6] asking us to follow the examples set by our Prophet. The duty that falls upon us is to learn about our Prophet's morals and His virtuous life and live according to his examples of moral action.

5. Şerhu'ş Şifa Aliyyu'l-Kari, Volume 1, Page 222
6. Surah Al-'Ahzab, 33/21

THE IMPORTANCE OF MORALITY FOR INDIVIDUALS

Nations are the communities that consist of families. Families consist of individuals. Therefore, a strong and happy nation depends on strong and happy families. Strong and happy families depend on individuals who fulfil their moral duties.

For this reason, it is very important before everything else that the individuals who bring about communities are formed with good morality. Just as ships cannot be built with rotten timber, strong communities cannot exist without people with the feelings of good morality and responsibility.

BUSSINESS LIFE AND GOOD MORALITY

Working is a command of our religion. A Muslim must work to earn their livelihood without being in need of anyone else. Sectors where people work in and income they earn are diverse. The issues that we must be careful in business and earning an income are: to derive our earnings from *halal* means and not mix any *haram* in our livelihood.

Our Prophet notified us of this by stating,

"On the day of judgment, a person will be brought to answer where they earned their wealth and where they spent it."[7] and warned those mixing *haram* in to their earnings stating:

"A person who deceives, causes harm or cheats Muslims is not one of us."[8] He gave the following joyful tidings to those working and earning by means of correct behavior:

"Those in trade who do not stray from integrity will be together with the Prophet on the day of judgment."[9] Integrity is a very important moral rule of being a Muslim. What befits a Muslim is to earn a living from clean means without straying from the true path in working life, without deception, refraining from black marketeering, and trafficking of all kinds.

---

7. Et-Terğib ve't-Terhib, Volume 1, Page 125
8. 250 Hadith, Page 159
9. 250 Hadith, Page 62

A manufacturer's duty is to manufacture a good product without deception. The duty of a worker or a civil servant is to carry out their responsibilities in full. A worker straying from the truth by thinking "no one can see me" hinders their duty acquiring ill-gotten gains. These actions are strictly forbidden in our religion. To steal the rights of another is robbery. Those who act like this cause their work to go to waste. As a result, the country is harmed and trust amongst people diminish. A Muslim with a clean heart and good morals avoids actions like these.

A person with good morals does things correctly, does not deceive anybody and does not cheat or carry out fraud. They duly carry out their responsibilities being useful to themselves and to their surroundings.

DOES MORALITY CHANGE?

A child comes to this world spotlessly clean. They will be raised with good manners if they are taught then by their parents. You cannot expect good morality and behavior if good manners are not taught and the spirit is covered with bad habits and black stains.

Just as we treat our physical illnesses with medication, we can cure our spirits by replacing the bad habits with good ones.

Our beloved Prophet indicated that bad habits could be corrected by stating; "**Beautify your morality.**."[10]

A person who hangs around another person who has a contagious disease can be infected with the same disease. Those who form friendships with people who have bad morals will be influenced by their actions and in time, they will lose their good habits and become people with bad morality. It is for this reason that in order to have good morality and sustain this, you need to be friends with people with good morals and refrain from associating with bad people.

Our beloved Prophet:

- Has likened friendships with good people to sitting in a shop that sells fragrances. Even if the shop owner does not offer you anything, you will benefit from its nice smell.

---

10. A. Hamdi AKSEKİ, Moral Lectures, Page 19.

- Has likened friendships with bad people to sitting in a shop that sells steel. A person sitting there becomes uncomfortable with either the sparks or its bad smell. [11]

People who make friendships with good people like this are influenced by their good morals and will also have good habits. People who make friendships with those with bad morals will be influenced by their bad behavior and that person's good habits will be spoiled and they will become a person with bad morals.

Our duty is to be careful when choosing friends, to be friends with good and knowledgeable people, to benefit from their words and conversations and to stay away from bad people. However, with the aim of saving people from bad behavior, we should become close to them and help them to possess good morality.

HIGH VALUE ISLAM PLACES ON REASON AND SCIENCE

Reason is a great blessing bestowed upon humans. Humans differentiate between good and bad with their reason. Reason is a characteristic that separates humans from other living creatures.

Reason is a condition that is required for accountability in our religion. To be sane is the first condition required by faith and worship. The importance of reason in Islam can be understood from the fact that people without intelligence are not responsible for religious commands.However, to find the true value of reason and for it to be of use to people depends on using it well. Those who do not use their reason are condemned in the holy Qur'an. Reason is one of the most important vehicles of knowledge.

Islam places great value on reason and knowledge. The Qur'an and prophetic tradition commands to always read and learn. "Read", the first verse of the holy Qur'an openly shows us the importance of reading. Allah the Almighty commands the following on the value given to knowledge and people of knowledge:

"**Say: Are those who know equal to those who do not know?**"[12] Our Prophet specifies that it is an important duty for Muslims to learn knowledge stating:

11. Cami'us-Sağir.
12. Surah Az-Zumar, 39/9

"It is *fard* for all men and women to learn."[13]

Appropriate to our religion, our ancestors gave much value to knowledge and showed great respect to scientists.

On the return from the expedition to Egypt, Yavuz Sultan Selim the great Ottoman ruler was passing through a muddy place with a religious scholar named Ibni Kemal.

Ibni Kemal was saddened when the mud from his feet splashed onto Yavuz dirtying his clothing.

Yavuz Sultan Selim who saw his teacher saddened showed great respect to scholars leaving a will stating, **"Do not be saddened teacher! The mud being splashed from the feet of a scholar is but an ornament for us. Save this kaftan with its mud and place it on my coffin."**

QUESTIONS

1) What is morality?
2) Explain the importance of morality in Islam.
3) Explain the role of good morality played by belief and worship.
4) What were the morals of our Prophet like?
5) Explain the importance of morality for individuals.
6) Explain the influence of morality in business life.
7) Can morality change?
8) Explain the value placed on reason and science by Islam.

13. Mişkatü'l-Mesabih, Volume 1, Page 233

UNIT II

OUR MORAL DUTIES

Topics:

- Moral duties in Islam
- Our duties towards Allah, our Prophet and the Qur'an
- Our duties towards ourselves
- Our duties towards our bodies
- Our duties towards our spirits
- Moral rules when eating and drinking
- To discipline and correct our tongues
- To discipline and correct the rest of our organs and limbs

MORAL DUTIES IN ISLAM

Moral duties in Islam are divided into five main parts:

1) Our duties towards Allah, our Prophet and the Qur'an,
2) Our duties towards ourselves,
3) Our duties towards our families,
4) Our duties towards our nation and people,
5) Our duties towards all of humankind.

1- OUR DUTIES TOWARDS ALLAH, OUR PROPHET AND THE QUR'AN

A) Our duties towards Allah

Allah created us from nothing equipping us with perfect organs and limbs allowing us to benefit from everything on the earth. The superior features that were given to humans have not been given to any other living creature. There are duties that we must perform in gratitude for such kindness.

These duties are:

a) To believe in the existence and oneness of Allah.

b) To fulfil our duties of worship.

c) To act in accordance with His commandments and refrain from what is prohibited.

d) To hold the love of Allah above all else.

e) To remember the name of Allah with respect.

f) To give thanks to the blessings given.

b) Our duties towards our Prophet:

Allah gave the duty of conveying Islam to humans to our Prophet Muhammad (salla Allāhu ʿalay-hi wa-sallam). Our beloved Prophet worked a lot for people's salvation. He encountered great difficulties for this purpose. He enlightened the world with Islam's light. He showed people the way to be happy.

It is for this reason we must perform these duties towards our Prophet;

a) To believe that He is the last and greatest Prophet,

b) To love Him a lot and to recite salawat upon Him,

c) To follow the path showed by Him,

d) To live following the example of His good morals.

c) Our duties towards the Qur'an:

a) To believe that the holy Qur'an is the last book sent to our Prophet by Allah,

b) To recite it beautifully in accordance with its methods,

c) To try and understand its meaning,

d) To be extremely respectful when reciting and listening to the Qur'an,

e) To carry out the commands of the Qur'an and to avoid its prohibitions.

2- OUR DUTIES TOWARDS OURSELVES

Humans are creatures that consist of bodies and spirits. For this reason, the duties towards ourselves are divided into two parts:

A) Our duties towards our bodies,

B) Our duties towards our spirits.

A) Our duties towards our bodies

a) Balanced nourishment: We must have a balanced diet and be careful of what we eat and drink. Having a strong and healthy body depends on this. The holy Qur'an commands: **"O humankind, eat from whatever is on earth that is lawful and good."** [1]

Our Prophet wanted Muslims to be powerful and strong stating: **"A strong believer Mu'min is better than a weak one and is more lovable in Allah's eyes."** [2]

b) To protect our health: Just as it is our duty to protect our bodies from illness and take precautions to prevent this, it is also our duty to seek treatment when we are suffering from an illness. In relation to this, our beloved Prophet commands the following:

"O Allah's servants! Be treated. Because Allah has created a cure for all illnesses." [3]

Islam has prohibited all substances that are harmful for our bodies, such as, alcoholic drinks and drugs. It commands that we refrain from all actions that put our health at risk.

The most important blessing given by Allah to humans is health. Humans are responsible for protecting this blessing their whole life. A person cannot live their life at ease if they are not healthy nor can they fulfil their duties of worship as required. For this reason our ancestors have said, "The start of all things is health."

We should understand the value of our health while we are healthy and take precautions against illnesses. This is because a person does not understand the full value of a blessing when they have it. On this topic, our Prophet stated, **"There are two blessings which people are deceived with** (that is, we do not understand its value). **One is health and the other is idle time."** [4]

---

1. Surah Al-Baqarah, 2/168
2. Meşariku'l-Envar, Volume 2, Page 112

3 Cami'us-Sagir.

4 Cami'us-Sagir, Article "Nun."

The attainment of happiness in this world and the hereafter is dependent on being healthy. Therefore, our religion has placed great importance on the topic of health and asked that precautions be taken against illnesses. In the event of illness, it has commanded us to obtain treatment.

We must eat adequately and observe cleanliness. We must try to strengthen our body by doing useful exercises and remember the words of our Prophet who stated, **"A strong Mu'min is better than a weak one and is more lovable to Allah."**

We should refrain from harmful things and avoid bad habits such as excessive tiredness, sleeplessness, use of alcohol, being in a polluted place, eating food and drinking water that is contaminated with germs. We must carry out immunization on time, especially for children against possible illnesses and take advice from specialists.

Our Prophet ordered that we should avoid people who have contagious diseases and commanded, **"Run away from a person who has leprosy like you would from a lion."** [5]

In another hadith, He ordered that we should be cautious of contagious diseases stating, **"Do not go there if you hear of the plague disease."** [6]

Our Prophet stated, **"Be treated. Allah the Almighty has created a cure for all diseases."** The meaning of this is that we should try to use all means to be treated if we catch any type of disease. This shows that to be treated is a command of our religion.

Our Prophet himself received treatment and recommended the use of some substances in his day for the purpose of treatment.

It is because of the importance placed on treatment by Islam that many medical practitioners were trained. The written pieces of work by the scholars Ibn-i Sina and Abu Bakr al-Razi have been studied in the field of medicine for hundreds of years in Europe.

To be treated is not against the beliefs of *tawakkul*. On the contrary, true *tawakkul* is when a sick person asks Allah to be healed after trying all that they can to be cured. Otherwise, people will say that they have *tawakkul* in Allah without looking for a cure, which is to misunderstand the Islamic

5. Bukhari, Medicine
6. Keşfu'l-Hafa, Volume 1, Page 104

understanding of *tawakkul*. This is similar to waiting for a plant to grow in the field without sowing a seed. This thought has nothing to do with *tawakkul*.

Everything is tied to a reason in this world. We should first adhere to reasons and then wait for results. To seek and use medication means to adhere to a reason, which results in the illness being cured. It is a reason to sow crops in the field when the time arrives and harvesting the crop is the result of this.

c) To pay attention to cleanliness: Cleanliness is one of the responsibilities that we have towards our bodies. A Muslim's body, clothing and environment must be clean. Cleanliness plays an important role in protecting our health. Our Prophet stated:

"Cleanliness is half of faith." [7] which indicates the importance that our religion places on cleanliness.

Our beloved Prophet also placed great importance on clean teeth. He recommended that we clean our teeth when he by stating the following: **"What is going on with you who comes next to me with yellow teeth? Use a miswak."** [8]

B) Our duties towards our spirits:

Our duties towards our spirits are:

a) To clean our spirits from unfounded and incorrect beliefs.

b) To establish true and strong beliefs.

c) To equip it with true and beneficial knowledge.

d) To purify it from bad thoughts and nasty habits.

e) To ornament it with good thoughts and beautiful habits.

We must clean our spirits from bad habits such as:

Animosity, anger, jealousy, deceit, not keeping promises, being two faced, lewdness, disrespect, misbehavior, mercilessness, cowardice,

7. Meşariku'l-Envar, Volume 2, Page 107
8. Beyhaki, Miswak: The "Arak" tree is a toothbrush that is grown in Saudi Arabia. Toothbrushes are today made from clean substances in the place of miswaks. The aim is to clean teeth.

laziness, stinginess, being patronizing, cruelty and injustice, breaching trust, impatience, rude and harsh behavior and being hard hearted.

We must adorn our spirits with beautiful habits such as:

Friendship, mercy, righteousness, generosity, courage, diligence, patience, shame, respect to elders, love for people, keeping promises, behaving politely and kindly, being soft hearted, just, polite and well-mannered, forgiving, humble controlling one's anger, being responsible for one's tongue, carrying the feelings of compassion to people and all living things.

MORAL RULES WHEN EATING AND DRINKING

1) For our food and drink to be *halal*,

2) To wash our hands before and after we eat,

3) To say "Bismillah" when starting to eat and "Alhamdulillah" after finishing,

4) To eat from in front of ourselves and to do so with our right hand,

5) To take bite size pieces and swallow after chewing properly,

6) Not to speak when our mouth is full,

7) Not to take another mouthful before finishing the previous one,

8) Not to blow into the food to make it cool down,

9) Not to breath into the glass when drinking water,

10) Not to say or act in a manner that is disgusting to others,

11) Not to waste food, to put enough food on a plate that we could eat and to actually eat all of it,

12) Not to rise from the food table until everyone has completed their meal,

13) To allow elders to start eating first,

14) Not to eat in public on the streets.

TO DISCIPLINE AND CORRECT OUR TONGUES

One of the duties towards ourselves is to discipline our tongues. Just as we must be careful of what goes into our mouth, we must also be careful of what comes out of it. Islam has taught us the manners of how to say things and how to speak.

The moral rules that we must follow when speaking are:

1) To speak understanding where the words will lead to,

2) Not to say things that will have no benefit in this world or the hereafter,

3) Not to hurt anyone's feelings with statements or interrupt them while speaking,

4) To speak to people in accordance with their status and position,

5) Not to be excessive when praising somebody,

6) Not to speak loudly next to elders,

7) Not to babble or prattle,

8) Not to sneer or twist our mouth when speaking, not to be pedantic or look for errors in other people's words,

9) Not to get accustomed to bad words, not to lie or promise things we know that we cannot deliver, to talk about other people, to be talebearer and to refrain from making incorrect promises.

10) Not to make fun of others or call them by bad nicknames,

11) Not to divulge secrets,

Our Prophet replied with the following when asked what the road to salvation is: **"To conserve one's tongue."** [9]

One of the Companions asked our Prophet; "*What is the thing I should fear most for myself*?" Our beloved Prophet replied by holding His blessed tongue with His hand: **"It is this."** [10]

Our Prophet (salla Allāhu ʿalay-hi wa-sallam) stated in a hadith: "A person who believes in Allah and Judgment Day should either say an auspicious word or remain quiet." [11]

---

9. Riyadh us Salihen, Volume 3, Page 107
10. Ibid, Volume 3, Page 106
11. Ibid, Volume 3, Page 103

It can be seen that we are responsible for our tongues and must be careful of what we say. This is an important moral rule.

TO DISCIPLINE AND CORRECT THE REST OF OUR ORGANS AND LIMBS

Just as we discipline our tongues, it is also our duty to discipline and correct our organs, limbs and actions in accordance with moral rules.

These duties in brief are:

1) To remove one's hands and feet from what is *haram* and not to do things that harm others,

2) Not to look at something that is not ours with jealousy, not to look seeking to find other people's defects or to disturb others by looking.

3) Not to listen to lies, gossip and words that will not be beneficial in this world or the hereafter,

4) Not to intrude or violate another person's wealth, life or honor.

READING:

Our religion has forbidden wastage

Our religion commands working and earning from halal and legitimate means. It has also forbidden wasting what one earns and unnecessary spending. The holy Qur'an commands the following:

"Eat and drink, but be not excessive. Indeed, Allah likes not those who commit excess." [12]

The words at the end of this ayah which commands; ***"Indeed, Allah likes not those who commit excess."*** *is an important warning to Muslims, which shows us clearly that wastage is haram. Without a doubt, no Muslim would want to be a person whom Allah does not love.*

Our religion commands that we should refrain from stinginess, always be restrained, have a moderate way of life and follow a reasonable path.

12. Surah Al-Araf, 7/31

The Qur'an commands that the good servants who want to attain the mercy of Allah through their way of life should follow this path by commanding:

"And they are those who, when they spend, do so not excessively or sparingly but are ever, between that, justly moderate." [13]

It can be seen that just as our religion teaches us how to earn, it also teaches us how to spend. The duty that falls upon us is to follow the appropriate recommendations of our mighty Lord and our beloved Prophet without being excessive and arranging our lives in a restrained and balanced way.

A person who squanders money, that cannot balance their income and expenses, who spends more than they earn, cannot reach the level of life that they desire. There will not be any tranquility in a family like this. We must use our wealth to satisfy our needs and needs that are to the benefit of the community.

Just as this is the case for a family, it is also the same for a nation. Wastage is an obstacle that stops the development of a nation, individuals and pushes communities towards poverty causing efforts to be in vain.

Nowadays, the amount of wastage of bread, which is a basic food that is thrown in the bin, is extremely thought provoking. Actually, it is not only bread that is being thrown in the bin. What is being thrown away is the farmer's sweat, the efforts of the workers making the bread and the money of the purchaser.

Our beloved Prophet commanded that we show respect towards bread.

By throwing bread into the bin, we do not show respect to the bread nor follow the recommendation of our Prophet.

It is a waste to put more food on your plate than you can eat, to have the light on more than is required and for the tap to drip water for nothing. No one has the right to waste and use these things excessively.

Wasting time is also wastefulness. It is likewise wastefulness to emulate the lives of rich people by throwing away cheap clothing and purchasing expensive marks and getting into debt trying to keep up with the latest fashion. These are the opposite principals of living economically in our religion, and they are actions that turn the social equilibrium upside down and cause the economy to collapse.

---

13. Surah Al-Furqan, 25/67

Nations who progress are ones that continually work and spend appropriately whilst refraining from wastefulness.

We must know well the value of the blessings that we own whilst refraining from wastefulness and squandering it away using our means, time, earnings, public and hidden treasures in an economical way.

Our beloved Prophet taught us an important principal that we should follow in life stating, ***"A thrifty person shall never fall poor."***[14] *Let us not forget that the damage caused by wastefulness is not limited to this world.*

We will be brought to account on the Day of Judgment about where we spent our life and our wealth.

Our Prophet commands: ***"People will not be able to leave Allah's presence on the Day of Judgment until they are questioned about four things:***

1) Where they spent their life,

2) Where they wore out their body,

3) Where they earned and spent their wealth

4) What deeds they did with their knowledge."[15]

QUESTIONS

1) How many categories of moral duties are there?
2) What are our duties towards Allah, our Prophet and the Qur'an?
3) What are the duties towards ourselves?
4) What are the duties towards our bodies?
5) What are the duties towards our spirits?
6) What are good and bad habits?
7) What are the moral rules whilst eating and drinking?
8) What are the moral rules that we must adhere to when speaking?
9) How do we correct the rest of our organs?

14. Keşfu'l-Hafa, Volume 2, Page 189
15. Et-Terğib ve't-Terhib, Volume 1, Page 125

UNIT III OUR DUTIES TOWARDS OUR FAMILY

Topics:

- The importance of family in Islam
- The duties of family members towards each other
- The duties of husband and wife towards each other
- The duties of mother and father towards their children
- The duties of children towards their parants
- A youth who is rebellious towards his mother encounters the danger of losing his faith in his last breath (Reading)
- The duties of siblings towards each other
- Our duties towards kin and relatives
- Our duties towards our neighbors
- A Muslim considers their neighbor as follows (Reading)

THE IMPORTANCE OF FAMILY IN ISLAM

The smallest unit of a community is the family, which consists of a husband and wife, mother and father, and children.

The combination of families makes up nations. The importance of the family for nations is great, because the basic structure of nations are families. If families are happy and peaceful then, nations are powerful and strong.

Families make nations what they are. The family is a school where moral values, traditions and customs are learned. Our responsibilities towards Allah, the homeland and the nation are learned in the home firstly. Children imitate the actions of family elders, and that unconsciously imitated behavior becomes their habits in the long run. Thus, the moral and personal foundations of a child are formed in the family.

Children are like cameras, recording everything around them. Therefore, family individuals must always behave well so that the clean soul of a child can capture good images. For this reason, mutual moral duties and responsibilities carry great importance for family members. The happiness of a family and the future of a nation depend on this.

THE DUTIES OF FAMILY MEMBERS TOWARDS EACH OTHER

Husbands and wives are the basis of a family.

Our Prophet (salla Allāhu ʿalay-hi wa-sallam) commanded the following:

"Be careful, your wives have rights over you just as you have rights over them..."[1]

A – The Duties of Husband and Wife towards Each Other:

Before everything else, there must be reciprocal love between a husband and a wife,

The husband must work to provide the requirements of his family, including food, clothing and other necessities. His earnings must be halal,

The husband must be helpful with his family's religious and moral duties. He must work to teach them their deficiencies,

The husband must be kind and soft towards his wife. He must not be rude or harsh.

On this topic, our beloved Prophet commands the following:

"From a faith perspective, the most perfect Mu'min is the one whose morals are the most beautiful. The most perfect of you is the one who behaves best to his wife." [2]

The woman must act with love and respect towards her husband. She must be helpful to her husband by managing the house and upbringing their children,

The woman must be thrifty and must not waste what her husband earns and must protect her house,

The woman must be bound to her home and protect her honor meticulously.

Our Prophet commands:

1 Riyadh us Salihen, Volume 1, Page 318

2 Riyadh us Salihen, Volume 1, Page 320

"If a woman performs the five daily prayers, fasts during Ramadan, protects her honor and behaves obedient towards her husband, then, she is said: 'Go to jannah through whichever door you wish." [3]

"Any woman who dies while her husband is content with her enters jannah."

B – The Duties Of Mother And Father Towards Their Children:

The ornament and the source of happiness of the family home are children. They are entrusted to mothers and fathers by Allah. Mothers and fathers are responsible for the upbringing of their children towards Allah and the community. The main duties of mothers and fathers towards their children are:

1) To feed and raise their children healthily and protect their body and spiritual well-being,

2) Not to feed their children with what is *haram*,

Our Prophet commanded: **"The most rewarding money spent in the path of Allah is that spent on family members."** [4]

He warned: **"It is sufficient as a sin for a person to neglect family members whom he/ she is responsible for to"** [5]

3) To name their child with a good name,

4) To discipline their child well and be a good example from a moral perspective,

Our Prophet stated the importance of disciplining children commanding, **"A father cannot grant a better gift to their child than good discipline."** [6]

1) To teach their children how to perform prayer and their other religious and moral duties,

2) To educate their children, help them attain a profession to earn a living,

---

3 250 Hadith, Page 186

4 Riyadh us Salihen, Volume 1, Page 329

5 Riyadh us Salihen, Volume 1, Page 331

6 Cami'us – Sağir

3) Ali stated the following, "Raise your children for a time other than the time that you live in, because they have been created for a time other than yours."

4) To love and be interested in their children, because children also require love just as much as food and drink,

Our Prophet loved children a lot and paid attention to them.

5) To be just and fair when showing love towards their children and giving them presents,

6) To marry off their children when they reach marriageable age,

C – The Duties Of Children Towards Their Parents

1) To do good towards their mother and father,

2) To provide them with a livelihood if they are in difficulty,

3) Not to hurt their mother or father with words or deeds in any way. Not to even say "uff",

4) To have a smiling face and to state pleasant words towards their mother and father. To not look at them in a harsh or angry way.

5) To run to them as soon as they call them,

6) To fulfil the commands of their mother and father provided these commands are not contrary to Allah's command,

7) To make them content with all that they do,

8) Not to speak in a loud voice next to them,

9) When their mother and father are at a stage of need, to serve them lovingly,

10) Not to walk in front of them on the road,

11) Not to go anywhere without their permission,

12) To remember them with mercy when they die, to supplicate, to give charity on behalf of their spirit, to fulfil their last will and testament, to do good towards the friends of their mother and father and not to be the reason for bad words to be said to their mother and father.

On the rights of mothers and fathers, our Prophet commands the following:

"The deed that Allah loves most are the prayer that is performed on time and to do good towards your mother and father." [7]

"On the Day of Judgment, one of the people whom Allah will not look at the face is the rebellious towards their mother and father." [8]

"Allah will postpone all the sins (penalties) that He wishes on the Day of Judgment except giving to the owner prior to dying, and the punishment for the rebellion committed towards one's mother and father." [9]

READING:

A young man who is rebellious towards his mother faces the danger of losing his faith in his last breath.

Abdullah bin abi Awfa narrates the following:

A person came to the Prophet when we were in His presence stating:

- *O Rasulullah, there is a lad lying on his deathbed. Even though he is told to state "La ilaha illallah", he cannot. Our Prophet asked:*

- ***Did he use to perform prayer?***

- *Yes, he replied. Upon this, our Prophet stood up and so did we.*

Our Prophet went to the youth and said, "Say La ilaha illallah"

The youth:"I cannot say this."

When our Prophet asked why, a man replied:
- *He was rebellious towards his mother.*

- ***Is his mother alive****?*

The people there stated: "Yes, she is alive."

Our Prophet: **"Tell her to come here."** *They called the lady and she came. Our Prophet asked the lady,* **"Is this (sick person) your son?"**

- *Yes (he is my son), she replied.*

7. Riyadh us Salihen, Volume 1, Page 347
8. Et-Terğib ve't-Terhib, Volume 3, Page 327
9. Selected Hadiths, Page 58

Our Prophet asked: ***"Look, if a big fire is prepared here and you are told" We will not burn your son if you intercede however, if you do not intercede, we will burn him in this fire", what would you do, would you intercede****?*

The lady said she would be his intercessor.

Our Prophet:" ***In that case*** *(to save this rebellious son of yours from the hellfire, forgive your rights)* ***show Allah and I as a witness that you are consenting of him****."*

The Lady: "O Allah, I hold you and your Prophet as a witness. I am consenting of my son (I forgave all of my rights). Upon this, our Prophet said to the youth to state: ***"La ilaha illallahu, wahdahu la sharika lah, wa ashadu anna Muhammadan abduhu wa rasuluh."*** *The ill youth immediately recited the shahada. Upon this, our Prophet said:*

"All praise be to Allah, that He has saved this youth from the hellfire using me as a vehicle." [10]

MOTHER

Mother! Mother! Lovely Mother!
My whole heart is yours mother...
My heart is a treasure
It is filled with love mother...
You are the owner of this love
You are the one that has made me live happily,
You are the one who gives me compassion,
One who looks sweet like an angel,
Always on the lap when small,
Later in the cradle on a swing,
You are the one that has raised me,
You are the one that gave me my first knowledge,
If I am sadden, your smiling face,
If I resent, your kind word,
They will give me joy and delight
My ill will melts suddenly.
You are mine yes mother
Of course I am yours mother!...

E. Ali SİPAHİ

10. Selection of Hadiths, Page 161

FATHER

You are the pillar of our home!
The apple of our eye!
How pretty, how good,
My dear father.

At nights when you come,
We are overcome with happiness
The days become nights for us,
My dear father.

We laugh if you laugh,
We eat with pleasure if you eat,
We always listen to whatever you say,
My dear father.

Rakım ÇALAPALA

D – The duties of siblings towards each other:

1) There must be sincere love and solidarity between siblings,

2) Siblings are like pieces that complement each other. Nothing should spoil this solidarity or separate siblings,

3) Things like inheritance, money, wealth and financial benefits should not come between siblings, it should not spoil their solidarity,

4) Elder siblings are like parents to their younger ones. The younger ones should show respect to the elder ones, refrain from arguing, stating harsh words and actions. The elder siblings should protect the younger ones and show love and compassion.

5) Siblings should do good towards each other, one should protect the benefits of the other as if it were one's own benefit.

E – The duties towards kin and relatives:

In a broad sense, there are moral duties that we must perform towards our kin and relatives, as they are part of our family.

These are:

1) To show love and respect towards kin and relatives,

2) To help those people in need,

3) To not forget them, to visit them from time to time, to give gifts,

4) To contact those far away by mail or telephone asking how they are, thus strengthening family ties,

Our aunties and uncles have a similar status like our mother and father. We should treat them with love and respect like our mother and father.

Our Prophet stated the importance of being interested in relatives by commanding:

"Those who cease to concern for people close to them will not enter paradise." [11]

Abdullah bin Abi Awfa from the Companions stated:

We were next to the Prophet when He stated:

"Those who cease to concern themselves about their relatives should not sit with us today." Upon this, a youth who felt resentment towards his aunty got up from amongst us and went to his aunt. He saw her and made peace. Later, that youth returned to our assembly. Upon this, our Prophet commanded:

"Mercy will not be given to the community of those who have ceased to concern themselves about their relatives." [12]

F - Our duties towards our neighbors

The people who are closest to us after our family and relatives are our neighbors. We encounter them just about every day. It is a command of our religion that we get on well with neighbors that we frequently meet.

Allah the Almighty commands in the holy Qur'an, that we should do good deeds towards our neighbors. Our beloved Prophet also commanded:

"Those who believe in Allah and the hereafter should do good deeds towards their neighbor." [13]

---

11. Riyadh us Salihen, Volume 1, Page 370
12. Selection of Hadiths Page 208
13. Riyadh us Salihen, Volume 1, Page 343

“Those who believe in Allah and the hereafter should not torment their neighbor.” [14]

Our Prophet informed us in a hadith that those who torment their neighbors cannot be true Mu’mins and cannot enter paradise.

Our main duties towards our neighbors are:

a) To respect the rights of neighbors, not to hurt them with words or actions,

b) To have a smiling face, to state kind words and to share happiness and sadness,

c) To try and resolve their sorrow and hardship, to help them as required, to give them loans, to give presents,

d) Not to disturb them with loud sounds and noise,

e) To visit the ill, to perform the prayer of those deceased, to wish condolences,

In summary: We should love and wish for them what we wish for ourselves. We should not do things to them that we do not want done to ourselves.

We should get on well with our neighbors even if they are not Muslims. We should refrain from tormenting them. It is our duty to perform good deeds.

This is a command of our religion. Appropriate to this command throughout history, Muslims have always behaved well towards non-Muslim neighbors.

One day, Abdullah, the son of the Caliph Umar asked his servant to sacrifice a sheep and distribute a part of it to their neighbors. He commanded that they start firstly from their non-Muslim neighbors and repeated this command for three times. [15]

READING:

A Muslim thinks of his neighbor highly as follows...

14. Riyadh us Salihen, Volume 1, Page 342
15. Aliyyu’l-Kari Şehru Aynu-l İlm, Volume 1, Page 291

One day, Fatih Sultan Mehmet changed his clothes (not to be recognized) and went to the market with the objective of inspecting the quality and the price of the food. He went into a shop, gave the salātu wa salām and said:

- *Give half a batman (a unit of weight) of oil, half a batman of honey and a half batman of cheese."* *After the shopkeeper weighed and calculated half a batman of oil he said:*

- *"My brother, buy your other need from my neighbor as his goods are better and he has not yet made a sale today." The Sultan went to the second shop and bought a half batman of honey. The shop owner said to him:*

- *"All thanks be to Allah my brother. I have made my first sale and have earned money to feed my children however my neighbor has not yet made a sale." Upon this, the Sultan said:*

- *"This people can conquer the whole world with good morals like this. May Allah damn those who would want to spoil the good morals of our people"* [16]

QUESTIONS

1) Explain the importance of the family in Islam.
2) What are the duties of husbands and wives towards each other?
3) What are the duties of mothers and fathers towards their children?
4) Explain the duties of children towards their parents.
5) What are the duties of siblings towards each other?
6) What are our duties towards our kin and relatives?
7) Explain our duties towards our neighbors.

16. Tahsin ÜNAL, Ottoman Struggles for Virtue

UNIT IV

OUR DUTIES TOWARDS ALL OF HUMANKIND

Topics:

- Our moral duties towards people
- Our duties towards animals
- A teary scene (Reading)
- Characteristics of a Muslim living in accordance with the Islamic Morality
- The things that are prohibited in Islam
- The great danger threatening humankind: Alcoholic drinks and drugs (Reading)

OUR MORAL DUTIES TOWARDS PEOPLE

1) Not to cause harm to others:

It is prohibited to invade people's life, property, house, freedom and honor in our religion. These are the sacrosanct rights of people. Muslims are duty bound to show respect to the rights of others while refraining from all acts and actions that harm people. This is a condition of being a true Muslim. Our Prophet commanded:

"A Muslim is the one who does not harm other Muslims with his tongue or hands." [1]

2) To help others

It is a command of our religion to act with kind words and a smiling face towards people, to help the poor, to fulfil the needs of the poor, to protect the lonely, to lift the fallen, to show the road to those who have lost their way and to have good morals.

3) To show respect towards the elders, and mercy to the young:

It is an important moral rule to show respect to our mothers and fathers, our elder siblings, our teachers, and to those who are older than us; and to

1. Riyadh us Salihen, Volume 3, Page 148

show mercy and be helpful to those younger than the lonely, the weak, the orphans and us.

Our Prophet (salla Allāhu ʿalay-hi wa-sallam) stated the importance of this topic in the following statement:

"He who does not have mercy on the young or respect the elderly is not one of us." [2]

4) To exchange salām:

Muslims exchange greetings when they encounter each other and shake hands. It is a *sunnah* to give wa salām but *fard* to respond to it. Firstly, the younger one should give the was salām to the elder and the person walking to the one sitting. Exchanging the was salām strengthens the ties of love and friendship amongst Muslims.

5) Not to be resentful

If Muslims become resentful amongst each other for any reason, they should reconcile themselves immediately.

Our Prophet stated that it is a bad deed to remain resentful by stating: **"It is not *halal* for a Muslim to remain resentful with a Muslim brother for more than three days."** [3]

He commanded that those who remain resentful for long periods are committing a great sin by stating: **"If a person remains resentful with their Muslim brother for a year, he will commit a sin as if he spilt that brother's blood."** [4]

6) To reconcile those who are resentful

If a person sees two Muslims who are resentful with each other, they are duty bound to make a reconciliation between them. On this topic, the holy Qur'an states:

7) "Muslims are only brothers. In that case, correct the relationship between the two brothers of you." [5]

---

2. Selection of Hadiths, Page 218
3. Riyadh us Salihen, Volume 3, Page 168
4. Riyadh us Salihen, Volume 3, Page 170
5. Surah Al-Hujurat, 49/10

Our Prophet (salla Allāhu ʿalay-hi wa-sallam) stated that reconciling the resentful parties is a very good deed:

"The most favorable *sadaqah* is to reconcile the resentful." [6]

8) To visit friends

At appropriate times, Muslims should visit close ones, elders and the friends of their parentsfathers.

During visits, we must pay attention to the following:

a) To choose an appropriate time to visit,

b) Visits should not be too frequent as to annoy people,

c) If possible, to notify the people who will be visited in advance,

d) To wear clean and tidy clothing,

e) Not to go into anyone's house or room without their permission.

9) To host visitors

To host visitors is a good deed that is recommended by our religion. Being hospitable has an important place in the customs of Muslims.

Our main duties towards visitors:

a) To welcome visitors with a smiling face and kind words,

b) To host them with the best things, to make offerings,

c) Not to scold servants or children in the presence of visitors, not to have a long face,

d) To say goodbye to visitors when they are leaving.

10) To attend invitations

If there is not an objectionable situation, Muslims should attend to the invitations of their religious siblings. In relation to this, our Prophet commanded the following:

---

6. Selection of Hadiths, Page 237

"If one of you receive an invitation to a wedding dinner or similar, they should attend." [7]

Our Prophet did not discriminate against the rich or the poor. He would even attend the invitations of servants.

11) To kiss the hands of elders:

As a sign of respect, Muslims can kiss the hands of scholars and elder people.

12) Not to investigate the faults of others

A Muslim is the one who does not pry into the private lives of religious siblings. They do not spread the faults that they see, nor gossip about their religious siblings. Rather, they try to fix errors that they see with inoffensive deeds or words.

13) To forgive those who have done harm

A person of good morals forgives those who have caused harm to them. Not only do they forgive them, but they also respond by doing well. These are very good deeds performed by Muslims who have mature morality.

Our beloved Prophet commanded: **"Whoever has these three habits, Allah will place that person in paradise with his mercy."**

When asked what these habits are, He replied:

- **Give to those who do not give to you,**
- **Go to those who do not come to you,**
- **Forgive those who act cruelly towards you.**[8]

14) To visit the sick

A Muslim should visit their religious siblings who are sick, make *dua* for them to recover and refrain from words or deeds that would sadden the sick.

15) To participate in the *janazah*

To perform the *janazah* prayer of their deceased religious sibling, to take them to the cemetery, to ask Allah for mercy for the religious sibling and to

7. Cami'us – Sağir
8. Selection of Hadiths, Page 211

make *dua* for them. These are the important duties of Muslims towards the religious siblings who have left this world for the hereafter.

16) To want good for your religious sibling

A Muslim must possess good thoughts about their religious siblings. They must desire the good things that they love for themselves also for their religious siblings and not desire for them that they do not desire for themselves.

This is a measure of being a Muslim with good morality.

OUR DUTIES TOWARDS ANIMALS

Our religion has commanded that we treat animals well. It is our moral duty not to torture animals, to look after them and show them mercy.

Our Prophet notified us of a woman who acted cruelly to a cat:

"A woman locked a cat up without giving it any food or drink. She did not even let the cat go and find its own food. The poor animal died of hunger some time later where it was locked up. It is for this reason that the woman saw torment and entered hell." [9]

Our Prophet commanded the following in relation to a man who showed compassion to a dog:

"One day whilst walking, a man became extremely thirsty. Eventually he found and entered a well, drank from its water and then exited it. At that stage, a dog that had its tongue sticking out and breathing heavily was licking the humid ground due to its thirst. Thereupon, the man thought "This dog is thirsty just like me." and went down the well. He filled his shoe with water (as there was no container) and climbed out of the well by holding the shoe in his mouth. He allowed the dog to drink. On account of this, Allah was content and forgave all of his sins. The Companion said:

- O Rasulullah, can we earn rewards (*sawab*) if we perform meritorious acts for animals? Our Prophet said:

- **You can earn rewards as a result of treating all living things well."** [10]

---

9. Riyadh us Salihen, Volume 3, Page 174
10. Riyadh us Salihen, Volume 1, Page 161

READING:

A teary picture...

Huzeyfat al-Adawi, a person fought in the Yermuk War, which was between Muslims and the Byzantines, explained the following:

I commenced looking for my uncle's son on the battlefield when the war finished. I found him heavily wounded. I thought that I would give him some water. Just as I was about to give him water, I heard groaning from another wounded person nearby. My uncle's son did not drink the water and signaled that I give the water to the injured person groaning. I took the water to him and saw that it was Hisham, the son of As. I heard the groaning of another injured person as I was about to give him water. Hisham did not drink the water either and signaled for me to give it to the other wounded person, so I took the water to him. I found that he had just surrendered his spirit so I returned to Hisham. I realised that he was also dead. I thought that I might as well allow my uncle's son to drink the water so I rushed back next to him but I also found him dead. Thus, I was not destined to give any of them water.

What high emotions, what noble actions. Even in their last breath while burning with thirst, they thought more of their brothers in religion, and thus displayed a true moral understanding. [11]

THE CHARACTERISTICS OF A MUSLIM LIVING IN ACCORDANCE WITH ISLAMIC MORALITY

A good Muslim:

1) Is the one who believes in the essentials of faith undoubtedly and expresses this belief verbally.

2) Performs his worship in the manner commanded by Allah and shown by our Prophet.

3) Avoids what is prohibited by our religion such as alcohol, gambling, theft and fraud.

4) Does not lie, act as a false witness, take a false oath and backbite.

11. A.Hamdi AKSEKİ, A Religious Guide for a Soldier Page 269

5) Does not harm others with his hand or tongue.

6) Stays true to their word and does not betray a trust.

7) Tries to perform the duties incumbent upon him in the best possible way.

8) Avoids all words and actions that will cause bad feelings amongst people.

9) Refrains from being double-faced and is true to their word.

10) Makes friends with people of high morals and does not seek the company of bad people.

11) Shows respect to their parents and refrains from words or actions that could upset them.

12) Shows love to those younger than themselves and respect to elders.

13) Does not hurt their neighbor and performs good deeds to the best of his ability.

14) Apologizes if he does injustice towards others and returns the rights to their owner. Asks for forgiveness from Allah.

15) Does not seek revenge from those that cause harm and seeks forgives for those who do injustice.

16) Works for this world as if they are never going to die, and makes preparations for the hereafter as if they are going to die tomorrow.

17) Works for the benefit of others, especially the poor, indigent and lonely.

18) If required he does not hesitate to do things unselfishly for Allah's sake, or for the homeland and the nation.

19) Does not mock or belittle others, gets on well with others and is modest.

20) Accepts that all Muslims are brothers.

21) Is patient and does not fall into despair when he faces difficulties.

DUA

My great Lord, these dark roads,
Make them roads that reach you!
Arms locked with ambition,
Make them arms that embrace each other!

Let the conversation in our hearts be swift,
Let it be a mark that reaches the justice that we harbor,
Let the cliffs in front of us be flat
Make the thorns in our path roses!

Do not leave a person in heresy,
Do not make them the most horrifying of animals in the world;
Do not let us forget honesty and conscience,
Make us your worthy servants!

Orhan Seyfi ORHON

THINGS THAT ARE PROHIBITED IN ISLAM

The things that are prohibited in our religion are called *"Haram."*

Just as there is much wisdom and benefit in Allah's commands, there is harm in the things prohibited for this world and the hereafter. Allah the Almighty has prohibited harmful things for us because of compassion and has asked that we stay away from these. Those who do things that are *haram* are disobedient and disrespectful towards Allah. Those who do *haram* will bear the penalty of these actions.

We must learn the prohibitions of our religion that carry great importance and discard the harm which is haram and not receive a penalty.

The things prohibited are:

1) To associate a partner with Allah,
2) To be disobedient towards one's parents and to defy them.
3) To kill a person unjustly.

4) To invade the wealth and honor of others and to commit adultery.

5) To consume all sorts of substances -alcoholic beverages, opium, marijuana, drugs, heroin etc., - that alter clarity of mind and consciousness.

6) To gamble, to engage in money exchange and usury.

7) To steal and cheat during trade.

8) To eat the meat of dead animals, pig meat and the meat of other animals that are not *halal*.

9) To lie, to make false promises, to talk about others negatively, to slander, to act as a false witness, to mock others, to affix bad nicknames and not to keep promises.

10) To be jealous (of the good fortune of others), bear grudges and to remain resentful.

11) To avoid military service, to betray the homeland.

12) To cause divisiveness amongst people, to cause bad feelings and to back bite.

13) To be double-faced, arrogant and disregard others.

14) To pass judgment on something that one does not fully understand.

15) To befriend harmful people.

16) To perform magic and believe in what it says.

17) To waste one's property and wealth, to be altogether stingy.

18) To invade the house of others, to enter someone's house or room without permission.

19) To perform worship or good deeds for show other than for the sake of Allah.

20) To investigate the shame or shortcomings of others.

21) To assist the one who does injustice or harm to others.

22) Not to protect what has been entrusted and to breach trust.

READING:

The great dangers threatening humankind, alcoholic drinks and drugs

Our religion has placed great importance on people's health. The things that we consume or use that are in any way harmful to our bodies and our mental health have been deemed haram and prohibited.

Nevertheless, in Muslim countries, the use of drugs has increased and the increase in its users should make us all think seriously about it. In Islam, our Prophet openly warns how destructive alcoholic drinks and all other intoxicated substances and states as follows:

"Avoid alcohol, the mother of all harms." [12] *and* ***"Avoid alcohol because it is the key to all harms."*** [13]

Indeed, alcoholic drinks and drug substances adversely influence the brain, which represents the headquarters of a person's body. It stops perception and thought processes that sometimes places a person without their knowledge in a laughable and sometimes pathetic state. It opens the road to various sicknesses that are destructive to the body.

How sad it is for a person to destroy their body with their own hands. Especially putting their ability of rational thinking, which puts them in an eminent position and distinguishes them from other living things in an unworkable condition. Alcohol sends some people to the grave and others to prison where sincere friends who sit at the table end up drawing guns against each other. Isn't it alcoholic drinks that cause many traffic accidents and as a result, drag many people to an unexpected early death?

Allah the Almighty by commanding, ***"So avoid it that you may be successful."*** [14] *prohibited alcohol and gambling notifying us that we must stay away from these to reach salvation. In a hadith, our Prophet wanted Muslims to escape these bad habits by stating:* ***"All drinks that cause drunkenness are haram."*** [15] ***"A little of what causes drunkenness is also haram."*** [16]

It is particularly and importantly necessary to focus on narcotics that are drug substances that ruin a person's mental balance, their nervous system, and destroys the body by leading it to certain death. We must inform everybody, especially the youth about the use and trade of this poison, which Islam prohibits. Everyone must do what is incumbent upon them for our youth not to fall into the traps of drug dealers and harmful friends.

---

12. Keşfu'l-Hafa, Volume 1, Page 382
13. Cami'us – Sağir
14. Surah Al-Ma'idah, 5/90
15. Bukhari , Al Ashriba
16. Cami'us – Sağir

It is very difficult for those drug users who begin by thinking that "nothing will happen with a single use" to escape this because they have already experienced the poison. Poison can only be experienced once. There is no second experience because the first experience ends with an eventual early death. Drugs are also like this, experience is not required. A person who commences the use of drugs is on a dangerous road of no return. At the end of this road, they touch death.

Now then;

Let us protect our children. Let us follow whom they are friends with, where they spend their time and where they travel. We must protect our children from this disaster that will cause us life-long agony and grief.

Let us not say, "My child would not do anything like this." Our child may be very good and we may trust them a lot. However, we may not be aware of the traps set for our children. How can we ensure that our children are not going to be affected by these evil, sly and insidious traps? As it is not possible to ensure this, we must be sensitive and cautious about this topic.

By numbing and deceiving our youth to achieve their sordid wish to destroy the Muslim nation by refuting our youth and denying the forthcoming great and powerful Muslim countries the strength of dynamic people who generate new plans and put forward new ideas. We must take lasting measures against these very sly and cruel traps of betrayal as soon as possible, as it carries the significance of life.

We must be very smart as a nation against the games of the enemy who want to blacken our future and handicap a generation by poisoning our children. We have to take radical measures against these traps of betrayal that are being woven around our children.

Our nation, especially our youth will come across a danger that is very insidious and forbidding if we do not take immediate and effective measures. This fire now is just a spark and must be extinguished before it gets to a stage where we cannot control it.

To use drugs is to intentionally fall off the edge of a cliff, to consciously go to one's death. Drugs are such a trap, that it is very difficult for those who are caught up in it to escape. It is almost impossible.

We trust the discretion of our youth who are our assurance for the future. We believe that they have a degree of faith and a strong will not to fall into these traps.

However, even though it is small in numbers, our stomach aches and our hearts are torn when we see them fade away.

For this reason, we often mention that we must be smart as a nation against the danger of drugs by understanding that the best precaution is to not go near this trap or fall into the claws of this cruel monster. The only and certain way to escape this trouble is never to use narcotics. We should not forget this.

We call out to our youth who are our one and only possession:
Beloved youth!..
Think of yourselves.
Think of your future.
There is a beautiful future ahead of you.
Do not ruin it for yourself in this youthful period of your life.
Think of your family who do not withhold any sacrifice from you.
Think of your country that awaits great service from you.
Think of the second and eternal life after death.
Do not make this world and the hereafter a dungeon for yourselves.
Do not distress your nation who awaits a lot from you.
Come, let's give an ear to this warning;
Let's say "Absolutely no to the death trap of drugs."

QUESTIONS

1) What are the duties that we have towards other people?
2) What are our duties towards our guests?
3) What should we pay attention to when visiting friends?
4) Explain the importance of acting with mercy towards animals.
5) What are the attributes of a Muslim who lives in accordance with the principles of Islamic morality?
6) What are the things that are prohibited (*haram*) in Islam?

CHAPTER FOUR
SIYAR
(Our Prophet's Life)

UNIT I

THE BIRTH OF PROPHET MUHAMMAD (salla Allāhu 'alay-hi wa-sallam) AND HIS CHILDHOOD

Topics:

- The situation in Arabia prior to Islam
- The ancestry of Prophet Muhammad (salla Allāhu ʿalay-hi wa-sallam)
- The birth of Prophet Muhammad (salla Allāhu ʿalay-hi wa-sallam)
- The childhood of Prophet Muhammad (salla Allāhu ʿalay-hi wa-sallam)
- The protection of the Ka'bah by Allah (Reading)

THE SITUATION IN ARABIA PRIOR TO ISLAM

The Arabs lived in extreme ignorance prior to Islam. Hardly any people could read or write. There was no respect for people's rights. The strong would crush the poor. Women who were deprived of many rights were being sold as if they were property. They made it a custom to kill female children by burying them alive and no one could prevent this heart-breaking situation.

The belief in the oneness of Allah was forgotten. They were worshipping the idols that they had made with their own hands. There were more than 360 idols in the Ka'bah although it had originally been built by the Prophet Ibrahim and his son Isma'il to worship Allah. Moreover, there was an idol in every home that the family members worshipped. The community was encompassed by alcohol, gambling and all kinds of immoral acts where fairness and mercy had been wiped from their hearts. The situation of people living in other countries in the world was much worse.

There was a great need for the last Prophet to arrive and rescue humankind from this fearsome situation, to show ways for people to achieve happiness in this world and the hereafter.

THE ANCESTRY OF PROPHET MUHAMMAD

(Salla Allāhu ʿalay-hi wa-sallam)

The father of the Prophet Muhammad (salla Allāhu ʿalay-hi wa-sallam) was Abdullah. The father of Abdullah was Abdul-Muttalib, the chief of the Quraysh tribe of Banu Hashim and a notable of Makkah. Our prophet's mother was Aminah, the daughter of Wahb from the Quraysh tribe of Banu Zuhrah.

The ancestry of Muhammad belonged to an honorable family on both the paternal and maternal sides. The ancestry goes back until Ibrahim.

THE BIRTH OF PROPHET MUHAMMAD (salla Allāhu ʿalay-hi wa-sallam)

The birth of our Prophet Muhammad (salla Allāhu ʿalay-hi wa-sallam) was on a Monday night on the 12th night of Rabi' al-Awwal before dawn in Makkah which coincides with April 20, 571.

The most attractive, the sunniest night since creation!
Will be born on this night, the greatest of all births!

The mountains, stones and trees... all rose for salām!
They began to give salātu wa salām from within!

What was awaited on the ground and the sky, it is equal never being born,
Was born on a night like this, the only sun of the Creator.

M. ASIM Köksal

On the morning of His birth, the world was filled with divine light. His father Abdullah who had died about two months before, did not see the birth of his only son.

When Aminah brought a radiant child into the world, his grandfather Abdul-Muttalib gave a huge feast and named him Muhammad.

When they asked: "What did you name your grandson?"

- Muhammad.

They said:

- There is not a name like this amongst your ancestors. What is your objective in giving this name?

Abdul-Muttalib replied:

- I hope that he is praised by Allah in the heavens and by the people on earth.

Many extraordinary events occurred on the night of the birth of our Prophet. Fourteen columns of the palace of the ruler of Iran (Khosrau) were ruined, the Lake Sava dried up, and after burning for a thousand years, the fire worshipped by the Zoroastrians (fire worshippers) suddenly went out. These events were signs that the reign of Iran would end, the Byzantine Empire would collapse and the idolaters would disappear. Indeed, that is what happened.

THE CHILDHOOD OF PROPHET MUHAMMAD (salla Allāhu ʿalay-hi wa-sallam)

The notables of Makkah had a custom. The newborn children were given to and remained with nursing mothers in tribes living in the vicinity of Makkah. This was because the climate in Makkah was harsh and hot, which was not good for the children.

Our prophet was nursed by Aminah three days and by Suvaybah khatun for two days. Later, our prophet was given to a nursing mother called Halima from the Sa'd tribe. Halima loved him more than she loved her own child, protecting him even from the blowing wind. Halima's small daughter Shaima, the nursing sibling of Muhammad, also loved him a lot and played with him. This orphan child brought good fortune to this family. One day, Halima's husband said:

"Halima, this child has brought great fortune to us. From the day He stepped foot in our house, the milk from our animals and the fat content of the milk has increased. Our house has filled with abundance. We have more wealth. I sense something different in this child."

After staying with this family for five years, Prophet Muhammad (salla Allāhu ʿalay-hi wa-sallam) was brought back to his family in Makkah.

Our Prophet's (salla Allāhu ʿalay-hi wa-sallam) mother Aminah had relatives in Madinah. Aminah went to Madinah with her son in order to visit her relatives and allow her son to visit the grave of his father. They stayed in Madinah for one month. They visited the grave of our Prophet's father Abdullah. Aminah, her son and her servant Ummu Ayman set off to return to Makkah. They reached the village of Abwa that evening and spent the night there.

Aminah fell ill there. She sat her one and only child next to her, kissed Him fondly and embraced Him longingly. The mother who sensed that she was going to die and be separated from her son, knowing that she would not see him again with a worldly eye looked into his face and said the following:

"Every new thing will get old and everything will disappear. I will also die but I will not grieve because I gave birth to a clean child. I am leaving this world a great and good being."

After these words, Aminah closed her eyes to this world. At that stage, Prophet Muhammad (salla Allāhu ʿalay-hi wa-sallam) was six years old. Ummu Ayman took the child and returned to Makkah.

Abdulmuttalib, Prophet Muhammad's grandfather, took in this orphaned child. Our Prophet remained with him for two years. When Abdulmuttalib's death approached, he delivered Him to our Prophet's uncle and asked in his last will and testament that he be looked after very well. At that stage, our Prophet had reached the age of eight. Abu Talib and his wife Fatimah looked after the child very well. They loved Him like their own child.

READING:

The protection of the Ka'bah by Allah...

The Ka'bah is the first place of worship built on this earth for the purpose of worshipping Allah. With the command of Allah, it was built by the Prophet Ibrahim and Isma'il. The Ka'bah is located in the city of Makkah in Arabia. It has kept its holiness and attracted attention throughout history.

Prior to Islam, the Ka'bah was used for other purposes than the reason for which it was built. It was filled with idols by the Arab idolaters. Our Prophet rid the Ka'bah of the idols when Makkah was conquered in the year 630.

Makkah was the trade center for the Arabs prior to Islam. Many people would come to Makkah each year with the aim of visiting the Ka'bah.

Abraha, the Governor of Yemen in Habeshistan (Abyssinia), built a great place of worship in San'aa to draw the attention of people from the Ka'bah to his country. However, the people would not abandon the Ka'bah. Upon this, Abraha decided to bring down and demolish the Ka'bah by mobilizing a strong army with elephants that came to the outskirts of Makkah. There was a huge elephant at the head of the army.

The people of Makkah did not have the power to oppose this army. Abraha's men looted all the property and animals owned by the Arabs and brought it to him. Amongst the looted property were 100 camels owned by Abdul-Muttalib, our Prophet's grandfather. The people of Makkah formed a committee to plea with Abraha. The committee also included Abdul-Muttalib. Abraha asked why they had come. Abdul-Muttalib said that they had come to ask that the camels be returned. Upon this, Abraha said:

"I thought that you had come to beg so that I would not demolish the Ka'bah. You however, are sorry for your camels."

Abdul-Muttalib gave Abraha the following answer:

"I am the owner of the camels and I want them back. The Ka'bah has an owner and its owner will protect it."

Abraha returned the camels to Abdul-Muttalib and then mobilized to destroy the Ka'bah. There was a great elephant at the front. The elephant did not take another step as it got close to the Ka'bah. It would walk when turned away from the Ka'bah, but not when facing the Ka'bah. Despite all efforts, the elephant would not walk towards the Ka'bah.

At this time, an unexpected event occurred. Groups of birds filled the sky flying above the elephant army. These birds threw small stones like bombs on the soldiers, which they carried with their beaks and claws. In the places where the stones hit, the bodies of the soldiers were riddled with holes and within a short time, the army was distraught and scattered. The Ka'bah was saved from being demolished. Saving his life with difficulty, Abraha returned to his country where he later died. As Abdul-Muttalib had stated, Allah the owner of the Ka'bah had indeed protected it.

Allah the Almighty punished those who wanted to continue their superstitious beliefs by demolishing the Ka'bah that was not defended by the people. He did not allow them to demolish it. This was because Allah's beloved servant, Prophet Muhammad (salla Allāhu 'alay-hi wa-sallam), was going to be born soon. This event took place in the year 571 and about

50 days later, our Prophet Muhammad (salla Allāhu ʿalay-hi wa-sallam) was born.

QUESTIONS

1) What was the situation prior to Islam in Arabia?

2) What were the names of Prophet Muhammad's mother and father?

3) Where and when was Prophet Muhammad's birth, who was his wet nurse?

4) What kind of events occurred around the world on the night Prophet Muhammad was born, and what were these an indication of?

5) Who called our prophet with the name "Muhammad" and what was his objective?

6) When did Muhammad's mother and father die?

7) With whom did our prophet grow up after the death of his mother?

UNIT II

THE PROPHET MUHAMMAD's (salla Allāhu 'alay-hi wa-sallam) ADOLESCENCE AND MARRIAGE

Topics:

- The travels of Prophet Muhammad (salla Allāhu ʿalay-hi wa-sallam)
- The trade life of Prophet Muhammad (salla Allāhu ʿalay-hi wa-sallam)
- Prophet Muhammad's (salla Allāhu ʿalay-hi wa-sallam) marriage to Khadijah and htheir children
- The arbitration of Prophet Muhammad at the time of the renovations of the Ka'bah

THE TRAVELS OF PROPHET MUHAMMAD (salla Allāhu ʿalay-hi wa-sallam)

His uncle Abu Talib was involved in trade. He took Muhammad with him on an expedition once. They stopped at a town called Busra near Damascus where they met a monk called Bahira.

Bahira saw the name and all the attributes that were written in the Torah and the Bible about the last Prophet in this child. Upon this, he told Abu Talib to take him back to Makkah because the Jews would cause him harm. Taking the advice of Bahira, Abu Talib cut his trade travel short and returned to Mecca rather than going to Damascus.

At the age of 17, Muhammad (salla Allāhu ʿalay-hi wa-sallam) went to Yemen with His uncle Zubair.

THE TRADE LIFE OF PROPHET MUHAMMAD (salla Allāhu ʿalay-hi wa-sallam)

There was a rich widow woman named Khadijah from among the notables of Quraysh. She would sometimes enter into partnerships with people giving them capital. Khadijah gave our prophet some money and sent him to Syria with a trade caravan.

During His trading life, our prophet (salla Allāhu ʿalay-hi wa-sallam) achieved success in his work due to his honesty and integrity. For this reason, he returned with more profit than expected from each trade caravan. Khadijah was very happy with her trade partnership with prophet Muhammad.

PROPHET MUHAMMAD'S (salla Allāhu ʿalay-hi wa-sallam) MARRIAGE TO KHADIJAH AND HIS CHILDREN

After returning from the travel to Damascus, our Prophet married Khadijah. At that time, Prophet Muhammad was twenty-five years old whereas Khadijah reached forty. A happy home was established.

Prophet Muhammad was the father of seven children, three of whom were boys and four were girls. Of these, six were born to Khadijah and one to Mariya. His sons were Qasim, Abdullah and Ibrahim. His daughters were Zainab, Ruqayyah, Umm Kulthum and Fatimah. Qasim and Abdullah died at a young age in Makkah prior to his Prophethood. However, Ibrahim was born in Madinah after the *Hijrah* and died there at a young age. All of His daughters grew up and married. Apart from Fatimah, his other three daughters died before our Prophet. Our Prophet's bloodline continued with Fatimah who married Ali.

THE ARBITRATION OF PROPHET MUHAMMAD AT THE TIME OF THE RENOVATIONS OF THE KA'BAH

The Ka'ba was damaged due to a big flood. The people of Makkah decided to repair the Ka'bah. As the walls of the Ka'bah got higher and the time came to place the holy black stone, which was called the "Hajar al-Aswad", all the tribes began to compete against each other in order to achieve this honor. In fact, there were fights and disagreements amongst themselves as a result of this. In the end, they agreed to appoint our prophet as an arbiter because they believed that he was the right person for he was truly reliable. They agreed that they would comply with whatever decision he made.

Prophet Muhammad put the *Hajar Al-Aswad* on top of a beam. He made the tribal leaders hold the ends of the beam. They lifted the stone up all together. Prophet Muhammad put the stone in its place on the wall with his blessed hands. His compromising behavior made everyone content and this way, a great disagreement had been averted. Our prophet was thirty-five at the time of this event.

Our prophet Muhammad (salla Allāhu ʿalay-hi wa-sallam) was an extremely honest and reliable person. Due to this attribute, He was called "Muhammad al-Amin", which means “"Reliable Muhammad" among the people. He had earned everyone's love and respect and he was thus like a shining star in the community with his clean and exemplary way of life.

Allah the Almighty instructed him in the best possible way. He equipped him with morality and virtue because he was going to be entrusted with prophethood for the salvation of humankind.

QUESTIONS

1) Where did Prophet Muhammad travel to during His childhood and youth?

2) Who did Prophet Muhammad marry and when?

3) How many children did our prophet have?

4) Explain the arbitration role that Prophet Muhammad played during the repair of the Ka'bah.

5) What was the reason for Muhammad being called "Muhammad al-Amin"?

UNIT III

THE PROPHETHOOD OF MUHAMMAD (salla Allāhu 'alay-hi wa-sallam) AND THE SECRET INVITATION

Topics:

- The first revelation
- The interregnum period
- The commencement of the invitation to Islam
- The first Muslims
- The first *Hijrah* to Habashistan
- The attitude of Al-Najashi, the King of Habashistan, towards Muslims

THE FIRST REVELATION

When Prophet Muhammad (salla Allāhu ʿalay-hi wa-sallam) reached the age of forty, he underwent some obvious changes. He would take with him food provisions and retreat to the cave of Hira on the outskirts of Makkah. He would stay there alone for days reflecting upon the greatness of Allah, the creator of the universe. Whatever He saw in his dreams would eventuate. He would see many truths that others could not and knew what they did not know. This situation continued for around six months. This way, Allah the Almighty was disciplining and preparing him for prophethood.

On a Monday night during the month of Ramadan in the year 610 of the Gregorian calendar, Muhammad (salla Allāhu ʿalay-hi wa-sallam) retreated once again to the cave of Hira where He turned with His whole being towards Allah. At this time, Jibril (Gabriel) (alayhi al-salām) appeared to Him and said:

- Read!

Muhammad (salla Allāhu ʿalay-hi wa-sallam) said:

- **I do not know how to read.**

Jibril said for a second time, "Read!" Muhammad (salla Allāhu ʿalay-hi wa-sallam) again said, **"I do not know how to read."**

When Jibril (alayhi al-salām) said "Read" for a third time, Muhammad asked, **"What should I read?"** Then, Jibril (alayhi al-salām) revealed the following verses at the start of Surah Al-'Alaq , which means the following:

"Recite in the name of your Lord who created -

Created man from a clinging substance.

Recite, and your Lord is the most Generous -

Who taught by the pen -

Taught man that which he knew not."

Thus, the first revelation was revealed to the Prophet Muhammad (salla Allāhu ʿalay-hi wa-sallam). The verses of the Qur'an began to be revealed. After this, the angel disappeared. He began to recite the verses as if they were placed in his heart.

He returned home under the heavy influence of the first revelation, the greatness of the duty taken in and the emotions of responsibility felt. He explained to Khadijah what he had experienced. Khadijah said the following to console him:

"Glad tidings! Show perseverance. Upon my oath to Allah who holds my life in His hands, you will be the Prophet of this *ummah*. Allah the Almighty will never leave you alone because you respect the rights of relatives, you are true to your word, you can endure difficulty, you host visitors and you run to assist those who face disaster. Allah will not leave such a servant alone.

THE INTERREGNUM PERIOD

The revelations stopped for a period after the first five verses of Surah al-'Alaq were revealed. Jibril (alayhi al-salām) was no where to be seen. This was the time for our prophet to prepare to receive the revelations. Thus, our Prophet wished for the divine revelation to come again with his whole heart and he was in a position to accept it.

Thereupon, Jibril (salla Allāhu ʿalay-hi wa-sallam) appeared to him and revealed the first few verses of Surah al-Muddaththir. The meanings of these verses are as follows:

"O you (Muhammad) who covers himself with a garment,

Arise and warn,

And your Lord glorify,

And your clothing purify,

And continue to keep away from bad things."

After this, the revelations continued incessantly and the revelation of holy Qur'an was completed in 23 years.

As explained above, the short period between the first revelation and the next is called the "Interregnum period of the revelation."

THE COMMENCEMENT OF THE INVITATION TO ISLAM

With the reception of the revelation and prophethood being assigned to Muhammad (salla Allāhu ʿalay-hi wa-sallam), he first told and invited people to Islam that He could trust. The first Muslims conducted their worship in secrecy. This situation continued for about three years. Meanwhile, the number of people who had accepted Islam exceeded thirty.

THE FIRST MUSLIMS

Our Prophet first made Muslims of his loyal wife Khadijah and then of the children Ali, Zayd ibn Harithah who attained his freedom after being a slave and of the elders, Abu Bakr.

THE FIRST HIJRAH TO HABASHISTAN

The torture to the Muslims by the polytheists increased with every passing day. The Muslims could not perform their worship freely or recite the Qur'an aloud. For this reason, our Prophet gave Muslims permission to make the *hijra* to Habashistan – which was a safer place.

The first group, which included eleven men and four women, went to Habashistan secretly from Makkah via the red sea road in the fifth year of Muhammad's prophethood. Amongst them were Uthman and his wife, the Prophet's daughter Ruqayyah. The Muslims were well received there, attaining a life of safety and tranquility.

After hearing that the first group of Muslims were well received, another group of about 80 people made the *hijrah*. They were led by Ali's brother Ja'far al-Tayyar.

THE ATTITUDE OF AL-NAJASHI, THE KING OF HABASHISTAN, TOWARDS MUSLIMS

The polytheists of Makkah were disappointed that the Muslims had found tranquility in Habashistan. To have them returned, they sent al-Najashi, the king of Habashistan many gifts together with two messengers. The messengers asked al-Najashi to give the Muslims to them so that they could return them to Makkah. Al-Najashi, who was a Christian himself, called for the Muslims in order to obtain information about Islam.

After listening to both sides, he found that the Muslims were right and so the messengers returned to Makkah empty-handed.

After this, al-Najashi protected the Muslims even more than before. The Muslims and the people of Habashistan got on with each other very well.

QUESTIONS

1) At what age, when and where did Prophet Muhammad receive his first revelation?

2) What is the Interregnum era?

3) Who were the first Muslims?

4) Why did the Muslims make the *hijrah* to Habashistan?

5) How were the Muslims received in Habashistan?

UNIT IV

THE ANNOUNCEMENT OF THE INVITATION TO ISLAM

Topics:

- The open invitation to Islam
- The tyranny of the polytheists against the Muslims
- Those who were the most hostile towards the the Prophet Muhammad (salla Allāhu ʿalay-hi wa-sallam)
- The reasons why Quraysh opposed Islam
- The polytheists' appeal to Abu Talib and our Prophet's response
- Hamza and Umar becoming Muslims

THE OPEN INVITATION TO ISLAM

Our Prophet called people to Islam secretly for three years. The period of calling people to Islam openly had commenced after the following verses with the following meaning were revealed:

"And warn, [O Muhammad], your closest kindred. And lower your wing to those who follow you of the believers. And if they disobey you, then say, "Indeed, I am disassociated from what you are doing." [1]

"Then declare what you are commanded and turn away from the polytheists." [2]

Thereupon, the Prophet Muhammad (salla Allāhu ʿalay-hi wa-sallam) first gathered his those near and dear to him at his home and gave a feast. He conveyed the messages received from Allah and invited them to Islam. His uncle Abu Lahab objected to our Prophet and scattered those who gathered.

A short time later, our Prophet (salla Allāhu ʿalay-hi wa-sallam) went on top of al-Safa hill with the aim of widening the invitation. From here, He called out to the people of Makkah. Those who heard Him gathered around Him.

Our Prophet (salla Allāhu ʿalay-hi wa-sallam) asked those around Him:

1. Surah Ash-Shu'ara'
2. Surah Al-Hijr

"Would you believe me if I said to you that behind this hill is the army of an enemy?"

They replied in unison:

"Yes, we would believe you because we have never heard you lie."

Thereupon, our Prophet told them:

"Then know that Allah has chosen me as a Prophet. He sent me his word with the intermediacy of an angel. He commanded that I invite people to Islam, the true religion. Allah is one. There is no deity except Him. I am his Prophet whom He has sent to you and all people."

Abu Lahab who was present stood up and said harsh words to our Prophet. Upon this, those who attended dispersed from the meeting. As such, no result could be achieved from the meeting.

THE TYRANNY OF THE POLYTHEISTS AGAINST THE MUSLIMS

The polytheists tried to turn them from Islam by extinguishing the divine light of Islam by torturing, tormenting and carrying out various acts of oppression against the Muslims.

Umayyah ibn Khalaf was one of the greatest enemies of Islam. He laid Bilal al-Habashi on the hot sand for hours under the sun, stacking stones on his chest and stated, "I will kill you like this if you do not give up being a Muslim." Achieving no result from this, he tied a rope around Bilal's neck and dragged him around Makkah from one side to the other. Even though he was crushed by this savage torture, Bilal shouted, **"Allah is one, Allah is one!"** Eventually, Bilal attained his freedom through Abu Bakr who bought him from the cruel hands of Umayyah.

Of the first Muslims, Ammar bin Yasir was beaten on the hot sands until he fainted. His mother Sumayyah was killed in cold blood after being beaten with a spear by Abu Jahl. His father Yasir was also killed by the torture of the polytheists. Yasir and his spouse Sumayyah were given the title of being the first martyrs of Islam.

Likewise, Habbab bin Erat underwent unbearable torture due to his belief by being laid on top of burning red coal and Abu Fukaihah was dragged across the hot sands tied by his feet. In addition to these, many more Muslims were dealt with cruelty by the polytheists. Nevertheless, the owners of true faith were not daunted. They did not leave Islam.

One of the greatest services to Islam that Abu Bakr did was to save Muslim slaves by buying them from their hostile owners after they had accepted Islam.

THOSE WHO WERE THE MOST HOSTILE TOWARDS THE PROPHET MUHAMMAD (salla Allāhu ʿalay-hi wa-sallam)

The polytheists did not hold back from tormenting our Prophet and the new Muslims.

The following people were the most hostile towards our Prophet:

1) Abu Lahab: Even though he was our Prophet's own uncle, he was the greatest enemy of Islam. He objected to our Prophet from the first day. At every opportunity, his wife would place thorns on the roads that our Prophet was going to walk through. Surah al-Tabbat was revealed in relation to them both. Abu Lahab was so distressed that he died after finding out that the Muslims were victorious at the battle of Badr.

On one occasion, Abu Lahab's son Utayba attacked our Prophet by grabbing him from the collar and ripping his shirt. His actions saddened our Prophet immensely and he then made the following *dua*: **"O Allah, set a monster upon Utayba."** Allah accepted His beloved Prophet's *dua*. A lion appeared on the road to Damacsus and tore Utayba apart. Thus, he was punished for insulting the Prophet.

2) Abu Jahl: The person who felt the most hostility towards our Prophet was Abu Jahl. He tormented Muslims a lot. He killed the mother of Ammar b. Yasir due to her beliefs. He was punished by being killed at the battle of Badr.

3) As b. Wayil: He was a man who outdid himself at being an enemy of our Prophet by upsetting him and mocking him when our prophet was in a deep agony upon the death of his son Qasim. He said, "The ancestry of Muhammad had dried up."

The following verse in Surah al-Kawthar was revealed upon this: **"He who is hostile towards you is actually the one whose name is forgotten**

and whose ancestry is ceased." As b. Wayil was thrown off the animal that he was on whilst he was going through a passage on a mountain near Makkah. The animal bit his leg and he died from this wound.

4) Walid b. Mughira

5) Umayyah ibn Halaf

6) Utbah bin Rabi'ah was at the head of those who were hostile towards our Prophet.

THE REASONS WHY QURAYSH OPPOSED ISLAM

1) Islam did away with class differences. It announced that people were equal like the teeth of a comb, that slaves were equal to their masters in the eyes of Allah. The notables of Quraysh did not accept this equality and became enemies of Islam because they were afraid that their positions would be taken away.

2) Makkah was the trade center of the Arabs. The Ka'bah was located in Makkah and had about 360 idols in it. They thought that the idols were drawing the Arabs to Makkah and believed that no one would come to trade if Islam took the idols away. Therefore, they felt that their livelihood would disappear.

3) Idol worship was deeply rooted in Arabia over hundreds of years. Primitive nations were struggling to differentiate between good and bad, they would not easily abandon the doings of their ancestors, and they were enemies to change. Islam forbid the idol worship that the Arabs had been accustomed to, and in its place it brought the belief in one God.

4) To be a leader of the Arab people, they would not seek qualities such as being worthy, virtuous or having merits. Only two conditions were sought. One of these was wealth and the other was to have many children.

As Prophet Muhammad (salla Allāhu ʿalay-hi wa-sallam) did not have these attributes, they were saying that they could not accept him as a leader. Moreover, there was a rivalry between the Hashimi and Amawi tribal leaders. As Prophet Muhammad (salla Allāhu ʿalay-hi wa-sallam) was from the Hashimi arm of Quraysh, most of his enemies were Amawis.

THE POLYTHEISTS' APPEAL TO ABU TALIB AND OUR PROPHET'S RESPONSE

The Prophet Muhammad's uncle, Abu Talib, loved him very much. He was always supporting and protecting his nephew during the spread of Islam. The polytheists and the notables appealed to Abu Talib aggressively by saying: "Either get your nephew to abandon Islam or stop protecting Him."

Abu Talib explained the situation to his nephew Muhammad (salla Allāhu ʿalay-hi wa-sallam). He replied as follows, **"I am put in charge by Allah to convey the right religion.**

I am not doing anything of my own accord. I am Allah's messenger. O uncle, to abandon this task, if they gave the sun in my right hand and the moon in my left hand, I still wouldn't abandon it."

After listening to this answer, Abu Talib gave an assurance to continue protecting our Prophet stating: "Continue your duty son. They cannot do anything to you while I'm around."

HAMZA BECOMES A MUSLIM

Despite all of the difficulties, our Prophet (salla Allāhu ʿalay-hi wa-sallam) continued His duty and the number of Muslims increased each day. It was in the sixth year of his prophethood. One day, while passing by our Prophet who was sitting on the Safa hill, Abu Jahl cursed him. Our Prophet did not respond to this rude behavior. A woman who saw this sad event explained this to the Prophet's uncle, uncle Hamza. Hamza had not yet become a Muslim but he was outraged at the insult of his brother's son. He immediately went to where the polytheists gathered and addressed Abu Jahl saying:

- Is it you who cursed and hurt my brother's son? He then hit Abu Jahl on the head with his bow.

After this event, Hamza accepted Islam and took his place next to our Prophet.

UMAR BECOMES A MUSLIM

The fact that Hamza became a Muslim and the Muslims grew stronger each day alarmed the Quraysh polytheists. To find a solution to this problem, they gathered at a place called *Dar al-Nadwah*. After reviewing the situation, they agreed to kill our prophet upon the suggestion of Abu Jahl. They charged Umar to carry out this awful duty, for he was the bravest amongst them. At that time, Umar was 33 years old. He put on his sword and set off to kill our prophet.

The Muslims had gathered at Arkam's house. Our Prophet was also there. On the way, Umar ran into Nuaym. He asked, "Where to oh Umar?"

Umar replied:

- I am going to dispose of Muhammad's body that is causing bad relations between people.

When Nuaym replied to Umar, "You have embarked upon a hard task." Umar scolded him saying:

- Are you also on Muhammad's side?

Nuaym replied:

- Oh Umar, leave me and look to your own family. Your brother-in-law Said and sister Fatimah have become Muslims.

Umar then changed his path and went to knock on his sister's door to kill them first. At that moment, his sister and brother in law had been reciting the verses of "Surah Taha", which was newly revealed to our Prophet. When they saw that Umar had come armed, they became fearful and hid the pages of the Qur'an.

When Umar entered, he asked them what they were reading. They replied, "Nothing." His anger increased even further and he said, "So what I have heard is true!" He grabbed his brother in law by the collar, threw him to the ground and started hitting him. He also slapped his sister Fatimah in the face as she was trying to save her husband. The poor woman lay on the ground with her mouth and nose covered in blood. With the strength that her faith had given her, Fatimah said the following to Umar:

- Be afraid of Allah. Look at what you have done to a woman. My husband and I have become Muslims. We will not turn from this even if you cut off our heads.

Umar replied:

- Bring me the thing that you were reading.

His sister brought it out and gave it to him. Umar began to read it carefully and his heart began to soften as he read it. The harmony of the Qur'an, the steepness of its meaning, the sweetness and beauty of its lines conquered Umar's heart. Now that Umar's heart was open to Islam, he went next to our Prophet. He kneeled before him and became a Muslim stating the *kalimah al-shahada*. Those who were there rejoiced and stated the *kalimah al-shahada* altogether.

Islam strengthened with Umar's inclusion into the Muslim community. Umar asked, "How many friends do we have?" and they replied, "40 people including you."

Upon Umar's request, all the Muslims went straight to the Ka'bah. There, they performed prayer together in the open. In the meantime, the polytheists were bewildered when they learnt that Umar, who they had sent to kill our Prophet, had become a Muslim.

The merciless and stone heart of Umar who had set out to kill our Prophet was softened with the verses of the Qur'an that he recited at his sister's house; his dark heart was filled with radiance. He turned his feelings of hostility towards the Prophet to feeling of friendship.

QUESTIONS

1) How and why did Muhammad invite people openly to Islam?

2) Explain the torment to the Muslims by the polytheists and what the Muslims did in answer to this.

3) Who were the most hostile people towards Prophet Muhammad?

4) What were the reasons for Quraysh becoming enemies with our prophet?

5) Who is Abu Talib and how did he protect the Prophet Muhammad?

6) How did Hamza and Umar become Muslims?

UNIT V THE YEARS OF BOYCOTT AND GLOOM

Topics:

- The boycott of Muslims by the polytheists
- The deaths of Abu Talib and Khadijah
- Travel to Taif
- The Aqaba Allegiance
- The miracle of Mi'raj
- Prayer, the gift of Mi'raj

THE BOYCOTT OF MUSLIMS BY THE POLYTHEISTS

Polytheists seriously were alarmed by Islam's spreading and getting stronger each day with Hamza and Umar becoming Muslim Thereupon, they got together and agreed to the following boycott decisions:

"From now on, everyone must cease relations with all Muslims, those protecting them and the Hashemites, the relatives of Muhammad. Noone is to have conversation, trade with them or give and take girls (in marriage) from them."

Of the polytheists, Mansour ibn Ikrima wrote down the agreement and they hung it on the wall of the Ka'bah together.

The boycott continued for three years. The Muslims suffered with great difficulties during this period. The polytheists did everything they could not to allow food or drink into the suburb that the Muslims were living in. They endured all sorts of hardship, hunger and thirst for the sake of Islam. They were forced to live by eating the leaves of trees. The state of children crying from hunger was heart breaking.

The polytheists could not achieve results from these inhumane actions. They could not prevent the spreading of Islam's divine light. At this time, a moth had eaten the agreement that was hung on the Ka'bah's wall except for the name of "Allah." All the other words were eradicated. Moreover, the hand by which Mansour ibn Ikrima wrote the agreement withered and he was left crippled. At that time, instead of "Basmala", they used "Bismikallahumma" in its place.

In the end, a few polytheists became kindhearted, pulled it down and ripped apart this cruel document. Thus, the boycott was lifted and the Muslims were saved from a great discomfort.

The boycotting the Muslims lasted three years between the seventh year to the tenth year of the Prophethood.

THE DEATHS OF ABU TALIB AND KHADIJAH

The Muslims and our Prophet could breathe a little easier with the lifting of the boycott. However, His uncle Abu Talib died and not long after, a few days later, death of His wife Khadijah followed this.

Abu Talib loved and protected our Prophet like his own child whereas Khadijah was the first to believe in our Prophet and she consoled Him during his most difficult times. She was a spouse who was helpful, loyal and faithful. Our Prophet felt great sorrow from losing these two valuable people who were always supportive. For this reason, this year of sadness was called "the year of sorrow."

After the deaths of Abu Talib and Khadijah, the polytheists increased the torment against our Prophet. A despicable person threw dirt on his head while passing through a street one day. Our Prophet went home in that state. When Fatimah saw her father, she became sad and cried whilst cleaning the dirt that was thrown on Him. Seeing His daughter cry, our Prophet (salla Allāhu ʿalay-hi wa-sallam) uttered His trust in Allah saying, **"Do not cry my child, Allah the Almighty will protect your father."**

TRAVEL TO TAIF

With the increase of torment after the deaths of Abu Talib and Khadijah against our Prophet by the polytheists, he went to Taif with Zayd ibn Harithah to invite people to Islam. Just as the people of Taif did not accept Islam, they wanted our Prophet to go. Not only that, they stoned our Prophet. The stones thrown wounded His feet and his feet covered in blood. He was in a state where He could not walk. Zayd was trying to shield our Prophet with his body from the stones that were being thrown.

Our Prophet returned to Makkah sadly after taking shelter and resting a little at a roadside vineyard. Our Prophet encountered the greatest torment of His life during this trip. However, he did not fall into despair nor was he daunted because of these events, rather, he continued in his duty.

THE AQABA ALLEGIANCE

For years, our Prophet invited the people of Makkah to Islam. However, he faced great difficulty due to the stubbornness and attitude of the people of Makkah. Yet, this was not going to prevent the Prophet of Islam from carrying out His duty. The divine light of Islam was going to continue to enlighten humankind. For this, Allah the Almighty opened a new horizon. For Islam to spread, He prepared a more suitable environment. This environment was Madinah.

Our Prophet went outside Makkah during the hajj season on the eleventh year of his prophethood. He encountered a group of six men who came from Madinah and told them that He was a Prophet. He recited the Qur'an and explained the commands of Allah. He invited them to become Muslims.

The people of Madinah were tactful. They became Muslims after coming to the conviction that what the Prophet was saying was reasonable and true. They tried to spread Islam on their return to Madinah.

The first Aqaba Allegiance (the twelfth year of Prophethood)

The following year, a group of twelve people came from Madinah to Makkah. They met with our Prophet at a place called Aqaba near Makkah. Their leader was As'ad ibn Zurarah. Amongst them were also the same five people as a year ago. They pledged their allegiance and their word to our Prophet on these matters: *"Not to associate a partner with Allah, not to steal, not to commit adultery, to avoid lying or slander and not to oppose the Prophet."* This is called the first Aqaba Allegiance.

The people of Medina asked our prophet to send someone who could explain Islam to them. Our prophet sent Mus'ab who contributed greatly to the dissemination of Islam in Medina.

The second Aqaba allegiance (the thirteenth year of Prophethood)

In this year, the number of people who came to Makkah from Madinah were 75. Of these, two were women. After meeting with our Prophet again at the place called Aqaba, the second Aqaba materialized. According to this, the people of Madinah promised to protect our Prophet as if they would their family. They held the hands of our Prophet and pledged allegiance.

After this, our Prophet wanted them to choose 12 representatives from amongst them. They then chose the 12 representatives. They all promised our Prophet that they would *"Abide by Him in good and bad times in all conditions and situations, to always speak the truth and not to be afraid of anything on the path of Allah."*

The Aqaba allegiances were an important turning point in the spread of Islam.

THE MIRACLE OF MI'RAJ

Mi'raj literally means to climb high and Isra means the night journey. One and a half years prior to the *Hijrah* on the 27th night of the month of Rajab, our Prophet was taken from Masjid al-Haram in Makkah to Masjid al-Aqsa in Jerusalem, ascended to the heavens and saw the *alam al-malakut*.

Mi'raj event was one of the great miracles of our Prophet and a demonstration of Allah's endless power. However, the polytheists did not acknowledge it. This is because they were incapable of understanding the greatness and the broad power of Allah. Due to their limited thinking and superstitious beliefs, they did not have the ability to comprehend the miracle of Mi'raj.

The believers accepted and believed in the Mi'raj without hesitation. When the Mi'raj event was explained to Abu Bakr, he ratified our Prophet saying, "If Muhammad said it, then it is true." After this event, Abu Bakr was given the title "*Siddiq*" which means "the ratifier."

PRAYER, THE GIFT OF MI'RAJ

Just as people bring back presents from a holiday to their loved ones, our Prophet returned from the holy Mi'raj trip with important glad tidings and gifts.

On the night of Mi'raj, our Prophet (salla Allāhu ʿalay-hi wa-sallam) ascended to Heaven, went into the presence of Allah and was bestowed with the divine revelation without any medium. He was given three things there:

1) The last two verses of Surah al-Baqarah (Amanarrasulu),

2) The glad tidings of *jannah* to His *ummah* to those who do not associate a partner to Allah,

3) The five daily prayers as a gift of Mi'raj.

One of the conditions of Islam and a pillar of the religion is prayer. It became *fard* on the night of Mi'raj.

QUESTIONS

1) What type of boycott decision did the polytheists agree to take upon the Muslims? How many years did this last?

2) When did Abu Talib and Khadijah die? What name was this year called?

3) Explain the travel of our Prophet to Taif.

4) Explain the first and second Aqaba Allegiances.

5) When did our Prophet ascend to Mi'raj?

6) What are the gifts of Mi'raj?

UNIT VI

THE HIJRAH AND THE FIRST YEARS IN MADINAH

Topics:

- The *Hijrah* of our Prophet from Makkah to Madinah
- How our Prophet was received in Madinah
- The construction of Masjid al-Nabawi
- The brotherhood between the Ansar and the Muhajirin
- The school of our Prophet and Ashab al-Suffa

THE HIJRAH OF OUR PROPHET FROM MAKKAH TO MADINAH (622)

In the history of Islam, the migration of our Prophet from Makkah to Madinah is called the *"hijrah."*

Upon the continuation of the suppression and tyranny by the polytheists, our Prophet gave Muslims permission to make the *Hijrah* from Makkah to Madinah. The Muslims commenced the migration to Madinah in groups. They left their homes they were born and they grew up, their property and wealth for the sake of religion. They ran to the light of hope that was burning in Madinah.

There was no one left in Makkah besides our Prophet, Abu Bakr, Ali and a few Muslims. Despite all of the difficulties, our Prophet carried out hHis duties completing 13 years of his prophethood in Makkah.

The polytheists were afraid that the people of Madinah would become Muslims and that the Muslims in Makkah would strengthen the development of a strong Islamic community by migrating to Madinah. They secretly gathered at a place called Dar al-Nadwah agreeing to a proposal by Abu Jahl to kill our Prophet in order to wipe out Islam from its root. To carry out this frightening decision, they selected one youth from each tribe. These youths who were armed, surrounded the Prophet's home and waited for him to emerge.

The secret decision of the polytheists to kill Him was notified to our Prophet by Jibril on behalf of Allah and Allah gave him permission to migrate. Our Prophet had Ali laid in His own bed and then walked to Abu

Bakr's house passing by the polytheists who had surrounded His house. Allah protected His Prophet. The armed polytheists did not see Him.

After getting ready for the road, our Prophet together with Abu Bakr went at night to Jabal Thawr and hid there in a cave. This was a distance of one and a half hours from Makkah. In the morning, they realized that our Prophet had left his home. Thereupon, the polytheists began to look everywhere. They promised to give a reward of a hundred camels to whoever found Muhammad.

The people looking for our Prophet followed the tracks on the road right to the front of the cave that our Prophet was hiding in. Yet, they saw that a spider had spun a web at the entry of the cave. They wanted to look inside until one of them said, *"If a person had gone inside, there wouldn't be a spider's web or the nest of a pigeon."* and then they turned away.

When the polytheists came in front of the cave, Abu Bakr anxiously said,

- They are going to see us oh Messenger of Allah.

Our Prophet replied:

- **Do not worry, Allah is with us.**

It is a miracle that a spider had spun a web and that a pigeon had made a nest and left an egg there on the branch of a tree. Allah the almighty protected His beloved Prophet with these miracles. Allah turned away the enemy who had come to the entry of the cave with a secret force.

After Prophet Muhammad and Abu Bakr stayed in the cave for three days, they left for Madinah. A tracker named Suraqa tracked them down. He rode his horse at them with all his strength. He got really close to them. Right at that moment the horse stumbled and he rolled on the ground. He stood up and rode his horse straight at them again however, this time the horse's legs were stuck in the sand up to its knees and he was hammered on the spot. A secret strength was pulling the horse back. When Suraqa saw this situation, he got frightened and regretted what he had done. He asked for forgiveness from our Prophet and returned. He stated to those coming from behind, *"I searched this area and there is no-one here."*, and made them return. Suraqa later became a Muslim.

Our beloved Prophet completed this historical journey in a week reaching the village of Quba near Madinah on Monday. He was welcomed here with great joy.

Our Prophet stayed here for more than ten days and had the Quba masjid built. As the masjid was being built, He carried stones with his blessed hands. He worked like a laborer.

This is the first masjid built in Islam's history. Ali, who left Makkah three days after our Prophet, reached him here.

HOW OUR PROPHET WAS RECEIVED IN MADINAH

Together with the Muslims who were with them, our Prophet left to go to Madinah from Quba one *jumu'ah*. When they came to the home of the Banu Salim tribe, it was time for zhuhr. Our Prophet informed Muslims that it was *fard* to perform the *jumu'ah* prayer. There, they performed the first *jumu'ah* prayer. After prayer, our Prophet later continued on the road to Madinah.

The people of Madinah lined both sides of the street with the joy of *Eid* to receive the honorable guest. As our Prophet passed, they said, "Please come in oh Messenger of Allah!", the little kids screamed with joy saying, "Allah's messenger has arrived!"

Our Prophet who was welcomed with great joy in Madinah stayed as a guest for about seven months at the home of Halid ibn Zayd, a.k.a. Abu Ayyub al-Ansari.

THE CONSTRUCTION OF MASJID AL-NABAWI

There was an empty piece of land next to Abu Ayyub al-Ansari's house. Our Prophet purchased this property and built a mosque on top of it with rooms around the sides to live in it himself. He then moved in to this house from where He was a guest.

This is the mosque that is visited by Muslims in Madinah, "Masjid al-Nabawi." While this mosque was being built, our Prophet carried mud bricks and worked on it himself.

THE BROTHERHOOD BETWEEN THE ANSAR AND THE MUHAJIRIN

The Muslims who migrated from Makkah to Madinah are called "*Muhajirin*." The native people of Madinah are called "*Ansar*" because they helped the *Muhajirin*.

The people of Madinah helped the *Muhajirin* who had left their wealth and property behind. They welcomed them warmly, provided them with shelter and shared their food.

In world history, it is impossible to find another community that showed such solidarity. This incident was an example to the world and is one of the great wonders of Islam.

Our Prophet made each *Muhajirin* a brother with another *Ansar*. This brotherhood was stronger than the ties of blood brothers.

In Islamic history, the *Ansar* and *Muhajirin* are always remembered with respect. They provided great service to our religion.

THE SCHOOL OF OUR PROPHET AND ASHAB AL-SUFFA

A covered area on one of the corners of Masjid al-Nabawi was called "Suffa." Those who sheltered there were called "Ashab al-Suffa."

The poor and the destitute who did not have a home stayed here. These people would work when they found a job to earn a living. When they could not find work, their needs were be met by our Prophet and the wealthy people of the Ashab. The people who married from this group would move to a different house and form a home.

Those who were here were always together with our Prophet. They would benefit from His wisdom. They would spend their days in worship and learning. The Suffa School was the first institution to provide Islamic education with our Prophet as the teacher of the *Ashab*. Abu Hurairah who narrated the most hadiths was a student of this school.

Those who were educated at the Suffa School included great scholars that could comprehend and explain Islam, the holy Qur'an and the hadiths very well. People who were assigned to explain Islam were sent from this school.

For this reason, this place carrying the name *Suffa* was the first Islamic school in history. The students who graduated from this school had an important responsibility in the spreading of Islam and the teaching of the religion.

QUESTIONS

1) What does *Hijrah* mean?

2) What were the reasons that our Prophet and the Muslims made the *Hijrah*?

3) Explain *Hijrah and* the miracles shown to the Prophet at the time of the *Hijrah*.

4) What was the name of the first mosque built in Islamic history?

5) How was our Prophet received in Madinah and whose house was He a guest in?

6) What is Masjid al-Nabawi and where was it built?

7) Who were referred to as *Ansar* and *Muhajirin*?

8) Who were the *Ashab al-Suffa* and what kind of service did they provide to Islam?

UNIT VIII

THE BATTLES OF OUR PROPHET (salla Allāhu 'alay-hi wa-sallam) (I)

Topics:

- The reasons for the battle of Badr
- The battle of Badr and its consequences
- The reasons for the battle of Uhud
- The battle of Uhud and its consequences
- The lessons to be learned from the battle of Uhud
- The reasons for the battle of the Trench
- The battle of Trench and its consequences
- The treaty of Hudaybiyyah
- The consequences of the treaty of Hudaybiyyah
- The "Invitation to Islam" letters sent to neighboring national rulers
- The conquest of Khaybar
- The visit to the Ka'bah (*Qada Umrah*)

THE REASONS FOR THE BATTLE OF BADR

Even after our Prophet settled in Madinah with the *Muhajirin*, the polytheists of Makkah did not abandon their hostilities. They came to the outskirts of Madinah and stole the camels of the Muslims. The polytheists sent a message to Abdullah ibn Ubbay asking him either to kill Muhammad or to remove Him from Madinah. They told that they would attack Madinah if he did not comply. On the other hand, they sent a big trade caravan to Damascus in preparation for a big war against the Muslims.

The Muslims had to be wise against this danger and take precautions. With the aim of stopping the departure of this caravan during the month of Ramadan in the second year of the *Hijrah*, our Prophet set off with an army of 305 people. The polytheists who heard this attacked Madinah with an army of 1,000 people. They stopped by when they arrived at a place called Badr taking control of the water supply there.

The Muslims had left Madinah not to start a war but to stop the caravan owned by the polytheists.

They heard that a great army of the enemy was coming from Makkah. Upon our Prophet consulting His Companions, He decided to encounter the enemy.

When they came to Badr, the army of Islam was forced to stay in a sandy field. There was no water here. The polytheists who had arrived earlier seized the place where the water was located. However, Allah helped them, it rained a lot that night and the Muslims were saved from water troubles.

Our Prophet tried to spread Islam with pleasant words showing them the right way without forcing anyone. However, the Muslims were given permission by Allah to wage war against the attacks of the polytheists.

THE BATTLE OF BADR AND ITS CONSEQUENCES

(2nd year of the Hijrah/Year 624 of the Gregorian calendar)

The polytheists were more superior to the Muslims in numbers (soldiers) and from weapons' perspective. For this reason, they seemed confident that they were going to win this battle without taking the spiritual strength of the Muslims into account. Justice and superstition, worship and curse would clashed there. The future of Islam was dependent on the result of this battle.

The following morning both armies confronted each other and the war started. At that moment, our Prophet raised His hands to the sky and made the following *dua*:

"O Allah! Give me the help that you promised today." Later, He performed the *sajda* and begged Allah the Almighty as follows; **"O Allah, if this handful of Muslims are destroyed today, there will be no one left on earth to worship you."**

Allah the Almighty accepted His Prophet's *dua*.

The Muslims fought as heroes due to the strength that they gained from their faith and with Allah's help, they vanquished the enemy army who were far superior. The enemy lost 70 lives and left 70 hostages behind. Islam's greatest enemy Abu Jahl was amongst the dead. As such, the war ended with certain victory for the Muslims. At this war, 14 Muslims became martyrs.

The army of Islam returned to Madinah with the joy of victory. Our Prophet commanded that the hostages be treated well. A portion of the hostages was released on the payment of a ransom.

Each of the hostages who could not find the ransom amount and knew how to read and write were released after teaching ten Muslims how to read and write. These actions of our Prophet showed the importance that Islam places on reading and writing.

THE REASONS FOR THE BATTLE OF UHUD

The defeat of the polytheists at the battle of Badr brought great sadness to Makkah. The polytheists had begun to mourn. Abu Lahab who was the most hostile towards our Prophet died because of this sorrow.

To avenge the loss at Badr, the polytheists prepared an army of 3,000 people this time. Many women who had lost their loved ones at the battle of Badr had joined the army. Abu Sufyan who was the commander of the army took off abruptly from Makkah and set up their headquarters at Mount Uhud, which was situated near Madinah.

Our Prophet's uncle Abbas was not yet a Muslim at that stage and was in Makkah. He secretly advised our Prophet with a letter that the polytheists were going to walk upon Madinah. (Abbas, whom our Prophet loved very much, later became a Muslim)

THE BATTLE OF UHUD AND ITS CONSEQUENCES

(3rd year of *Hijrah*/Year 625 of the Gregorian calendar)

As it was stated in the letter, the enemy army had actually come up to Mount Uhud and set up their headquarters there. Thereupon, our Prophet discussed the situation with His companions and took off to Mount Uhud where the enemy army was located with the strength of 1,000 people. On the way, a group of 300 hypocrites left the army and returned leaving the count of Muslims at 700 people.

When the Muslims arrived to where the enemy was located, they organized themselves keeping Mount Uhud behind them. The army of Islam had a valley located on their left. To avert a threat that could come from that direction by an enemy attack, our Prophet placed a force of fifty archers and gave them the following command: **"No matter whether the enemy wins or loses, do not leave your places without receiving a command from me. When the enemy cavalier arrives, fire your arrows."**

The Muslims clashed gallantly against the enemy army and defeated them. The women who were part of this army began dispersing towards the mountains.

However, the battle was not won yet. They were supposed to follow the enemy to make sure of the result.

However, the Muslims had thought that the battle had been won and people began collecting the booty that the enemy had left behind.

The group of fifty archers saw this and moved (except for a few) from their positions without listening to their commanders. However, our Prophet had told them not to move from their spots without receiving a command from him.

It served the polytheists well for the archer force to move from their spots. They quickly gathered themselves and attacked through the valley that had been left by the archers. The Muslims were in a difficult predicament against this attack. Because of the carelessness of the Muslims, it caused the loss of the battle that had already been won and the lives of many heroes of Islam who became martyrs, together with our Prophet's uncle, Hamza. Our Prophet's tooth was broken and His face was injured. Even at its most intense time of the battle, our Prophet was making *dua* as follows while wiping the blood off his face; **"O my Lord, forgive my nation... They do not know what they are doing."**

Here is the mercy and the love of people in our Prophet's heart...

The Muslims gave 70 martyrs at the battle of Uhud. The count of the dead polytheists was 22. The women in the Islamic army had shown great devotion during the battle servicing the soldiers by handing out water and bandaging their wounds.

Many years later while passing through the place where the battle of Uhud took place, our Prophet remembered that bitter day and spoke to those next to Him as follows: **"O Muslims! From now on, there is no possibility of worshipping the idols again. I am not worried about this at all. What I am afraid of is for you to worship this world."**

From this battle, the polytheists were victorious but withdrew from Uhud without achieving the results expected. The Muslims, who regathered, followed the enemy for a while. The enemy could not risk another battle and continued their road towards Makkah and the Muslims returned to Madinah.

THE LESSONS TO BE LEARNED FROM THE BATTLE OF UHUD

When the Muslims had won the battle initially, why did they later suffer defeat?

There are important lessons to be learnt by the Muslims from this.

Not listening to the word of elders, not following the orders of commanders and leaving guard duty, which is a sacred duty for personal benefit, are causes for an army to lose a battle. Not only do the people who make the mistake suffer, but also the whole nation suffers.

This is what occurred at the battle of Uhud. The archers placed on the valley did not follow the commands of the Prophet, they left their places of guard to collect the booty and caused the army of Islam to lose and fall into disaster.

This historic event is a warning for the Muslims.

THE REASONS FOR THE BATTLE OF THE TRENCH

After making the hijrah to Madinah, our Prophet made a treaty with the Jews who lived there. The people of the Banu Nadir tribe who lived near Quba started to make them feel uncomfortable after the battle of Uhud. They wanted to cancel the treaty with the Muslims. Besides, they even arranged an assassination to kill our Prophet. Upon this, the Jews were exiled from their homeland.

The notables of the Jewish community used this as an excuse, went to Makkah and made an agreement with the polytheists. Two years after the battle of Uhud, the polytheists marched upon Madinah with an army of 10,000 people under the command of Abu Sufyan. When our Prophet heard the news, he discussed the situation with His companions as usual. They decided to defend themselves by using a different strategy against the enemy.

THE BATTLE OF THE TRENCH AND ITS CONSEQUENCES

(5th year of *Hijrah*/Year 626 of the Gregorian calendar)

In defense of the city, the Muslims were going to dig trenches around the city and stop the enemy outside of Medina. In an intensive work, the trench was dug in six days with the help of our Prophet.

The enemy army were surprised when they came to Madinah and saw the trench. They looked for a place to pass but they did not succeed. The Muslims held guard night and day preventing the advancement of the enemy. Our Prophet himself would hold guard until mornings.

As the siege of the enemy army dragged on, famine and drought began to appear in Madinah. The Muslims suffered great difficulties. They were in trouble with the cold and hunger as the season was winter.

It had been twenty-seven days since the siege had started. On the last day of the siege, our Prophet begged Allah as follows:

"O Allah, My Lord who sent us the Qur'an... The one who settles accounts with the enemy swiftly! Break this enemy society... Pulverize them... Shake their willpower O Allah..."

When our Prophet finished his *dua*, signs of happiness appeared on his face. His *dua* was accepted.

He gave the glad tidings to Muslims that Allah was going to help them.

Towards that evening, a very violent wind appeared on the side of enemy. Within a short period of time, this wind turned into a hurricane. The sand was striking into the face and eyes of the enemy and ripping off their tents. It knocked over the saucepans and blew out the fires. It was as if the strength of nature was battling with the enemy. This situation scared the enemy immensely. They could not endure anymore and the army of 10,000 people was defeated. They ran away that night in fear and terror leaving behind lots of food and property.

By morning, the hurricane had died down and there was no enemy left in Madinah or its vicinity. The Muslims praised Allah for saving them. After not achieving the results at the battle of Badr, Uhud and the Trench, the polytheists of Makkah realized that they could not extinguish the divine light of Islam. After this, they did not attack the Muslims again.

THE TREATY OF HUDAYBIYYAH

(6th year of *Hijrah*/Year 628 of the Gregorian calendar)

The Muslims who migrated from Makkah to Madinah had yearned for the homes that they had grown up in and wanted to visit the sacred Ka'bah. Our Prophet set off to go to Makkah and visit the Ka'bah in the sixth year of the *Hijrah* with a group of 1400 people. When the people of Makkah received news of this situation, they agreed not to let the Muslims in.

Upon this, the Muslims stopped at a place called Hudaybiyyah. Our Prophet sent Hazrat Uthman to Makkah as a messenger to state that they wanted to visit the Ka'bah. The people of Makkah did not give permission for the Muslims to visit and wanted them to delay this to the following year.

After long meetings, the Muslims and polytheists made an agreement with the following conditions:

1) The Muslims were going to return to Madinah this year without visiting the Ka'bah.

2) They could come to Makkah the following year but not stay there longer than three days.

3) The Muslims were to come to Makkah without weapons.

4) The Muslims were not allowed to take any Muslims from Makkah to Madinah however, if the people of Madinah wanted to stay in Makkah, they would be able to.

5) If any Muslims or polytheists of Makkah were to go to Madinah, they were to be returned. However, they did not have to return any Muslims if they return to the Quraysh side.

6) The Arab tribes could join in whichever side they wanted.

After the treaty, our Prophet returned to Madinah together with the Muslims without visiting the Ka'bah.

THE CONSEQUENCES OF THE TREATY OF HUDAYBIYYAH

The treaty conditions at first looked very harsh for the Muslims. Nevertheless, our Prophet accepted these conditions because He knew that this treaty would be very beneficial to the Muslims. Indeed, it eventuated like this. On the return to Madinah, Surah Al-Fath was revealed. In this *surah*, Allah the almighty was giving the glad tidings of a great victory to the Muslims. By signing this treaty, the polytheists of Makkah recognized the existence of Muslims for the first time.

After a short while, some of the people of Makkah became Muslims and came to Madinah. However, in accordance with the conditions of the treaty, the polytheists wanted them to be returned. After this, those who became Muslims and escaped Makkah commenced gathering at a place between Makkah and Madinah as they were not allowed to go to Madinah. This was an important place where the caravan of traders of Makkah passed.

In time, a strong Muslim community developed here. They started to fear this situation as the roads of the traders of Makkah were in danger. By sending a messenger to our Prophet, they wanted to change a clause of the treaty and allow the Muslims of Makkah to go to Madinah. Our Prophet accepted this request. This way, a clause that initially seemed to be harmful to the Muslims was changed and removed at the request of the polytheists.

With the Treaty of Hudaybiyyah, the tension between the Muslim and polytheists was defused. The danger that might come from the polytheists' side was disappeared. The Muslim found peace. The voice of Islam started to be heard. Some important people of Makkah came to Madinah and became Muslims. This treaty provided Muslims to increase and get stronger. It provided Islam to spread everywhere.

THE "INVITATION TO ISLAM" LETTERS SENT TO NEIGHBORING NATIONAL RULERS

Our Prophet (Sall Allāhu ʿalay-hi wa-sallam) was sent as a Prophet to all of humankind. For this reason, after the treaty of Hudaybiyyah, the duty of conveying Islam to the world commenced. Messengers were sent to the Byzantine emperor, the leaders of Iran, Egypt, Habashistan, Oman and Bahrain. He sent them letters of invitation to Islam. Our Prophet had made a seal out of silver with the sentence **"Muhammadu'r Rasulullah"** on it. He stamped the bottom of the letters with this seal.

The ruler of Habashistan accepted Islam upon receiving the letter of invitation. The Byzantine emperor and the ruler of Egypt treated the messengers well, but did not accept Islam. Whereas the ruler of Iran acted disrespectfully and ripped up the letter with great anger. Not long after, this ruler was killed by his son hence receiving punishment for the disrespect showed towards the Prophet.

THE CONQUEST OF KHAYBAR

(6th year of *Hijrah*/Year 628 of the Gregorian calendar)

Khaybar was a place on the way to Syria where mainly Jews lived. There were seven castles there. Some of the Jews that were exiled from Madinah resided there. The Jews of Khaybar prepared a plan to attack Madinah.

Our Prophet sent a messenger to them and proposed an agreement. The Jews did not accept the proposal of our Prophet. They agreed with the Gatafan Arabs and attacked the Muslims. Before they could attack, the Muslims acted sooner setting off with an army of 1,600 people. They arrived to Khaybar within three days. When the Jews saw the Muslims, they retreated into their castles.

Here, our Prophet made the following *dua*:

"O my Lord, we want from you only what is good for this nation and this community. We take refuge in you from all the evil of the people of this place and what is inside."

Our Prophet first offered an agreement however, the Jews refused this. Upon this, the war commenced. The intense clash continued for 10 days and the castles were taken one by one. Hazrat Ali showed great bravery during this war. At one stage, he continued fighting after dropping his shield using a door as a shield that was there. 10 Muslims and 93 Jews died during the battle.

Some of the Muslim women contributed to the war by helping the soldiers with what they had earned by knitting, giving medication to the ill and distributing water to the soldiers in the battlefields.

The Jews were desperate and wanted peace. They offered to stay on their land and continue farming offering the Muslims half of the crop that they produced. Their requests were accepted. Our Prophet acted kindly towards the Jews. The Jews, however, gave a feast with the purpose of poisoning our Prophet. Our Prophet was informed by Allah that the food in the feast had been poisoned so He spat out the mouthful and escaped being poisoned.

THE VISIT TO THE KA'BAH (QADA UMRAH)

(7th year of *Hijrah*/Year 629 of the Gregorian calendar)

In accordance with the treaty of Hudaybiyyah one year ago, the Muslims were going to visit the Ka'bah on the seventh year of *hijrah*. Our Prophet departed from Medina for Makkah with a group of 2,000 Muslims. When they saw the Ka'bah, the Muslims were all in a big excitement. They called out the *takbeer* altogether. They visited the Ka'bah in accordance with the requirements and exited *ihram*. The following day our Prophet entered the Ka'bah. When the time for the *adhan* came, Bilal-i Habashi recited the *adhan* for Zhuhr with his sweet strong voice. Two thousand Muslims performed the Zhuhr prayer together with the congregation.

The Muslims returned after staying three days in Makkah. During this visit, the people of Makkah monitored the Muslims carefully.

The Muslims left a positive impact on the people of Makkah, with their cleanliness and good morality. The love for Islam began to grow inside them. Shortly afterwards, the Quraysh notables Khalid ibn Al-Walid and Amr ibn Al-As went to Madinah and became Muslims.

QUESTIONS

1) When and with whom was the battle of Badr done?

2) What were the reasons for the battle of Badr? What were its results?

3) When and where was the battle of Uhud?

4) What were the reasons for the battle of Uhud? How did it result?

5) What sort of lesson should the Muslims take from this battle?

6) When was the battle of The Trench, what were its reasons and its results?

7) When and with whom was the treaty of Hudaybiyyah and what sort of results were born?

8) Which national rulers did our Prophet send letters of invitation to?

9) When and how was Khaybar conquered?

10) When was the visit of the Ka'bah performed?

UNIT VIII

BATTLES OF OUR PROPHET (Sall Allāhu 'alay-hi wa-sallam) (II)

Topics:

- The conquest of Makkah
- The battle of Hunayn
- The battle of Autas and the siege of Taif
- The expedition of Tabouk
- Demolishment of Masjid-i Dhirar (Reading)
- Characteristics of our Prophet's battles
- Hajj Amirship of Hazrat Abu Bakr
- The Farewell Hajj
- The Farewell Khutbah
- Sections from our Prophet's historical farewell khutbah (Reading)
- Our Prophet's illness and death
- The events after our Prophet's death
- Our Prophet's children
- Asharah mubasharah
- Our Prophet's companions
- Our Prophet's high morality that holds light to humankind

THE CONQUEST OF MAKKAH

(8th year of *Hijrah*/Year 630 of the Gregorian calendar)

The people of Makkah did not adhere to the treaty of Hudaybiyyah. Our Prophet sent them a notice wanting them to adhere to the conditions of the treaty. The people of Makkah insisted not to adhere to the treaty conditions. After not being able to achieve the results from the meetings held, our Prophet (Sall Allāhu ʿalay-hi wa-sallam) decided to conquer Makkah. He prepared an army of 10,000 soldiers in the 8th year of the *Hijrah* and marched upon Makkah in the month of Ramadan.

The people of Makkah did not have the strength to oppose the Muslims. The army of Islam entered Makkah through four sides. Our Prophet wanted

Makkah taken without any bloodshed. Therefore, He told the following to the soldiers:

"Do not spill blood, do not engage in armed battle!"

It eventuated as He said and Makkah was conquered without any bloodshed. Our Prophet went to Al-Masjid Al-Haram, had the idols cleaned out of the Ka'bah and gave an important sermon to the people gathered there. In His sermon, our Prophet mentioned:

After explaining the oneness of Allah, the equality of people and the previous feuds being lifted, He then recited the *ayah* with the following meaning:

"O humankind! We have created you from a male and a female, and made you into nations and tribes, that you may know one another. Verily, the most honorable of you with Allah is the most righteous of you. Verily, Allah is All-Knowing, All-Aware." [1]

The people of Makkah who heard these words were the ones who had tried to kill our Prophet; inflicted unbearable torments on the first Muslims; and tried their best to extinguish the divine light of Islam. Now, they had bowed their heads and were waiting for the verdict about themselves.

Our Prophet (Sall Allāhu ʿalay-hi wa-sallam) asked the following:

O people of Quraysh! What do you think I am going to do with you?

They said,

"You are a noble and honorable brother."

Our Prophet (Sall Allāhu ʿalay-hi wa-sallam) showed His greatness here by stating, **"You will not be condemned today, you are all free."** and forgiving them all.

The great Prophet, who conquered Makkah with immense mercy and forgiveness, also conquered the hearts. He gave people great lessons of good morality and virtue. Bilal-i Habashi recited the *adhan* from the roof of the Ka'bah for the Zhuhr prayer on the day Makkah was conquered. After performing prayer, our Prophet went on top of the Safa hill where the new Muslims had gathered. First the men and then the women pledged their allegiance to our Prophet.

1. Surah Al-Hujurat 49/13

THE BATTLE OF HUNAYN

(8th year of *Hijrah*/Year 630 of the Gregorian calendar)

With the conquest of Makkah, the Ka'bah was cleaned from the idols and most of the polytheists became Muslims. The light of Islam was spreading quickly throughout the world.

The Hawazin tribe lived on the outskirts of Makkah. They were a large tribe who worshipped idols. After the idols were broken in Makkah, they decided to fight with the Muslims thinking that the turn of their own idols had come.

In preparation for an attack, an army of 20,000 gathered at a place between Makkah and Taif called Hunayn.

Our Prophet had not yet returned to Madinah from Makkah. After receiving word of the enemy's preparation, He gathered an army of 12,000 soldiers and set off to where the enemy was at Hunayn.

The enemy had set a trap in a narrow valley. The Muslims relied on their numbers and did not take the required precautions. As the army of Islam passed the valley during the twilight hours of the morning, they were violently attacked by the enemy who had ambushed them. The army of Islam was spoiled and they began to disperse. This situation was very dangerous for the future of Islam.

There was only one hero left standing on that battlefield resisting the violent attacks of the enemy army with courage. That person was our Prophet Muhammad (Sall Allāhu ʿalay-hi wa-sallam).

Our Prophet (Sall Allāhu ʿalay-hi wa-sallam) called the dispersed Muslim soldiers next to Him. The army of Islam who heard His voice regathered and moved to attack the enemy. The enemy army were surprised against this ruthless attack. They began to disperse and run away. Whilst the Muslims were almost defeated briefly at the start, they were triumphant again later which they were very happy about. The enemy ran away leaving many hostages, thousands of camels, sheep and a large amount of silver on the battlefield.

This battle was won with the courage, determination and perseverance of our Prophet (Sall Allāhu ʿalay-hi wa-sallam).

THE BATTLE OF AUTAS AND THE SIEGE OF TAIF

(8th year of *Hijrah*/Year 630 of the Gregorian calendar)

The Muslims chased the enemy who ran away from Hunayn to a place called Autas. There, they caught and knocked out the army who were regathering, and acquired certain victory. The enemy could not regather after this. The Muslims had four martyrs and they had killed 70 soldiers of the enemy.

THE SIEGE OF TAIF

At the battle of Hunayn, Malik ibn Avf, the leader of the polytheists' army, took refuge at the castle in Taif. Upon this, the army of Islam surrounded the castle of Taif. The people of Taif closed the gates of the castle and defended themselves. The siege lasted about one month without a success. The Muslims called off the siege, and returned to Makkah.

Later on, however, the people of Taif abandoned worshipping idols and accepted Islam.

Our Prophet left behind Muadh ibn Jabal to teach the new Muslims in Makkah the holy Qur'an and Islam, and returned to Madinah together with His companions.

THE EXPEDITION OF TABOUK

(9th year of *Hijrah*/Year 630 of the Gregorian calendar)

Tabouk is a place between Madinah and Damascus. After Makkah was conquered, Islam began to spread very quickly.

To prevent the spreading of Islam, the Byzantine emperor commenced preparations for war and the Arab Christians gave their support to him.

The Muslims who heard this started to gather volunteer soldiers. Hazrat Abu Bakr and Hazrat Uthman gave great assistance in supplying the army. The women participated by donating their ornaments. To disperse the enemy forces, our Prophet set off from Madinah with an army of 30,000 soldiers. They came to Tabouk after passing over the desert for hundreds of kilometers in the heat of summer. The enemy avoided battle and retreated into their castles. When no one confronted the Muslims, a battle was not required and the army of Islam returned. Thus, they intimidated the enemy and achieved the expected result from the expedition.

READING:

DEMOLISHING OF MASJID AL-DHIRAR

The munafiqs built a masjid in the vicinity of Madinah to split the congregation of the Quba masjid in order to disunite the Muslims and to prepare a place for Abu Amir, an adversary of Islam.

Abu Amir was at war against our Prophet at Uhud and Hunayn and when he could not get a result, he ran away to Damascus. He sent a message to the munafiqs stating; ***"Arm yourselves as much as possible, be prepared, build me a place of worship, I am going to the Byzantine Emperor, I will come with a great army to expel Muhammad and His companions from Madinah."***

With the encouragement of this man, the munafiqs built the Masjid al-Dhirar. The Munafiq wanted to gather here rather than at our Prophet's masjid, saying that they could not travel there due their old age and illnesses. This building, which looks like a mosque from the outside, was actually a sinister home built to disunite the Muslims.

The munafiqs invited our Prophet to come and open the masjid that they had built. Allah almighty notified through Jibril that the masjid was built for evil purposes to disunite the Muslims. Upon this, our Prophet on return from the Tabouk expedition had the masjid knocked down and burnt. Thus, the munafiqs could not attain their evil wishes. In the meantime, Abu Amir died in a miserable state in Damascus.

CHARACTERISTICS OF OUR PROPHET'S BATTLES

Our Prophet invited people to Islam with kind words without being rude or harsh. On the contrary, the polytheists carried out all sorts of harm to our Prophet and His followers. Many Muslims suffered an unbearable degree of torture due to their religious beliefs and some were ruthlessly killed.

The Muslims endured this inhumane treatment for exactly thirteen years. In the end, they were forced to leave the nation where they were born and grew up, and migrate to Madinah. However, they did not leave the Muslims in Madinah in peace. In this situation, the Muslims had no choice but to fight and defend themselves. Upon this, the *ayah* that gave permission to battle was revealed in the second year of the *hijrah*. The meaning of these *ayahs* were:

"Permission to fight has been given to those who are being fought, because they were wronged. And indeed, Allah is competent to give them victory." [2]

"Fight in the way of Allah those who fight you but do not transgress. Indeed, Allah does not like transgressors." [3]

Whether from these *ayahs* or the battles that our Prophet fought, we see the following characteristics.

1) Our Prophet's battles did not have the intention of attacking because Islam is a religion of peace.

2) These battles were to prevent the attacks of the enemy and exalt the name of Allah. They were defensive battles to protect the religion, lives and the wealth of Muslims.

HAJJ AMIRSHIP OF HAZRAT ABU BAKR

(9th year of *Hijrah*/Year 631 of the Gregorian calendar)

When the *hajj* season arrived in the 9th year of the *Hijrah*, our Prophet (Sall Allāhu ʿalay-hi wa-sallam) sent Hazrat Abu Bakr as the *hajj amir* with the 300 people who had gathered to make the *hajj*. He also sent Hazrat Ali from behind.

Hazrat Ali explained how the *hajj* was going to be performed notifying them:

"From now on, it has been banned for anyone who worships idols to perform hajj and to make tawaf the Ka'bah in a nude fashion."

That year, for the first time in the history of Islam the *hajj* was performed in accordance with the principals of Islam.

2. Surah Al-Haj, 22/39
3. Surah Al-Baqarah 2/190

THE FAREWELL HAJJ

(9th year of *Hijrah*/Year 631 of the Gregorian calendar)

After Makkah was conquered, Islam spread quickly. The belief in the oneness of Allah settled thoroughly in the hearts. The people who saw salvation in Islam came themselves in groups and became Muslims. Our Prophet (Sall Allāhu ʿalay-hi wa-sallam), who saw the auspicious results of the honorable struggle for 23 years, performed the *hajj* in the tenth year of the *Hijrah* with more than a hundred thousand people.

Our Prophet (Sall Allāhu ʿalay-hi wa-sallam) addressed roughly 124 thousand Muslims at Arafat and recited His renowned khutbah. This was called His "Farewell Khutbah." After this khutbah, the *ayah* with the following meaning was revealed,

"This day I have perfected for you your religion and completed my favor upon you and have approved for you Islam as religion."[4]

Our Prophet realized that His journey to the hereafter had approached. He farewelled the Muslims here as He knew that He would not be able to perform the *hajj* again. For this reason, it was called the "Farewell hajj" by our Prophet.

Our Prophet returned to Madinah after completing His *hajj* duties together with other Muslims.

THE FAREWELL KHUTBAH

This khutbah notified the principals of equality laying the foundations of the true meaning of tranquility and happiness. As there were no devices like speakers then, each sentence our Prophet spoke was repeated by another person loudly which the whole congregation could hear instantly. This khutbah brought important provisions to protect the rights of humans much before the universal charter of human rights.

The provisions in the farewell khutbah includes:

1) Pre-Islamic customs of ignorance are abolished.

---

4. Surah Al-Ma'idah 5/3

2) All people are equal. A person can be superior to another only with his taqwa in Allah.

3) Life, wealth and honor are sacred and protected from all sorts of breach.

4) Entrustments are advised to be returned to their owners.

5) All forms of interest are made haram.

6) Blood feuds have been lifted.

7) The men must protect the rights of women and the women must respect the rights of men. Both men and women must avoid adultery.

8) All Muslims are made brothers. It is haram to breach the rights of your religious brother.

9) All servants must be treated well.

READING:

Parts from our Prophet's historical farewell khutbah:

O People!

Lend me an attentive ear, for I know not whether after this year, I shall ever be amongst you here again.

PEOPLE!

Just as you regard this day as sacred, just as you regard this month as sacred, just as this city (Makkah) is sacred;

your life, property and honor are also sacred, it is protected from all invasions.

MY COMPANIONS!

You will indeed meet your Lord tomorrow and will certainly be interrogated on your situation and actions. Do not return to your previous perversions after I go and decapitate each other. Those who are here listening to my last will should notify those who are not here. It could be that the person conveyed could better understand and protect than those who were here.

MY COMPANIONS!

Return the goods entrusted to you to their rightful owners. All forms of usury (interest) is lifted and is under my feet. However, you are still required to pay your actual debt. Do not inflict nor suffer any cruelty. From now on, usury is prohibited with the command of Allah. All types of these ugly customs of ignorance are under my feet.

MY COMPANIONS!

All blood feuds harbored from the era of ignorance has been completely lifted.

PEOPLE!

Today, satan has lost all hope that he will ever be able to influence or control you forever. However, you will make him pleased even if you obey him with the small sins asides from the things I have lifted. Avoid these to protect your religion.

PEOPLE!

I recommend you to look after women rights and be afraid of Allah with regard to this. You have taken them as your wives only under Allah's trust. Their honor and chastity became halal to you after promising in the name of Allah. You have rights over your women and they have rights over you. Your rights over your women is for them not to let anyone you dislike violate your family.

O MU'MINS

I leave behind me an entrustment to which if you hold on tightly, you will not stray from your road. That entrustment is Allah's book, the holy Qur'an. MU'MINS! Listen to my words very carefully and learn by your hearts. Every Muslim is a brother to every Muslim. As such, all Muslims are brothers. Nothing that belongs to a fellow Muslim shall be legitimate to a Muslim unless it is given freely and willingly.

MY COMPANIONS!

Do not act cruelly to yourselves. You also have rights upon yourself.

PEOPLE!

Allah almighty has given their rights (in the Qur'an) to their rightful owners. There is no need to bequest the successor.

PEOPLE!

Your Lord is one, Your father is one. All of you are the sons of Adam and He is from clay. The most valued among you is one that shows the most respect to Allah. An Arab has no superiority over a non-Arab except with taqwa. PEOPLE, tomorrow they will ask me of you, what will you say?

"We will witness that you have executed the role of Allah's messenger, you have fulfilled your duty, you gave us bequests and advice." *(Upon this, our Prophet raised His index finger towards the sky and then turned it towards the congregation and commanded the following)* ***Be witness O my Lord. Be witness O my Lord. Be witness O my Lord.***

OUR PROPHET'S ILLNESS AND DEATH

(10th year of *Hijrah*/Year 632 of the Gregorian calendar)

Our Prophet performed the farewell *hajj,* returned to Madinah and soon after became ill. He realized that His duty had come to an end and that He would migrate from this world. His illness was getting worse each day. Whilst he was ill, He would go and perform prayer at the masjid when the adhan was recited. However, three days prior to His death, His illness became even worse. He could not go to the masjid. He commanded that Hazrat Abu Bakr be the imam for the congregation and lead the prayer.

His daughter Hazrat Fatimah visited her father every day. He gave His daughter this advice on His deathbed:

"O the daughter of the Prophet, look to carry out auspicious deeds to save you from the responsibilities of the hereafter. You will not gain anything from being the daughter of a Prophet. I cannot save you from the terror of that day."

On a day His illness advanced, He said to His companions as follows, **"You will reunite with me again. The place that we will meet is on the edge of the Kawthar pond. Anyone who wants to meet me there should protect his hand and tongue from unnecessary tasks and words. It has been notified to me that my time to migrate from this world has come. I am happy that I will meet my Lord but I am also sad that I will be leaving my *ummah*. I have received my news. I am going to Allah."**

With the help of some of His companions, He came to the masjid two days prior to His death. He turned His face towards the congregation and said:

"O Muslims! If by chance I caused any of you harm, I am ready to receive its reciprocation.

- **Whomever I have hit, here is my back, come and hit it.**

- **Whoever has a debt owed by me, here is my wealth, come and get your right.**

When our Prophet's illness eased a little one Monday morning on June 8, He went to the masjid. He performed the Fajr prayer with the congregation following the lead of Hazrat Abu Bakr from where He was sitting. His illness increased when He returned home from the masjid. At mid-morning that day, He supplicated as follows: **"O my Lord! Give me ease against the severity of death. Take my life with sweetness."** There was water in a container next to Him. He put His hand in the water and cooled down His blessed face.

Finally, towards noon He raised His hand. He pointed His shahada finger upwards and said, **"To the Highest Companion (Refik-i Ala)."** This was His last words.

Allah's messenger submitted His blessed soul to His Lord at the age of 63 (Monday, 12th Rabi Al-awwal 10th year of Hijrah –June 8, 632 of the Gregorian Calendar).

Our Prophet (Salla Allāhu ʿalay-hi wa-sallam) was buried where He died. The place in Madinah where His grave is located is called "Rawda-i Mutahhara." Of the 23 years of Prophethood, our beloved Prophet (Salla Allāhu ʿalay-hi wa-sallam) spent 13 years in Makkah and 10 years in Madinah. He worked for the happiness of people. As the last Prophet, He duly performed His duties and migrated from this world.

Whatever the world owns, is a given from Him;
His community is indebted to Him, the individual is indebted to Him,
All of humankind is indebted to this Innocent
O my Lord, assess us with this confession at Armageddon.

Mehmet Akif ERSOY

THE EVENTS AFTER OUR PROPHET'S DEATH

The death of our Prophet brought about deep sorrow among Muslims. Al-Madinah Al Munawwara was wrapped in mourning. Some of the Companions did not want to believe in his death. At that time, Abu Bakr approached, uncovered our Prophet's face, kissed it and then cried. Later, he made a short statement and calmed the Companions down.

After long meetings the same day, Abu Bakr was selected as the first caliph. The following Tuesday the Muslims gathered at the *masjid* and pledged allegiance to Abu Bakr.

On Tuesday, one day after the death of our Prophet (salla Allāhu ʿalay-hi wa-sallam), he was buried where he had died.

When our Prophet (salla Allāhu ʿalay-hi wa-sallam) became ill, he had seven dirhams with Him. He had this money distributed as sadaqah among the poor. When he died, he did not have any money so he did not leave behind any monetary inheritance.

The greatest inheritance that he left was to pull the world out of darkness and enlighten it through the divine light of Islam, morality, which attained true tranquility and happiness for people and the principals of virtue.

How happy it is for people going through the divine road shown by the holy Qur'an and drawn by our Prophet....

Days of bliss however,
Absolute judiciary seen in the world,
Your wings spread to the ground,
It is mercy, to everybody,
Morality attained the era of spring,
The ground was beautified, the horizon cleared,
Your virtue spread to the universe,
The ground perished to the sky,
There is no example in the history of humankind,
His imagination lives in every language,
Take a summary of the feature word;
It was humankind, however more virtuous than angels.

Mustafa Femi GERÇEKER

OUR PROPHET'S CHILDREN

Our Prophet was father to seven children. Of these, three were male and four were female.

His male children; Qasim, Abdallah and Ibrahim.

His female children; Zainab, Ruqayyah, Umm Kulthum and Fatimah.

Six of them were from Khadijah and his son Ibrahim was given birth to by Maria.

Qasim and Abdallah died at a young age prior to His prophethood. Our Prophet (salla Allāhu ʿalay-hi wa-sallam) was saddened by the death of his children. Another *kunya* (name) for our Prophet was "Abu al-Qasim." That means, the father of Qasim. Our Prophet (Salla Allāhu ʿalay-hi wa-sallam) liked this name. He found consolation because it was a reminder of his son who had passed away.

His other son Ibrahim was born in Madinah after the *Hijrah*. He also died at a young age. Upon the death of his son, our Prophet wept with sadness and said:

"The eye fills with tears, the heart saddens. We cannot say a word except what is appropriate with Allah in attaining His consent. Oh Ibrahim, we are in deep sorrow for losing you."

There was an eclipse of the sun on the day Ibrahim died. Some people said, "The eclipse of the sun had occurred because of Ibrahim's death." Our Prophet notified them that this thought was incorrect and said:

"Without a doubt, the sun and the moon are two orders of the signs of Allah. They do not eclipse because of anybody's death or birth."

All of our Prophet's daughters grew up and married. Apart from Fatimah, his three other daughters passed away before him. His youngest daughter Fatimah married Ali. Our Prophet's progeny continued from her descent.

ASHARAH MUBASHARAH

Our Prophet (salla Allāhu ʿalay-hi wa-sallam) gave the glad tidings that ten of his Companions will enter paradise directly. They are called "Asharah Mubasharah", which means "The ten people who are given the glad tidings of paradise."

Their names are as follows:

1) Abu Bakr
2) Umar
3) Uthman
4) Ali

5) Talha

6) Zubayr

7) Abdurrahman ibn Auf

8) Sa'ad ibn abi Waqqas

9) Said ibn Zayd

10) Abu-Ubaida ibn al-Jarrah

OUR PROPHET'S COMPANIONS

The people who die as Muslims after seeing our Prophet are called "Companions" (*Ashab*).

There are two types of companions:

1) Muhajirin: With the aim of performing their religious duties in order to escape from the torment of the polytheists, the Muslims who migrated from Makkah to Madinah are called "Muhajirin."

2) Ansar: The people of Madinah who helped the Muslims who migrated from Makkah are called "Ansar."

The name "Ansar" was given to them due to their assistance to the *Muhajirin*.

OUR PROPHET'S (salla Allāhu ʿalay-hi wa-sallam) HIGH MORALS THAT BROUGHT LIGHT TO HUMANKIND

Our Prophet Muhammad (salla Allāhu ʿalay-hi wa-sallam), the most loved servant of Allah, the last and greatest Prophet was born as the bliss of sunshine. Just as water revives the land, Allah the Almighty gave life to the world again with our Prophet.

Thanks to the light of faith that He placed in the hearts, incorrect beliefs were erased, instead of ignorance education is flourished, instead of cruelty justice is dominated, instead of hostility and enmity friendship is grew. In a true sense, the Islamic brotherhood has been formed. Women reached their true value they are worth in the family and community.

Our beloved Prophet showed people the ways to attain happiness in this world and in the hereafter. While teaching, He led the best example, by applying the principals of morality firstly on his life. Our Prophet's heart was filled with the love of people. He was so merciful that He would give what He had in His hands to the poor and remain hungry himself. He was also compassionate and merciful towards animals, and gave water to a thirsty cat in his own hands and commanded that we treat animals well.

Our Prophet loved His children a lot. He would caress them and sit them on his lap.

A man who saw our Prophet kiss and love a child said, "I have ten children and I have never kissed any of them."

Our Prophet replied, **"Whoever is not merciful to others will not be treated mercifully."**

Even whilst performing prayer, He showed tolerance when His grandchildren Hasan and Husayn climbed on His shoulders to play games, by keeping still until they had finished

He was extremely humble. He did not differentiate between rich or poor. He would go even if a maid invited him, and he would sit and eat with the poor. He would go to the house of the poorest people and ask about their situation and feelings.

He would visit the poor and make *dua* for them to recover. When He went into a gathering, he would sit wherever he found an empty spot and never stretched His legs towards others.

A man came to visit our Prophet and started to shiver when he became excited in his presence. Upon this, our Prophet said to him, **"Do not shiver my friend! I am not a ruler. I am the son of a Qurayshi woman who fed herself with dry bread."**

He would patch his own clothing, fix his shoes, go to the market and buy the things he needed and take it back home himself. He would not be a burden on anyone.

Our beloved Prophet was an exemplary family head. He would act extremely kind to women and assist them in their household chores. He commanded:

"The best of you are the ones who treat women well."

Our Prophet loved visitors and He would serve them himself. He would also act the same way towards non-Muslims who would visit him.

He never said any harmful words to anybody, never acted harshly or scolded anyone throughout his life.

Enes who was a servant of our Prophet for ten years said, *"Our Prophet never even said "uff" to me. He never said to me for something that I did, why did I do it or for something I did not do, why did I not do it, He never scolded me.*"

Our Prophet was smiley-faced and soft-worded. He would listen to others when they spoke without interrupting. He would not throw the faults of others in their face.

Our Prophet's lifestyle was plain and clean. He would always keep his body and clothes clean and would use a *miswak* to clean his teeth. He would dislike messiness and dirtiness. He would tell his Companions to come to the *masjid* in a clean state.

On one occasion, he said to those that came in a dirty state to the mosque: **"It would have been better had you have come after washing."**

Our Prophet spoke truthfully. He would keep His promises all the time. He disliked liars. Due to his rightness and trustworthiness, He was called "Muhammad al-Amin", i.e. "Trustworthy Muhammad."

He was the most generous of all people. He would not turn down anyone who asked something of him, saying, "**I am only a distributor, the giver is Allah**." However, he did not like beggars and showed them ways that they could escape from poverty.

He would not seek revenge from anybody and loved to forgive. He would even do well to those who treated Him badly. He would never forget any good deeds done towards him and he would always remember those who did good deeds. He would act respectfully towards the elderly and would show love and compassion towards the young ones. He would stand when he saw his nursing siblings, lay his vest on the floor and have them sit on it.

Our Prophet disliked laziness and those who sat idly. He carried stones when the *masjid* was being built and He worked like a laborer. Even when his Companions wanted him to rest, he continued to work.

During a trip that he embarked on with his companions, they stopped the night to rest. They shared work duties amongst themselves to prepare dinner.

Our Prophet said, "**In that case, I will collect some stuff to burn.**" He did not want to stay idle whilst his friends were working.

Even though our beloved Prophet had financial opportunities, he lived a simple life distributing his property and money among the poor. As such, He is an exemplary person for humankind showing people with his actions that social justice in the community is not simply words.

How happy it is for those following his path.

QUESTIONS

1) When was Makkah conquered and how did our Prophet (salla Allāhu ʿalay-hi wa-sallam) treat the polytheists?

2) Where was the battle of Hunayn fought? What were the causes and results of this battle?

3) What were the results of the battle of Autas and the siege of Taif?

4) When did our Prophet return from Makkah to Madinah?

5) What were the characteristics of the battles of our Prophet?

6) What is the *hajj amirship* of Abu Bakr?

7) When was the farewell *hajj* performed?

8) What principals were focused on during the farewell *khutbah*?

9) When and where did our Prophet (Salla Allāhu ʿalay-hi wa-sallam) die?

10) Where is our Prophet buried and what name was given to His grave?

11) How many children did our Prophet have and what were their names?

12) What is meant by *asharah mubasharah* and who were they?

13) Who were the Companions of our Prophet?

14) Explain the high morals of our Prophet.

WUDU *DUA*S

1) When commencing *wudu*: Recite the following *dua* after the "Auzu" and "Basmala":

اَلْحَمْدُ لِلّٰهِ الَّذِي جَعَلَ الْمَاءَ طَهُورًا وَجَعَلَ الْاِسْلَامَ نُورًا

Pronunciation: **Al hamdu lil lahil lazi ja'alal ma'a tahuran wa ja'alal islama nura.**

Meaning: All praise is due to Allah, Who made water purifying, and Islam with radiance.

2) While rinsing the mouth:

اَللّٰهُمَّ اسْقِنِي مِنْ حَوْضِ نَبِيِّكَ كَاْسًا لاَ اَظْمَأُ بَعْدَهُ أَبَداً

Pronunciation: **Allahumma'skini min huvzi nabiyyika ka'san la azmau ba'dahu abada**.

Meaning: O Allah! Allow me to drink with a bowl from the pool of our Prophet so that I shall never be thirsty again.

3) While washing the nose:

اَللّٰهُمَّ لاَ تَحْرِمْنِي رَايِحَةَ نَعِيمِكَ وَجَنَّاتِكَ

Pronunciation: **Allahumma la tahrimni rayihata naimika wa jannatik.**

Meaning: O Allah! Do not deprive me of the smell of your blessings and paradise.

4) While washing the face:

اَللّٰهُمَّ بَيِّضْ وَجْهِي بِنُورِكَ يَوْمَ تَبْيَضُّ وُجُوهٌ وَتَسْوَدُّ وُجُوهٌ

Pronunciation: **Allahumma bayyid wajhi binurika yawma tabyaddu wujuhun wa taswaddu wujuh.**

Meaning: O Allah! On the day when some faces will become white and some faces will become black, allow my face to be white.

5) While washing the right arm:

اَللّٰهُمَّ اَعْطِنِي كِتَابِي بِيَمِينِي وَحَاسِبْنِي حِسَابًا يَسِيرًا

Pronunciation: **Allahumma a'tini kitabi bi yamini wa hasibni hisaban yasira.**

Meaning: O Allah! Give me my book of deeds from the right hand side and judge me with an easy account.

6) While washing the left arm:

اَللّٰهُمَّ لاَ تُعْطِ كِتَابِي بِشِمَالِي وَلاَ مِنْ وَرَاءِ ظَهْرِى وَلاَ تُحَاسِبْنِي حِسَابًا شَدِيدًا

Pronunciation: **Allahumma la tu'ti kitabi bishimali wa la min wara'i zahri wa la tuhasibni hisaban shedida.**

Meaning: O Allah! Do not give me my book of deeds from the left side or from behind. Do not make my account difficult.

7) While performing the *masah* on the head:

اَللّٰهُمَّ غَشِّنِي بِرَحْمَتِكَ وَ اَنْزِلْ عَلَيَّ مِنْ بَرَكَاتِكَ

Pronunciation: **Allahumma ghashshini bi rahmatika wa anzil alayya min barakatik.**

Meaning: O Allah! Cover me with your mercy and bring upon me your blessings.

8) While performing *masah* over the ears:

اَللّٰهُمَّ اجْعَلْنِي مِنَ الَّذِينَ يَسْتَمِعُونَ الْقَوْلَ فَيَتَّبِعُونَ اَحْسَنَهُ

Pronunciation: **Allahummajalni minallazina yastami unal'kawla fa yattabi uno ahsanah.**

Meaning: O Allah! Allow me to hear the words of justice and conform to the best of the words.

9) While performing *masah* over the neck:

اَللّٰهُمَّ اَعْتِقْ رَقَبَتِي مِنَ النَّارِ

Pronunciation: **Allahumma a'tik rakabati minannar**.

Meaning: O Allah! Free my body from the hellfire.

10) While washing the feet:

اَللّٰهُمَّ ثَبِّتْ قَدَمَيَّ عَلَى الصِّرَاطِ يَوْمَ تَزِلُّ فِيهِ الْاَقْدَامُ

Pronunciation: **Allahumma thabbit qadamayya alassirati yawma tazillu fihil aqdam**.

Meaning: O Allah! Keep my feet firm on the bridge (to paradise) on the day when the feet will slip.

*DUA*S RECITED DURING PRAYER

Subhanaka:

It is recited during prayers whilst standing.

The places it is recited:

1) Always in the first *ra'kah* after the *iftitah takbir*,

2) When you rise at the beginning of the third *ra'kah* of the *sunnah* of the *asr* prayer prior to the *Fatihah*,

3) When you rise at the beginning of the third *ra'kah* of the *sunnah* of the *isha* prayer prior to the *Fatihah*,

4) When you rise at the beginning of the third *ra'kah* of the *Tarawih* prayer if it is being performed giving the *salām* in lots of four,

5) During the *janazah* prayer after the first *takbir*.

سُبْحَانَكَ اللّٰهُمَّ وَبِحَمْدِكَ وَتَبَارَكَ اسْمُكَ وَتَعَالٰى جَدُّكَ وَجَلَّ ثَنَاؤُكَ وَلَاۤ اِلٰهَ غَيْرُكَ

Pronunciation: **Subhanakallahumma wa bihamdik, wa tabarakasmuk, wa ta'ala jadduk (wa jallah thanauk), wa la ilaha ghayruk**.

Meaning: O Allah, how perfect You are and praise be to You. Blessed is Your name, and exalted is Your majesty. There is no god but You.

Note: The words "wa jalla thanauk" in brackets is recited during the *janazah* prayer.

Al-taḥiyyāt:

The places it is recited:

It is recited upon every sitting during prayer.

اَلتَّحِيَّاتُ لِلّٰهِ وَالصَّلَوَاتُ وَالطَّيِّبَاتُ اَلسَّلاَمُ عَلَيْكَ اَيُّهَا النَّبِيُّ وَرَحْمَةُ اللّٰهِ وَبَرَكَاتُهُ اَلسَّلاَمُ
عَلَيْنَا وَعَلٰى عِبَادِ اللّٰهِ الصَّالِحِينَ اَشْهَدُ اَنْ لآ اِلٰهَ اِلاَّ اللّٰهُ وَاَشْهَدُ اَنَّ مُحَمَّدًا عَبْدُهُ وَرَسُولُهُ

Pronunciation: **Attahiyaatu lillahi wassalawaatu, wattayyibaat. Assalaaamu alayka ayyuhan nabeeyu wa rahmatullahi wa barakaatuh. As salaamu alaynaa wa alaa ibaadilaahis saliheen.**

Ashhadu an laa ilaha illallah wa ashhadu anna muhammadan abduhu wa rasuluh.

Meaning: All worship performed with the tongue, body and wealth are for Allah. Peace be upon you, O Prophet, and the mercy of Allah and His blessings.

Peace be upon us and upon the righteous servants of Allah.

I bear witness that there is none worthy of worship but Allah and I bear witness that Muhammad is His servant and His messenger.

Allahumma Salli and Allahumma Barik:

The places it is recited:

1) After *al-taḥiyyāt* during the final sittings of each prayer,

2) After *al-taḥiyyāt* during the first sitting of the *sunnah* of the *asr* and *isha* prayers,

3) After *al-taḥiyyāt* during the sitting on the second *ra'kah*, where the *Tarawih* prayer is being performed giving the *salām* in lots of four,

4) During the *janazah* prayer after the second *takbir*.

اَللّٰهُمَّ صَلِّ عَلَى مُحَمَّدٍ وَعَلَى اٰلِ مُحَمَّدٍ كَمَا صَلَّيْتَ عَلَى اِبْرٰهِيمَ وَعَلَى اٰلِ اِبْرٰهِيمَ
اِنَّكَ حَمِيدٌ مَجِيدٌ

Pronunciation: **Allahumma salli ala Muhammadin wa ala ali Muhammad. Kama sallaita ala ibraheema wa ala ali ibraheem. Innaka hameedun majeed.**

Meaning: O Allah, let your mercy come upon Muhammad and the family of Muhammad as You have showed mercy upon Ibrahim and the family of Ibrahim. Surely You are the Praiseworthy, the Glorious.

اَللّٰهُمَّ بَارِكْ عَلَى مُحَمَّدٍ وَعَلَى اٰلِ مُحَمَّدٍ كَمَا بَارَكْتَ عَلَى اِبْرٰهِيمَ وَعَلَى اٰلِ اِبْرٰهِيمَ
اِنَّكَ حَمِيدٌ مَجِيدٌ

Pronunciation: **Allahumma barik ala Muhammadin wa ala ali Muhammad. Kama barakta ala ibraheema wa ala ali ibraheem. Innaka hameedun majeed**.

Meaning: O Allah, bless Muhammad and the family of Muhammad as You blessed Ibrahim and the family of Ibrahim. Surely You are the Praiseworthy, the Glorious.

Rabbana atina and Rabbana aghfirli

The places it is recited:

1) During the sittings after *Allahumma Salli* and *Allahumma Barik*,

2) Those who do not know the Qunut *dua* can recite the "Rabbana Atina" *ayah* during the *witr* prayer.

3) After the third *takbir* during the *janazah* prayer, those who do not know the *dua*s to be recited can instead recite the "Rabbana atina" verse with the intention of *dua*.

رَبَّنَا اٰتِنَا فِى الدُّنْيَا حَسَنَةً وَفِى الْاٰخِرَةِ حَسَنَةً وَقِنَا عَذَابَ النَّارِ. بِرَحْمَتِكَ
يَا اَرْحَمَ الرَّاحِمِينَ

Pronunciation: **Rabbana atina fiddunya hasanatan wa fil akhirati hasanatan waqina adhaban-nar. Birahmataka ya arhamarrahimin**.

Meaning: Our Lord, give us in this world that which is good and in the Hereafter that which is good and protect us from the punishment of the Fire.

رَبَّنَا اغْفِرْلِى وَلِوَالِدَىَّ وَلِلْمُؤْمِنِينَ يَوْمَ يَقُومُ الْحِسَابُ

Pronunciation: **Rabbanaghfirli wali waali dayya wa lil mu'minina yawma yaqumul hisaab.**

Meaning: Our Lord, forgive me, my mother, my father and the *mu'mins* on the Day of Judgment (the day in which everyone will give account).

The Qunut Duas:

After the hands are raised and the *takbir* is given after reciting the Fatihah and a surah during the third *ra'kah* of the *witr* prayer, the hands are again tied and the *Qunut dua* is recited.

اَللّٰهُمَّ اِنَّا نَسْتَعِينُكَ وَنَسْتَغْفِرُكَ وَنَسْتَهْدِيكَ ۝ وَنُؤْمِنُ بِكَ وَنَتُوبُ اِلَيْكَ ۝ وَنَتَوَكَّلُ عَلَيْكَ ۝ وَنُثْنِى عَلَيْكَ الْخَيرَ كُلَّهُ نَشْكُرُكَ وَلاَ نَكْفُرُكَ ۝ وَنَخْلَعُ وَنَتْرُكُ مَنْ يَفْجُرُكَ ۝

اَللّٰهُمَّ اِيَّاكَ نَعْبُدُ وَلَكَ نُصَلِّى وَنَسْجُدُ وَاِلَيْكَ نَسْعٰى وَنَحْفِدُ نَرْجُو رَحْمَتَكَ وَنَخْشٰى عَذَابَكَ اِنَّ عَذَابَكَ بِالْكُفَّارِ مُلْحِقٌ ۝

Pronunciation: **Allahumma inna nasta'inuka wa nastaghfiruka wa nastahdik. Wa nu'minu bika, wa natubu ilayk. Wa natawakkalu alayka wa nuthni alaykal-khayra kullahu nashkuruka wa la nakfuruk wa nakhlahu wa natruku man yafjuruk.**

Allahumma iyyaaka na'budu wa laka nusalli wa nasjudu, wa ilayka nas'a wa nahfidu narju rahmataka wa nakhsha adhaabaka inna adhaabaka bil kuffaari mulhiq.

Meaning: O Allah! Truly, we seek Your help and Your forgiveness of our sins. We seek guidance in the things that you are content with. We believe in and repent to You. We trust You. We praise you knowingly for all the blessings that you have given us. We thank You and are not ungrateful to You knowing that it is not from someone else.

We abandon those who deny Your blessings and disobey You.

O Allah! You alone do we worship and for You do we perform prayer and prostrate and we betake to please You and present ourselves for service in Your cause. We perform Your worship with joy. We hope for Your increased and continued mercy. We fear Your chastisement. Undoubtedly, Your torment will reach the infidels and the non-believers.

SURAHS RECITED DURING PRAYER[1]

***Surah al-Fatihah*:**

بِسْمِ اللّٰهِ الرَّحْمٰنِ الرَّحِيمِ ﴿١﴾

اَلْحَمْدُ لِلّٰهِ رَبِّ الْعَالَمِينَۙ ﴿٢﴾ اَلرَّحْمٰنِ الرَّحِيمِۙ ﴿٣﴾ مَالِكِ يَوْمِ الدِّينِۜ ﴿٤﴾ اِيَّاكَ نَعْبُدُ وَاِيَّاكَ نَسْتَعِينُۜ ﴿٥﴾ اِهْدِنَا الصِّرَاطَ الْمُسْتَقِيمَۙ ﴿٦﴾ صِرَاطَ الَّذِينَ اَنْعَمْتَ عَلَيْهِمْۙ غَيْرِ الْمَغْضُوبِ عَلَيْهِمْ وَلَا الضَّٓالِّينَ ﴿٧﴾

It is recited whilst standing during prayer.

Pronunciation: **Al hamdu lillaahi rabbil 'alameen. Ar-Rahman er-Raheem Maaliki yaumid Deen. Iyyaaka na'abudu wa iyyaaka nasta'een, Ihdinas siraatal mustaqeem Siraatal ladheena an 'amta 'alaihim Ghairil maghduubi 'alaihim waladdaalleen.**

Meaning: All praise is due to Allah, Lord of the worlds - The Entirely Merciful, the Especially Merciful, and Sovereign of the Day of Judgment. It is You we worship and You we ask for help. Guide us to the straight path - The path of those upon whom You have bestowed favor; not of those who have evoked Your anger or of those who are astray.

---

1 **Important explanation:** The pronunciation of the *surahs* has been written in English to make it easier to memorize for those people who do not know how to recite the Qur'an.

However, as the English alphabet does not encompass all the letters in the Arabic alphabet, it is not possible to learn the exact pronunciation with these letters. For this reason, it is necessary to learn these *surah*s and *dua*s without error from knowledgeable teachers by listening to their pronunciation from them.

One of the *fard*s of prayer is to recite the Qur'an. If we consider that incorrect pronunciation, where the meaning changes, could invalidate our prayer, then the importance of memorising these *surah*s correctly can be appreciated.

***Surah al-Fil*:**

This and the following *surahs* are recited after *al-Fatihah* whilst standing during prayer.

بِسْمِ اللّٰهِ الرَّحْمٰنِ الرَّحِيمِ

أَلَمْ تَرَ كَيْفَ فَعَلَ رَبُّكَ بِأَصْحَابِ الْفِيلِ ﴿١﴾ أَلَمْ يَجْعَلْ كَيْدَهُمْ فِي تَضْلِيلٍ ﴿٢﴾ وَأَرْسَلَ
عَلَيْهِمْ طَيْرًا أَبَابِيلَ ﴿٣﴾ تَرْمِيهِمْ بِحِجَارَةٍ مِنْ سِجِّيلٍ ﴿٤﴾ فَجَعَلَهُمْ كَعَصْفٍ مَأْكُولٍ ﴿٥﴾

Pronunciation: **Alam tara kayfa fa'ala Rabbuka bi ashabil fil. Alam yaj'al kaydahum fi tadlil. Wa arsala alayhim tayran ababil. Tarmihim bi hijaratin min sijjil. Faja alahum ka'asfin ma'kul.**

Meaning: Have you not considered, [O Muhammad], how your Lord dealt with the companions of the elephant? Did He not make their plan into misguidance? And He sent against them birds in flocks, striking them with stones of hard clay, And He made them like eaten straw.

***Surah al-Quraysh*:**

بِسْمِ اللّٰهِ الرَّحْمٰنِ الرَّحِيمِ

لِإِيلَافِ قُرَيْشٍ ﴿١﴾ إِيلَافِهِمْ رِحْلَةَ الشِّتَاءِ وَالصَّيْفِ ﴿٢﴾ فَلْيَعْبُدُوا رَبَّ هَٰذَا الْبَيْتِ ﴿٣﴾
الَّذِي أَطْعَمَهُمْ مِنْ جُوعٍ وَآمَنَهُمْ مِنْ خَوْفٍ ﴿٤﴾

Pronunciation: **Li ilafi Quraysh'in. Ilafihim rihlatashshitai wassayf. Falya'budu Rabba hadhalbayt. Alladhi at'amahum min ju'in wa amanahum min khawf.**

Meaning: For the accustomed security of the Quraysh - Their accustomed security in the caravan of winter and summer - Let them worship the Lord of this House(Ka'bah), Who has fed them, saving them from hunger and made them safe, saving them from fear.

Surah al-Ma'un:

بِسْمِ اللّٰهِ الرَّحْمٰنِ الرَّحِيمِ

اَرَاَيْتَ الَّذِي يُكَذِّبُ بِالدِّينِ ﴿١﴾ فَذٰلِكَ الَّذِي يَدُعُّ الْيَتِيمَ ﴿٢﴾ وَلَا يَحُضُّ عَلٰى طَعَامِ الْمِسْكِينِ ﴿٣﴾ فَوَيْلٌ لِلْمُصَلّ۪ينَ ﴿٤﴾ اَلَّذ۪ينَ هُمْ عَنْ صَلَاتِهِمْ سَاهُونَ ﴿٥﴾ اَلَّذ۪ينَ هُمْ يُرَٓاؤُنَ ﴿٦﴾ وَيَمْنَعُونَ الْمَاعُونَ ﴿٧﴾

Pronunciation: **Ara aytal-ladhi yukadh-dhibu biddin. Fadhalikal-ladhi yadu-u'l-yatim. Wala yahuddu ala ta'amil miskin. Fawaylul lil-musallin. Al-ladhina hum an salātihim sahun. Al-ladhina hum yuraa-'un. Wa-yamna-'unal-ma'un.**

Meaning: (O Muhammad) Have you seen the one who denies the Recompense? For that is the one who drives away the orphan and does not encourage the feeding of the poor. So woe to those who pray but who are heedless of their prayer. Those who make show of their deeds. They withhold simple assistance.

Surah al-Kawthar:

بِسْمِ اللّٰهِ الرَّحْمٰنِ الرَّحِيمِ

اِنَّٓا اَعْطَيْنَاكَ الْكَوْثَرَ ﴿١﴾ فَصَلِّ لِرَبِّكَ وَانْحَرْ ﴿٢﴾ اِنَّ شَانِئَكَ هُوَ الْاَبْتَرُ ﴿٣﴾

Pronunciation: **Innaa a'taynakal kawthar. Fasalli li Rabbika wanhar. Inna shani aka huwal abtar.**

Meaning: Indeed, We have granted you, [O Muhammad], *al-Kawthar*. So pray to your Lord and sacrifice to Him alone. Indeed, your enemy is the one cut off.

***Surah al-Kafirun*:**

بِسْمِ اللّٰهِ الرَّحْمٰنِ الرَّحِيمِ

قُلْ يَٓا اَيُّهَا الْكَافِرُونَ ﴿١﴾ لَٓا اَعْبُدُ مَا تَعْبُدُونَ ﴿٢﴾ وَلَٓا اَنْتُمْ عَابِدُونَ مَٓا اَعْبُدُ ﴿٣﴾ وَلَٓا اَنَا

عَابِدٌ مَا عَبَدْتُمْۙ ﴿٤﴾ وَلَا اَنْتُمْ عَابِدُونَ مَا اَعْبُدُۜ ﴿٥﴾ لَكُمْ دِينُكُمْ وَلِيَ دِينِ ﴿٦﴾

Pronunciation: **Qul yaa ayyuhal kafirun. Laa a'budu ma ta'budun. Wa laa antum abiduna maa a'bud. Wa-laa ana abidun ma 'abadtum. Wa laa antum 'abiduna maa a'bud. Lakum dinukum waliya din.**

Meaning: (O Muhammad) Say, O disbelievers! I do not worship what you worship. Nor are you worshippers of what I worship. Nor will I be a worshipper of what you worship. Nor will you be worshippers of what I worship. For you is your religion, and for me is my religion.

Surah an-Nasr:

بِسْمِ اللّٰهِ الرَّحْمٰنِ الرَّح۪يمِ

اِذَا جَٓاءَ نَصْرُ اللّٰهِ وَالْفَتْحُۙ ﴿١﴾ وَرَاَيْتَ النَّاسَ يَدْخُلُونَ ف۪ي د۪ينِ اللّٰهِ اَفْوَاجًاۙ ﴿٢﴾ فَسَبِّحْ
بِحَمْدِ رَبِّكَ وَاسْتَغْفِرْهُۜ اِنَّهُ كَانَ تَوَّابًا ﴿٣﴾

Pronunciation: **Idha jaa a nasrullahi walfath. Wara aytan nasa yadkhuluna fi dinillahi afwaja. Fasabbih bihamdi Rabbika wastaghfirh. Innahu kana tawwaba.**

Meaning: (O Muhammad) When the victory of Allah has come and the conquest, And you see the people entering into the religion of Allah in multitudes, Then exalt Him with praise of your Lord and ask forgiveness of Him. Indeed, He is Ever Accepting of repentance.

Surah al-Tabbat:

بِسْمِ اللّٰهِ الرَّحْمٰنِ الرَّح۪يمِ

تَبَّتْ يَدَٓا اَب۪ي لَهَبٍ وَتَبَّۜ ﴿١﴾ مَٓا اَغْنٰى عَنْهُ مَالُهُ وَمَا كَسَبَۜ ﴿٢﴾ سَيَصْلٰى نَارًا ذَاتَ لَهَبٍۚ ﴿٣﴾
وَامْرَاَتُهُۜ حَمَّالَةَ الْحَطَبِۚ ﴿٤﴾ ف۪ي ج۪يدِهَا حَبْلٌ مِنْ مَسَدٍ ﴿٥﴾

Pronunciation: **Tabbat yadaa abi lahabin wa-tabb. Ma aghna anhu maluhu wama kasab. Sayasla naran dhata lahab. Wamra atuh hammalatal hatab. Fi jidiha hablun min masad.**

Meaning: May the hands of Abu Lahab be ruined, and ruined is he. His wealth will not avail him or that which he gained. He will enter to burn in a Fire of blazing flame.

And his wife [as well] - the carrier of firewood. On her neck is a twisted rope of *masad*.

Surah al-'Ikhlas:

بِسْمِ اللّٰهِ الرَّحْمٰنِ الرَّحِيمِ

قُلْ هُوَ اللّٰهُ اَحَدٌ ﴿١﴾ اَللّٰهُ الصَّمَدُ ﴿٢﴾ لَمْ يَلِدْ وَلَمْ يُولَدْ ﴿٣﴾ وَلَمْ يَكُنْ لَهُ كُفُوًا اَحَدٌ ﴿٤﴾

Pronunciation: **Qul huwallahu Ahad. Allahus Samad. Lam yalid walam yulad. Walam yakul lahu kufuwan Ahad.**

Meaning: (O Muhammad) Say, He is Allah who is One. Allah is *Samad* (the Self-Sufficient Master, whom all creatures need, He neither eats nor drinks). He neither begets nor is begotten. Nor is there to Him any equivalent.

Surah al-Falaq:

بِسْمِ اللّٰهِ الرَّحْمٰنِ الرَّحِيمِ

قُلْ اَعُوذُ بِرَبِّ الْفَلَقِ ﴿١﴾ مِنْ شَرِّ مَا خَلَقَ ﴿٢﴾ وَمِنْ شَرِّ غَاسِقٍ اِذَا وَقَبَ ﴿٣﴾ وَمِنْ شَرِّ
النَّفّٰاثَاتِ فِي الْعُقَدِ ﴿٤﴾ وَمِنْ شَرِّ حَاسِدٍ اِذَا حَسَدَ ﴿٥﴾

Pronunciation: **Qul audhu bi Rabbil falaq. Min sharri ma khalaq. Wa min sharri ghasiqin idha waqab. Wa min sharrin naffathati fil uqad. Wa min sharri hasidin idha hasad.**

Meaning: (O Muhammad) Say, I seek refuge in the Lord of daybreak. From the evil of that which He created. And from the evil of darkness when it settles. And from the evil of the blowers in knots. And from the evil of an envier when he envies.

Surah al-Nas:

بِسْمِ اللّٰهِ الرَّحْمٰنِ الرَّح۪يمِ

قُلْ اَعُوذُ بِرَبِّ النَّاسِۙ ﴿١﴾ مَلِكِ النَّاسِۙ ﴿٢﴾ اِلٰهِ النَّاسِۙ ﴿٣﴾ مِنْ شَرِّ الْوَسْوَاسِ الْخَنَّاسِۙ ﴿٤﴾
اَلَّذ۪ي يُوَسْوِسُ ف۪ي صُدُورِ النَّاسِۙ ﴿٥﴾ مِنَ الْجِنَّةِ وَالنَّاسِ ﴿٦﴾

Pronunciation: **Qul a udhu bi Rabbinnasi. Malikinnasi. Ilahin nas. Min sharril waswasil khannas. Al ladhi yuwaswisu fi sudurinnasi. Minaljinnati wannas.**

Meaning: (O Muhammad) Say, I seek refuge in the Lord of humankind. The Sovereign of humankind. The God of humankind. From the evil of the retreating whisperer. Who whispers evil into the breasts of humankind. From among the jinn and humankind.

HOW WUDU IS PERFORMED – WITH PICTURES

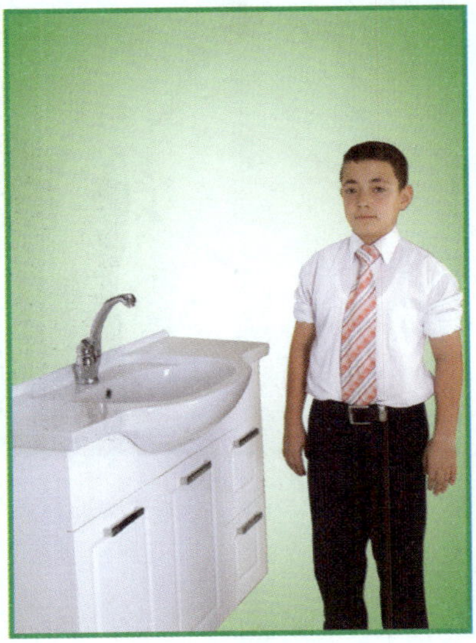

Picture: 1

1) Firstly, state the *niyyah "I intend to perform wudu for the consent of Allah"* and recite *"Auzu billahi Minashaitan Nirajeem, Bismillahir Rahmanir Raheem."*

(Picture: 1)

2) Wash your hands up to the wrists three times, pay attention to wash between the fingers. If there is a ring on a finger, move it so as to ensure that the area under the ring is washed.

(Picture: 2)

Picture: 2

3) After this, scoop water into your mouth three separate times with your right palm rinsing it properly on each occasion.

(Picture: 3)

Picture: 3

4) With your right palm, sniff water into your nose three separate times.

(Picture: 4)

Picture: 4

5) Clean your nose with your left hand by blowing it.

(Picture: 5)

Picture: 5

6) Wash your face completely three times from where the hair on your forehead finishes, to your ear lobes and under your chin.

(Picture: 6)

Picture: 6

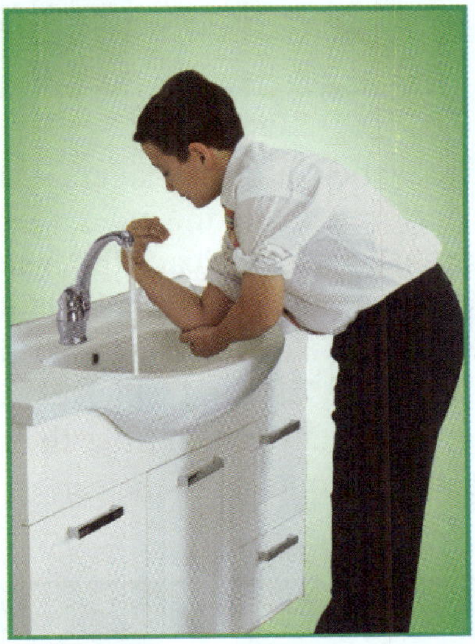

Picture: 7

7) Wash your right arm three times together with the elbows. Rub all over the arm while washing to ensure that no dry place is left.

(Picture: 7)

8) Wash your left arm together with the elbows three times. Rub all over the arm while washing and ensure that no dry place is left.

(Picture: 8)

Picture: 8

Picture: 9

9) The hands are wet with new water; the *masah* is performed with the inside of the right hand by wiping the top of your head.

(Picture: 9)

Picture: 10

10) The hands are wet again. The *masah* is performed with the index finger of the right hand which cleans the inside of the right ear and the thumb which washes the outside of the ear; With the index finger of the left hand which cleans the inside of the left ear and the thumb which washes the outside of the ear.

(Picture: 10)

Picture: 11

11) Without needing to wet the hands again, the *masah* is performed on the neck with the back of the three remaining fingers.

(Picture: 11)

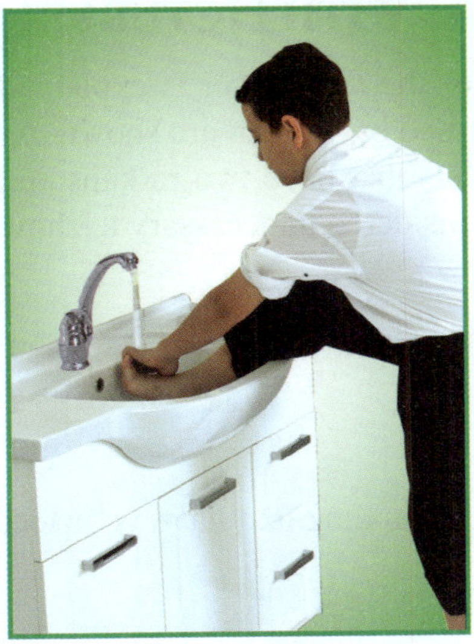

Picture: 12

12) The right foot is washed three times together with the heels. Start to wash from the tips of the toes then between the toes.

(Picture: 12)

13) The left foot is washed three times together with the heels. Start to wash from the tips of the toes then between the toes.

(Picture: 13)

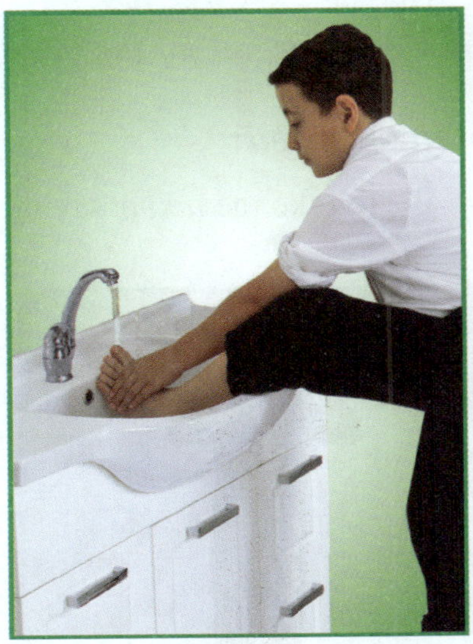

Picture: 13

When the *wudu* is completed, the *kalimah al-shahada* is recited facing the *qibla*.

HOW PRAYER IS PERFORMED - WITH PICTURES

As an example, the two *ra'kahs* of *fard* of the *fajr* prayer is explained with pictures and the different actions performed by women are shown. As there is no difference between the way prayers that have two ra'kahs and those that have more are performed, it was considered unnecessary to show them.

How the *fajr* prayer is performed:

The first *ra'kah*:

1) Face your feet towards the *qibla* when standing and have your feet four fingers apart.

2) Recite the *iqama.* (for men only)

The *Niyyah*:

3) The *niyyah* is performed stating: *"I intend to perform the fard of today's fajr prayer for the sake of Allah."*

***Iftitah takbir*:**

4) To take the *takbir* saying "Allāhu akbar."

Picture: 1

Men, when men say the *takbir*, the inside of the hands face the *qibla* while holding the fingers apart normally. The hands are raised so that the thumbs are raised to the height of the ear lobes.

(Picture: 1)

Picture: 2

Women, when women make the *takbir*, the inside of the hands face the *qibla* while holding the fingers normally apart and raise the hands with the level of the finger tips reaching shoulder height.

(Picture: 2)

Qiyaam:

1) Tie your hands after the *takbir*. Look at the place of *sajda* whilst standing.

2) State the following in order whilst standing:

a) Subhanaka,

b) A'uzu Basmala,

c) Surah al-Fatihah,

d) Another surah from the Qur'an.

Picture: 3

Men; place the palm of their right hand on top of their left hand, wrap their thumb and little finger of the right hand around the left wrist and place the hands just below the belly button.

(Picture: 3)

Picture: 4

Women; place the right hand over the left hand and place both hands together, one on top of the other, on their chest.

They do not wrap the wrist as men do. **(Picture: 4)**

Ruku:

7) Perform the *ruku* by stating "Allāhu akbar" and state "Subhana rabbi al-azeem" three times. Look at the tops of your feet while performing the *ruku*.

Men, hold the knees during *ruku* while the fingers are kept apart and the back is straight. They must keep the knees and elbows straight.

(Picture: 5)

Picture: 5

Picture: 6

Women, bend their backs slightly whilst bending less than men. They place the hands (without keeping the fingers apart) on the knees whilst bending the knees slightly.

(Picture: 6)

Rising from *ruku*:

8) Rise to the feet from *ruku* saying “Sami Allāhụ liman hamidah” and “Rabbana lakal hamd” when standing upright.

Men, To rise and straighten from *ruku*.
(Picture: 7)

Picture: 7

Picture: 8

Women, To rise and straighten from *ruku*.

(Picture: 8)

***Sajda*:**

9) The *sajda* is performed by saying "Allāhu akbar." The *sajda* is performed by firstly touching the knees, then hands and then face to the ground. During the *sajda*, the head is placed in alignment between both hands. The feet are not raised while performing the *sajda*. During the *sajda* you look at the sides of your nose. Here, "Subhana rabbi al ala" is recited three times.

Picture: 9

Men, keep the elbows away from the sides during the *sajda* and keep the arms up above the ground. The feet are placed upright with the toes facing the *qibla*.

(Picture: 9)

Women, keep the hands by the sides during the *sajda*. The feet are placed upright with the toes facing the *qibla*.

(Picture: 10)

Picture: 10

The sitting between both *sajda*s:

10) You sit up on your knees by raising your head from *sajda* stating "Allāhu akbar." While sitting, the fingers are placed level with the knees with the hands on the thighs whilst looking at your lap. Here, you sit for a period short enough to at least state "Subhanallah."

Picture: 11

Men, when sitting, spread their left foot on the ground, sit on it, keep the right foot upright and make the toes face the *qibla*).

(Picture: 11)

Women, spread their feet to the right side and sit like that.

(Picture: 12)

Picture: 12

11) The second *sajda* is performed after stating “Allāhu akbar” and “Subhana rabbi al ala” is stated three times.

12) After “Allāhu akbar” is stated, you stand to commence the second *ra’kah* by tying your hands.

(Picture: 3-4)

When rising from the *sajda*, you first raise your face, then hands and later your knees with your hands placed on them.

Everything done up until this point from the *iftitah takbir* is called one *ra'kah*.

Second *ra'kah*:

1) To recite in order whilst standing;

a) *Basmala*,

b) *Surah Al-Fatihah*,

c) Another *surah* from the Qur’an.

2) Perform the *ruku* stating “Allāhu akbar” just as in the first *ra’kah* stating “Subhana rabbi al azeem” three times.

(Picture: 5-6)

3) Rise to the feet from *ruku* stating “Sami Allahu liman hamidah” and state “Rabbana lakal hamd” when standing upright.

(Picture: 7-8)

4) Perform the *sajda* stating “Allāhu akbar.” Here, recite “Subhana rabbi al ala” three times.

(Picture: 9-10)

5) Sit up on your knees from *sajda* by stating “Allāhu akbar.” Here, sit for a period short enough to at least state “Subhanallah.”

(Picture: 11-12)

6) Perform the second *sajda* after stating “Allāhu akbar” and state “Subhana rabbi al-ala” three times.

Al-qa'da al-akhira **(Sitting at the end of prayer):**

7) Sit up on your knees from *sajda* stating "Allāhu akbar."

When sitting, the fingers are placed level with the knees with the hands on the thighs whilst looking at your lap.

8) **In order during the sitting;**

a) *Al-Taḥiyyāt*,

b) *Allahumma Salli*,

c) *Allahumma Barik*,

d) *Rabbana atina... dua*s are recited.

Picture: 13

Picture: 14

(**Men**; when sitting, spread the left foot on the ground, sit on it, keep the right foot upright and make the toes face the *qibla*).

(Picture: 13-14)

Women; spread their feet to the right side and sit like that.

(Picture: 15)

Picture: 15

Giving the *salām* to the right side:

9) Firstly, turn the head to the right and state "Assalamu alaikum wa rahmatullah." Look at the shoulder whilst giving the *salām*.

Picture: 16

Men, the way the *salām* is given to the right side.

(Picture: 16)

Women, the way the *salām* is given to the right side.

(Picture: 17)

Picture: 17

Giving the *salām* to the left side:

10) Then, turn the head to the left stating "Assalamu alaikum wa rahmatullah." Thus, the second *ra'kah* of prayer is completed.

Picture: 18

Men, the way the *salām* is given to the left side.

(Picture: 18)

Women, the way the *salām* is given to the left side.

(Picture: 19)

Picture: 19

DUA

The hands are raised to chest level when performing the *dua*. The hands are opened towards the sky with the insides of the palms are tilted towards the face slightly and the two hands are kept apart. (Picture: 20-21)

Picture: 20

A boy performing *dua*.

(Picture: 20)

A girl performing *dua*.

(Picture: 21)

Picture: 21